Praise for *Dark Wine at Dusk*

"A gripping paranormal romance that will leave readers aching for more. Passionate, breathtaking and beautifully written."

~InD'tale Magazine

"The chemistry between Henry and Cerissa will keep you turning the page. Powerfully written and totally unputdownable!"

~A 'Wishing Shelf' Book Review

"With a superb plot and its edgy narrative, *Dark Wine at Dusk* is sure to be well received by discerning fans of the genre and is recommended without reservation."

~BookViral Book Reviews

"If you enjoyed the first two books in this series, you're going to love this one…*Dark Wine at Dusk* picks up with the continuing mysterious murders of the residents of Sierra Escondida. [Cerissa's and Henry's] passionate romance alights everywhere throughout his mansion. One of the most inventive love romps I've ever read is the hide-and-seek game they play in his vineyard…I won't tell more as story spoilers are not in my toolbox, but the tension and shock of the mounting climax will keep you riveted."

~Sharon Bonin-Pratt's Ink Flare

ALSO BY JENNA BARWIN

The Hill Vampire Series

DARK WINE AT DUSK (Book 3)

DARK WINE AT SUNRISE (Book 2)

DARK WINE AT MIDNIGHT (Book 1)

DARK WINE AT DUSK

A Hill Vampire Novel
Book 3

Jenna Barwin

Hidden Depths Publishing

Dark Wine at Dusk by Jenna Barwin
Copyright © 2019 Jenna Barwin. All rights reserved.

This book or any portion of it may not be reproduced in any form or by any means, or used in any manner whatsoever, without the express written permission of the publisher or author except for the use of brief quotations in a book review.

This is a work of fiction. Names, characters, businesses, products, places, events and incidents are either the products of the author's imagination or used in a fictitious manner. Any resemblance to actual persons, living or dead, or actual events is purely coincidental. Any trademarks, service marks, product names, or named features are assumed to be the property of their respective owners, and are used only for reference. Opinions of the characters are not necessarily those of the author.

Printed in the United States of America
First printing & ebook edition, 2019

Hidden Depths Publishing
Orange County, California
www.hiddendepthspublishing.com

Cover design: Covers by Christian (Christian Bentulan)
Images used under license from Shutterstock.com and Depositphotos.com

Interior Design by Author E.M.S.

Editing team: Katrina Diaz-Arnold, Refine Editing, LLC; Trenda K. Lundin, It's Your Story Content Editing; Arran McNicol

Library of Congress Control Number: 2019939688

ISBN 978-0-9986549-7-3

1) Urban Fantasy 2) Paranormal Romance 3) Science Fiction & Fantasy 4) Romance

Join Jenna Barwin's VIP Readers

Want to know about new releases, and receive special announcements, exclusive excerpts, and other FREE fun stuff? Join Jenna's VIP Readers and receive Jenna Barwin's newsletter by subscribing online at: https://jennabarwin.com/jenna-barwins-newsletter

You can also find Jenna Barwin at:

Facebook: https://www.facebook.com/jennabarwin/

Twitter: @JennaBarwin https://twitter.com/JennaBarwin

Instagram: JennaBarwin https://www.instagram.com/jennabarwin/

Pinterest: https://www.pinterest.com/jennabarwin/

BookBub: https://www.bookbub.com/profile/jenna-barwin

Email: https://jennabarwin.com/contact

DARK WINE AT DUSK

Chapter 1

The Scarlet Brethren Headquarters—The last week of May

The corporation's president could hold a cross without being harmed by it. As he twirled the necklace, light glinted off the shiny gold and a smile curled his lips.

How amusing that such a simple symbol could display his power to the superstitious. They feared him, but that didn't stop them from flocking to him. They coveted what he had to offer.

While he'd happily welcome them, their ever-increasing numbers presented a challenge: how to stay hidden. So far, mortal institutions had provided the best camouflage. It made his organization easy to establish and easier to hide, at least, up until now.

Of course, being careful never hurt. He had survived this long *because* he took precautions. He called his operatives by titles used in any ordinary corporation and insisted they call him President.

If treaty vampires monitored his phone calls, they would assume he was conversing with a subordinate, a director of operations for his business. They would hear nothing to suggest otherwise, nothing to lead them to his true organization, nothing to reveal that the Director was the field marshal in the President's war.

Besides, he'd always liked the sound of "president" on the Director's lips. When the time was right, he would make a good president to rule his people. For too long vampires had been without strong leadership, becoming corpulent and lazy, hiding in the shadows, pretending to be...*mortal*.

He shuddered at the thought.

No, that wouldn't do. They had relinquished their personal power too easily. If he had his way, they'd man up and claim their rightful heritage.

Now.

Patience was more than a virtue; it was a way of life. For many, many years, he had sat on his grudge. To accomplish his goal, he had to kill those who stood in his way without anyone suspecting he was behind it. Even the mere whiff of suspicion would jeopardize his ultimate aim.

He placed the crucifix on the center of his Danish modern desk and picked up the list.

Alpha
Beta
Gamma
Delta
Epsilon

The foremost rule: never write down real names—never create any tangible thing that might connect him to the plan. He had come of age in an era when private schools taught classical Greek. The first five letters of their alphabet served as the code words for his targets.

The Director had been briefed on their true identities. Other than the Director, the President's only link to the unsavory part of the scheme was his IT expert and the anonymous burner phone the President carried. He replaced it regularly with a new one. It was a slight inconvenience, but a necessary one.

Slowly, cautiously, he had put the key components of his plan into motion. A back door to the Hill's computer system—installed years ago—had waited for the perfect moment to exploit it. Then he met the Director—a serial killer trolling the bars for a victim. At the time, the President had been pleased to find someone with the predatory skills he needed to execute his plan.

And the rest had fallen into his lap without any effort on his part. He sometimes toyed with the idea that he was on a mission from God.

At least he had, until nothing had gone as planned—thanks to the Director's many failures. The President laid the list of code names aside and twisted the heavy ruby ring around his left index finger. The ornate crest imprinted on the ring's side belonged to his maker.

What to do, what to do...

A carved ivory chessboard sat near him. He plucked a white pawn and white bishop from the game.

He'd lost Blanche and Frédéric.

Unfortunate.

He placed the white pieces on his desk and seized a black pawn. All he had to show for their work was the meaningless death of one inconsequential Hill resident: Kim Han.

He set the pawn aside and stared at the board.

The beauty of playing chess—he could wait a long time between moves. Time used to fortify his defenses, close the gaps in his strategy, and attack when everything was right. The pressure of time felt by mortals didn't register for him—an advantage of being immortal.

Except the playing field was changing. New technology made it harder to stay hidden. Government crackdowns on fake IDs meant changing his identity would be more difficult in the next five years. If he didn't hurry, mortals might learn about his people before he took control of the treaty communities. And of course, the more followers he had, the more chance that loose lips would sink his ship.

Back when he was turned, he'd tried to convince his colleagues that nothing would do but a complete restructuring of their society. A benevolent dictatorship, with vampires in charge. The leadership hadn't listened.

Fools.

He could see what others did not. Mortals couldn't be trusted to run world governments. War after war, their aggressions were never-ending. His predictions had been right. And now, his people were slowly being squeezed into the light of day. Once outed, they'd be slaughtered by the superstitious.

Even though his methods may seem unsavory to some, his approach would produce a smaller body count than all-out war. He didn't want his people to die. If anything, he wanted to save as many as he could, to bring them over to his side, to see *his* way was right.

Persuading them was more gratifying than converting them by force.

But a few had to die for the greater good. They stood like a clog stopping a drainpipe. Once he flushed them down, the way would be cleared for him to rise.

He stared at the chessboard. Quite a mess so far. Would he have to dispose of his right-hand operative and start again sometime later? Or would the Director be able to redeem himself? The President growled. Yes, he'd been patient before, waiting for the right time to attack. But the idea of more delay was not appealing, not with mortal government snooping into every aspect of his life.

He pushed the chessboard aside, squared the crucifix, and punched the phone number.

"Yes?" the Director answered.

"You're late."

"I was about to call."

The President ignored his excuse. He'd learned to never acknowledge their reasons—nothing justified failure.

"We have new intelligence on Project Epsilon," the President said. He picked up the coded report and leaned back in his plush executive chair. "Have you made contact with the courier I recommended?"

"Yes. He's perfect for the job."

"I hope so, for your sake."

"I'll make sure the courier has everything he needs to complete the delivery."

The President surveyed the chessboard and wrapped his fingers around the white queen. She could move without limitation: sideways, diagonally, forward and back. The Director was his queen—not that he'd ever tell him that.

"You better hope the courier successfully delivers the package on time, if you want your promotion," the President said.

"I'm sure he will."

"Do not bungle it this time."

"Nothing will go wrong. I'll see to it."

The President returned the white queen to the board, centering it precisely on the black square. The Director would stay on the board—*for now*.

"Did you receive my gift?"

Ah, the President relished the Director's attempts to ingratiate himself with gifts. But then, the Director sent the best gifts. Two gallons of adrenaline-spiked blood had arrived, disguised as a delivery of gourmet food.

"Yes, it was quite delicious. But you must be careful. Don't let your extracurricular activities distract from your primary project. Not if you want your promotion."

"Of course, sir."

The President disconnected the call. Better to leave his subordinate feeling rattled. The Director would do nothing to interfere with his promotion into their ranks. The fool thought once he had his reward, he would never have to worry about the police meddling with his avocation.

But the Carlyle Cutter had it all wrong. After the President turned the serial killer into one of his elites, the Cutter would never be free. He was far too useful.

During the Tudor reign of England, psychopaths were used as court torturers. An admirable practice, one the President would soon reinstitute, with the Cutter as his chief torturer.

The Cutter might as well enjoy his captivity.

The President swiveled his chair and gazed over at the hardwood shelves filled with history books. He'd studied war and revolutions. He understood what made them work:

Lies.

Lies to the peons, lies to those who wanted to be like him, lies to those he'd already turned. Give them someone to hate, someone to *fear*, and tell them what they wanted to hear. Then they would follow you to their death.

Not that he wanted his loyal followers to die. No, he had better ways to ensure a relatively peaceful transfer of power. Only a few had to die to make way for the future.

The President lifted his glass and took a sip. The victim's blood *sizzled* through his veins. He closed his eyes, remembering the thrill of slicing into live flesh, of bleeding out his prey—a pleasure he'd soon be free to indulge in again.

He took another drink, rolling the blood in his mouth.

Yes, he'd be free to indulge—once *he* was in charge.

Chapter 2

Rancho Bautista del Murciélago, Sierra Escondida—The Next Day

Dr. Cerissa Patel swept the driveway in front of Henry's home before turning on the hose to wet the pavement. Chalk would stick better to a damp surface. Getting on her hands and knees, she laid out a grid, nine dots wide by nine dots high: the pattern for creating a *kolam*.

Cerissa's family—her father's family—had created a daily *kolam* to bring prosperity to their home in Surat, India. When her *pita*—her father—died in the late 1700s, she had abandoned the practice.

Earlier in the day, her best friend Karen had helped her pack and move from Gaea's guestroom. There was so little stuff to box that Cerissa could have done it herself, but working together gave her an excuse to check in on Karen—and get caught up on the local gossip.

Karen seemed all right, showing no signs of trauma from being kidnapped by the Carlyle Cutter. Karen's emotional links to those memories had been erased, so Cerissa wasn't surprised, but she was glad to confirm it.

They enjoyed their lunch out, and then Cerissa used the afternoon to unpack her things in Henry's master bedroom—now her bedroom.

Would she ever get accustomed to the idea? The Lux Enclave had been where she'd lived for so long that it felt strange to think of anywhere else as home. Yet here she was, officially moved in with her boyfriend. She looked around.

Now what?

The sun had passed its zenith, but Henry wouldn't wake until dusk, and her fingers itched to do something. Then the idea came to her. What better way to celebrate than to revive the ancient ritual and make her own *kolam*?

The local stores failed to carry colored rice flour—the traditional material used—so she chose white and red chalk for her design. The colors were complementary to his Spanish Colonial home. The house had smooth white stucco walls, the roof topped by terra cotta tiles. The heavy wood beams supporting the eaves were stained in the same dark walnut color as the double front doors.

The house reflected Henry's cultural origins—he had been born Enrique Bautista Vasquez in Veracruz, Mexico, over two hundred years ago.

Kneeling on the driveway's concrete, Cerissa drew curving lines around each dot, creating a pattern, a mix of shapes for animals and humans. A triangle pointed up for man, and another pointed down for woman—her and Henry, their beginning living together.

She invented her own symbol for vampires, and for her mother's people, the Lux, until the *kolam*'s whole design represented a diverse harmony.

Her *dadi ma*—her father's mother—had taught her the traditional art.

Dadi ma had been there, someone to comfort her three-year-old self when her mother abandoned her.

Until that point, Cerissa had been the anchor that had kept *amma* tied to a mortal man. The Lux had forced her mother to live with humans to bear a child, and as soon as she thought Cerissa was old enough to get along without her, *amma* returned to the Lux Enclave, leaving Cerissa behind and breaking her young heart.

She now understood why *amma* left. Living with humans had never been her mother's choice. *Amma* hadn't loved Cerissa's father; she didn't think of humans as equals.

The other women in *pita*'s household had pinched the three-year-old Cerissa and blamed her for *amma* running away. Cerissa had initially believed them—had believed it was all her fault.

"That is enough," *dadi ma* had scolded the women. "It's not the child's fault." She pulled Cerissa into her lap, holding her close against her silken sari, which smelled of sunlight, coriander, and love.

As young Cerissa cried, feeling like her whole world had fallen apart because *amma* left, *dadi ma* picked up Mungi, the household mongoose, and held the sharp-faced animal so Cerissa could pet him, distracting her from her hurting heart.

"Hold your hand flat," *dadi ma* said, and then dropped cooked egg on Cerissa's palm. Mungi's tongue tickled her hand as he delicately picked up the choice tidbit, and she squealed with delight, forgetting her sadness for the moment.

Everyone in the family pampered the mongoose. Not only did he kill the deadly cobra, he caught and ate rats, keeping the pests out of their rice bags.

Cerissa had wished she could be Mungi—able to roam where she wanted and be welcomed by the entire household, even by the mean women who pinched her.

But Mungi and *dadi ma* weren't the only ones who cared for her.

Cerissa's *pita* cherished her and loved her, and she idolized him. He told her stories about the Hindu gods and goddesses, taught her to meditate, and showed her how to be still and open to the universe.

But it was *dadi ma* who protected her.

She hadn't thought of *pita* and *dadi ma* in ages; both were long dead. A tear formed and dripped on the *kolam*, marring the pattern. Cerissa dried the spot with her palm and went about repairing the design, small chalk strokes to fill in the white line erased by her tear.

Pita had died when she was ten years old. Her heart had ripped open, the pain unbearable, and it was to *dadi ma*'s lap she ran. Huddled against her grandmother's sari, tears had bled down Cerissa's face.

A few nights after *pita*'s funeral pyre, *amma* returned, stealing Cerissa from her bed. She had cried and begged to stay.

Dadi ma, roused from sleep by the noise, came out of her room and knelt before Cerissa, hugging her fiercely, as Cerissa's tears wet *dadi ma*'s brown neck and fell into her dark braid, which was shot through with gray.

"I love you, my little *pihu*. I'll always love you. But it's time for you to go with your *amma*—to go to her people. I'll see you again; we'll visit, and I'll tell you all the kitchen gossip, and you can show me what you've learned."

Dadi ma unwrapped Cerissa's clutching fingers and placed her hand in *amma*'s palm. "Take good care of my granddaughter," she had said sternly.

Except her mother hadn't. *Amma* dropped her at the Enclave's nursery, leaving her in the custody of strangers and never returning for her. There, she learned for the first time what she was—a member of the Lux.

She had always worn a crystal band around her wrist. "Never take it off," her *amma* had scolded her as a toddler. "You can't risk losing it. The jewels are too valuable."

Growing up, Cerissa had believed it was a bracelet from *amma*'s dowry—the only thing she had left when *amma* abandoned her.

When the band was removed by a Lux guardian, Cerissa morphed into her true form for the first time. Relief had swept through her ten-year-old body, relief at finally being comfortable in her own skin, relief to flutter her small, immature wings and count six fingers on her blue-skinned hand.

But she never saw *dadi ma* again after that night. Later, Cerissa realized the old woman had misled her. To convince her to leave with her mother, *dadi ma* made a promise she couldn't keep. An early lesson learned: love and complete candor didn't always go hand in hand.

Cerissa shook her head. What was causing these deep thoughts to blow through her mind today, the day she moved in with Henry? She took a breath and blew the air out again and again, until she set her thoughts free on the warm afternoon wind. Balanced on her heels, hovering over the *kolam*, she let peace infuse each chalk stroke.

The intercom's crackle broke her concentration, and she fell back, landing on her butt in surprise.

"I'm sorry, *cariña*." Henry's voice came over the front-door intercom. "I didn't mean to startle you."

The tungsten bracelet he wore now muted the crystal embedded in his wrist. The bracelet had been adjusted so she no longer experienced his emotions when he woke. The crystal still protected him from Lux interference, marking him as her mate, but it no longer transmitted their feelings to each other.

Most of the time, she liked the emotional privacy. But sometimes she missed having insight into what he was experiencing—and she missed the spark of his consciousness alerting her when he rose from his deep sleep in the basement crypt.

She brushed her hands on her jeans, dusting off the white chalk, and stood, glancing over her shoulder at the sun. The fiery globe hung low in the horizon—too soon for a vampire to be awake. "What are you doing up?"

The front door remained closed. "Early moonrise."

"Oh, I forgot to check the astronomical tables."

The security camera moved, the servo making a *whirring* sound, and the lens pointed at her artwork. "What are you drawing?"

"I hope you don't mind…"

"Cerissa, this is your home now. If it makes you happy, it makes me happy."

"Do you like it?"

"The design is lovely."

"It's a *kolam*." She knelt again and touched an elaborate *S* curve. "These knots bring good luck to new relationships. The other symbols represent all of us in harmony."

"Is it finished?"

She tucked a stray hair behind her ear. Her long, dark hair was bound in a single braid, but some strands had come loose in the afternoon breeze. "I have a little more work to do. I'll join you inside in a few minutes."

"I'll make dinner while you complete the design."

"You don't have to—"

"It's my pleasure to cook for you."

She could almost see the gracious bow accompanying his words.

"What would you like?" he asked. "Enchiladas? Grilled chicken? Pasta? I had the delivery service stock the refrigerator today."

"Ah, enchiladas sound nice."

"Very good," he said. "Take your time. Dinner will be ready in"—there was a slight pause—"thirty minutes."

"Thanks, Henry."

She knelt by the design, smiling to herself, a shimmer of happiness coursing through her chest. Henry was a master chef. He had the skill to prepare liver—a food she despised—and make it desirable. But his Mexican dishes were to die for. And having him cook for her gave her the same "wrapped in warm blankets" feeling she used to get when *dadi ma* made spicy biryani with pomegranate seeds—her favorite as a child.

She selected the red chalk and resumed filling the space inside a square, the square representing culture.

Her life had been nomadic, a blend of cultures: first South Asian, then Lux, and then European. She'd spent most of her intermediate *karabu* stage—the Lux equivalent to an extended early adulthood—living with families in Europe and learning to mimic a broad range of human behavior, while spying for the Lux.

Now, she had transitioned to her *principatus* stage—a full adult—and was making her home with Henry in a vampire-controlled town. All the vampires in Sierra Escondida lived in a gated community, with two mountain ranges forming a V, and a tall block wall completing the Hill's protective triangle, giving them a private base from which they could hide in the open. Henry's substantial vineyard estate, affectionately named *Rancho Bautista del Murciélago*, or Bautista's Ranch of the Bat, covered forty acres.

She moved to a circle in the *kolam*—nature—and filled it in using short red strokes against the concrete's grain. Of all the environments she'd lived in, nature produced the least anxiety. Morphing into an animal was almost as good as meditation. As a cougar, she could let her mind relax and her senses fully experience the wilderness in the Central California foothills bordering the Hill.

She took in a deep breath, and something settled inside her. The warm breeze carried wild sage mixed with the musty scent of the sprawling vineyard that bookended the house. She looked out at the lush, verdant fields beyond the small lawn, took another deep breath, and smiled.

It smelled like home.

Chapter 3

Henry's Kitchen—A Short While Later

Cerissa took her place at the mahogany kitchen table. *Pollo enchiladas verdes* with rice and vegetables filled a stoneware plate.

Yum.

A wine glass sat next to her plate. Slices of fruit floated in the deep ruby liquid. When she lifted it, the fruit bounced off the glass, and she took a sip. Henry had made sangria.

"Very nice," she said, returning the glass to the table.

He nodded at the compliment, his ponytail bobbing with the motion, his long black hair held back with a leather string. He strode to the stove.

Her gaze followed him. Whoever had designed skinny jeans had his tight butt in mind, and the fitted t-shirt he wore showed off his broad shoulders and narrow waist—a physique shaped by hard physical labor. He had been building his California ranch in the weeks before he was turned in the early 1800s.

She snickered when she read his t-shirt: *Alpha Vampire* was printed in red gothic letters on black cotton.

Using scissors, he snipped off the corner of a shiny blue pouch and poured the heated blood into a tall mug. The blood came from her genetically engineered non-sentient human clones.

She tore her gaze away from his ass and sliced into the enchilada. "You know, once we start producing blood for the treaty communities, I need a name to print on the bags."

He eased into the chair across from her and placed his mug on the table. "What about keeping it simple and using 'Dark Wine'?"

She cocked her head. Dark wine was the euphemism Hill vampires used for blood. It would be recognizable, at least to those from Sierra

Escondida, but was the term misleading? "I wouldn't want a mortal to think the contents were for them."

"Why not add a warning label?"

She laughed. "Not for human consumption?"

"Something like that."

They fell silent as she savored her dinner—the chicken filling tender, the green sauce tangy, with just a little fire—and he slowly sipped his drink. Their silences still made her nervous, like she had an obligation to fill the air with words. She controlled the urge by taking another sip of the delightful sangria, letting the alcohol relax her.

After he finished his drink, he put his mug in the dishwasher and then picked up the large frying pan.

"Leave it," she said. "You made dinner—I'll do the dishes."

"It's no bother. Take your time and enjoy your meal." He scooped the leftover enchiladas into a plastic container. "I made extra in case you want them for lunch."

"Thanks. Tomorrow I have to go into Mordida, so maybe I'll eat them for dinner."

"Whatever works best for you." He slid the leftovers into the refrigerator. "I noticed you had brought your bags over from Gaea's. When will you move the rest of your belongings?"

"Ah, I don't own very much. I have a small room at the Enclave…the Lux aren't into acquiring possessions."

"Whatever you have, you should bring here. This is your home now."

"Do you want to go with me tonight? To the Enclave, I mean, to get them?" She took her empty plate to the sink, rinsed it off, and added it to the dishwasher.

"Are you sure it's all right if I go with you, *cariña*?"

"Now that we're working together to stop the VDM"—the vampire dominance movement—"the Protectors have no objection if you come to the Enclave with me. It won't be like last time."

Henry slowly nodded at her, though the wariness didn't leave his expression. She couldn't blame him. The last time he had flashed to the Enclave was to save her from the Protectors, who were punishing her for disobeying their directives. He had grabbed the Scythe of Justice out of Agathe's hand and stood ready to do anything to protect her.

My champion.

Her root chakra opened at the memory, warmth heating her core, and tingles ignited across her skin. She wanted to take him to bed to show him how much she loved him. But he was right: she should finish moving in first. Then they could celebrate.

"I do own a few mementos I'd like to keep in our room here." She closed the door and started the dishwasher. "Although it doesn't make sense to pack my sarongs." They were designed to wrap under her wings—all Lux wore them.

"Very well," he said. "Let's go get your things—including a few sarongs. You told me it isn't healthy for you to stay in human form for long periods of time."

He was right. She hadn't understood it when she was a child, but the Protectors' decision to lock her in human form hadn't been good for her. As an adult, overuse of the stabilizing hormone would make her ill. She used the medicine sparingly—mostly when she needed to stay in one form for an extended period—or whenever he was going to bite her.

Henry took her into his arms and kissed the side of her neck. She shivered pleasantly as he laid three more kisses along her collarbone.

"You're welcome to take on your Lux appearance anytime we're alone," he whispered against her skin, his warm breath tickling her.

"Henry—" she said, starting to object.

"Since I first saw your Lux wings, I've wanted to stroke your feathers. Are they as soft as they look?"

She sighed. There was no avoiding it.

She touched her watch, triggering the transport device to flash them to her room at the Enclave. Carved from volcanic rock, the walls of her bedroom were black and smooth. A few decorations hung on them, including her most prized possession: a charcoal drawing of her *pita*.

Henry stepped back and looked around nervously.

She stripped off her t-shirt, removed her bra, and unbuttoned her blue jeans. "I guess it's time."

Fear had stopped her before, fear he'd reject her on religious grounds, given his deep Catholic beliefs. But he'd already seen her Lux form. He knew she looked like a biblical angel, although she believed her people were ancient astronauts.

A flash of memory invaded her mind: a stiff brush being roughly pulled through her wavy hair, her *amma* bemoaning how three-year-old Cerissa looked in mortal form. A sharp pain welled in her chest. The fear Henry might reject her for how she *really* looked pricked at that tender spot.

She stiffened her spine.

Henry won't reject me.

He loved her unconditionally. He'd told her so, and she believed him. With a sigh of determination, she morphed to her Lux body. From her bedside drawer, she removed a translator crystal. Her blue jeans and thong slid off her thin Lux hips, falling to the floor, and she stepped out of them.

"Touch away," she sang in her native language, and the crystal repeated her words in English.

Henry swept his gaze across her, letting his eyes do the touching first.

So beautiful.

Her skin shimmered blue, her wings were ecru rather than white, and her hair was the same shade. She had the face of an angel. Her two large eyes were solid silver—they had no pupils or white sclera. It almost made her look blind, but he knew better. A multifaceted third eye sat on her forehead, a bit above and between her silver ones. Her nose was but a button, her mouth a tiny bud—humanlike, but not quite the same.

For the first time, he saw her truly naked. She'd been covered up in surgical scrubs the last time he'd seen her like this.

She had small breasts, androgynous in appearance—if indeed they functioned as breasts. He had no idea. Yet, other than her breasts, she had no apparent sex organs. Was she female or male, or something completely different?

Where a woman would have a cleft, she was smooth, no hair, her hips narrow, her legs thin but muscular. A flap of skin hugged her belly like a kangaroo's pouch. He wondered what it was for but refused to ask. Small steps. He sensed her discomfort and didn't want to be intrusive.

He lightly stroked her neck with his fingertips, and she flinched.

"Sorry," she sang. "Human fingers are like sandpaper."

"Would it hurt you if I touched your wings?"

She did an about-face, presenting her wings, her small buttocks visible where the feathers curved away, with taut muscles evident beneath her smooth skin. The wing tips hung to her knees.

Two scars ran in parallel along the length of her spine and crossed the well-built muscles supporting her wings.

When he hesitated, she sang, "Go ahead. Touch."

He brushed his palms over the tops in the direction the feathers tapered.

Soft. So soft.

He pinched a feather, stroking its edge with his fingertips, and inhaled deeply, taking in the scent of her—sunlight, ocean spray, and a hint of jasmine.

Like he imagined heaven would smell.

He froze.

Is she really a fallen angel? Or are the Lux lost astronauts?

As much as the first thought bothered him, it didn't matter. He loved her and accepted her as she was.

He bent toward her back and kissed the scars where the so-called Scythe of Justice had cut her. To mar such a beautiful body—the injustice ground at him. "Will they ever heal completely?"

She exhaled a musical note, sounding like a sigh, and turned to face him. He stared into her large, round eyes, molten silver swirling with an iridescent quality, waiting for her answer. Her multifaceted third eye—in three shades of brilliant blue—emitted a bright blue glow, creating a halo effect over her head.

"The Protectors want the scars to remain permanently as a reminder of my disobedience," she sang, and the crystal translated.

She morphed back suddenly. Seeing her naked female body sent a *zing* right through him in a way her Lux body didn't. Her Lux body inspired love—but her human body stirred both love and lust.

Her intense green eyes were what he first noticed when she was clothed. Like rare emeralds, they seemed to sparkle when light hit them. Her thick, luscious, very kissable lips came next, barely beating out her long mink-brown hair, which flowed loose to her waist.

But naked? His gaze immediately traveled lower, to the figure of a buxom goddess, dark brown nipples topping her sienna-colored breasts and full hips he loved wrapping his fingers around.

He was a man—he wouldn't apologize for being aroused by such beauty.

He took her in his arms and traced the scar lines on her back. Remorse crawled up his spine.

"Henry, it's all right."

She pressed against him. He grew hard despite his guilt.

"Really," she continued. "They're no different from the scar on my arm. I just have to remember to re-create them each time I become human."

He ran his fingers over the ridge girding her bicep. She'd been shot protecting him. Like a warrior, her mortal body carried too many battle wounds. "And your wings? Are they all right?"

"They droop if I don't work out, but exercise strengthens the muscle beneath the scars."

"I am sorry." He squeezed her tightly to him. "I'm sorry you were punished on my account."

She hugged him back. "It's not your fault. I knew I was forbidden from having a relationship with you, but I was all too eager to believe Ari when he screwed up my orders and told me we had permission to mate."

Ari was her cousin and mission supervisor, and a bit irreverent for Henry's tastes.

"Still," Henry said, "I am sorry you suffered because of me."

A peaceful feeling suddenly flooded him—she had used her aura to make him feel better, to lighten his guilt. He didn't object. She didn't do it often enough to be unacceptable, and it was part of who she was, one of the Lux powers she had.

Her fingers slid around to the front of his waist and slipped under his t-shirt's hem, raising it, her fingers gliding seductively across his abs. Sex? Here? He grasped her hands to stop her. "Do you think this is a good idea?"

She smiled at him, a possessive grin, like a cat eyeing a piece of salmon. "I'm naked. I don't see any reason you shouldn't be."

"We should go back to my place, no?"

"This room is private, although I've never had a man here before. We've already broken in your bed. Why shouldn't we try mine?"

I will be her first here?

The corner of his mouth turned up. He wanted as many firsts with her as he could gather. "But let's pack beforehand. Then we can take our time."

She nuzzled his chest, kissing his skin where she'd lifted his shirt. "If you insist."

"I do." He gave the room a quick scan. "We should have brought boxes with us."

"There isn't much." She put on her underwear, shimmied into jeans, and pulled the t-shirt over her head. "My duffel bag should hold most of it to take back to your house."

"Our house." He grasped her shoulders, his gaze meeting hers. "Our house, *cariña*."

Our house. Her heart gave a little crazy pitter-patter at his words. And the way he'd accepted her Lux appearance had left her almost giddy with relief.

She kissed him one more time and then hauled a large canvas bag from the closet. She laid out things on the bed and he packed them, including a couple of her more colorful sarongs, the fabric printed with big Polynesian flowers.

When she reached for the charcoal portrait hanging on the wall opposite the bed, Henry crossed the room, placing his hand over hers, stopping her. "Who is that man?"

Henry seemed jealous and slightly suspicious, but the tungsten bracelet he wore blocked the crystal's connection.

"My *pita*." She touched the glass lovingly. "My father."

Henry released her hand. "Must he be in our bedroom? We could hang the picture in the upstairs hallway, perhaps? I don't know if I could perform with your father watching over us."

She bit her lips together to suppress her smile. Henry unable to perform? The thought was laughable. But all relationships required compromise, and his proposal was acceptable. "The wall outside the master bedroom is fine."

"Thank you," he said.

She laid the framed portrait on her bed and resumed packing. A touch of bittersweet sadness overcame her as she worked. The sketch had been one of the few things she'd been allowed to keep after *pita*'s funeral when she moved to the Enclave. There, she learned the Lux had food and medicines that would have healed him.

Snakes of guilt had hatched in her young stomach—if only she had been older when *pita* fell ill, she could have used Lux medicines to save his life.

Years later, when she passed her exams, she was offered her choice: medical research or computer science. Either task suited her. Math and science were like a second skin.

But she chose medical research. She would never sit by powerless again while someone she loved died.

She gave her head a little shake. Too many deep thoughts today. "That's everything," she said.

Henry looked puzzled. "But there are still bottles in the bathroom."

"I'll have to work in the Enclave lab occasionally, to supervise the care of the blood clones. So, I'll need some toiletries and sarongs here."

Henry frowned. "I don't like you keeping a second home."

She patted the bed, inviting him to sit next to her. When he did, she slid onto his lap and hooked her arms around his neck. "Why does it bother you?"

"Having this room"—he glanced around—"makes it too easy for you to leave."

She melded her body against his. "I'm not going anywhere but to our home. I wish you wouldn't wear the bracelet all the time. I can't tell what you're feeling…and I feel so lonely without you in my head."

Her cousin had provided the bracelet to block the connection and give them emotional space. Initially, Henry had expressed reservations about the crystal, concerned the link would allow her to control him. His fears were groundless, but she couldn't push—she had to let him come to his own conclusion.

After a quiet moment of contemplation, he said, "Ari told me the dampening circuit can be adjusted to a comfortable level of exchange. Would that make you happier?"

"Indeed, it would." Cerissa's phone rang—"Send in the Clowns" played. "Speak of the devil."

She sat up, dug her phone out of her purse, and punched the speaker button so Henry could hear. "Hi, Ari. I'm at the Enclave with Henry. What's the emergency?"

"I need your help."

"I thought we agreed—you're only supposed to contact me during the day."

"Don't snap at your supervisor, sweet cheeks. I know you'd like some playtime, but I need your help right now. Tig wants to see you."

Cerissa's shoulders sagged. Yeah, she had hoped to settle in and enjoy being with Henry before other demands interfered. But they couldn't ignore a summons from the police chief for Sierra Escondida. "What's so important that Tig needs us now?"

"You got to vouch for me at tonight's council meeting, *and* you need to explain why I know about vampires. Tig has started asking tough questions."

Henry cleared his throat. "I may have the solution for Ari's problem." He laid a hand on her shoulder and squeezed gently. "But I'm not sure you'll like it."

Chapter 4

Sierra Escondida Police Department—One Hour Later

Captain Jayden Johnson raced out of the police station, his concern growing over his mate's disappearance. Chief Tigisi "Tig" Anderson was scheduled to give her report to the town council in one hour, and she wasn't in her office at home or at the police station. No scribbled note, either. She usually left him a note if she was going off the Hill.

Where was she?

Then it dawned on him. She had to be in the one place she always went when upset. He jogged across the parking lot and over to the Hill gym.

A few minutes later, he found her alone and pummeling a punching bag. She resembled an African warrior, all lean muscle, as she gave another rapid triple punch. It was a testament to the manufacturer that she didn't put her fist right through the damn thing—must be rated for vampire strength.

The way she attacked the heavy bag was not a good sign. He ticked through the events of the past few nights. Had he done something to piss her off? He didn't think so, but as her second-in-command and her mate, he had double the opportunity to get under her skin.

He waited by the door a moment, watching her hit the leather-covered bag with all her strength, watching it dent under her force.

"Hey, Tig," Jayden called out, and strode toward her. "You didn't wake me when you got in last night."

"You needed your sleep," she said, taking another swing.

"Easy there." He jumped back, away from the bag's rebound. "What's got you so mad?"

"Everything. The Carlyle Cutter could strike at any moment, and I have to wait on the council's damn political bullshit before I can get anything done." She hit the bag, sending it swinging wildly.

He stepped a few paces back to give her room to vent. "Maybe with his last botched attempt at killing Henry, he's gone for good."

She punched again. Twice. "The lion always returns to the watering hole," she said, using one of the Kenyan sayings he'd heard before. "Count on it. The hunting is too easy." She threw a right cross and sent the bag swinging. "I swear—I'll kill him with my own hands when I catch him."

Yeah, a familiar sentiment. After the Cutter shot Jayden, Tig's fierce determination to capture the serial killer had magnified. Add in Kim Han's murder and Karen's kidnapping, and Tig was ready to mete out justice the old-fashioned way.

He didn't agree with her—but he understood how she felt.

"What about Ari, the computer geek?" Jayden scratched at the five o'clock shadow on his chin. His receding hairline meant less hair grew on his head, but his face didn't have the same problem. "I thought Ari was going to track down who hijacked Henry's email."

"That's the subject of tonight's town council meeting—getting Ari's contract approved."

"Then you need to shower right away if you're going to be on time."

She grasped his arm with her gloved hand and turned his wrist so she could see his watch. "Crap. You're right."

Jayden helped her take off the boxing gloves. He was glad to see her using them. In the past, he had nagged her about it. No reason for her to bust her knuckles just because she needed to work out some anger. Although she'd heal fast even if she did—unlike his mortal body. It had been over two weeks since a bullet went through his leg, and the pain still came back anytime he sat or walked for too long.

"Thanks," she said, angling her head to kiss him.

He wrapped his arms around her and deepened the kiss. The smell of leather and sweat took him right back to the first time they made love.

Releasing her, he said, "Next time, wake me if I fall asleep."

"Now I have something to look forward to." She met his lips one more time before disappearing into the women's shower room.

Tig sat through the first hour of the council meeting tapping her foot. When would Ari show? The next item on the agenda was his contract.

She stood and eased open the council chamber's exit door, peering outside—no one waited in the lobby.

Where are they?

She glanced back to the dais, where the four council members sat behind a curving U-shaped desk. Frédéric's chair was empty, pushed to the end. The all-vampire council had reorganized their seating chart to avoid a gap. They wanted to distance themselves from the dead traitor.

She scanned the crowded room—more people than normal were attending the meeting.

Frédéric's co-conspirators could be among them.

That notion stuck in her craw, churning her gut, making her jaw ache like she had cracked dried maize with her teeth. She'd vacillated between thinking Frédéric was the ringleader, and thinking he'd killed himself to protect someone else.

Could she trust anyone here? Jayden, certainly. But the remainder of her list could be jotted on a business card. The entire council served as reserve police officers. Councilwoman Liza Ehrgott was the brightest of the bunch and the highest-ranking reserve officer. Liza made the list right under Jayden.

Tig had dirt on both Rolf Müller, the vice mayor, and Zeke Cannon, who wasn't on the council but was part of her reserve force. She knew their weak spots and her knowledge was enough to hold those two part-time officers in line. If they turned on her, hell would rain on them.

She didn't possess any dirt on the mayor, but her sixth sense told her to trust the mayor—as far as she could trust any politician.

And Carolyn Cubbedge, the fourth council member, was a good friend—but a lousy reserve officer. Chain of command didn't sit well with the former slave.

At this point, Tig's faith also extended to the victims who had survived the attacks: Henry Bautista, Yacov Eliahu, and Chen Méi, along with mortals Cerissa Patel and Karen Hunter.

That left close to fifty Hill vampires who might be backing the traitors, not to mention their mortal mates. Most Hill residents had mates, with a few notable exceptions, like Liza, Zeke, and the mayor. Did being leaders in a community leave no time for romance? Or in Zeke's case, was being a contract killer for the federal government a bit of a dating dampener?

The longer the Hill went without another attack, the more Frédéric looked like the ringleader. Maybe. Or was some underground group still out there, waiting for the right moment to strike? Tig's informant, Petar

Petrov, claimed a clandestine group was planning to decimate the mortal population and keep the rest for food. Unfortunately, Petar had heard no new rumors since Frédéric's demise.

From the dais, Liza was speaking about a proposed ordinance to impose an emergency curfew on Hill residents. The council had already implemented a Rule of Two. Vampires had to travel in pairs when visiting other cities adjacent to Sierra Escondida. Substantial resistance had sprung up in the community over the Rule of Two. The curfew was unlikely to gain support.

Tig motioned to Liza, giving her the universal sign to stretch it out. The councilwoman gave a short nod in reply, her perfect brunette hair, cut in a pageboy style, undisturbed by the motion.

Tig slipped out the exit door and into the lobby to scan the parking lot through the floor-to-ceiling windows. She spotted Henry's black Viper arriving with Cerissa in the passenger seat. Ari's rental car parked next to them a moment later. Tig waved at them to hurry, ushering them into the council chambers. "We're up next."

The mayor held his gavel poised, the overhead lights reflecting off his bald head as he stretched forward to pound the sound block. His puffy gray eyes appeared unhappy. He wasn't alone.

"The public portion of our meeting is now adjourned," the mayor said. "We'll move right into closed session."

The spectators took their cue and made their way out the exit door. Tig watched for stragglers, for any sign that one of them was part of the conspiracy, but nothing struck her as suspicious.

Once the room had emptied, the mayor tapped his gavel again. "Closed session is convened. Chief Anderson, is the consultant you want to hire here?"

Tig strode to the podium. "Yes, your honor."

"Then give your report," he said with an impatient wave.

Can't they read? My memo's in front of them.

Just one more formality she hated—the mayor wanted both a written and oral report. She brushed a hand along her dark blue dress uniform, smoothing out the jacket, and began.

"The police department is seeking permission to hire a computer consultant, one who is aware of the facts behind our unique community."

No one ever used the word "vampire" in the council chambers—the meetings were recorded—and she wasn't going to break with tradition.

"An organized group of conspirators, including Blanche Larson and former council member Frédéric Bonhomme, hijacked Mr. Bautista's email and hacked the police department computers. Using the information they gleaned, they launched attacks against our founders."

Rolf nodded at Tig from the dais. He brushed his straight blonde hair out of his icy blue eyes and kept his focus trained on her. Not only did she know his secret—he was addicted to adrenaline-spiked blood—but she had his gratitude for rescuing his mortal mate, Karen Turner, after the conspirators kidnapped her.

With Rolf, his gratitude would soon be forgotten, but his secret wouldn't be. He had to stay on her good side if he didn't want her spilling the beans. And staying on her good side meant supporting her proposal to hire Ari.

"Because of the emergency nature of the situation," Tig continued, "I hired a consultant Mr. Bautista recommended. Ari Dumont was instrumental in finding critical data pointing to Councilmember Bonhomme's involvement in Karen's kidnapping."

The mayor raised his bushy eyebrows. "But you didn't clear it with me first."

"I'm sorry, Mr. Mayor; there was no time." She had to suck it up, much as she hated kowtowing to him. At the point Ari offered to help, she didn't know whom to trust and had acted on her own. "The consultant is Dr. Patel's cousin and was vouched for by Mr. Bautista."

"Harrumph. How can we trust Mr. Dumont? He isn't bonded to any of us."

Henry stood. "If I may approach the podium?"

The mayor snorted. "Go ahead."

Tig stepped aside and swiveled the gooseneck toward Henry. He said into the microphone, "Mr. Dumont is my envoy."

The mayor's puffy eyes opened wider. "When did you hire an envoy? Our community hasn't used envoys in the past—"

"We had no choice but to do so the night Karen was kidnapped," Henry replied. "We needed help tracking the kidnapper's email, and Cerissa offered her cousin, an expert in the information technology field." Henry extracted a folded document from his suit coat. "He has signed an envoy contract, and I've hired him to figure out who placed a trap on my email. We suspect the saboteur worked in the IT department at the winery Rolf and I own."

"But how do we know Mr. Dumont won't disclose, ah, confidential information?"

Henry gestured to Ari. "If you could join me for a moment?" When Ari reached the podium, he slid back his sleeve, revealing fang marks, and showed Tig. "He is bonded to me, and I will continue to renew the bond for the duration of his service. Will that satisfy the council?"

Tig nodded her approval, hoping they would agree. The bond would prevent Ari from speaking about vampires to outsiders. In her view, the bite was more reliable than an envoy contract to compel Ari's silence.

"I'm satisfied," Rolf said.

"But I'm not," the mayor said. "The consultant should be bonded to a member of the council and not under Henry's control."

Tig didn't like that idea. She trusted Henry not to interfere with her work. If a council member bonded Ari, they might take advantage of the consultant's loyalties and pump him for confidential information. But she remained silent. Better to let Henry duke out this one. As a founder of the Hill community, he had more gravitas than she ever would.

"Mr. Mayor—" Henry began, his face clouding over.

"No offense intended, Henry," the mayor blurted out. "It's just that Mr. Dumont will be working for us."

"He is also working for me. We have a trap—"

"A back door," Ari whispered.

"Yes, a back door on the winery email server. Mr. Dumont is going to fix the problem for us."

"Still, the Hill's interest trumps yours," the mayor said.

The town attorney, Marcus Collings, rose to his feet. Some mortals on the Hill had compared Marcus to a young Bradley Cooper, with his dishwater-blonde hair combed back.

"If Henry is willing, I would be happy to bond the consultant to me," Marcus said, tugging at the corner of his neatly trimmed mustache.

His tell. He only tugged at his mustache when nervous.

Tig raised an eyebrow. What did the town attorney have to be nervous about? His idea was a smart move. He and Henry were close friends—Marcus had been part of the group that founded the town in the late 1800s. If anyone who worked for the current government could persuade Henry, it would be Marcus.

Henry glanced over at Tig, and she signaled her agreement. She didn't care who blood bonded Ari so long as that person wasn't on the council.

"That would be acceptable with me," Henry said. "If Mr. Dumont agrees."

Ari raised his hand. "All good here."

The vote went as planned. Passed four-zero.

Tig took the microphone back. "Thank you. If we may be excused, we have work to do."

The mayor waved his dismissal. She led her group outside and said to Henry, "If Ari doesn't mind working tonight, I'd like him to join me back at the police station."

Henry paused, appearing to consider her request. "After he stops by Marcus's house. They should take care of formalities first."

"Sounds like a plan," Tig said.

"But please allow time for him to meet with me later." Henry looked at Ari. "He needs to fix the computer server at the winery, too."

"I should be able to do both," Ari said. "Give me a moment to speak with my cousin before I go."

Ari crossed the parking lot to his car, with Cerissa following. Tig watched them go.

Hmm. Her new computer consultant warranted watching. He better not leak any confidential information to the town attorney before she was ready to disclose it. Sometimes, timing was everything. She would impress the need for secrecy on Ari as soon as the bite was over.

Yes, Marcus was a better choice than a council member, and she didn't doubt Marcus's loyalty to the Hill. But if she'd learned anything during her decades on the Hill, everyone had an angle and worked it to their benefit. Even the town attorney. So both men would be on her radar until the case was solved.

CHAPTER 5

Town Hall Parking Lot—Moments Later

Cerissa stopped by Ari's rental car. He held up his hand and tilted his head in Tig's direction, who stood talking with Henry. Tig was almost as tall as him and looked sharp with her hair cut into a short afro. Her skin was the color of espresso, much darker than Cerissa's own nutmeg tone or Henry's lighter brown. From Tig's command of English, it was hard to believe she had been born in Kenya over four hundred years ago.

Moments later, Tig nodded her goodbyes and strode off in the direction of the police station. Once she was out of hearing range, Ari gestured to the bite on his wrist. "Why didn't you tell me fang serum contains a sexual stimulant?"

"I did. You weren't listening."

"Shit, that stuff is powerful." He smoothed out his sleeve over Henry's bite, tugging at the cuff. "I'm still sporting a woody."

"Ewww." Cerissa covered her ears. "I don't want to hear about it."

It was bad enough she'd had to consent to Henry biting Ari. A thread of jealousy had wrapped around her heart while she watched Henry's fangs penetrate her cousin's wrist. The council's decision to let Marcus take over the bite was a win in her book.

"Come on, Ciss. Fang serum is powerful. How does that stuff work?"

"I suspect one of the component compounds causes the reaction. The sample I had was a small one from Blanche, and the test I ran consumed it. I need more to complete my studies."

She had tried running simulations on the various complex molecules found in Blanche's fang serum, including the morphing hormone—a substance she was far more interested in than the sexual stimulant. She just couldn't reconcile why the Lux morphing hormone was produced by a vampire's body.

She suspected the morphing hormone somehow turbocharged the healing properties of vampire blood—the two together were required to turn a mortal into a vampire.

But why did vampires produce the same specialized hormone that the Lux did? Her scientist's mind wouldn't let go of the mystery.

"Hey, Ciss, over here." Ari snapped his fingers in front of her face, and she focused on him again. "Don't you see the potential? This is big."

"What are you talking about?"

He leaned back against the rental car, stretching like a cat. "And you call yourself a biochemist. Decode the fang serum and produce the sexual stimulant commercially. The research lab you're building…you get a potency drug to market, and you won't need investors—you'll be rich."

"I don't need to be rich." She had a purchase option on a land parcel on the public side of the Hill's wall and preliminary architectural plans.

But town approval was required to build her lab. "What I need is community support. We want vampires eager to try clone blood even though it'll cost more than the expired donor blood they usually feed on. They need to be excited about paying the difference."

Ari made a funny face, like she'd missed an obvious point. "The potency drug profits could subsidize clone blood production, letting you charge the vamps less for the blood." He waggled his eyebrows. "And you can't tell me you aren't curious."

She frowned at him. "Curiosity isn't the issue. How do you think Henry would feel if I asked, 'Can I have a sample of your serum to experiment with?' That's just rude."

The one time she'd examined Henry's fangs, he'd consented, but his body language had communicated his displeasure at being poked and prodded. She didn't want to subject him to that again. He was her boyfriend, the man she loved—not a test subject.

"Look, kid, I'm not saying to do this today, but think long term. There must be a way to get a sample without offending him—or ask your sponsor, Leopold."

She wrinkled her nose. Too much would have to be explained if she sought Leopold's help. "Ari, I'm not going to—"

"Now, Ciss, don't pass on this one. Do you know how many drugs for erectile dysfunction are sold annually? I can tell you this: the number is high, and it's not because they can't get it up. They're using those drugs recreationally, to decrease the time between repeat bouts of sweaty, blissful sex."

"Ari—"

"Come on, Ciss."

"You need to drag your mind out of the gutter and back on business." She opened his driver's door and gestured for him to climb in. "And speaking of which, it's time for you to go."

He stepped into the car but didn't sit. Instead, he leaned against the doorframe. "Not so quick. The Protectors are getting impatient. With you and Henry teamed up to find the VDM, we need a plan."

"But it's not like a bomb is ticking. With Blanche and Frédéric dead, the conspirators are more likely to pull back and regroup than strike again so soon. Of course, the attacks could end with them."

Ari raised his head from the doorframe. "You better hope you're right, kid. If I were the VDM, I wouldn't wait."

The Protectors had sent her to Sierra Escondida to uncover the group intent on turning mortals into blood slaves. There had been no hint of another impending assault, and she had no real clues to go on. What was she supposed do, wiggle her nose and magically reveal the VDM conspirators? It didn't work that way.

"Look, Ari. I need to up my spy game, which means getting everyone accustomed to my presence here and becoming part of the wallpaper. Then I'll work on wooing investors for the lab as a way to meet vampires from other communities and broaden our net."

"That's not the real reason. You want time to nest with tall, dark, and bitey over there," he said with mirth in his eyes and a jerk of his chin in Henry's direction.

She glowered at Ari. "Give it a rest. I've had a rough few weeks. I deserve some time off. Besides, you're in the best position to discover a new lead—find out who hacked Henry's computer."

"That's not the real reason you want to delay." He clasped his hands and held them to the side of his face, his eyes mocking her. "My little cousin's in love. It's so cute."

Now she knew why Henry hated being called *cute*. She scowled at Ari. "You have an appointment to get to. Or do you want me to go with you to Marcus's house?"

He snorted. "A little awkward, don't ya think? Hey, I understood why you wanted to be there when Henry bit. But Marcus is a stranger—no reason for you to chaperone."

She furrowed her brow. "I was going to leave before the bite. I just wanted to make sure everything went smoothly."

"What's the big deal?" Ari sat down in the driver's seat. "Five minutes, in and out. I think I can handle this without you."

"Well, Nicholas will probably be there, anyway."

"Nicholas?"

"The assistant town attorney. He and Marcus are dating."

Henry had filled her in—the town council had granted a dispensation to allow the two men to date. Normally, mortals had to be mated before coming to the Hill, as dating on the Hill was forbidden. But exceptions were made for certain hard-to-fill job categories, and assistant town attorney was one of them.

"Hmm," Ari murmured, raising an eyebrow.

"Get that gleam out of your eye. You are not seducing them."

"*Moi*? How can you even suggest that?"

"Because I know you too well. *Behave*, Ari. Don't make me regret not going with you," she said, and closed the car door, shutting off whatever flip remark was on the tip of his tongue.

Chapter 6

MARCUS COLLINGS'S HOME—TEN MINUTES LATER

Marcus pulled his Mercedes into the garage. He rushed through the house—a folder with Ari's background clutched in his hand—and opened the front door for the computer consultant, who had arrived ahead of him.

"Come in, come in," Marcus said.

He led Ari into the living room and offered him a seat on the black leather couch. Ari scanned the surroundings and gestured to the Andy Warhol painting across from him. "Very nice. Gives the room a modernistic yet retro feel."

"Thank you." Marcus lounged back on his favorite egg chair, which was covered in white leather. The monochrome furniture let his colorful and bold art collection stand out.

"Is Nicolas here? Perhaps he'd like to join us?"

Why is Ari interested in Nicolas? "He left for New York this afternoon on business."

A flash of disappointment crossed Ari's face.

Odd.

Marcus leaned back and brushed his fingers over his mustache. He had never placed faith in giving an envoy access to the Hill. Sure, his advice to the mayor when Cerissa first arrived was they had to let her stay—the treaty didn't provide any other choice.

In truth, any mortal who became involved with vampires—mated or envoy, it didn't matter—wasn't to be trusted.

Marcus had learned that lesson the hard way. His only offspring had used him to become a vampire and dumped him. The whole experience made it difficult for him to trust anyone's motives—including Cerissa's and Ari's. And something about Ari reminded Marcus of the man he had once called *his prince*. Another reason to be suspicious.

He opened the file folder and scanned the list of credentials and projects the mortal had worked on. "From your curriculum vitae, you appear well qualified to provide computer consulting services."

"I've worked in the field for a long time," Ari said, his forest-green eyes bright.

Ari balanced a briefcase on his knees and flipped the latch open. His thick head of unruly, dark hair, his square jaw, and the way he held himself with confidence fit Marcus's idea of a fantasy lover. An eight out of ten.

And he never slept with anyone less than a seven.

When it came time for the bite, well, the experience would be pleasurable for at least one of them, even if he didn't trust Ari. After all, he never let distrust get in the way of seduction.

"Here's my contract." Ari removed a document from the briefcase. "I figured you'd want to review the legalese before the mayor puts his John Hancock on it. The terms from my proposal are incorporated—you should find it a fair restatement."

"I thought we might chat first." Marcus set the pages aside. "So, you are Cerissa's cousin?"

"Yes, I'm her older cousin. Her mother and my father are brother and sister."

Cerissa and Ari's coloring were enough alike to validate Ari's statement. In fact, Marcus could imagine his own white skin pressed against Ari's brown tones—a nice image. "Were you close as children?"

Ari placed his briefcase on the floor. "Yes, but I don't understand what my childhood has to do with my consulting contract."

"I was curious whether your background and upbringing are the same as hers."

"Why?"

Marcus didn't reply, simply waited.

Ari cocked his head. "Look, Marcus, I'm not sure why my upbringing matters. If you want to ask something specific about me, then go for it."

"Fine." Marcus narrowed his eyes. "I just thought to ease into the topic."

"Which is?"

"How you learned about vampires. Unless, of course, Cerissa simply told you?"

"Ahh, now I get it." Ari crossed his legs. "Cerissa didn't break her envoy agreement with Leopold, if that's your beef. I found out about vampires before she became Leopold's envoy. A relative saved a vampire's life back in the 1800s. The story is well known to my family."

"Who was this vampire?"

"Leopold."

"Did you meet Leopold—"

"Nope, never met him."

"Then you knew nothing but a family tale."

"When I was introduced to Henry, I recognized the signs. The rings on his fingernails were a dead giveaway," Ari said, smirking.

His bad pun deserved a demerit. Marcus pressed his lips together and downgraded Ari to a seven. If everything else checked out, the young man was still in the running for paramour status, but only barely.

"And Henry's slightly cool handshake confirmed the fact," Ari continued. "But I kept my mouth shut. I've told no mortal about him. When Karen was kidnapped, Henry had to disclose too much to enlist my help, so he asked me to be his envoy. Simple."

Marcus sat back. "I see."

Something about the story seemed off. Was Ari covering for Cerissa? Had she violated her contract with Leopold and created this fiction to conceal the breach? Too much was at stake if Marcus guessed wrong. Now was not the time for the world to learn about vampires.

Ari's look remained smug. "Anything else?"

"Your credentials as a computer expert are in order, but your personal life is…very interesting."

"Oh?"

"You're based out of Miami—"

"South Beach, actually."

"Yet you appear on the West Coast at a moment's notice whenever Cerissa needs you."

"Nothing strange about it. I travel a lot on business. As a consultant, my schedule is flexible."

"And wherever you go, there appears to be a trail of lovers left behind."

Ari scrunched his dark eyebrows. Even frowning, the man was handsome. "Why the interest in my sex life? What does that have to do with my qualifications?"

"It might make you a security risk."

Ari interlocked his fingers over his crossed knee. "Marcus, I don't need this job. I'm doing this as a favor to Cerissa. If you don't want my help, I'll leave. You can deal with the problem yourself."

"I meant—"

"Just remember, you guys were your own worst security risk—running your email through unsecured ISPs with no firewall between your PCs and the outside world. I'm going to build a server system here on the Hill, one your town will control. I've already migrated Henry's personal email to my private system, but you would be better off acting as your own ISP."

Ari stood. "Until your server room is constructed, I was going to do my best to secure the police department's existing email system. But I don't need the noise. So, if you'll excuse me, I'll go."

"Don't be in such a hurry," Marcus said, indicating with a wave of his hand for Ari to return to the couch. "My question was not intended as an insult. But it is reasonable to ask whether your indiscriminate sexual liaisons might lead to someone learning about us through you."

"You're joking, right?" The consultant resumed his seat with a show of reluctance. "I thought Henry's bite would seal my lips when among the uninitiated."

Marcus tugged at his mustache. "It's supposed to."

How much to say? Repeatedly wiping a mortal's mind made them resistant. And then there had been rumors—nothing proven, of course—that at least one bonded mate had *allegedly* told his family. His memory had never been wiped, so it couldn't be that.

But the vampire may have been at fault. Her relationship with her mortal mate was on the rocks, and she wasn't renewing the bite frequently enough. The two ultimately broke up and the mortal's mind was wiped, ending the threat. Still...

"Supposed to?" Ari repeated. "Doesn't the bite always work?"

"Some in our community believe the loyalty bond is less than perfect."

Ari stared at him silently, looking skeptical.

Marcus held up his hands. "I'm just being thorough. Which is what I get paid to be."

Ari huffed out a frustrated sound. "I know how to use lip glue, or I wouldn't be top in my field. Check my references—you aren't the first client to keep sensitive secrets. Not to mention, I've known about vampires for years and never posed a security risk to any of the communities. But if you have concerns, I'll go on my way. My loyalty will be secured by Henry's bite, even if you don't think that's a perfect fix."

As Ari spoke, an intoxicating scent reached Marcus's nose. Anger had stirred the mortal's blood. Marcus's mouth watered in anticipation, and he shifted in his chair to hide his arousal.

"Please don't leave," he said, giving his best imitation of a friendly smile. Despite Marcus's mistrust of mortals, nothing Ari had said so far warranted dismissing him. "Not only are you smart, you held your ground nicely. And you are a very handsome young man."

The consultant eased back in his chair, looking surprised. "Are you coming on to me?"

"Perhaps. My investigator led me to believe you are bisexual."

"You could put it that way. I consider myself 'omnisexual'—I'll eat anything. But I thought you had a boyfriend. Nicholas, right?"

"Nicholas and I haven't reached the committed stage yet. We aren't mates; we aren't *exclusive*. We are taking things slowly."

"And what would you be looking for with me?"

"I thought you might enjoy the benefits that come with the bite."

Ari grinned a big, sloppy, I'll-fuck-anything grin. "Call me curious. I've wondered what Cerissa finds so fascinating about vampires."

"You mean to say, even knowing about us, you've never had a vampire lover?" Marcus started envisioning the possibilities. He'd score fresh blood *and* introduce a newbie to the delights of their world. A win-win. "Perhaps we should correct your oversight."

"Why don't we finish the contract first? Then we can see what comes up," Ari said with a laugh. "Although I usually put play before work, Cerissa would kill me if I didn't make sure all the paperwork was finalized tonight."

"Of course. That sounds like a perfect plan." Marcus picked up the document and skimmed through it. Nothing in the contract raised any concerns. He took out his Montblanc and signed on the line for the town attorney. There was also a space for the mayor to sign, but with Marcus's approval, the mayor wouldn't even bother reading it.

"Done." Marcus returned his pen to his suit coat pocket. "Now, let's see about our playtime."

He stared into those forest-green eyes, using his gaze to both seduce and freeze his prey. He had no intent to force himself on Ari, but freezing the mortal would let him know what kind of powerful creature he was playing with.

For some, danger was an aphrodisiac.

Marcus stood and sauntered toward where Ari sat, keeping his gaze riveted on those sexy eyes.

Except Ari didn't freeze. He bounced to his feet. "I'm easy, in more ways than one."

Marcus hid his surprise. "That's very good information to have."

He pulled Ari into his arms. Later would be soon enough to figure out why his gaze had failed to hold Ari in place. Right now, Marcus needed to get out of his head and enjoy the banquet before him.

After Marcus demonstrated the pleasures that went with the bite and they both had their releases, he surveyed Ari's naked body lying next to his. Not a bad conquest, even if he had yet to learn anything new about Ari or Cerissa. And then there was the other matter—Ari's failure to freeze. Had Henry's recent bite somehow interfered? It seemed the likely explanation.

Ari rolled off the bed. "As fun as you are, I should start working on Tig's computer soon. I'm going to clean up."

"Of course."

Nice to know. Some guys were slobs and would go into the office straight from bed. Marcus was more on the fastidious side. He had suggested they shower together beforehand, and they had, much to his delight. An entertaining appetizer. Though there had been a brief pause in the fun when Ari had insisted on using the bathroom—alone—before they made love.

Was Ari pee-shy, or had he needed a moment to collect himself before taking the plunge and having sex with a vampire? Either way, the break hadn't cooled the heat between them.

Speaking of which, wow.

Returning clean and dry from the bathroom and showing off his best attributes, Ari picked up his pants from where they were draped over a chair and pulled them on. A silver cylinder fell out of his pocket and rolled across the hardwood floor to stop short of Marcus's toes. The device looked like a fat pen but had four thumbwheels, and the end was similar to a tire pressure gauge.

Marcus bent to pick it up.

Ari swept in fast to beat him to it. "Don't touch that."

"Why? If it's silver, you're not allowed to bring it to the Hill."

Ari stuck the wandlike cylinder in his back pocket and waved his empty hand. "No worries on that front. Stainless steel."

Then why didn't he want me to touch it?

Marcus reached around to grab it.

Ari dodged and plopped onto a chair, trapping the device underneath him. "Naughty, naughty, Marcus."

"What is it?"

"A calibrating tool. Computer stuff, ya know? I don't want you inadvertently messing with the current setting."

Ah, tech geeks and their toys.

Ari stuck his foot in a shoe and leaned over to tie the laces. "One thing, Marcus. I should have asked this up front. When we combined the bite with sex, was some sort of commitment involved? I'm not into regular relationships. I'm seeing other people, and I don't plan on stopping."

"So am I." With the council's blessing, Marcus had taken Nicholas as a lover and had no intention of giving him up, but they had yet to combine sex with the bite. Father Matt was currently playing a surrogate role, biting Nicholas on a regular basis to ensure the loyalty bond.

"Are you sure it's okay?" Ari looked doubtful. "Cerissa had led me to believe the Hill was kind of conservative about these things."

"Nothing to fear, dear boy," Marcus reassured him. "There is a small loophole in the rule. We can jump through it and avoid the problem."

"And, being the fine attorney you are, you've found and exploited that loophole before?"

"You are correct. Everyone knows my bite is to secure your loyalty, and technically, no other vampire may *bite* you. But it does not make us *mates* unless I assert the claim publicly within seventy-two hours of the occasion. And while I've had a splendid time and would welcome an encore when we renew the bond, I will not assert any claim. So, you are safe."

The same couldn't be said for Nicholas. The young mortal had made it clear—once they combined the bite with sex, he expected Marcus to announce they were mates and become an exclusive couple. But Ari? From the investigator's report, Marcus had no fears Ari would make a similar demand and give up his wild ways.

Ari frowned. "Cerissa seemed certain another vampire would be able to tell."

"While a vampire can tell whether a person has been *recently* bitten and presumed to be mated, they cannot easily discern the identity of the biter. For me to guess, I would need to get close to the vampire in question, remember their scent, then get close enough to their mate to smell the same scent in their blood. That's why our tradition requires the vampire asserting the claim to do so publicly. Avoids mistakes."

"I bet Cerissa isn't aware of your loophole."

"No reason to mention it to her, is there?"

"None I can think of," Ari agreed. "With your knowledge of vampire law, and my knowledge of computers, we can have an arrangement meeting both our needs."

"As any good alliance should."

Chapter 7

Rancho Bautista del Murciélago—the next day

Cerissa caught some sleep and then examined the basement room Henry had offered her. With the right furniture and equipment, it would become a temporary lab to work in until the real one was built. The room ran thirty feet long by twenty feet wide and lay right underneath Henry's spacious drawing room—no, *their* drawing room.

It's going to be a while before I think of the house as ours.

Bare cinderblock lined the basement. White trails streaked down the gray blocks, signs of water intrusion. A quick trip to the local hardware store solved that problem, and she spent most of the morning applying a waterproof sealer over the bricks. She waited four hours for the primer to dry and started rolling on a base coat of Swiss Coffee.

The hot spring day turned the usually cool basement into a sauna. How could Henry sleep in this heat? The paint fumes made breathing difficult, so she switched on the air conditioner.

Henry rested nearby in one of the locked crypt rooms. The crypts ran underneath the kitchen and game room. He had insisted she stay away from him during the day. While the crystal in his arm prevented him from causing her any real harm, and vice versa, he refused to let her catch a few Zs with him.

Silly fears. He would never hurt me.

Halfway through the second coat of paint, she felt him stir to consciousness—another early moonrise. It would be a while before he was showered and dressed.

The dampening bracelet had been adjusted, so she now received a trickle of his emotions whenever he was awake, unless he wanted to block her. He had a list of exercises to do to gain control over the bracelet, allowing him to cut the connection if he needed to.

But it didn't work the other way around. She had no control over the connection mentally—only the recipient of the crystal did. But an app Ari installed on her phone allowed her to switch to the *no connection* setting.

Everyone deserved emotional privacy, although being connected emotionally didn't bother her as much as it did Henry. The Lux were accustomed to sharing emotions with each other—that was what their third eye was for. So far, he was still learning to master the blocking techniques Ari taught him.

Thinking about Ari reminded her—exploring the components of fang serum was still on her "to do" list. Despite his taunts over creating a sexual stimulant—which she had no intention of doing—she did need to run more tests to make sure the potent serum wouldn't hurt her over time. She tried not to sigh at the thought. It just seemed so invasive to ask Henry for a sample.

So far, all she knew was that when he bit, the morphing hormone his fangs injected would force her back to Lux form, interrupting their lovemaking and his bite. She had no idea what drinking her Lux blood would do to him and didn't want to take the risk to find out.

She kept working from the short ladder, dipping the roller into the tray, running the paint up the wall, watching the brick's crevices sop up the liquid latex.

"Aren't you being productive?"

"Oh," she squeaked, and spun around, gouging the wet paint with the roller's handle. "I didn't expect you so soon."

He stood there shirtless, wearing pajama bottoms, looking sexy as hell, and the temperature in the room rose a few notches despite the air conditioning.

"When I realized you were in the basement, I wanted to see all was well. You didn't have to do this by yourself. I could have hired a contractor to finish the room."

"I didn't want a stranger down here while you slept."

He stretched and yawned, his muscles rippling, his hair hanging loose to his shoulders. "There are vendors vetted for the Hill, and I have other places to sleep."

She set the roller in its drip tray, climbed down the ladder, and pulled off her latex gloves. "I don't mind the work. It's kind of nice—I feel like I'm accomplishing something."

"I think your nose would disagree." He wet his fingers against his tongue, used them to scrub the tip of her nose, and then displayed the white paint.

She shrugged. "I'll shower when I'm done."

He wrapped his arms around her, drawing her close. His cheek felt soft against hers—he'd shaved already. The enticing scent of his spicy cologne started a tingle in her belly.

"Would you like to go upstairs?" he whispered in her ear. His deep voice, his Castilian accent riding his words, sent a shot of excitement straight through her.

"What about the paint?" Her bare arms were dotted with splatter.

"The smudges make you sexier, if such a thing were possible."

They made a brief stop in the kitchen to allow Henry to feed first. He insisted on taking the edge off his hunger before biting her. When they reached the bedroom, Cerissa stripped, and he was out of his pajama bottoms just as fast.

She thrilled at the sight of him naked, pulled him into bed, and swept her fingers across his well-defined pecs, letting them linger on his nipples, pinching each lightly.

His crucifix necklace hung around his neck. He lifted the chain over his head and stretched to drop it on the nightstand, giving her a great view of his tight ass. When he twisted back around to face her, his erection brushed her thigh.

An idea occurred to her, and she touched his shiny tungsten bracelet. "Take it off too."

"Why?"

"I want you to feel what I feel." She ran a finger over the solid metal. "While we make love."

He raised one eyebrow and gave her a cocky smirk, a look saying he was game if she was. He unlocked the clasp and set the bracelet aside.

As soon as it was off his wrist, the warm caress of his love wove through her mind, twining around her love for him. He pulled her to him, brushing his lips against hers. She opened to him, and his tongue delved in, strong and masculine.

Copper and salt flavors invaded her mouth along with his tongue—remnants of the blood he'd drunk before they came upstairs. In the past, he'd been compulsive about rinsing his mouth so she wouldn't taste blood when they kissed. Had they passed one more level of intimacy?

Before they were done tonight, they'd pass another.

She ran her fingers through his silky black mane, gripping his hair to pull him tight against her mouth, the passion of his kiss sending a sexy shiver through her. He tweaked her nipple, and the tingles pooled in her core.

Pushing him on his back, she straddled his stomach, her knees digging into the soft cotton bedspread. She gazed into his dark brown eyes. *Brown* was too plain a word to describe them. They glowed like stained glass, a deep shade of chestnut, and were framed with long, full black lashes.

"Cerissa, are you forgetting something?"

"Oh. Yeah." *The fang serum.* "Be right back."

She ducked into the adjoining bathroom. From the medicine cabinet she removed a hypo injector—the size of a fat silver marker pen—that held various Lux medicines. She dialed in the code for the stabilizing hormone and pressed the blunt end to her neck, injecting it.

Returning to bed, she liked what she found: the covers pulled back and him stretched out naked on the sheet. She straddled him again. "Now, where was I?"

"Right here," he said seductively, his hands on her back bringing her closer.

She dangled a breast over his mouth, and he sucked her in, rolling the nipple, tickling her with quick flicks of his tongue.

She moaned as excitement sparked deep inside her.

His teeth scraped over the nipple before he released it to give the other equal treatment, his fingers replacing his lips on the first.

The way he suckled her—much more, and she'd melt into a puddle on his chest.

His erection lay pressed against his belly, her wet sex holding it down. She raised her hips, and his hard length sprang upright. Hovering over him, she rested her opening over his tip and brought her breasts to his chest, arching her back like a cat, rubbing her nipples on his skin.

He groaned. "You do love torturing me."

She wrapped her hand around his wrist where the crystal was embedded, pinning his arm to the bed by his shoulder, and murmured, "Watch this."

The words had barely left her mouth when their minds linked. The physical sensations his body experienced flooded her—his balls tightened as his penis twitched, aching for entry.

She impaled herself on him, enjoying the exquisite scrape of his erection entering her, followed seconds later by what he felt: the sensation in his sensitive tip as it slid along her inner wall, his shaft moving through her tight opening, squeezed by her.

She froze for a moment with him deeply inside her, her eyes closed, letting her mind absorb and adjust to the dual experience. When she opened her eyes, his were solid black.

"*Madre de Dios*," he said. "Is that what it's like for you?"

She smiled and raised her hips to slide almost to his tip and then down again to rock her wet cleft against his skin, the contact sucking on her, the slick skin letting loose with a gentle tug.

She closed her eyes to focus on two sets of sensations—his and hers—angling her hips to make sure the sensitive nerve bundle in his tip rode along her inner wall with each thrust, the crystal feeding her his excitement as she hit the right spot over and over.

He ran his fingers through her hair, fisting the strands, and brought her neck to his mouth. His hunger for her blood rushed through their connection, an uncontrollable urge, and his fangs pierced her neck—a quick sting, and then the potent chemical combination in his fang serum sent her into overload.

She rode him with a fierce speed, losing herself, no longer aware where his body stopped and hers began.

They were truly one: one mind, one body, one orgasm. She peaked first, but she'd barely started when he exploded within her, a single shot of mind-blowing intensity, as hers kept going, the ecstatic shudders strong. She held on, moving with him, until the last tremor died out completely.

Panting, she rested her face on his chest. His heart beat at a much slower pace, even when her pulse raced with passion. She released his wrist, and his body's intense sensations slipped from her mind.

But his powerful love remained.

Her eyes welled with tears. She had him back. He was hers again, and they had forever to share their love.

He stroked her hair, moving the waves away from her face, and kissed the top of her head. "What are you feeling, *mi amor*? Your emotions…are confusing."

She swiped at her tears and rose to meet his soulful eyes, which had returned to normal. "Happy. Grateful. Deeply in love with you."

"Then why are you crying?"

She stroked his cheek and traced his lips with her thumb. "I came so close to losing you."

The Protectors had almost separated them forever. Henry's quick thinking and negotiation skills had backed the Protectors into a corner—they had no choice but to let Cerissa return to him or they'd have to go to war against the vampire communities.

"You'll never lose me, *cariña*. I'll follow you no matter where you go."

She rolled off him and snuggled in close. His body was cooler than hers, but not cold, and she pressed closer, the heat from her workout quenched against his skin. She followed the curve of his pecs with her fingers until she drifted off.

CHAPTER 8

RANCHO BAUTISTA DEL MURCIÉLAGO—MOMENTS LATER

Henry gently held Cerissa as she dozed. She was making soft, contented sounds. As much as he'd like to let her sleep, the hour was too early, and she needed to refuel after he fed on her blood. He nuzzled her neck, kissing the mark left there by his fangs.

"That feels nice," she murmured.

"Good. But you should shower and eat dinner."

"I want to stay right here, cuddled next to you."

"Your body needs calories, particularly after I bite. You said so yourself."

"Beast," she said, slapping his shoulder lightly. "It's not fair using my words against me."

"Come on." He pulled back the sheet she had tucked under her chin.

"All right." She slid out of bed. "Aren't you coming with me?"

"I'm going to strip the bed. You left a trail of dry paint flecks on the sheets."

"Hey, I offered to shower first."

"And I had no patience to wait. So, I'll do penance by stripping the bed, while you shower and go downstairs to eat."

"Sounds fair to me."

She came back to the bed to kiss him. When she turned to leave, he lay there a moment longer, watching her nicely round butt move with each step. He let out a satisfied sigh as the bathroom door closed behind her.

After he finished changing the sheets, he directed another mental burst of love in her direction and then snapped on the tungsten bracelet, reducing their connection to a mild trickle. As fun as it had been to connect through the crystal, he needed some *head space*, to use Ari's term.

Henry showered in his own bathroom. He rinsed off the paint flecks that had transferred to his skin and pictured the way she had looked naked and splattered: so beautiful, so loving, so perfect. How did he get so lucky?

He shut off the water, grabbed the towel, and wrapped it around his waist.

I am not worthy of her.

A chill crept into his solar plexus, the hair rising on his wet arms, his happiness retreating as a long-buried memory surfaced. He fought to force the vision away, stepped from the shower, and stared at himself in the mirror.

"I am not that person," he said to his reflection, gripping the sink's edge.

The recollection usually had an aura like a nightmare—horrific, but surreal and distant, easy to suppress and forget. Now, the worst moment of his life was back in high definition.

"I have changed. It will never happen again."

He tensed his muscles, forcing the memory away until it receded to the dark place where it lived.

Gone.

By the time he left the bathroom, he'd managed to lock up his emotions and pocket the key, his mind emptied of the disturbing vision.

Dressed in blue jeans and a short-sleeve shirt, he strode into his mansion's kitchen carrying the dirty sheets and towels. Cerissa stood by the center island, wearing a lovely summer set, capris and a sleeveless blouse. The May night had become unseasonably warm; June was a few days away.

"I put fresh towels in your bedroom," he told her.

"Our bedroom."

"Of course, *cariña*." He balanced the dirty linens in one arm and slipped the other around her waist, pulling her gently to him. "Our bedroom."

He kissed her, enjoying her warm lips on his. The scent of *enchiladas verde* was on her breath.

Good. She's eaten.

He crossed the kitchen and opened the closet doors concealing the washer and dryer. He loaded the sheets into the washer and started them, leaving the towels on top of the dryer. They would go in the next load.

"This feels kind of weird," she said. "What do we do now?"

He gave her a lopsided grin. "Whatever we want to do. This is no different from any other evening we've spent together, except you stay here to sleep, instead of returning to Gaea's house."

Cerissa tilted her head and smiled—a look he recognized: she wanted something, and he suspected he wouldn't like what followed.

"All right," she said, "then I have a request."

He fanned his fingers, gesturing for her to continue.

"I, ah, I need fang serum and blood specimens," she said. "Do you mind?"

He eyed the odd medical implements spread out on the granite counter. "I was wondering what those were for. Why do you need these samples?"

"For testing. I want to do additional tests on fang serum, compare it to what I got from Blanche, make sure the components are the same, to ensure your bite causes me no harm in the long term. As for the blood sample, if I'm going to help Rolf find a solution to his need for adrenaline-spiked blood, yours will provide a baseline for comparison to his."

She patted a tall seat by the kitchen island.

He took the offered stool, resting his arm on the granite counter and facing her. "You will need samples from Rolf as well."

"True. I was going to ask Karen to arrange a time."

He held up his hand. "The request will be better coming from me."

"All right. And after you donate, I have a surprise for you."

He raised one eyebrow. He usually liked her surprises. "Where do you want to start?"

"With fang serum." She handed him the cup. A rubbery material was stretched over the top and held on with a band. "Bite into the latex and pull forward to release the serum."

He sniffed it.

Unappetizing.

She looked at him quizzically. "What's wrong?"

"They don't pop out on demand."

She stepped between his legs and moved her hair aside, inviting him to nuzzle her. He set the cup down and took her into his arms, kissing her soft neck. Her blood's scent did what the cup could not: his fangs sprang into place, and he sighed. He'd rather plunge them into her warm vein than into a sterile container.

"The cup, not me."

Had she read his feelings through the crystal's connection? Or was he that transparent? He palmed the container. "As you wish."

"Wait." She raised a swab toward his mouth. "Open." She swabbed around his fangs, and the light touch of cotton tickled the sensitive area. Finished, she dropped it in a tube. "Now I'm going to put my finger in your mouth. Don't bite."

"I suggest you hurry."

"Open wider." She ran her fingertip along the roof. "The gland feels engorged. How long does it take to refill?"

She removed her finger, and he answered, "I've never timed it. Less than an hour."

"Okay," she said, motioning to the cup in his hand. "Bite down on the latex."

The stretchy material *popped* as his fangs pierced the drum-like cover, creating an odd sensation when it gave way. He pushed the container forward, and his fangs drained, accompanied by a disconcerting tingle.

When the tingle stopped, he held up the cup. A clear liquid, tinted yellow, covered the bottom. He handed it to her, and she screwed on a lid. He ran his tongue across the back of his teeth, scraping his taste buds to lose the bitter chemical taste left by the latex.

"Let me take another look." She swabbed around his fangs and then pressed the gland.

"Hey," he said, pulling back.

"Did my touch hurt?"

"No, but it didn't feel good, either."

"Please let me try again. I'll be more careful."

He opened his mouth and let her. It was part of the deal, being mated to a scientist. She pressed, and expecting her touch this time, he didn't pull back.

"The gland is less turgid, less round." She withdrew her finger and selected a tube with a fat needle. "Now for the blood sample."

The procedure was nothing new. In the past, he had donated to help other injured vampires heal. She was smooth with the needle.

"There," she said, pressing a cotton ball over the punctured arm vein. Completely unnecessary. For a small wound like this, his skin would grow back in ten minutes. She capped the needle and set the tube aside. "And now your reward."

She handed him a shiny silver pouch. Usually, she used a blue bag to package blood from her human clones and a red one when she drew a higher concentration of red blood cells. What did the silver bag contain?

"If you don't mind being my guinea pig," she added.

"Guinea pig?" He started a pan of water heating on the stove. The pouch wasn't wrapped in a self-warming bag. "What is different about this blood?"

"While I was away, I figured out how to induce the clones to produce a higher concentration of stress hormones—adrenaline, as well as cortisol and norepinephrine, if you want to be technical—to create the blood Rolf craves."

"You think this will satisfy him?"

"We'll have to experiment to find out. I don't know what the cause is. It could be a substance addiction he can be weaned off, with support. If his problem is akin to a deficiency, more like a diabetic who needs insulin to survive, then I'll have to determine the proper dosage. Just because the blood produces a mental high doesn't mean it's bad for him."

Henry turned off the flame under the pot and slid the bag into the warm water, swishing it around so the contents would heat evenly without cooking. Cooked blood was disgusting.

"There is an exhilaration that comes from drinking adrenaline-spiked blood—"

"I'm calling it 'adrenaline-enhanced' for now. The other term has baggage."

"You could be right." He fished the bag out of the water, cut the corner with scissors, and poured it into an insulated coffee mug. A quick sniff told him it smelled like the blood of a victim who'd been hunted.

Is this a good idea?

He sniffed again, and a thread of apprehension brushed his skin. He took a sip and closed his eyes. The sudden rush pounded through his veins, followed by an ice-cold chill. He dropped the mug on the kitchen island. It toppled, and the blood spread across the granite counter.

Cerissa rushed to his side. "Henry, are you all right?"

He stumbled back, fighting the surge, the power, the desire for *more*.

"Y-you made it too s-strong," he stammered, and clutched the edge of the island's granite top. The spilled blood flowed between his fingers, invoking images he'd rather forget.

"I'm sorry," she said, clinging to his arm.

Her scent beckoned to him. He gripped the counter harder and fought the driving desire to plunge his fangs into her. "Please, *cariña*, step back."

"Henry—"

"Step back. I don't need new sins to repent for."

She took a few steps away, looking at him strangely. "Will you be all right?"

His heart pounded in his chest, and he squeezed the countertop harder. "Just get something to clean the spill."

She hurried across the kitchen to grab a roll of paper towels and returned to sop up the blood puddle. She gave him a towel.

Wiping his hands, he said, "Whatever you do, do not give that to Rolf."

"Don't worry. I won't. I can dilute it with regular blood. But by how much?"

"Cut it in half, at least." His head swam as he walked to the trash can to dispose of the paper towel. "A normal mortal, even one afraid of us, would never taste that strong."

"Would you like some regular blood?"

"Yes, thank you."

She took another sample from him while the blue pouch heated. "I'm sorry," she said, as she slid in the needle. "But I need to compare, before and after, to see if I can understand the effect ingesting stress hormones has on vampires."

A few minutes later, she handed him a mug. He wrapped his hands around the hot ceramic, warming himself, and took a deep drink.

"Did it help?"

"Better." He gulped down the rest. The swirling dizziness receded, the rush slowed, and the chill faded. "I hate admitting I miss the blood of a victim. There is something special about it. But that was too much—even for me, someone who doesn't have Rolf's problem. I'm sorry you had to see how I reacted."

"When I morph into a predator species, I take on their love of the hunt." She put her arms around his shoulders. "To chase, to kill, to eat raw flesh, I, ah, I enjoy it as much as they do."

He pulled back, shocked by her revelation.

"Did I overshare?"

"It never occurred to me. You hunt when you morph into a *puma*?" He pondered the idea. Could she really understand what he went through, what he gave up when he formed the community? "So, you know what it's like to be the hunter."

"Yes."

He stared beyond her, his vision glazing over. "To stalk your prey, to see them run, to give chase, knowing their running is futile. To smell their fear as they stand paralyzed and you close in. To sink your teeth in and taste their terror, to hunt but not kill…"

He stopped.

His mind's eye saw his life when he'd first been turned vampire. Back then, he had accidentally killed before gaining control of his hunger. Cerissa knew this. He'd been honest about his early days.

But once his hunger was under control, once he no longer killed his victims, he *still* had enjoyed the chase. Shame washed through him. As a young vampire he'd forced himself to abandon hunting, no matter how much he'd relished the adrenaline-enhanced blood.

Cerissa was looking at him curiously, her head cocked to the side.

"I am sorry," he said. "It triggered old memories for me, what my life was like before we formed the Hill community."

"You miss the chase."

Did his yearning show in his eyes? Hers showed only sympathy. "We have abandoned the old ways."

"You can always chase me," she said, shrugging.

"It would not be the same."

"Perhaps not." She ran a finger over his chest, looking coy. "But then, you might not be able to catch me."

He grasped her chin, turning her to gaze directly into his eyes. "If you stayed in human form, I guarantee I would catch you."

She smiled. "You sound so certain."

"I am."

"You like to bet, don't you?" She took a step back. "Want to put a wager on it? I'll hide in the woods, and you'll try to find me. If I manage to evade you for twenty minutes, you'll be my love slave, whatever I want. But if you find me before the twenty minutes are up, then I will be your love slave and you may do anything you want with me."

"*Anything?*" he asked.

"Anything."

The corners of his mouth twitched up. "Would you like to try tonight?"

A thrill ran right through Cerissa, and she couldn't suppress a big grin. Henry seemed so sure of himself. But she had a few tricks up her sleeve. She wouldn't make it easy for him to win.

"I'm game." She gave a light laugh. "Literally, I guess."

"Yes indeed, you will be my prey tonight."

"But only if you catch me."

"You mean, *when* I catch you."

Ah, the arrogance of the male vampire. "No, I had it right the first time."

His grin grew more lopsided. "Do you need a few minutes to prepare first? I'll give you a head start. But one rule: no morphing. You must remain in human shape, so I have a chance of finding you. If you changed into a tree, how would I sense it was you?"

"A tree?" She wrinkled her nose at him. The very idea repulsed her. "I can only morph into animal form. We'll both stay in human shape, but I get to enhance my abilities, so we have a more even playing field."

"That would be equitable."

"And I get a five-minute head start."

"If you are going to enhance your abilities, you get three minutes."

"Deal. But we'll set the finish time using the clock by the pool. You don't win unless you've captured me within twenty minutes and returned me poolside so we can confirm the time. I don't trust your watch. You might be tempted to cheat."

"I would never cheat in matters of love," he said with mock seriousness, a hand to his chest as he bowed to her.

She raised one eyebrow skeptically. "Oh, and no using the crystal in your wrist to flash to me. In fact, we should leave our phones here." She laid hers on the counter. "No technology."

His phone joined hers, and he wrapped his arms around her. His kiss left her breathless.

"No fair," she said.

"For good luck." He leered at her. "May the best vampire win."

She stuck her tongue out at him. He flashed his fangs at her, and she took off at a fast walk. "No biting until you catch me," she said over her shoulder.

On the way out, she grabbed her purse from the foyer, continuing through the drawing room and out the French doors leading to the pool. She fished a hair band from her pocket and tied back her long hair before discarding her sandals. Running barefoot would be easier.

She dropped her purse on a poolside table. Another hypo was inside—she would need a second dose of stabilizer before he bit again. Regardless of who won, she suspected there would be more biting involved.

"Okay, I'll start at nine oh seven, and you go at nine ten," she said, looking at the clock on the wall that was framed by a decorative sunburst. Considering he never saw the sun, the clock always struck her as an odd choice. "You have to return me here by nine thirty to win."

She took a deep breath and planned her strategy. Beyond the pool patio, Henry's vineyard was lit by floodlights, one at the end of every tenth row. The oak grove to the east was shrouded in darkness. That was where she would hide.

Henry counted down the seconds.

"Go," he said, his low-pitched voice making the word a predatory warning. The sound sent lust shooting through her.

She took off running and raced toward the dense forest. As a cougar, she had memorized those oak woods like the back of her paw. But it was different being human; she didn't see as well. She enhanced her night vision and morphed the soles of her feet until they were tough enough to withstand running over the hard dirt and debris littering the forest floor.

She picked her footing carefully and avoided leaving an obvious trail, careful to step lightly, to run along fallen logs, to hopscotch onto rocks. She even masked her body odor, so he wouldn't locate her by scent.

But there was one telltale sign she was powerless to fix—the night insects stopped their clicking and chirping as she sprinted past them, giving away her location.

Damn. There's no way to avoid the cricket alarm.

Running swiftly, she knew he couldn't be far behind. All she had to do was evade him until 9:30 and then he'd be hers to command.

Chapter 9

Sierra Escondida Police Department—One Hour Earlier

Thanks to an early moonrise, Tig had fed, dressed, and gotten caught up with her email before dusk. Once the sun blipped behind the coastal mountains, she walked to the police station to meet with Ari, a follow-up to last night's discussion. By 8:20 p.m., they concluded their meeting.

Ari's plan to make the police department's email communications secure seemed solid. A separate building would be constructed to house the server system with a good firewall installed. The council might have kittens over the expense, but the costs could be passed on to the residents through their cable TV bills, and that should put the council's complaints to rest.

She waited until Ari left the station. He headed for the town hall offices across the parking lot. His plan was to spend the night shoring up the mayor's computer system. Later, he would go to Vasquez Müller Winery to work in the winery's IT department. Like many computer geeks, he tended to stay awake into the early morning. The Hill was fortunate he kept vampire hours so easily.

After she saw him disappear into the building where the mayor's office was housed, Tig grabbed the keys for one of the police cruisers and locked the station's outer door. She was overdue for a break. Since the attacks on Hill residents began, she and Jayden had spent little private time together.

She was determined to make time for him tonight, and started the car, signaled left on Robles Road, and made the turn to head home.

A crackle on the two-way radio warned her of an incoming message. "All units, shots fired at the guard gate. Repeat. Shots fired—one dead. All available units to the gate."

Tig's stomach dropped to her feet, *déjà vu* enshrouding her. With a screech of tires, she made a U-turn and sped down Robles Road, past fields of grapevines and vineyard estate homes. She keyed the radio. "This is Chief Anderson. I'm on my way. Two minutes out. Dispatch, phone Jayden. Make sure he heard the call. He's off duty."

"Ten-four. Two other reservists are on their way," the dispatcher responded.

At the crime scene, a pink convertible sat skewed on the road, the top open. A hundred feet behind the BMW stood the tall block wall, covered in painted stucco, protecting the Hill.

Or, at least, the wall was *supposed* to protect it.

The ornate wrought-iron entry gates were closed. The decorative lights lit up the area like it was daytime. The guard on duty was huddled inside the guardhouse, and Tig skidded to a stop next to Abigale Cherrill's convertible—the pink BMW had to be hers; the car was the only one of its kind in the community.

Gun in hand, Tig got out and used Abigale's car for cover, inching her way to the empty driver's side. The coppery smell of blood was strong, and she suppressed the urge to let her fangs extend. A quick peek over the car door—one of Abigale's mates was slumped in the front passenger seat, resting over the center console.

Ducking back down, Tig opened the driver's door and reached over to check the body for signs of life. Too late—Nina was dead from a gunshot through the head.

The mushy thud of fists on flesh reached Tig's ears. A cold rush of fear charged through her.

I need the perp alive.

She sprang up and sprinted across the asphalt. The next meaty punch echoed, and she raced toward the sound, leaping over the decorative planter bordering the road. Holding her Beretta at her side, she ran up the grassy knoll and into an oak grove bordering the association's wall.

The flashing emergency lights from her car bounced off the shadowy tree branches. The effect made everything seem surreal, like a flickering silent movie, as her feet crunched the dry leaves.

"Abigale, don't kill him," Tig yelled, even as her brain registered the scene's incongruity: Abigale wore a pink knit dress with matching high-heeled shoes, not a blonde hair out of place, while she held a man with one hand and delivered slap after slap with the other.

Despite Tig's command, the beating continued.

Tig holstered the Beretta and, having no choice, launched herself at them. The three slid across the grass, then Abigale rolled over and jumped to her feet, dragging the unconscious man with her. Her lacquered blonde bouffant now looked punked out.

"He's mine," she snarled.

Tig sprang to her feet and closed the distance between them. "Abigale, stand down. We need him alive to question him."

Abigale's eyes were solid black, madness clouding her face.

Tig raised her hands. "You'll get your chance to avenge Nina. We need him alive for now. Please. Let him go."

The widow stood there, frozen in place, her expensive knit dress splattered with blood.

Tig took a step closer. "You'll get your chance, I promise."

The black in Abigale's eyes slowly receded, letting her blue irises show. With a disgusted sound, she released the unconscious man, tossing him to the ground like a piece of trash.

"Thank you." Tig placed her hand on Abigale's shoulder and pointed her toward the road. "Go back to the car. Jayden should be there by now. I'll take care of this."

Abigale descended the slope on tiptoe, keeping her spiked heels from sinking into the soft grass, and stopped at the car where Nina's body slumped.

Tig shook her head in disbelief. Another Hill founder attacked. That made four out of the five. Only Marcus had gotten by unscathed, with no attempt on his life so far.

But the night is young.

Tig clenched her jaw.

Investigate now, cynical jokes later.

She spotted where the shooter had lain in wait. A natural blind created by two oak trees at the top of the rise, where he could rest the rifle on a low branch, be perfectly hidden, and take a clear shot at the road below. At first, it hadn't made sense why he risked coming over the wall, but now it did. There wasn't enough cover outside the wall to protect him from view and give him the same elevation to sight from.

She snapped a few photos of the location with her phone, then removed nitrile gloves from her back pocket and pulled them on. She hoisted the man onto her shoulder, dropped her badge to mark where the rifle lay, grabbed the firearm, and hurried downhill to the road.

The gunman was still unconscious when she laid him across the police car's hood, slapped on the handcuffs, and then threw him into the back seat. Fortunately for him, Abigale was practiced at inflicting pain without causing permanent injury. Tig locked the car's doors in case he regained consciousness and then removed the ammo cartridge from the rifle, bagged it, and put everything in the trunk.

She jogged over to the guardhouse. The Spanish-style building sat next to the wrought-iron gates, and a man was huddled down inside. "The shooter's in custody," she said. "Keep the gates shut. If anyone wants in, tell them we have an active crime scene and to come back in an hour."

"Yes, ma'am."

The guard was one of the contract regulars, provided by a security company. No one working for the security company knew vampires existed.

She took out her phone, tapped the record icon, and held it between them. "What did you see?"

If he saw Abigale *whoosh* up the Hill, or Tig carry the man like a sack of potatoes, his memory would have to be altered.

The guard scratched his head. "Not much. I heard the gunshot, saw the car skid to a stop, and then I ducked down and called dispatch." His eyes moved to the left, like he was trying to remember something. "Our watch orders are to call for police if there's a problem and stay inside the guard shack. I, ah, I crouched down and didn't see anything else. I'm sorry."

"You did the right thing." She exhaled a sigh of relief. His mind wouldn't need wiping. She stopped the recording. "Phone me if you remember anything, no matter how strange. And for now, stay inside with the door closed. We'll let you know when it's safe to come out."

She pulled the blinds shut so he wouldn't see anything out the back window. Wiping a mortal's mind became more difficult each time it was done, so it was better if she kept him from seeing anything in the first place.

When she walked back to the crime scene, Jayden's police van was parked on the other side of Tig's car, tactically positioned at an angle. No cars would be able to pass by to exit.

Good. She didn't want anyone leaving yet. She phoned dispatch and instructed them to send out a reverse-911 alert, notifying the community what happened and telling them no one was allowed to leave while she investigated.

Abigale was sitting in the driver's seat and holding Nina's hand.

Jayden stood by her, his notepad and pen in hand. "Did you see anyone else with the shooter?"

"No."

"Have you ever seen the shooter before?"

"No."

"Did you notice anything unusual while you were driving?"

"No."

Abigale delivered her staccato answers through gritted teeth, her fangs hanging out over her lower lip, her body rigid with repressed rage.

Not good.

In her condition, Abigale could strike out at anyone. "Captain, please go search the area where the shooter laid in wait." Tig pointed to the stand of oak trees on the small rise. "I left my badge as a marker."

"Sure, chief." He dropped the notepad into his investigator's kit, grabbed the case's handle, and, with his flashlight in the other hand, jogged up the grassy knoll.

Two reserve officers arrived in a white Ford pickup truck. She sent Zeke to help Jayden and kept Liza with her. Tig trusted the councilwoman more than she trusted Zeke when it came to processing a crime scene, and she stole a glance in the direction of the guardhouse. The mortal was peeking through the blinds. Abigale's back was to him, and at this distance, he wouldn't see her fangs out.

Tig opened the driver's door. "I'm sorry, but I need you to get out of the car."

Abigale stayed frozen, the splatter pattern on her pink knit suit strafing from right to left, like a paintball had hit and exploded out—Nina's blood from the gunshot.

"We have to collect the evidence. Please. Go sit in Jayden's van. We'll drive you back to your house in a few minutes."

Abigale continued to stare straight ahead. "I don't want to leave her."

"I'll put her in the back of the van. She'll ride with you back to your house."

The widow gave a hesitant nod and then leaned over to kiss Nina's bloody cheek. With a hiccupped sob, she swung her legs out of the car and stood, raising her perfectly manicured hand to her mouth. Another short sob escaped.

Tig gently gripped Abigale's shoulder and walked her to the van.

When Tig returned to the convertible, Liza had the camera out and was photographing everything. "Can you hand me a pair of tweezers from your kit?" Tig asked.

Liza passed them over. Tig dug out the bullet lodged in the driver's-side headrest and deposited the silver lump into a plastic envelope.

Abigale was lucky. The bullet must have traveled through Nina's head and deflected enough to plow into the side of Abigale's headrest cushion, barely missing her. Blood spray was everywhere.

After Liza finished taking photos, they bagged Nina's body and put her in the back of the van. Yeah, only the coroner was supposed to handle the body, but Dr. Clarke had yet to appear. He would conduct a pro forma autopsy later, but it was clear what Nina died from.

A purse lay on the passenger-side floor. Tig placed it in the van with Nina. Abigale would want it.

A short while later, Jayden and Zeke returned from the assassin's perch. Tig signaled them over.

"We found the ladder the shooter used to scale the wall," Jayden reported. "But nothing else. No trash, so I doubt he was there for long. No sign of any other footprints."

Damn. Cameras had been ordered for the walls but not yet installed.

Tig looked toward the oak grove. The thicket provided a buffer between the nearest vineyard estate and the Hill's wall. "My guess—he arrived alone shortly before dusk."

"He probably hiked to the wall from the business district." Jayden gestured to the gate. The business district started a few blocks away. "I can search the parking areas to see where he left his car."

"Do that. Zeke, go with Jayden. I need to get Abigale home."

"Sure, chief," Zeke replied.

"Liza, would you mind driving the van? I don't see your car here." Liza usually drove a Mercedes roadster, and the car was nowhere in sight.

"No problem. Zeke and I were at Jose's Cantina when the call came in, so I rode with him."

"Good. I'll take the suspect, then. We'll question the assassin at Abigale's house."

Her basement had a room especially suited for interrogating the killer. Tig had toured the room on occasion to ensure Abigale didn't abuse the mortals she lived with, but there had never been a reported problem—the dominatrix believed in consent and safe words.

Tig had an idea how she might use Abigale's special room. No safe word would protect the killer from what she had planned. Not to mention it would be easier to interview Abigale there, rather than have everyone stand around the small suite of offices at the Hill's police station. She told Abigale her plan and the widow agreed with a nod.

Another police car pulled up, and Lieutenant Bailey got out. Tig left him to wait for the tow truck and stop anyone from leaving. She then signaled the others to go. As they headed to their vehicles, Tig stood there for a moment, looking at Nina's body bag in the back of the van. A tragedy—the mortal was too young to die.

A growl escaped Tig's throat as she slammed the doors shut.
This has to stop.
Now.

Chapter 10

Abigale's House—Ten Minutes Later

Tig drove down the street on which Abigale lived, dreading the moment when the rest of the widow's family learned about Nina's murder. She always hated delivering the death news, watching the family's world shatter—the transition from "all is well" devolving in an instant to horrific grief from which they would never fully recover.

She turned the police car slowly onto the wide driveway in front of a Mediterranean-style mansion. The shooter was still passed out in the back seat. Abigale's other mates were crowded together on the porch. Someone must have phoned ahead to warn them.

Tig slammed the gearshift into park and stomped on the parking brake. Liza stopped the police van next to her.

"Take him to the basement," Tig ordered her, handing the unconscious man to Liza.

Liza slung the killer over her shoulder and carried the evidence from the trunk in her other hand. Abigale's mates parted to let Liza pass—two were sobbing; the other four seemed paralyzed with shock. Abigale stayed frozen in the police van's front seat, her eyes tracking the man.

Tig carefully lifted Nina's bagged body from the back of the van and carried her reverently up the front porch stairs. The passenger door *snicked* open, followed by the tick of stiletto heels on pavement. She waited for Abigale to catch up. "Where should I take Nina? Her room?"

"The—the basement crypts."

Tig walked ahead and, when she didn't hear Abigale follow, glanced over her shoulder. Abigale stood at the front door, her gaze vacant.

"Abigale?"

The widow straightened her spine and stepped into the foyer. They went downstairs and through a hallway to a crypt containing a stone slab.

Tears streamed down Abigale's face. "I'll take her now."

Tig held the body while Abigale unzipped the bag and lifted Nina out, lovingly laying her on the stone slab. Nina's strawberry-red hair was matted with blood—Abigale brushed the fine strands back to cover the wound and caressed Nina's face.

"Do you want me to call her family?" Tig asked. Someone had to deliver the bad news. It went with the job.

"Yes," Abigale said. She dropped onto a chair next to the stone bier. Someone knocked at the crypt's door, and Tig swung around.

Luis, one of Abigale's mates, stood at the opening. Of all her mates, he'd been with her the longest, over fifteen years. He held up a black dress. "Mistress, you should change."

Abigale brushed her hands over the front of her knit suit. Nina's drying blood was turning the pale pink knit a darker shade, creating the face of a gruesome, lopsided jack-o'-lantern.

The image reminded Tig—she'd almost forgotten. "We'll need your clothes as evidence. And Nina's."

Abigale blinked, her wet gaze returning to the dead girl.

"I'll make sure you receive them," Luis said.

"One of my officers will drop off bags." Tig stepped into the hall, and Luis closed the door, staying behind. She strode to the basement room where Liza had taken the killer.

The large room was divided into different sections. One side was decorated as a Victorian boudoir, with a woven rug covering the cold stone floor. A nearby door led to a bathroom. The far wall was outfitted with chains and manacles.

Liza had chained the unconscious gunman to the wall, and a chest band held him upright. A table stood nearby—Abigale's gear was pushed to one side. The crime scene kit was open and the laptop computer running.

Tig picked up the killer's rifle: a Nam Hunter 900.

She understood why he'd used that model. You could walk into any gun store and buy one without a wait, and millions had been sold for hunting. A few tweaks and the 900 was the best assassin rifle on the consumer market, with a twenty-round cartridge to boot. If the killer hadn't been caught at the scene, and her forensics team had figured out the kill gun was a Nam Hunter 900, it would have been like looking for the killer knowing he preferred Coke to Pepsi—good luck finding him based on that.

"We have his wallet," Liza reported. "Angelo Pascala. I ran his prints, and they match. He's an ex-felon."

"Good work, thanks."

Tig would check the rifle's serial number later. Still wearing leather gloves, she picked up the magazine and thumbed the silver bullets into a glass evidence container. Touching the silver would necrotize her flesh, instantly reversing the vampire effect. A silver bullet through the heart resulted in instant death.

She held out the container for Liza to see. "They're similar to the ones used in the prior shootings."

"Yeah." Liza motioned to the unconscious man. "Do you think we'll get more information from this guy than we did from the men who kidnapped Rolf's mate?"

"I have every confidence we will."

The perps they had captured before—the ones who had kidnapped Karen—knew little. They had worked for a man they called the Director who used the first name "Chuck." Based on what the Director did to Karen, Tig figured out he was the serial killer that mortal police had nicknamed the Carlyle Cutter.

She had higher hopes with this perp. A paid killer was unlikely to take a job without learning whom he was working for. She continued to browse through the evidence collected from the scene, looking for any clue to break the case and tell her who was really behind this.

"What else was in his wallet?"

"A blank white plastic card." Liza held the rectangle by the edges and pivoted it so Tig saw both sides.

"Looks like the type used by automated garages," Tig said. "But it could be a local hotel key, too. Mordida hotels have started using unmarked electronic cards. That way, if a guest loses their room key, the finder won't figure out which hotel to try."

Liza put it in an evidence bag. "You're probably right. No one would drive here from San Diego and commit murder in one day. He'd want to be well rested, alert."

The killer was getting plenty of rest now.

Hmm. Should I ask Dr. Clarke to examine him?

Voices in the hallway outside caught Tig's attention—Abigale and Luis. Tig took a small evidence bag from the table and joined them. "I'm sorry to disturb you. Does this mean anything to you?"

She held out a small object, an enameled hair clip with a grapevine theme.

Abigale accepted the barrette, rotating it with her long white fingers. "Where did you find it?"

"On the floor of your car, next to a purse."

"It may be what Nina was reaching for. She said she had something for me and leaned over to open her purse. She knew I liked to wear my hair pinned back. When she sat up…"

Nina caught the bullet meant for Abigale.

The widow choked back a sob and wrapped her hand around the hair clip, her knuckles turning whiter under the strain, and then opened her fingers, holding it out to Tig.

"No, keep it. I photographed it. It won't lead us to the real killer."

Abigale clutched the hair clip to her chest. "Thank you."

Tig returned to the room and took a moment to scrutinize Pascala. His lip was cut, one eye swollen, and other bruises were beginning to form.

An idea occurred to her. "Wait here," she told Liza.

Tig ran up the stairs, taking them two at a time, and asked directions to the kitchen from Stephen, one of Abigale's mates. An industrial-sized vacuum pot held brewed coffee. With seven—now six—mortals living there, they probably drank enough coffee to justify the large dispenser.

She rummaged through the cabinets, found a mug, and pumped coffee in, filling it halfway, and added ice from the freezer to cool the hot beverage. She slid a sharp blade from the wooden knife block. Slicing open a vein in her arm, she allowed her blood to flow into the cup.

Not enough blood to kill him; maybe enough to heal him.

When the liquid was almost to the top, she brought her forearm to her mouth and licked the wound. The cut clotted and closed. In a few minutes, not even a scar would be left.

Carrying the mug, she returned to the basement. Pascala moaned as he started to rouse.

Liza raised an eyebrow, silently questioning what the plan was. Tig showed her the healing wound and then held the cup to Pascala's nose. All he would smell was coffee.

"Drink," Tig ordered him.

Pascala looked punch-drunk but sipped the coffee. Moments later, the lacerations on his face scabbed over and the swelling around his eye receded. It would be a while before he was completely healed, but this was an acceptable start.

His gaze focused on her, a good sign he was coming back to his senses. "Where am I?" Tig waited and didn't reply. He tugged at the chains and eyed her uniform. "I want an attorney."

"It doesn't work that way here." She held the mug to his lips again. "Drink more."

After he finished the coffee, his gaze swung to Liza and then back to Tig. He tugged at the chains. "You can't keep me here like this."

"Yes, I can."

"You're police. You gotta follow the law."

"Does this look like a police station to you?"

Pascala swiveled his head, taking in Abigale's unique taste in decorating. Tig's decision to bring him here was rewarded when the sharp smell of fear rose from him. His eyes became big and round, reminding her of an antelope facing a lion.

He yanked harder at the chains. "But I got rights."

She said nothing. Technically, he did have rights, and he would get them—eventually. The Hill tried hard to follow the law, but questioning him in front of a mortal attorney was forbidden, not if he knew vampires existed. The trade-off was simple: what she learned this way couldn't be used at *his* trial.

Not that his trial mattered. The information would be used to get the bigger fish. Whatever Pascala said would be entered into evidence against the vampire behind this once she caught him or her.

Tig continued to study Pascala as he tested the limits of his restraints: the *clink* of the chains being pulled, his grunts as he strained at them, his sweat souring as he realized how helpless he was, and then his movements became even more frenzied.

"Let me go, you fuckin' bitch!" he yelled.

Not the smartest thing to say.

Tig motioned to Liza. "Start the camera recording."

The bruises on Pascala's face had faded sufficiently to record the interview. Damage to veins and arteries always healed first, which only made sense. If the victim's circulatory system was compromised, how else could she turn them vampire?

But without the serum in her fangs, he'd stay mortal. And too much vampire blood—well, his body would self-destruct trying to change without the catalyst. It was why she had given him a small amount to drink.

"What's your name?" She already had the answer but wanted to start him down a road of telling the truth.

He sneered at her and spat in her face. Not the most intelligent suspect she had ever questioned. She wiped off the spit as she sauntered over to a cabinet in which Abigale kept various implements.

Liza made eye contact with her, and with a slight grin, the councilwoman gave her blessing to what Tig had planned. "I'm going outside," Liza said. "I'll leave you two alone."

"Do you mind running upstairs and getting my iPad out of the car?"

"Glad to."

"Oh, and bring a couple of large evidence bags to Abigale for her clothing."

"Sure, chief." Liza gave a jerk of her chin in the perp's direction. "Let me know if you need any help persuading this trash to talk."

After the door closed, Tig selected a bit gag and strode back to Pascala. He thrashed his head back and forth, trying to resist her efforts to shove the bit in his mouth. She grabbed his hair in one hand so he couldn't move, forced his jaws open, and strapped the rubber bar in place.

Still holding his hair, she locked eyes with him. "When next you speak, it will be to answer my question truthfully."

She took out a knife from the crime scene kit then cut away the shooter's clothing, sliding his shirt out from under the bellyband. She couldn't get his shoes and socks off without removing his leg manacles. They would stay on for now. She also left on his Jockey briefs. It would be one more level of humiliation, stripping him of the last bit of protection, which was an option should he prove resistant.

She returned to Abigale's cabinet and surveyed the choices. She picked a riding crop—something to cause pain but not damage—and strode back to the shooter. She flexed the crop and cracked the leather-woven cane against her own hand.

Using more extreme measures was out. The council had reamed her for beating the kidnappers, even though it got the perps to confess the location where Karen was being held.

She had ruptured the spleen of one perp, and Jayden had to fast-talk it when he handed the guy over to the county jail. The injured kidnapper had received too much damage for vampire blood to fix without killing him—or alternately, biting and turning him—and no one was willing to do that.

She poked Pascala in the side with the tip of the riding crop. "I'm going to remove the gag, and you're going to answer me. But know this: I can beat you night after night and you won't die. I can heal you each evening, and inflict pain until you beg for death, and then heal you again. Think about it. You were badly beaten when I brought you in here. Do you remember? Nod if you do."

The shooter jerked his head up and down, his eyes wide.

"Very good. I gave you something to drink to heal your injuries. I can beat you, and then heal you, over and over again. If you try what you did before, if you spit at me, I'll gag you and beat you, do you understand?"

The shooter nodded again.

She unfastened the strap, removed the bit, and stepped in close, inches from his face. Would he be a frightened lamb or fight back? To gauge his compliance, she gave him the chance to head-butt her.

He didn't.

"What's your name?" she demanded.

"Angelo Pascala."

"How many times have you been in prison, Angelo?"

"Twice. Been in prison twice. Jail more'n that; caught a few times and not convicted."

Good to see he wasn't a hardened soldier. Tig's former comrades would never surrender so easily. She stepped away from him and checked to make sure the camera was recording his confession.

"Who were you trying to kill?"

"The blonde, drivin' the convertible—Abigale Cherrill. When I learnt her girlfriend was working at the winery today, I took a chance Cherrill might drive out to get her."

"Who told you her girlfriend was working there?"

He didn't answer. Tig lifted the gag. She'd started to put the leather bit in his mouth when he yelled out, "Wait!"

"You want to tell me something?"

"If I do, he'll kill me."

"And if you don't, I'll beat you until you wish you were dead."

He set his mouth in an angry line. To get him to open, she squeezed his jaw joint and slipped on the gag again. He went crazy and tried to pull the chains off their eye bolts, but Abigale had done too good a job installing them securely. Panting and sweating, he eventually exhausted himself. Tig waved the riding crop in front of his face and brought it down fast, a sharp crack against the wall. He flinched.

"Are you ready to cooperate?"

He nodded rapidly like a bobblehead doll. The fear in his eyes told her she'd gotten through this time.

Grasping his hair firmly, she said, "Just because I ask you a question doesn't mean I don't know the answer. If I catch you in one lie, I'll beat the shit out of you, do you understand?"

Another nod.

She undid the gag and released his hair. "Now, you were going to tell me how you knew Abigale's girlfriend would be working at the winery."

"I had her name—it's Nina." He barely croaked out the words. "I asked about her at the gift shop. They told me she'd be workin' until eight tonight."

"Good boy." She had brought a bottle of water from the kitchen and gave him some to drink. "Who told you her name?"

Pascala didn't hesitate this time. "Charlie."

Interesting. The Carlyle Cutter had used the name "Chuck" when he kidnapped Karen—probably the same man. "And what is Charlie's last name?"

"He didn't tell me."

She let that go for now. "What does Charlie look like?"

"About six feet tall. White. Short, wavy black hair, clipped mustache, real preppy." Pascala tried to brush the hair out of his eyes, but the chains didn't stretch far enough. He used his shoulder instead.

Tig stepped back and thought for a moment. The description matched the town attorney—except for the black hair—or a handful of other vampires on the Hill, but she already knew the Carlyle Cutter wasn't a vampire.

"What was Charlie wearing when you met him?"

Pascala looked off to his left. "Ah, like he worked in an office."

"Suit and tie?"

"No, long-sleeve shirt and slacks." He gripped the chains, holding himself upright, and leaned back on the wall. "Like he bought them at a hipster store, you know, real stylish."

"How did you meet Charlie?"

"Through Tony DeLuca. Tony and I were in prison together."

Damn. Why couldn't they catch a break?

Tony was one of the dead men who had attempted to kill Yacov. Yacov had drained him—in self-defense, of course.

"How do you contact Charlie?"

"He calls me. We meet at a bar."

"What's his phone number?"

"He wouldn't give me one. The number was blocked when he called."

She held up his phone in a plastic bag. "If you're lying, I'll know soon enough. You won't like the consequences."

"I ain't lying."

She put the phone back on the table and crossed her arms. Ari would examine the device later and confirm it. "What has he promised you for doing this?"

"Two million."

"Anything else?"

"Ah—a passport for Uruguay."

She furrowed her brow. "If you can't track him, why do you believe he'll deliver on his promises?"

"He already gave me fifty thousand dollars in cash. He said he'd wire the rest afterwards to a bank in the same country and put the money in my name."

"You're awfully trusting."

Pascala shrugged. "I have his first name and I know what he looks like. And DeLuca knows where he lives."

"Tony DeLuca?"

"Yeah."

The dead guy. Tig cursed inwardly. "I'll be back in a moment."

She needed her tablet, so stepped outside to get it from Liza. When she returned to Pascala, she held up the iPad so he could see the screen. "I'm going to show you three sketches. I want you to tell me if any of them are Charlie."

He studied them for a moment. "Sort of like the one on your right."

The drawing based on Karen's description—Tig swiped the screen to discard the other two sketches.

"This one?" she asked, enlarging the picture he chose.

"Yeah, he's the one. But he had black hair and wore glasses."

Was Pascala lying? Karen had described Chuck as having brown hair. "You're sure? Black hair?"

"Yeah, and the color looked wrong, you know?"

The light bulb came on for her. "Like a bad dye job?"

"That could be it—too much black."

She placed the iPad on the table and stepped in close to Pascala, her gaze locked on his. "Who does Charlie work for?"

"He didn't tell me."

"Why is Charlie targeting people who live on the Hill?"

"He didn't—"

She cracked the riding crop against the wall. "And just when I thought you had decided to cooperate. You see, I think you do know and you're just not telling me."

She narrowed her eyes and continued to stare into his. Too bad her mesmerizing skills couldn't compel him to tell the truth.

"I don't know," he wailed, struggling against the chains. "Really, I don't. You got to believe me."

His last words were muffled as she raised the gag back to his lips. During her four hundred years, most of it as a mercenary, she had used pain to loosen tongues. She had also been on the receiving end. She knew the benefits and drawbacks.

The fear in his eyes, the panicked way he pulled at his chains—he had guessed what came next.

A knock on the door stopped her.

What did Liza want now?

Tig opened the door and Jayden walked in. His gaze swept the room and froze on the riding crop in her hand. He pivoted around and left without saying a word—the look on his face said it all.

Not good.

She followed him and closed the door behind her. Exposed bulbs cast shadows in the narrow hallway. Liza still leaned against the bare block wall, doing something on her phone.

"Give us a minute."

"Roger that, chief." Liza pushed off the wall and loped up the stairs, closing the door at the top behind her.

Storm clouds had formed on Jayden's face. "This isn't the 1700s. We don't torture people."

"The Hill has been attacked repeatedly—we're at war." Tig crossed her arms. "This is the only way I can get him to talk."

"Not in this country," he said, shaking his head. "We don't torture perps."

"Will you feel better if we call it 'enhanced interrogation techniques'?"

"What you call it doesn't matter. Stripping a man naked qualifies as torture. We learned that much at the academy."

"Then let's be clear. This isn't a police issue. These are terrorist attacks. We are at war with an unknown entity, and I'll use every tool at hand to find out who is behind this."

"This country doesn't torture, even during war. We signed the Geneva Convention."

"You haven't been keeping up on what happened after 9/11."

His frown deepened and anger sparked off him. "Not everyone agreed with those techniques, and there was no proof they worked. No reliable information was ever gleaned. And the studies I read in the academy—torture dehumanizes the torturer as well as the person being tortured. Hill vampires say they want to retain their humanity, but it's just lip service."

When she didn't respond, he added, "And you wouldn't be doing this if Pascala was a vampire."

Shit. Jayden had been upset by some of the propaganda Frédéric had distributed, propaganda aimed at glorifying vampires as superior, making mortals feel less-than. Was he angry because she was using pain to extract information from a *mortal*?

She met his eyes. "I'd use different techniques, but yes, I'd use pain, hunger, and humiliation to convince a vampire perp to talk."

"Still doesn't make it right, *chief*. We shouldn't risk our *honor* to win. Our honor has to mean something. Security can't be our only touchstone, or the founders' ideals in forming this community become meaningless."

"Well, *captain*, we're going to have to agree to disagree on this."

"Really? Agree to disagree? No way, Tig. Only a psychopath can torture and be unaffected. And I didn't fall in love with a psychopath."

She exhaled loudly and gave up. Words weren't going to win this argument. "Do you have something to report?"

"Yeah." He pursed his lips, still not looking happy. "No sign of any accomplices. We searched all the surrounding streets. If anyone was waiting for him, they must have taken off before we got there."

A voice interrupted them. "Ma'am?"

Tig looked up to see Zeke speaking from the stairs. *Shit.* Had he been standing there while they argued? Why hadn't Liza stopped him? Last thing Tig needed was anyone witnessing tension between her and Jayden over this. They worked too hard to show a united front to the Hill.

"We chalked the car tires," Zeke said. "The captain can check 'em tomorrow and find out which ones are still there. I reckon it may tell us which car the perp drove."

"Good," Tig said. "His name is Angelo Pascala."

Jayden took out a small notebook. "I wrote down the license plate numbers of the cars parked near the wall where he scaled it. I'll check the DMV database to see if he owns one of those. If we get a match, we can tow the car to impound."

"Sounds like a good plan."

"And the guard at the gate wants to know when he can open them for normal traffic."

She gave it a moment's consideration. "Go ahead and let people through. But tell the guard to keep a careful log of who comes or goes and the time. Even if they have an RFID sticker on their car, I still want him to note it."

The radio frequency identification sticker activated the gates to automatically open, but the computer logs weren't always reliable if two cars went through at once.

Tig checked her watch. It was 10:20 p.m.—two hours since Nina was killed, and no solid leads yet. She needed to get back in there with Pascala and dismissed Jayden and Zeke.

After they left, she pounded her fist on the concrete brick wall. No, she wasn't a psychopath, although sometimes she wondered why she hadn't become one after everything she'd been through.

Was Jayden right? Was torture a slippery slope she didn't want to slide down any further than she already had? The ticking-time-bomb theorem was bogus; no real-life situation ever mimicked the perfect circumstances under which a so-called ticking bomb justified torture—it presumed facts she could never know with enough certainty.

The slippery slope idea held more traction. She'd taken a shortcut with the kidnappers, using pain to get them to talk, and it had gone okay—she'd gotten reliable intel from them. But the problem with any shortcut was that it became easier to use until the shortcut became the first and not the last technique applied.

Shit.

She licked at the back of her bloody knuckles, glancing at the damage she'd done to the wall. Jayden was right. In her anger, she'd gone for torture first. Time to back up and try her other skills. She knew how to pry the truth out of Pascala—and she'd do it without using any *enhanced* techniques.

Chapter 11

Mordida—a short time later

Chuck unbuckled the metal clip to his waterproof watch and scrubbed the band with a mild bleach solution. His heart still raced from the kill—a quick victim taken to ease his anxiety.

The death blow delivered by this own hand had left him lightheaded.

The washing ritual grounded him. He rinsed the watch one more time and dried it on the white towel by his bathroom sink.

An alarm chimed. Five minutes to ten thirty.

Uneasiness seeped back into his consciousness, disturbing his ritual. The vampire who controlled him would call soon.

Dread sank its claws into him.

Pascala had screwed the pooch. The *tool* the President recommended wasn't as sharp as promised. Not that the President would care where the tool came from. The failure would be dumped on Chuck—the boss never accepted responsibility for his own fuck-ups.

How to explain what happened? With binoculars trained on Pascala, Chuck had observed from the roof of a nearby business as the damn vampire bitch leapt from the car and moved like lightning up the slope after him. And then Tig Anderson had arrived and walked off with Pascala's limp body over her shoulder.

Fuck that. Pascala was supposed to be my *toy.*

Chuck slipped the watch back over his wrist and cleaned his knife, the one he'd *inherited*—he always wore its scabbard on his belt, a symbol of his power. He inspected the blade closely. One more use and it would need sharpening.

Finished with his ritual, he took three steps, which put him in the living room. His small apartment was plain and neatly furnished. No clutter, no debris. An impersonal room for an impersonal man.

Upon entering, even a friend would conclude no one lived there. But he had no friends—and very few desires. The one he did have was an overpowering one. His obsession was the reason he worked for a vampire.

He put on clean gloves from the box on the counter and grabbed a glass from the kitchen cupboard, removing it from the straight row of identical glasses. He lifted a bottle of whiskey from under the sink. The same place his grandfather had kept his whiskey until Chuck killed him.

He poured, stopping when the golden-brown liquid filled the bottom inch. Enough to take the edge off, but not enough to make him stupid. He didn't like feeling stupid, and he hated being out of control. He shot back the liquor. It burned going down his throat.

The pain felt good.

Warmth flooded him as he studied the empty glass. *What will drinking human blood be like?* Smooth? Harsh? Tasteless? Metallic? He didn't care. He just wanted the power—the power to live forever and do whatever he wanted to do with no one able to stop him.

He'd already had a taste. Vampire blood. Enough repeated doses to make him stronger, faster, smarter. It made his pursuit of happiness—his version of that pursuit—so much easier.

Tonight, he'd pursued it with an unplanned playmate, thanks to Pascala's incompetence. But to be on time for the President's call, he had rushed the kill, leaving his desire unsatisfied. It felt like a meal half eaten.

Chuck washed the glass and returned it to the cupboard where it lived. He screwed the cap on the bottle and returned the whiskey to the under-sink cabinet, squaring the bottom perfectly with the indentation it had made on the shelf paper.

He parked himself by the phone and waited, clenching a pen in his hands. He hated being under the President's control.

It reminded him of being under his grandfather's control. The old bastard had molested him regularly when he was a child.

The last time it happened, they were living in that little shack, a two-bedroom house on Alameda Street. Paint peeled off the walls, and the brown shag rug was thick with grime. They were poor because the asshole drank all the time and wouldn't work.

All his grandfather had was the house—he'd bought the old residence after serving in the military—and somehow managed to pay off the mortgage free and clear before Grandma died.

His father had abandoned them when he was a baby, so his mother moved back in with her father—who never ceased reminding Chuck he was a *real* bastard.

Yeah, but you earned the name.

"Charlie, get in here," the old man would bellow.

His mother wasn't there to protect him the last time it happened—she was at her waitressing job—not that she was any good at stopping her father when he was in *that* mood.

The large man had to be in his fifties, mostly blubber but some muscle left—enough to swing a belt and leave welts. He towered over them and had beaten his mother so much as a child that she would try halfheartedly to protect Charlie and then disappear when her father started yelling "slut" at her.

On other occasions, she would warn Charlie to go to him, to stay quiet and "not risk the roof over our heads."

His mother wasn't exactly consistent with her motherly protection, but then, the thin bitch had looked like a strong breeze would tip her over.

"Charlie, don't make me ask twice," the old man bellowed. Chuck hated his childhood nickname—particularly on the lips of his grandfather.

He slunk into his grandfather's room. If he didn't come when called, the old man got out the belt and then did him. He'd learned it wasn't worth the extra pain to resist.

The old man pushed him face down on the bed, yanked down Charlie's pants, and fingered him while jerking off. Charlie gritted his teeth. He didn't cry, didn't make any noise, didn't show his anger.

All to avoid a beating.

After the old asshole finished, he waddled to the bathroom and scrubbed his hands with soap—yeah, right, as if his shame could be washed away. Charlie silently snuck off to his bedroom.

A short time later, the television in the living room blared loudly. Creeping along the hallway, he hid in the shadows by the doorframe and watched his grandfather drink himself into a stupor.

When the loud snores started, he knew the bastard had passed out in the recliner. Charlie snuck into the dirty kitchen, a few silent steps past the old man's back. He carefully unhooked the butcher knife from a cheap metal rack. He crept outside and used the sharpening stone until the knife gleamed.

Returning to the kitchen, he stripped off his t-shirt, leaving him naked—he hadn't bothered to put his pants or underwear back on—and laid the t-shirt on the grimy Formica table. He slipped on his mother's rubber gloves, the yellow ones she used to wash dishes on the rare occasion she wasn't too exhausted from working long hours.

Charlie tiptoed up behind his grandfather's chair, his junk hanging out and his innocence gone many years ago.

His heart pounded with each step, and he was afraid the noise would wake the old man. He was dead if his grandfather woke up. His hands shook when he raised the knife. In that moment, he ceased feeling the pain from his grandfather's last fingering.

He thrust the long knife down, stabbing the bastard.

Never again.

The point pierced the old man's right breast, angling downward. Bone stopped the blade. He wiggled it until he found an opening, and kept pushing, putting his weight behind the thrust, driving the metal deeper, until something gave way.

His grandfather's eyes sprang open, a choking, gurgling noise arising from his throat, and he tried to stand, but the lard in his ass and the whiskey in his veins made it easy to keep him pinned down. Old hands grasped at Charlie's arms, scratching the rubber gloves, trying to break Charlie's hold on the knife handle.

It didn't work.

The old man sputtered. A mist of blood sprayed out.

Jerking one last time, he died.

Too quickly for Charlie's tastes.

The boy took a deep breath and let the air out. It was a good feeling and set his dick tingling as the excitement buzzed through him—he was *alive*.

His yellow-gloved hands released the knife, leaving it in his grandfather's chest. Blood dripped onto the Naugahyde easy chair. Charlie's gaze moved to the ring on the dead man's index finger.

The diamond ring. When his grandfather used him, he'd feel the diamonds rub against his skin. He had to have it.

Trying to remove the gold band was fruitless. The fat fuck's fingers were swollen like sausages. A butcher knife from the kitchen remedied the problem. He chopped the finger off—actually, two fingers—with one blow. The ring easily slipped off the bloody stump.

His first souvenir.

He ran to the washroom—the little porch where the clothes washer was kept—and rinsed off the gloves and the ring. The blood mixed with the water and spiraled down the washbasin drain. A pretty image.

Now for the DNA. He may be poor, but he wasn't stupid. He sloshed bleach over the gloves to destroy the blood.

The OJ murder trial—who named their son Orenthal?—had been broadcast nonstop for the past few months, and between the trial and television news, he'd received a crash course on how not to get caught.

He rinsed himself off in the laundry room with a weak solution of bleach, making sure the large white plastic bottle with the blue label was also wiped clean. The window over the washbasin was open, fresh air blowing in, diluting the fumes.

He dried the gloves and returned them to the dish rack where he had found them. He dashed outside and buried the ring in the backyard flowerbed next to the laundry room door.

A quick shower, using the cheap shampoo his mother bought, covered the smell of bleach with a fake floral scent.

After he dried off and changed into his pajamas, he called 911, trying to sound panicked. It wasn't hard. His heart thrummed fast. He was both afraid of being caught and excited over his success.

A woman answered. "What's your emergency?"

"My grandfather—he's been hurt."

When the paramedics arrived, they pronounced the old bastard dead, and then the police took over. Charlie told them he had been asleep in the other room and loud voices arguing woke him. He left his bed to peek around the corner and saw two men wearing masks and gloves kill his grandfather. The one who stabbed the old man had stood behind him. They chopped off his fingers and took the diamond ring.

The boy cried as he told the police how scared he was.

The coroner later confirmed his story based on the angle of the blow—it had indeed come from behind the victim's right shoulder.

No one thought a scrawny fourteen-year-old like Charlie had the balls to murder his grandfather in cold blood, even though he was the same height as the killer.

The old man had owed people money, so the police assumed loan sharks took the diamond ring in an attempt to collect on those gambling debts. No one ever suspected the teen. After the funeral, Charlie rifled through his grandfather's closet, finding the cherished bowie knife at the back on the floor. It was his second souvenir and always hung from his belt.

Killing his mother without getting caught had been a bit harder.

The phone's trill made him jump. The President. That was what the vampire insisted on being called. Chuck's own code name was "the Director." He liked the power in it—he was the director of other people's destinies.

"Mr. President, the courier came very close to delivering the package as instructed, but there was an accident," Chuck said without preamble before the President could say anything.

"What happened to go wrong this time, Director?"

Chuck hated that condescending cultured voice. It ground at him almost as much as the fake IDs and credit cards using his childhood nickname. The President insisted he go by Charlie. There was no reason to do so, except to make fun of Chuck—when the vampire first trapped him, the dickhead had forced him to tell the Grandfather story and knew how much Chuck hated the name Charlie.

"My associate tells me the package was delivered to her companion instead," Chuck said, using the double-speak he'd been forced to practice. "The courier has since been detained due to the accident."

"Detained. In what condition?"

"The accident left him alive but no longer available to redeliver the package."

"How reliable is your associate, given he's on the competition's team?"

"Very. I've been slowly cultivating his loyalty. He's hoping for a year-end bonus like the one you promised me." The naïve chump lived with a Hill vampire but desperately wanted to be turned—something those assholes would never do.

"He may prove to be useful," the President said. "Did you meet with the courier in person before the delivery was attempted?"

"We met three times."

"I see."

"Nothing to worry about. I used our standard protocol, Mr. President." The standard protocol involved wearing colored contacts, glasses, and dyeing his hair to make it difficult to identify him. But he had to get the President's focus away from Pascala's failure. The President wasn't known for mercy—especially when blaming others. "Do you want me to continue to personally monitor our competition's location?"

In other words, did the asshole want him to watch the community's gate for their targets?

"Yes. We no longer have remote access."

Chuck scowled at the phone. *Tell me something I don't already know.* The Hill had figured out their email was tapped and closed the leak, so he had installed a wireless camera near the gated entrance, which was how he'd discovered Epsilon's pattern.

"I'll keep monitoring things," Chuck said.

"Good. There will be other opportunities. We want to make sure our future deliveries reach their intended destinations."

"Of course, Mr. President." He paused, fear creeping up his throat. "Ah, I'll need another box of our product if I'm to make another delivery."

"If you hadn't wasted what I gave you, you would have plenty left to make additional deliveries," the President shot back. "Your cavalier treatment of our product is inexcusable."

Chuck squirmed—the silver bullets he'd given Pascala could be linked to the President. "I had planned on using the courier to make multiple deliveries. Next time, I'll keep tighter control of the product."

"Very well. It's a good thing I ordered a second box. I'll make arrangements to have the *merchandise* delivered."

"Don't worry. The next one will be successful. I'll make sure of it."

"See that you do," the President said. "See that you do."

The call finished. It left Chuck with the same churning gut he would feel after his grandfather used him. He despised the feeling. He tried to suppress his fear, to make the anxiety go away. But there was only one way to make the pain go away. He would have to kill again, and soon.

Chapter 12

Sierra Escondida Town Hall—earlier that evening (around the time Tig apprehends Pascala)

Marcus strode down the hallway bisecting the town hall office complex and glanced at his phone: *8:45 p.m.* Earlier, he'd received an interesting "out of office" notice saying the mayor would be gone while Ari worked to secure his computer.

So…Ari is alone in the mayor's office.

A pleasant tingle ran through Marcus at the thought. He smiled to himself as he reached the mayor's door, which was partway ajar, and peered in. Surprise shot through him. Ari wasn't alone. Haley, Vishon's mortal mate, was standing next to the consultant, a folder in her hand, a colorful photo of the Hill's vineyards imprinted on the glossy cover. What was she doing here?

Marcus pulled back into the hallway and watched the two.

"Since you're working for the town as an envoy, I wanted to give you this," Haley said, laying the folder on the desk and tossing a strand of her long blonde hair over her shoulder.

"Uh-huh," Ari mumbled. He kept looking at the computer screen and typing.

"You should know your rights." She flipped open the cover to reveal the brochures inside. "This is a list of what they can and can't make you do under the Covenant. This is an FAQ, you know, frequently asked questions by mortals new to the Hill. If you have any questions not covered, I'm happy to answer them anytime."

Ari glanced over at the literature and returned his gaze to the computer screen. "Thanks. I already saw the brochure you gave Cerissa."

"This is different from the one I gave her. We wrote a packet especially for envoys, and I included our proposal to open one council seat for a mortal."

"Right, right. Leave it there. I'll look at it later," Ari replied distractedly.

Haley released a slight huff in response. Ari's gaze briefly slid to her, and he smiled.

His fingers flew over the keyboard, and then he hit the return key with a flourish. "There. Now we can chat."

Chat? Marcus didn't like the sound of that. He didn't need more mortals clamoring for equal rights, let alone his new paramour.

"So, beautiful lady," Ari began, walking his fingers across the slick folder toward Haley, "what are you, like, the union steward?"

"Uh, no—"

"You sure talk like one. Watching out for everyone's rights, making sure everyone's being protected."

"We're more of a political movement…"

"Is that so? What are you doing later? Maybe we could, I don't know, read through the literature together—or other things?"

Marcus's gut twisted with jealousy. He should never have mixed business and pleasure. It left him open to the same kind of betrayal his prince had perpetrated.

Pull yourself together, Marcus. You had one interlude with Ari. Nothing at all like what happened with Oscar.

Right. But first, he would stop this before the flirtation went any further.

He stepped into the small office. "Haley is mated, Ari. And she shouldn't be here. Your work for the council is confidential."

"Come on, Marcus," Ari said, leaning back and resting his head against his interlaced fingers. "In this town, you could fart and they'd hear the toot on the other side of the valley before you could say 'excuse me.' You can't be angry with—" He turned to look up at the mortal. "What's your name again?"

"Haley."

"You can't blame Haley for learning about my work here. Everyone working for the town knows, which leaves, what, twenty people who don't?"

"More than that," Marcus said.

"Still, you get my point. In a small town, it's hard to keep anything a secret."

It didn't matter how many found out. They had no business flapping their lips. Marcus glowered at Haley. "Who told you?"

She threw back her shoulders. "I don't have to answer your questions." She turned to Ari. "And don't let him bully you into doing anything you don't want to do. I heard about the blood bond thing. If you feel you're being mistreated, you can turn to Father Matt or Gaea Greenleaf for help."

"Mistreated?" Ari cocked one eyebrow, keeping his gaze on Marcus. "Good to know."

"I would never mistreat a thrall," Marcus shot back.

"A bonded, not a thrall," Haley said indignantly. "*Thrall* is so eighteenth century."

"I don't care what you call it. Ari is on the clock. We're paying him by the hour—" Marcus's phone buzzed. He glanced at the reverse-911 alert and pursed his lips. "Please leave," he said to Haley, pointing at the doorway.

She gave a little *humph*. "I'm only leaving because I was ready to go anyway." She handed Ari a business card. "Call me. We'll talk."

Ari used the card to give her a mock salute. She walked out with her hips rolling, her red-soled high heels tapping on the tile floor.

Once she was gone, Marcus closed the door. He scrolled through the alert on his phone, and every muscle in his face tensed. What he read angered him.

"What's got your jockstrap in a twist?"

"There's been a shooting." Marcus clipped his phone back on his belt. "A mortal—Abigale's mate."

Ari sat up at attention. "I should call Tig and see if she needs any computer help."

Marcus held up his hand. "She's still busy at the scene. If she wants anything, she'll contact you. In the meantime, I need to phone the mayor. He'll try to take action, and whatever he does will spread panic through the community. It's my job to talk him down."

"You're sure I shouldn't report to Tig? I'm almost done updating this computer. When I finish, I was going to stop by to see Cerissa before returning to the winery to work, but I could help Tig instead—."

"Don't bother the chief."

"Whatever, man."

"Good."

Marcus opened his mouth to say something about Haley, but then brought his lips together. He didn't need to say anything. Ari's flirtation with her hadn't hurt him.

Keep telling yourself that.

Marcus turned to leave.

"Hey," Ari said.

"Yes?"

"Don't I get a kiss goodbye?"

"The way you were flirting with Haley, I thought you'd forgotten about me."

Dammit. Why had he let that slip out? *So much for not caring.*

Ari rose to his feet. "Dude, how could I forget about you?"

Before Marcus said another word, the consultant stalked to him and attacked his mouth, parting Marcus's lips with his tongue.

Blood rushed to Marcus's groin, and an overwhelming peace flowed through him at the same time. Ari's hips pressed forward as he grabbed Marcus's ass.

When they broke from the kiss and stepped back, they were both breathless. Ari shut his briefcase and strode to the door. "Toodles, good lookin'. I'll see you soon when you're not too busy."

"Stay away from Haley." Marcus waved a finger after him. "I should have put a no-poaching-the-locals clause in your contract."

Ari turned and shot him a cocky smile. "Then where would *we* be?"

Marcus paused, and then laughed. He couldn't help himself. Ari was right. Writing a contract exception to allow *only* Marcus to screw the consultant would have made their affair too public. He had no choice but to accept Ari's loose ways. After all, he benefited from them.

Ari closed the door behind him, and Marcus raised his finger pads to his lips, catching Ari's masculine scent on them. That hot kiss was still in his blood. While the arousal stayed with him, the sense of peace began to wane, and a hint of guilt crawled up his chest.

He pictured Nicholas in his mind. They weren't mates yet, so they weren't exclusive, and being with Ari wasn't cheating...

Then why did Marcus feel guilty?

He shook off the emotion, returned to his office, and phoned the mayor. The mayor was likely to go nuts and demand all sorts of new rules to protect the Hill. It rarely worked. The Rule of Two hadn't protected anyone. Stupid rules only made it more difficult for Marcus to get his work done.

But he'd try to keep the council from going off the rails. Someone had to do the job. It might as well be him, for now.

Chapter 13

Rancho Bautista del Murciélago—near the time Tig arrives at Abigale's house

The predator in Henry watched as Cerissa disappeared into the woods. He had lived here for over a hundred years and knew those woods better than she did. Centering himself, he suppressed the crystal's connection completely. She wouldn't sense him coming.

This is going to be fun.

He had hunted human prey before, and as much as he wanted to deny the truth, no attempt to civilize him would ever pacify his desire to hunt. Cerissa's suggestion—that he hunt her—had made him hard the moment the words left her lips.

He kicked off his sneakers and used his thumbs to strip away his socks. She was right—running shoeless would be easier.

The clock's hand snapped to nine ten. He took off, darting at vampire speed on a parallel course to the one she took.

He sniffed the air, and surprise ribboned through him. "Enhanced human" included the ability to mask her scent.

Excellent. This wouldn't be too easy after all. He crossed over to the path she had taken and examined the forest floor for disturbances. He spotted the direction she had run and, picking up her trail, poured on the speed.

Long-dormant skills came back to him easily. Even without the full moon's light, he had no trouble seeing the tracks she left. He sniffed at the air as he ran.

Still no scent.

It didn't matter. She was good—there were moments when her footprints disappeared entirely—but he'd been at this longer than she had, much longer. He lasered in on her trail and found where her tracks ended at the base of a large oak tree. The glimpse he caught of her was so fast—a quick tilt of his head as he approached—that she would never know he had seen her on a high branch. He kept running and passed beneath her.

Would she climb down to flee? Or would she believe herself lucky and stay put?

Either way, he would enjoy playing with her as he closed in. He had plenty of time.

Deep into the forest he ran, and when he figured she had lost sight of him, he circled around, approaching the tree from the other side. He spied her silhouette on a branch, and his smile grew larger.

To take her unaware, he would have to climb silently. His fingernails elongated into claws to give him purchase on the tree's bark. That wasn't cheating—if she could use enhanced abilities, so could he.

Claw over claw he climbed, his bare feet giving him silent support, and he ascended straight up the trunk until he reached the branch she crouched on.

Her back was to him.

She was focused on trying to catch sight of him, her face pointed in the direction he had disappeared. Even with her superior hearing, she didn't look over her shoulder, didn't realize he was coming.

One knee after the other, he crawled along the sturdy branch. His focus was on her sexy backside. Anticipation caused his fangs to elongate and his *pene* to strain against his blue jeans.

Almost there. He retracted his claws before wrapping his arms around to keep her from falling and pulled her into his embrace.

"Henry!" she screeched.

"Easy, *mi amor*," he whispered.

The scent of her fear rolled across his tongue like tart lemonade on a hot summer's day. His tongue curled, caressing the scent, his taste buds standing at attention.

She struggled at first, her pulse racing, but he held her tight and pushed her ponytail aside to kiss her throat. The sound of blood rushing through her veins taunted him. His fangs ached to plunge into her then and there.

But he wanted to take his time.

She pressed a hand against her neck, blocking his lips. "You have to get me back to the pool to win."

"That should not be too hard." He kissed her knuckles before swinging her over his shoulder caveman style. He jumped, bending his knees to cushion their landing.

She tried to worm free, giggling in the process. "Put me down. This isn't fair," she said with mock anger and a couple of sharp wallops to his butt.

Perhaps he should have restrained her hands. "I didn't realize swatting was allowed under our rules," he said, and slapped her delightfully firm ass. "Good to know."

"Hey," she squealed, as she continued to spank him with both hands.

He aimed for her other cheek and slapped just hard enough to sting.

"Stop that," she yelled.

With his hand cupping her ass cheek, he enjoyed the exquisite roundness. "If you continue to misbehave, turnabout is fair play. Or would you like me to take off my belt and hogtie you?"

She stopped slapping at his butt. He took her silence for an agreement to quit fighting him. A quick glance at his watch—he had less than seven minutes to return her to the pool. It had taken her ten minutes to run to this tree, and while she was a fast runner, he was even faster.

He arrived with two minutes to spare and let her slide down his chest. Her body rubbed against his trapped erection as he lowered her until she stood on the flagstone patio.

"Do you concede?"

She pursed her lips, looking in the direction of the clock. "Yes, but just barely."

He wanted to kiss those sultry lips. But first, he had preparations to make. He opened the towel cabinet by the pool, took out two towels, and spread them over a double-wide lounge chair designed to hold two people.

Her gaze had followed him as he worked. "What's that for?"

"You'll see."

He scooped her up, laid her on the lounger, and pulled the band from her ponytail, allowing her hair to hang freely over her shoulders to her waist.

In her purse, he found the hypo. He dialed in the stabilizer—an easy code to remember: 1-2-3-4—pressed the tip to her arm, a light hiss sounded, and, finished, he dropped the cylinder on the glass tabletop.

"Ready?"

She nodded.

His eyes focused on the pounding vein in her throat. Her blood's tart scent, her musky arousal, and her breathless excitement threatened to overpower him. He wanted to devour her, in more ways than one.

"I hope you are not too fond of this blouse."

He gripped the collar and ripped it down the front.

Cerissa gazed into his captivating eyes as he tore the fabric. His pupils enlarged to wipe out the chestnut-brown irises, and she rose toward him, drawn like some imaginary cord pulled her. Her blouse fell down her arms and her smile grew.

He could do anything he wanted, and she'd let him. She both loved and trusted him.

Gently pushing her back on the lounge chair, he peeled off the remnants of her shredded blouse and then stripped off his shirt. He slipped his gold chain over his head, briefly brought the Christ to his lips, and set the crucifix on the nearby table.

"However shall I remove these?" he asked, touching the straps of her bra.

When she started to answer, he laid a finger against her lips, directing her to remain silent, and reached into his pocket. He pulled out a large folding knife and flipped it open, locking the five-inch blade in place. Sliding it under her right strap, he cut the elastic in two, and then cut the left.

She sharply inhaled with the thrill of the implied threat.

His answering smile was predatory. He placed the blade underneath the small piece of cloth holding the two cups together, the blunt metal cool against her skin, and goosebumps bloomed across her chest. He sliced toward himself and then set the knife aside. Her nipples crinkled as he palmed the cups and lifted them away.

"Lovely," he said in a breathy, masculine voice.

She grew wetter just from the way he looked at her.

He peeled off her capris and then fingered the elastic of her thong. With a quick *snap*, he tore the band in two at her hip, and did the same to the other side, sliding away the thin fabric, removing the unneeded barrier.

She now lay naked under the stars. He ran his hands along her body, starting at her neck, caressing her breasts, then the tender flesh of her stomach, across her hips and down her thighs. A light tingle followed the tracks his fingers left behind, the excitement building between her legs. She reached out to him, wanting to pull him to her, the exposure overwhelming.

"Not yet, *mi corazón*," he said.

He captured her wrists and brought each to his lips, sending another exciting shiver through her as he licked her pulse, and then pressed his lips to her amethyst and moonstone bracelet, the bracelet he had given her. The moonstone marked her as being mated to a Hill vampire.

Him.

He returned her hands to her sides. She gave in, letting him continue to lead.

After all, he'd won.

He pulled the string holding back his ponytail, and his ebony hair fell to his shoulders. Leaning over her, he suckled one breast and then the other, his silken cascade of hair brushing her skin, sending tingles right through her. His red-hot passion, his desire for her, seeped into her consciousness. On purpose? Or was he losing control?

He took his time, laving the hard nipple with his tongue, sucking until she couldn't take any more, her breath coming faster and faster, and just when she thought she'd explode, he sat back.

A bulge filled out his jeans. His face was a picture of controlled lust.

He bent and trailed kisses along her rising and falling ribcage, his mane of messy hair hiding his face. He edged downward, and those silken strands swept over her stomach, until he stopped to lick between her legs. A spasm of pleasure shot through her, and he slid two fingers inside, rhythmically stroking her.

His tongue threatened to send her over the edge quickly. It was like a cat's tongue, rougher than a human's, and he soon had her lost in the sensations.

"Henry, oh Henry," she said, trying to hold off the inevitable.

But he licked one more time, and waves of ecstasy overcame her. She arched her back, gripping the armrest and rising off the lounge chair, as pulse after pulse shook her.

When the waves receded, he kissed along her thigh until he gently plunged his fangs into her leg vein.

Liquid fire shot through her, reaching her core instantly, and she moaned again, her thoughts racing.

Need more, want more, must have more right now.

He drew out a few big gulps of her blood, and she tugged at his arm.

"Naughty, naughty," he said, licking the wound closed. He released her thigh and unbuttoned his jeans. "Hands at your sides."

Hard as it was, she obeyed.

"So beautiful," he said, his gaze sweeping her naked body. He slipped off his jeans and then spread her legs, kneeling between them, and, bracing his hands on the lounger, hovered above her.

She couldn't stand the wait. The potent fang serum and her love for him made self-control nearly impossible. Her arms wanted to rise, to grab him, to plunge him into her. It took all her willpower to be still.

He kissed her breasts and her neck, his erection bumping her opening, teasing her as he slid in an inch and then pulled back.

She whimpered and lifted her hips, trying to meet him. He pulled back again, licking her nipple as he did.

When he rose, he locked gazes with her. "I love you," he said.

Before she could respond, he plunged between her legs, burying himself to the hilt.

She gasped. "I love you too."

Her passion was ready to explode, but he moved so slowly, it was agony to be close to coming and yet not have enough friction to get there. He grinned cockily at her. He knew exactly what he was doing.

Damn that crystal.

She raised her hips with him, trying to hasten his thrusts, but he wouldn't speed up, keeping a rhythm that built her arousal higher without letting her peak.

I can't stand it anymore.

She grabbed his hips, moving them faster and faster, rocking him against her clitoris. She started to come, and felt him let go at the same time, losing herself in their shared orgasm.

When she emerged from the haze, she realized Henry had collapsed on top of her, though he had been careful not to crush her with his weight. She tenderly stroked his back, running her fingers over his strongly defined trapezius muscles and corresponding latts. His face was buried in her hair, his breath brushing her neck, their bodies slick with her sweat.

She loved him with all her heart.

After a few minutes, he slid out of her and lay on his side next to her. She faced him, looking into his crystalline brown eyes, and smiled.

If he desired the thrill of the hunt, she would happily give it to him—anytime.

Chapter 14

RANCHO BAUTISTA DEL MURCIÉLAGO—MOMENTS LATER

Henry held Cerissa close, enjoying the warmth of her face on his shoulder. He considered getting up to grab another towel to cover her so she wouldn't become chilled, but she didn't seem bothered by the evening air, and he was loath to release her from his embrace.

Footsteps on the stone patio broke the silence.

Henry's animal brain reacted. He jumped to his feet, snatched the knife from the table, and flipped the blade open. With his free hand, he threw the towel he'd been lying on over Cerissa to cover her nakedness.

"Well, now that you're done, I need to talk with you," Rolf said.

Baring his fangs, Henry growled. "Leave."

Rolf sniffed the air, and his eyes turned solid black. He clenched his hands, his fangs peering out over his lip, his knees bent as if ready to leap, but his face looked like a man struggling with himself. He didn't move.

Her blood. He smells her adrenaline-spiked blood.

Once triggered, it took a while before a mortal's body filtered out the stress hormones. She seemed no different in that regard.

Henry took a step closer, circling the knife in the air to draw Rolf's attention. "Leave now."

Rolf moved backward, his gaze still fixed on Cerissa. "N-no need to get defensive. I don't want her."

"I won't tell you again," Henry snarled. "Leave."

Rolf held up his hands and shifted his gaze away from Cerissa to the knife. "Ah, something happened. I tried to call. Your phone was off."

"If I have it off, I have it off for a reason."

"I thought you would want to hear what happened—right away."

It had better be something major to justify Rolf's interruption. Henry grabbed his jeans from where they were draped over a chair. "Go inside the house and wait for me in the drawing room."

Rolf pivoted and climbed the stairs. When the French doors closed behind him, Henry turned to Cerissa and said, "I am sorry, *mi amor*. I was not expecting him tonight. If I had, I would never have exposed you in this way."

She got off the lounger and kissed him. "Everything's all right. It's not your fault. And until he arrived," she said, blushing, "I was having fun."

"Why don't you go into the pool house and shower there? There will be a robe or something you can change into. I'll try and get rid of him as fast as I can."

"You do that. I'm not done with you yet," she said, a twinkle of mischief in her eyes.

He blew her a kiss, pulled on his jeans and t-shirt, and opened the French door to the drawing room.

Rolf paced back and forth in front of the river stone fireplace. "You smell like a whorehouse."

Henry closed on him, grabbing him by the collar. "If you ever do anything like that again, I will thrash you until you beg for death."

Rolf raised his palms, surrendering. His hair—long on top, shaved on the sides—fell forward into his eyes. "I didn't think it would matter. She isn't human—"

"She is my mate, and you won't disrespect her that way."

Rolf kept his hands raised. "All right, I won't."

Henry pushed Rolf away, and his business partner stumbled backward. Henry moved to the sideboard and poured a glass of Grey Goose. Taken straight, the vodka would give him a high for a minute or two before his blood detoxified the alcohol.

He shot the glass. The pungent liquid settled uncomfortably in his stomach, and his anger eased.

"What do you want?" he asked, wiping his mouth. They'd been business partners for so long that their relationship was like a marriage, but Rolf had never been this, well, invasive before.

Rolf swept his bangs back and started pacing. "From what I've pieced together, one of Abigale's mates was killed by a sniper about thirty minutes ago."

Henry's throat constricted. "Who?"

"Nina."

"*¡Dios mío!* Is Abigale all right?"

"Unharmed." Rolf ran a hand through his hair. "Tig is questioning the shooter in Abigale's basement."

The French doors opened, and Cerissa rushed in wearing a bathrobe. "Your anger changed to sorrow. What happened?"

She must have sensed his feelings through the crystal. "There's been another shooting," Henry told her. "One of Abigale's mates is dead."

"Oh, damn, not another murder." Her shoulders drooped, and then her eyes opened wide. "Wait—*one of?*"

"She has—had—seven mates."

"Right, right—I read about her, ah, arrangement." Cerissa crossed the room to him and touched his sleeve. "I'm sorry. How can I help?"

"I need to go see Abigale." He scrubbed his hand over his face. Abigale would be distraught and need his support. "Nina is—was—her youngest mate."

"It won't take me long to shower and change. I can go with you."

"Thank you, *cariña*. I would appreciate your company."

"I'm on my way over there now," Rolf said. He plucked nervously at his sleeve. "Karen's at home, calling others to tell them what happened. She'll join me at Abigale's later."

Cerissa stepped closer to Rolf, peering into his eyes. "When was the last time you fed?"

Rolf's gaze darted from Henry to Cerissa.

"You're acting like it's been weeks, not hours," she said. "I may have a solution to your feeding problem."

Rolf scrunched his face in an angry scowl. "You told her?"

Henry shook his head. Why hadn't she waited? He had wanted to break the news gently. "It was during Karen's kidnapping. She guessed something was wrong. I couldn't lie to her." He turned to Cerissa. "But you can't give him what you gave me."

"No, but I can dilute the concentration and he can try it. I'll take blood samples before and after. I need to figure out what it is about adrenaline-enhanced blood he needs. Don't worry. I'll work quickly and then we can go to Abigale's."

Cerissa suggested they go to the kitchen. She still had her medical bag there. "Which arm do you want me to use?" she asked Rolf.

Rolf looked taken aback, like he'd never heard the question before.

That's right—he's probably never had a blood sample taken before.

But Henry seemed familiar with the procedure. Why? "When you give another vampire your blood, how do you do you usually do it?"

Rolf held out his wrist. "I cut a vein with a knife."

"Rolf is younger than I am," Henry said. "The older vampires donate first."

"Hmm, well, this will be easier," Cerissa said, screwing a vacutainer needle onto the translucent plastic holder. "The extraction needle is so sharp that he shouldn't feel it."

Rolf put his fists on his hips. "I'm not afraid of pain."

But by the way he eyed the needle, his face paler than normal, his declaration seemed like a child facing the monster under the bed. It didn't make sense.

He's okay with a knife, but a needle puts him on edge?

Then it dawned on her. He grew up in a time when injections were very painful. A fear developed in childhood was hard to overcome.

"Sit there." She pointed to a chair at the kitchen table. She didn't want him falling if he fainted. While it would be his just desserts if he took a nosedive—given the way he interrupted them—he was her patient. His well-being was her priority now.

Rolf stared at his arm as she prepped it.

With a flick of her chin, she said, "Watch Henry, not me."

Henry helped, asking Rolf about winery business while she tied a rubber tourniquet above Rolf's elbow and took four samples. She put the full vacutainers in the refrigerator and measured out a tablespoon of adrenaline-enhanced blood, adding a cup of regular blood.

She handed Rolf the mixture. He raised the wine glass to his lips.

"A sip," she said. "A small sip. We need to see how you react."

He sniffed the liquid.

Instantly, his eyes became solid black, and he knocked back the entire glass in one gulp and licked his lips. "Now that's what I call *dark wine*."

Cerissa grimaced. "I said a small sip." She took the glass back from him. "How do you feel?"

He stood, holding on to the table. "Great. Where did you obtain adrenaline-spiked blood? It's illegal here."

"It's illegal if taken from a mortal, but this adrenaline-*enhanced* blood was from my clones. And sit back down. We're not through yet."

She took another blood sample from Rolf. "I want you to keep a notebook," she said, marking the second sample and placing it in the refrigerator. "A journal detailing how you feel each night and when the craving comes back. I'll provide you with a pouch of enhanced blood—already diluted. You usually hunt a live mortal once a week, right?"

He looked uncertain and swallowed hard. "Y-yes."

"Well, for now, you can drink one pouch a week, but no more. And no live hunting."

Rolf opened his mouth to reply, but Henry cut him off.

"We can talk later," he said, and escorted Rolf out.

Cerissa leaned against the kitchen island and rubbed her temples. Vampires were at war with each other, and a mortal had paid the ultimate price. She gritted her teeth.

Were the Protectors right? Were vampires so inherently evil that they weren't to be trusted?

The Lux believed they had a moral obligation to protect humanity, a duty that superseded any individual desire. She'd bought into their belief until she fell in love with Henry and claimed her own free will, refusing to be a slave to duty any longer. But she still wanted to protect humanity and stop the VDM.

And now Nina was dead—probably because of the VDM. Why couldn't vampires be more like the Lux?

We watch out for humanity. We don't seek to enslave them.

By their very nature, vampires were terribly flawed. But the Lux…

No, I can't give in to those thoughts. Henry is a good man. Look at the Hill and what he's built. Not all vampires are like the VDM.

She looked up at the sound of Henry returning to the kitchen. "*Cariña*, are you all right?"

"I will be when the killings stop."

A bright light appeared, and Cerissa lunged toward the shimmer, putting herself between Henry and the intruder. Someone from the Enclave had flashed in.

When Ari materialized, she shook a finger at him. "What did I tell you about using the front door?"

"I didn't want to run into Mr. Sourpuss. Rolf looked like he was in a bad mood." Ari offered his hand to Henry. "Hi, old man." He then raised his eyebrows at her. "Hey, cute outfit."

She wrapped her arms across her chest, holding the robe tighter. The last thing she wanted was a wardrobe malfunction in front of her cousin. "Why are you here?"

"I heard about the shooting—we need to talk about next steps. I can't leave—I'm still working on the town's email system, which means you need to go to San Diego *right now*."

"Hold on. Did you find out something new?"

"I emailed it to you an hour ago."

"Do I look like I have my phone on me?"

"No, you look like... Well, never mind." Ari tapped something on his phone and handed it to her. "I snapped this photo of a flyer lying on Tig's desk. The local priest told her a stack of them was left on the Hill Chapel's literature table by parties unknown."

The printing was a little blurred on his phone, like he'd tried to photograph the flyer surreptitiously. Why hadn't he held up the page and used his lenses to capture it on video? She could barely make out the words.

"'Be the wolf you were meant to be'?" she slowly read aloud.

The flyer offered a "new path" and encouraged vampires to quit hiding what they were. Printed at the bottom was a PO box address in San Diego.

She locked eyes with Ari when she finished reading the flyer. "Why are we just learning about this now?"

"If they don't save it electronically, I don't have access." His voice had an edge. "But now we have it."

She grabbed a chair at the kitchen table and motioned to Ari to do likewise as she read the words a second time. *Hmm.* Knowing what she did, the flyer sounded ominous. A group named New Path had paid Blanche to kill Henry, and New Path Church had picked up the previous shooters when they were paroled from prison. The Lux suspected New Path was involved with the VDM.

"You think 'new path' is a reference to the group that paid Blanche?"

"Yeah, since Jim Jones is New Path's contact person—"

"Wait. You're telling me Jim Jones, the religious cult leader who killed his followers in Guyana, is behind the VDM?"

"No, no." Ari waved his hand. "Tig thinks either the guy had the bad fortune to be born with the same name as the cult leader, or he took it as an alias, as an inside joke. The real Jim Jones killed all his followers—just like a vampire kills those he turns."

"Oh." She skimmed the flyer again. "But nothing here mentions Jim Jones."

"He's the one who registered the website New Path Church uses, and the PO box on the flyer is the same address the church's website is registered to, so it all links up now. Tig is trying to locate Jim Jones to question him about the assassination attempts. You have to track him down before she does—especially if he's involved in the VDM."

"All right, I'll make arrangements to give presentations on the lab to potential investors in San Diego." She handed the phone to Henry so he could read the flyer too. "Barney Morrison seemed interested. I'll see if he's willing to sponsor me."

"*Cariña*," Henry said, standing behind her and wrapping his fingers over her shoulders. "I know Wilma Wagner, the CEO of the San Diego community. Let me set up a meeting. We'll travel there together."

"You have your winery to run. You don't have to go with me."

He took the chair next to her. "But I insist. Rolf can handle winery business. Besides, there are a couple of distributors in San Diego I've wanted to speak to in person."

She crossed her arms. "You've been targeted by the killers—twice. It would be safer if you stayed home."

Henry's eyes became solid black, and the chill of his anger threaded through her. "I will not be made a prisoner of the Hill by the VDM," he said, and inhaled. His anger receded from her mind. "Do not worry about me. We'll stay for Nina's memorial service and then leave for San Diego the next night."

She didn't like his idea.

He leaned in, and his lips pressed against hers. Determination rolled off him like thunder. She wouldn't be able to talk him out of going, at least not right now.

"You two make such a cute spy team." Ari clapped his hands together. "Oh, and I almost forgot. You have to start wearing your lenses—the Protectors want video recordings of everything."

"What? Everything? No way am I wearing them when I'm with Henry." Her lenses recorded everything she saw and heard using nanotechnology.

He shrugged. "Everything except your bedroom. You can shut them off for nookie."

"How magnanimous."

"Hey, I went to the mat with the Protectors. After what you hid from them, they wanted twenty-four-hour video. I knew you'd blow a cork. So, lenses off in the bedroom only"—Ari eyed her robe again—"or wherever it is you make love. The rest of the time, we have to deliver videos."

She glanced over at Henry. He valued his privacy higher than most people. "Are you okay with that?"

"For the time being," he replied. "The Protectors understand we're working together. Once we track down the VDM, I may talk with Agathe about loosening their requirements."

"Yeah," Ari said with a laugh, "you handled her well the last time."

Cerissa squeezed Henry's hand. "All right," she said. "We'll make the arrangements tonight to go to San Diego—after we visit Abigale. The sooner we figure out who is behind the conspiracy, the sooner everyone will be safe, and we can get back to a normal life together."

Ari smirked. "With you two, life will never be normal."

Yeah, but with a little less interference, we could try.

She shoved her chair back and motioned to Ari. "It's time for you to leave."

"Not so fast. I had another reason for stopping by. I'm getting pushback at the winery. I need admin access to their computer server. The geek in charge refused."

"I'll email Suri," Henry said.

"Suri?"

"The winery's manager. She'll see my email in the morning. You should have what you need by noon."

"Okay, I can wait, but I have another question you may be able to answer now. Who was working for you nine years ago?"

"Suri was assistant manager at the time."

"I mean in IT—someone smart enough to install a back door in your email server."

Henry looked thoughtful. "A lot of people had access to our computer system back then. We had been using an IBM mini-mainframe to handle our stock inventory and shipping. We eventually hit the point where it wasn't cost-effective to stay with an obsolete technology. So, we hired an outside consultant to transition us from the old system to new hardware and software. We started around 2007, and the whole thing was running by 2009."

Cerissa was impressed. How did he remember so much? In addition to his tight butt and to-die-for eyes, she had to admire his keen mind and attention to detail.

Ari made a note into his phone. "Can you put together a list of everyone who had administration privileges during the transition?"

"Suri can. I will ask her."

"Great, that's a start. ¡Adiós, amigos!" Ari said, and left the same way he came in.

Cerissa gave Henry a quick kiss and then hurried upstairs. She couldn't wear an oversized bathrobe for a condolence visit. But what should she wear? Black was the color for mourning in this culture.

Shame slithered through her stomach.

Abigale wouldn't be mourning if I had stayed on mission and stopped the VDM by now.

She gave her head a little shake. This wasn't about her; she had no time for guilt. Henry needed her support.

She took a quick shower and then rifled through her closet. With a sigh, she put on black slacks, along with a black and navy blouse, the colors swirled. A somber outfit. She hoped she'd made the right choice, for his sake.

A short time later, she slid into the passenger seat of his Viper. He drove down the curving driveway, past the grapevines running across the slope where a lawn would normally be. At Robles Road, he made a left.

The evening sky was clear, and stars filled the night. The early full moon had already set. After passing six vineyard estates, he made a right turn onto a side street. A cluster of expensive homes sat on a cul-de-sac, no vineyards behind them.

Cerissa flipped down the visor mirror and freshened her lipstick while she used her lenses to check Abigale's dossier. The photo revealed a beautiful blonde woman who worked as a dominatrix—it was why she had seven mates and no vineyard.

"Why are we visiting so soon?" Cerissa asked. "Are you close friends with Abigale?"

"It's part of our tradition to visit the bereaved right away to make sure they retain the will to live."

Ah. That made sense.

Henry parked at the curb behind Rolf's car in front of a large Mediterranean-style home—a beautiful structure with bougainvillea vines outlining the roofline, their blooms a bright fuschia, and balconies girded by stone work.

Cerissa's gut tightened. She didn't move. It felt wrong, being here. She was a stranger. She shouldn't intrude on the grieving family.

Henry opened the car door for her. "Let's go."

Tonight, she would do this for him. And after paying their respects, they'd track down the VDM and put an end to this, once and for all.

Chapter 15

ABIGALE CHERRILL'S HOME—MOMENTS LATER

Henry escorted Cerissa along Abigale's elegant stone walkway, dreading the visit. What could he say to comfort his friend? Abigale had doted on her youngest mate—a pretty woman with a pleasant disposition.

Words seem useless.

He had first met Nina when he hired her to work in the winery's gift shop as a favor for Abigale. The young mortal was well liked by the staff there. How would they react to her murder? Should he find a grief counselor to help them process their loss?

I'll deal with it later.

He reached past Cerissa to press the large brass Victorian doorbell, and Rolf opened the door. "Abigale is downstairs with Nina's body."

They went through the foyer and into the living room. After a short wait, Abigale joined them wearing a mourning dress, with deep sorrow etched on her face.

Henry stood. "Please accept our condolences on your loss."

The others got to their feet a moment behind him.

Abigale crossed the room and collapsed onto a low-backed couch—Louis XVI, if he remembered correctly—which was covered in magenta velvet, the straight back trimmed with carved wood. The couch was as old as she was.

Henry sat next to her, and Rolf and Cerissa took the two matching chairs.

"Thank you." Abigale blotted her eyes with a flowered handkerchief. "Thank you all for coming by. I still can't believe she's gone."

"What happened?" Rolf asked.

Henry shook his head at his partner. Rolf's blunt question showed no empathy or decorum.

Abigale stared at her closed fist—something was clutched tightly in her hand. Tears streamed down her face as she told the story.

Tension wound in Henry's gut as he listened.

Powerless. Powerless to protect those I care about.

The memories came in rapid succession.

He could still hear *papi*'s meaty hand thudding against *mami*'s face, her strangled cry as she tried not to wake the *niños*. Only five years old, he would stay huddled in his bed, knowing if he tried to stop *papi*, he would just make it worse.

Powerless.

He could still see Simona left helpless in a strange country, frantically looking for him on the San Francisco docks, to forever wonder what happened to him. After Anne-Louise ripped away his mortal life, his maker forced him to abandon his betrothed. Grief had choked him as he hid in the dock's shadows, unable to protect the woman he should have married from the shame and pain of desertion.

Powerless.

He could still feel his maker's grip on him. Escape from her was like a fish dangled over a starving alley cat. Anne-Louise would act bored with him, let him think he might finally win his liberty. By the time he got five miles away to the next town, she would call him back. With every thudding step, he clenched his fists and struggled against her siren's call. And when he finally made it back to her hiding place, the punishment…

Powerless.

He hated the feeling with all his might.

Abigale was almost finished telling them what happened when Luis appeared from the hallway. The mortal was easygoing and friendly, and had treated Henry as a contemporary until learning his true age.

"Abigale," Luis said when she finished the story. "May I speak with you for a moment?"

She beckoned to him. "Join us."

Luis's eyes were red-rimmed, and his shoulders slumped as he hurried to her.

"What do you need?" She stood and slipped an arm around him.

"It's Carrie."

"How is she doing?"

"Not well. She wants to see you."

Carrie emerged from the hallway and hesitated. Her short blonde hair had been streaked blue since the last time Henry saw her.

"Come here, my dear." The young woman flew to Abigale, burrowing into her shoulder and sobbing.

"Could you give us a few minutes alone?" Abigale asked, looking in Henry's direction.

"Of course." He stood. Rolf and Cerissa followed him when he began to leave. Carrie emitted another loud sob.

"Henry, on second thought, I'd like Cerissa to stay. I understand she's a doctor."

He paused to look over his shoulder at Abigale, but before he could reply, Cerissa said, "Certainly," and returned to her chair.

Rolf cast a dark look in Cerissa's direction. Henry caught Rolf's arm and propelled him from the room, through the hall and into the kitchen.

"Your mate should not be left alone with Abigale," Rolf said once they were out of earshot.

Henry raised one eyebrow. What was his problem? "Luis and Carrie are there. Nothing improper will happen."

"A grieving vampire in Abigale's position shouldn't be exposed to any temptation."

"With all due respect, you put too much emphasis on strict adherence to the rules."

Rolf pounded his fist on the kitchen counter. "They are rules for a reason."

"Abigale will not attack Cerissa. She will not do anything to jeopardize Luis's respect for her. If any of us understands how to control the beast within, it is Abigale." Henry turned to leave. "Please pardon me, but I need to talk with Tig."

Rolf grabbed his arm, stopping him. "Mark my words. You need to keep a close eye on your mate. She doesn't realize how her actions might be perceived. She doesn't understand our community." Rolf poked Henry in the chest. "It's your job to make sure she does."

Henry glowered and brushed Rolf's hand away. Was he reacting this way because Cerissa had learned about his problem? "I'll make sure she has read the Covenant."

"You'll do more than that—you need to drill into her head she isn't an equal on the Hill. If she keeps acting like she is—"

"Rolf," Henry said, clenching his fist. "I'm not having a political debate with you." Cerissa was equal to anyone on the Hill, but arguing the point while making a condolence visit was unseemly.

Rolf narrowed his eyes. "Yeah? Well, what about her initiation ceremony? You've been mated three weeks and you haven't scheduled it."

Henry sighed. There were reasons he'd delayed, and not just because of Karen's kidnapping and Cerissa's trouble with the Lux Protectors. His mate hated surprises. She wouldn't understand why he was required to keep the ceremony secret from her.

No, I can't hide it. I must *tell her first. The rules be damned.*

He took out his phone and opened his calendar. "I'll schedule it for after we return from San Diego. I need to talk with Cerissa about the date, to ensure she's available."

Rolf crossed his arms. "You'll do no such thing. You know better. No mate can be told in advance—how else can we test their fitness? We must see their genuine instincts—to make sure they truly belong here."

Henry glowered at him. "Cerissa belongs here."

"So you say. She needs to prove she does. And you need to schedule it." Rolf pointed at him. "And you can't tell her in advance. If you do, you'll be facing a hundred lashes at the whipping post. I guarantee it."

Henry harrumphed and left. His trial for violating the Covenant had resulted in that damn archaic penalty, the sentence suspended with a year's probation, but the punishment would be reinstated if he violated the Covenant during the year.

He refused to argue with Rolf right then, not with Abigale grieving in the next room—but they would have words later.

Cerissa sat for a few moments in uneasy silence while Luis and Abigale tried to comfort Carrie. The young woman continued to sob uncontrollably.

"I'm so sorry, my pet. I should have protected her," Abigale said, rocking Carrie in her arms. Even in her grief, Abigale had the poise and grace of a blonde, blue-eyed Jackie Kennedy.

What can I do to help them?

Cerissa's guilt raised its head and hissed the answer. She'd let her desire for Henry distract her from her mission. Falling in love and starting a relationship with him had eaten valuable time—time she should have spent tracking the VDM.

Nina would be alive today if I had just done my job.

Abigale lifted her chin, catching Cerissa's eye. "She's been like this ever since she received the news. She and Nina were very close. Can you give her a tranquilizer? I hate seeing her in such pain."

Medicating the mortal didn't sound like a good idea. "She needs to process her grief. A drug might interfere."

"Are you sure?"

It felt strange to talk about Carrie with her sitting right there—better to ask the patient. "Carrie, do you want me to give you something to help you sleep?"

"No, thank you," she said, between hiccupping sobs.

Cerissa hesitated for a moment, not certain what to say. Then it occurred to her. There was someone more skilled in these matters who might help. "Would you like to talk with Father Matt?"

The young woman stopped crying for a moment and looked at Abigale for direction. "If you want to talk with Matt, it is entirely up to you. Just ask."

"He's Episcopal?"

Cerissa nodded. "He is, but he takes an ecumenical approach these days. He's also a trained psychologist. I would prefer he speak with you before I prescribed any medication."

"Nina was Episcopal. Could he give her last rites?"

Cerissa had no idea what Episcopal practices were. "Let's call him and ask." She took her phone out of her purse and tapped his number. "Matt, I'm over at Abigale's. Did you hear what happened?"

He hadn't. She stepped away to tell him, not wanting Carrie to be upset at hearing the details repeated.

A few minutes later, she returned and handed the phone to Abigale. "He wants you to confirm the invitation."

"Of course, Matt, you are welcome," Abigale said. "I would appreciate whatever you could do to comfort Carrie."

Was this another vampire rule? Did Matt need Abigale's permission before speaking with one of her mates? That seemed wrong. Wasn't he an ombudsman for mortals on the Hill?

After the call ended, Abigale handed back the phone. "Thank you."

Then it dawned on Cerissa. Carrie wasn't the only one who needed a trained psychologist. Abigale had been present when Nina was killed. That kind of trauma could lead to survivor's guilt. "You've been through a terrible experience. Talking with Matt may help you, too."

Abigale grimaced. "I will tell Henry if I need anything further from you."

Cerissa stood. She'd done her duty; she couldn't force treatment on Abigale. "My condolences to both you and your family over your tragic loss."

"Thank you. You may wait for Henry in the foyer."

Henry pressed his ear to the door. He heard no voices through the wall in Abigale's dungeon and knocked. Tig didn't look happy when she opened it a crack.

"What?"

"I'm sorry to bother you with such a small matter, but I need a travel pass."

She swept her hand over her short afro, a look of disbelief in her eyes. "Fuck, Henry, you're interrupting me for that? Send me an email request."

"We're leaving for San Diego right after the memorial service. I didn't want any misunderstandings, not with the threat of the whipping post hanging over my head."

He had to walk on eggshells to avoid a whipping. In the end, the trial had been an irksome power play by the council, the mayor determined to make an example of him. Henry wasn't going to give the mayor any excuse to do so.

Tig furrowed her brow. "You said 'we.' You and Rolf?"

"No, Cerissa and I. We both have business in San Diego."

"You can't go without a guard."

"I'll ask Rolf—"

"No, I can't risk a founder and a council member traveling together. It must be Zeke. I need Liza to stay here to help with the investigation. I can't spare Jayden, and I don't have anyone else I trust."

Every muscle tightened in Henry's jaw. "I don't need an escort, and if I did, *he* would be the last person I would take."

How to explain it to Tig? He hadn't told her what happened: Zeke had challenged him to a duel over Cerissa. The chief would have brought the dispute to the town council, and a trial would have been too embarrassing.

Now Henry wished he had. "There must be someone else who can go with us."

Tig rubbed her eyelids with one hand, like she was suppressing the need to explode. "Look, I spoke to him about his behavior weeks ago. He won't bother Cerissa. She's chosen you, you're blood bonded, and he's promised to back off. He understands what will happen if he doesn't."

"I really must object—"

"Either take Zeke, or no travel pass."

"What have we become?"

"A community at war. If you didn't believe it before, believe it now."

"War?" If Tig convinced the council, a whole list of onerous restrictions would limit travel. "A conspiracy, yes. But—"

"There's been a concerted effort to kill the founders of Sierra Escondida. If that's not a declaration of war, I don't know what is. I expect the council will recognize the truth soon."

"Fine," he said. Better to agree now than wait for the council to make travel impossible. "We will take Zeke, but on one condition. Deputize me. I may hear something in San Diego, and—"

"Henry, we're a police department, not county sheriffs," she said, sounding exasperated. "I can't 'deputize' you. At most, I can make you part of my reserve force."

"Then do so. Give me authority on your behalf. And rank superior to Zeke's."

She snorted. "Even if I did, San Diego is outside my jurisdiction."

"I'm not talking about state law. Under our treaty, it would give me status to ask questions."

"Fuck," she said, and pursed her lips. "All right."

Good. Being a reserve officer would give him cover to help Cerissa. His shoulders relaxed, and he let go of the tension he'd been holding. "Thank you."

"Let me contact Quentin and brief him on the situation. He's a good guy; he's been their security director for twenty years. I trust him, but watch your back."

"You may count on it." He started to leave.

"Wait," she said, and he stopped. "There are a few things you need to know." She closed her eyes for a moment and pinched the bridge of her nose, seemingly lost in thought. "Keep an eye out for anything to do with a church called New Path, or a man named Jim Jones—mortal or vampire. If you learn anything, report back to me immediately. Jones may be the person behind the attacks, so consider him dangerous—use extreme caution."

Henry schooled his expression. He couldn't reveal he had already learned about New Path and Jones.

"Okay, spill it," she said.

"Spill what?"

"Whatever you're hiding. I know your poker face when I see it."

"The only thing I'm hiding is my irritation at having to take Zeke."

Tig huffed. "I don't buy it, but I have a prisoner to interrogate. See Jayden tomorrow night. He'll give you a badge and kit. Read the book that goes with it. You need to follow basic procedures under the treaty."

"Have no fear. I negotiated the treaty. I will have no problem following it."

Cerissa found Rolf talking with other vampires in the foyer, and closed the doors to the living room behind her to give Abigale privacy.

They all fell quiet at the sound of someone at the front door. Karen swept in, kissed Rolf on the cheek, and nodded to the others. "Hey, everyone. How is Abigale and her family doing?"

"About as well as can be expected," Rolf said. "We're waiting here until she is ready to receive guests again."

"Sounds good." Karen walked over to Cerissa and gave her a hug and air kisses.

Cerissa held on to Karen's shoulders and studied her eyes as they stepped back from the hug. "How are you doing?"

"I'm fine."

"You're sure? I was concerned Nina's death might bring up some issues for you."

"I'm good. Don't worry about me."

Karen had been tortured by the Carlyle Cutter. Cerissa had used Lux technology to heal her physical injuries and desensitize her memories to process the emotional trauma, but the Lux touchstone had never been used on a mortal's emotions before, and Cerissa remained watchful for any unexpected side effects. After all, Karen still remembered the kidnapping and torture.

"Just as a precaution, maybe you should make an appointment with Matt. He's on the way over—"

"Now stop. You're being a mother hen, you know?" Karen used her pinkies to hook her straight auburn hair behind each ear.

"It's just—"

"I don't need a shrink."

Cerissa let out a small sigh. Patients didn't always follow their doctor's advice. "Well, Henry and I are going to San Diego right after the service for Nina. If you need anything, call, day or night—"

"Enough," Karen said loudly, planting her fists on her hips. "I'm fine."

Rolf looked their way, concern in his eyes. With a flip of her wrist, Karen dismissed him. "Go back to your conversation. Nothing's wrong."

Cerissa averted her gaze, embarrassed. "I'm sorry. I didn't mean to make a scene."

"No worries, girlfriend. If I need help, I'll reach out, okay? There's other people to worry about right now."

"Okay."

"And I'm sorry, too. I shouldn't have snapped at you. I guess I'm edgy because Rolf keeps bugging me about the same thing." Karen slewed her eyes in Rolf's direction. "He seems more anxious than normal. I mean, he's never anxious and now he's jumpy, like he can't sit still for five minutes. Has he said anything to Henry?"

Cerissa couldn't give away doctor-patient information. But she also couldn't lie to her friend. "Did you ask him?"

"Yeah, and he brushed me off."

"Ah, he may have post-traumatic stress disorder—PTSD—over the kidnapping. He was very anxious the whole time you were gone."

Karen smirked. "Maybe he's the one who needs to see Matt."

Cerissa held her lips together. *Nope. Not my place to say anything.*

"What about you?" Karen asked. "How are you and Henry doing?"

Heat rose to Cerissa's cheeks as an image popped into her mind: Henry hovering over her naked on the lounge chair, his pecs tight, his hair wild, and his eyes solid black.

"That good, eh?" Karen laughed and hurriedly covered her mouth. "Sorry, I shouldn't laugh here, not under the circumstances."

"I'll call you when I return from San Diego. We can go out to lunch and laugh all we want."

"Deal." Karen glanced in the direction of Rolf, who was still deep in conversation. She leaned in to Cerissa. "Did you hear the new rumor going around about the mortal rights group? With Frédéric dead, they want a mortal to take his council seat."

"Not a bad idea."

"Are you kidding? Rolf is absolutely opposed, and so am I."

"How can you be? You have as much right to be on the council as Rolf does."

"Not really." Karen fiddled with the moonstone ring she wore. "We'll live another fifty years if we're lucky. They'll live hundreds, so they plan long term. It makes no sense for one of us to make decisions for them."

"But we're part of the community too."

"Yeah, and they take care of us."

Cerissa crossed her arms. "Is that all you aspire to? To be taken care of?"

"Why not?" Karen giggled and then grew serious. "Aside from the kidnapping, living here—being a mate—hasn't been so bad. I kind of like the perks. And I work a job. Rolf doesn't pay for everything."

Cerissa cringed. How could Karen relinquish her independence? It made no sense.

Before Cerissa formulated a polite response, Henry appeared. She would talk with Karen about her views another time.

Henry exchanged pleasantries with Karen. When he finished, Cerissa said to him, "We should leave. Abigale needs to be with her mates more than she needs these visits. I called Father Matt—he's on his way over."

"My respect for you only deepens," Henry said. "I will suggest the idea to the others, that they be brief and leave."

After conferring, they decided Méi—Henry's vampire sister through Anne-Louise—would act as a proxy for Abigale, accepting visitors and freeing Abigale to be with her family. Karen left to return home to email the community. She would ask them to hold off visiting tonight.

Rolf pulled Henry aside. "I need to talk with Tig before I leave. Where is the shooter being kept?"

"In Abigale's basement. Her dungeon." He led Rolf down a hallway, and Cerissa followed. When they reached a flight of stairs going down, Henry added, "It's the first door on your left."

Cerissa raised her eyebrows. Why did Henry know where Abigale's dungeon was?

Rolf began the descent. "I'll call you later and tell you what I find out."

As she and Henry walked to the car, Cerissa pondered it. When between mortal mates, vampires would sometimes hook up with each other. Had Henry and Abigale been lovers? Was that why he knew exactly where her dungeon was?

None of my business.

He had told her about his past sexual relationship with was his maker, Anne-Louise. He had been bluntly honest, and Cerissa's skin crawled just thinking about his confession. She was not going to ask him anything about Abigale.

No, I'm not.

She had learned the hard way—it was far better to let a vampire's past lie in peace than to dig it up.

Chapter 16

The Hill Chapel—Next Day

Nina's body was cremated the following day. Her ashes were transferred to a wooden box for burial. Cerissa had asked Henry about the tradition and gotten a vague answer: "It's required by the Covenant."

Karen was much more direct over the phone.

"Vampires don't like to be reminded of coffin burials. Some were buried and had to dig their way to the surface when they woke from death's sleep. Not a pleasant memory, I'm sure you can understand. Not to mention, it made some of them a bit mental. And then there's the other issue."

"The other issue?" Cerissa repeated.

"If they cremate the remains, it eliminates any possibility the deceased was turned without permission of the council."

"Oh, my." Shock rattled through her. "I'll see you and Rolf at the funeral."

That evening, wearing a sleeveless black dress, she sat in the passenger seat of Henry's Viper. Henry put the car into gear and circled past the driveway fountain.

They hadn't made love again since Nina's death. Desire curled in her stomach, and she brushed her hand along his sleeve. He looked so handsome in his black suit and crisp white dress shirt, his tie in the community's blue, and his ponytail neatly tied back with a black ribbon. His suit fit perfectly: the pants snugged his butt, and the coat was tailored in at the waist. The satin ribbon added an old-fashioned but formal flare.

She wanted him.

A frisson of guilt struck her. She should be focused on the deceased instead of Henry's broad shoulders and sexy ass.

"I spoke with Wilma." He must have sensed her eyeing him, as he gave her a sideways smile. "We're cleared for San Diego."

A little of her tension eased. At least the pieces to their plan were falling into place. "That's a relief."

"We'll fly there tomorrow."

"Why not drive?"

"You may need a car during the day. I didn't think you knew how to operate a stick shift."

"I could be flip and say I learned before you did, but I'll be nice and say, 'Yes, I know how.'"

He steered down the steep driveway, pulled onto Robles Road, and put the car into second. "It's best if I fly us."

She raised an eyebrow. He could transform into a bat, but she doubted he meant that. "Fly?"

"Ah, I suppose I didn't tell you. I'm a licensed pilot. I own a few planes, and the winery owns a corporate jet. We can rent a car for you in San Diego. The people behind Karen's kidnapping may be watching for my car. It is distinctive."

"You just don't want me driving your baby."

"She requires a special touch, just like you do."

She stuck her tongue out at him. He flashed a little fang, and she quickly shut her mouth. Tongue bites weren't her thing.

After parking, they walked hand in hand and silently joined the other mourners headed for the chapel.

The building was constructed from river rock, the light gray stones worn round and smooth, with rough mortar holding them together. A trellis covered the walkway and formed an arch draped in grapevines loaded with green fruit. Electric lights pointed upward and gave the archway a halolike glow.

The two large oak doors stood open. Inside, Hill residents and their mates filled the pews. Each person wore the community's color—a vivid ultramarine—their way of honoring the deceased as one of their own. Henry had clued Cerissa in to the tradition, and she had selected a deep blue ribbon, which she pinned to the shoulder of her black dress.

Father Matt waited near the altar while community members took their seats. His brown hair hung straight, stopping at his strong jaw line, and his beard was closely trimmed. Gold wire-frame glasses outlined his eyes—he looked like a young John Lennon, only thinner.

If both men hadn't been killed, they would have been around the same age.

Matt appeared so peaceful, his eyes closed, his lips moving slightly, like he was saying a final prayer before starting the service. His vestments had the community's blue color woven into the embroidered cross.

When everyone was seated, he took the pulpit and said, "Please stand."

He began chanting *a cappella* the anthem from the rite for burial of the dead.

She removed a prayer book from the pew holder to follow along. The memory of her *pita*'s funeral pyre rose unbidden, even though his *mukhagni* service had sounded nothing like this.

During those last days before his damaged heart gave out, she'd sat as a child by *pita*'s bedside, holding his hand and watching his labored breathing. His thick brown hair was matted to one side and sweat beaded on his forehead.

She had mopped his brow with a cool cloth, trying to give him some comfort, while tears formed in her eyes. The *vaidya* had been by and left some traditional medicines to try. The herbs did nothing to ease his suffering.

He reached up and his large hand cupped her face. "Why do you cry, little one?" he asked, in a hoarse whisper.

"I don't want you in pain." She bowed her head, ashamed of her tears. "I—I don't want you to die."

He stroked her face again. His touch should have comforted her, but it didn't.

"Pain and death are part of the cycle of life."

She brought her lips into a moue. "If I were a goddess, they wouldn't be."

"You'd make a fine goddess, little one." He raised her hand to his mouth, kissed it and closed his eyes.

"Please don't leave me." Tears choked her voice.

"I'll never leave you." His hand shaking, he tapped his fingers over her heart. "I'll always be right here."

His eyes closed again, and his hand dropped to his side.

That was their last conversation.

Her heart clutched—over two hundred years and she still missed him. His tragic death could have been prevented with Lux medicines. A wisp of guilt still hung in her chest. If only she could have saved him.

She focused on Henry, trying to suppress her own grief. It was the first time she had seen him practice his religious beliefs. He joined in the Episcopalian service, rarely glancing at the prayer book that prompted the congregational responses.

It seemed odd, given he was Catholic and not Episcopal. Had he been to enough funerals to learn the denomination's rite by heart?

She'd had an easier time convincing him to talk about being vampire than to get him to talk about his Catholicism. All she knew was Father Matt was his confessor, despite their difference of opinion when it came to the Pope and religious canon.

After the service was over, she walked by Henry's side to the country club's ballroom. The stone pathway was illuminated with tea lights in small, sand-filled paper bags. The large ballroom—the room where she'd first locked eyes with Henry—was decorated somberly, one half with dining tables, and the other half with only chairs. Flower sprays on stands sat against the walls, long gladiolas interspersed with white and pink roses.

Zeke paced back and forth through the room's center, an automatic rifle slung over his shoulder. He was dressed in all black, a blue string tie at his throat, his honey-blonde hair swept loose to the right.

Even Liza and Rolf had automatic pistols holstered at their belts—Cerissa recognized the Glock 18's extended magazine.

Has it really come to this? Armed guards at a funeral reception?

What was happening to their community?

Henry gestured to the kitchen, where a buffet was spread out. "*Cariña,* you should have something to eat with Karen and the other mates. I will join you later."

"All right," she said reluctantly, and released his hand.

He strode past Zeke to where the vampires were gathered around Abigale. Cerissa joined the mortals in the ballroom's kitchen, pleased by what she saw. With less than twelve hours' notice, the community had filled the buffet table to overflowing.

She found Luis standing at the back of the line, thanking those who came.

"I'm so sorry." She offered him a hug.

He accepted, hugging her stiffly. "Thanks."

"Is there anything I can do to help?"

The sadness weighed heavy on him. "Not right now."

"Why don't you grab something to eat?" she suggested. "You don't have to stand here and greet everyone."

His brown eyes looked uncertain. "I don't know. Abigale expects me to stay here."

"Come on." She took his arm, pulling him to the back of the buffet line. "I'm sure she didn't mean for you to starve. Besides, Henry and I were the last couple to leave the chapel."

As the line moved forward, they filled their plates. At the beverage table, where wine and soft drinks were being served, Cerissa selected a Cabernet.

"Let's find a place to sit." She spotted Gaea's boyfriend at a table across the room and gestured in his direction. "I stayed with Gaea when I first arrived here, and Dylan was very helpful and friendly."

Luis walked with her toward Dylan's table. "He's a nice kid—he sometimes helps out when we need an extra set of hands to deliver banked blood."

"You and Dylan work for Olivia? He seemed too busy with college to hold a job."

"He fills in so infrequently, he doesn't mind if he has to skip a class."

Gaea stood on the other side of the room near Henry, deep in conversation. The Rubenesque vampire reminded Cerissa of a brown-haired Mae West. Cerissa hadn't visited her former landlady since returning to the Hill. After the trip to San Diego, she would correct her oversight. Gaea loved to gossip to whomever would listen.

As they wove through the tables, Cerissa asked, "You don't work for Abigale?"

"She insists we all take a job, something to keep us occupied in the afternoons and interacting with other people. She doesn't want us to become too isolated."

At the table, they greeted the six people already there. Luis took the chair next to Gaea's mate. "How's school?"

Dylan scooted his chair over to make room. "We're on a break, but it seems like I keep running from one deadline to another."

"Welcome to the adult world."

"Hey, man, I... Well, I don't know what to say." Dylan squirmed in his seat. "I'm sorry about what happened to Nina."

The other people at the table offered Luis their condolences and returned to their conversations.

"Are you coming to work tomorrow?" Dylan asked.

"I haven't decided yet," Luis said. "Can you fill in for me if I don't?"

"Of course, man. Glad to. Summer classes at the junior college don't start for another week yet." Dylan picked up his wine glass. "You know, I've always wondered what drinking blood is like."

For a moment, the pall lifted from Luis's face, and he chuckled. "To hear them tell it, it's ambrosia."

"Yeah, I imagine everything changes when you're turned, even your taste buds." Dylan sipped his Chardonnay. "What I wouldn't give to be one of them and live forever. Anyone hear whether the council has plans to replace Kim Han?"

No one at the table responded.

Cerissa sliced into the ham. Dylan had the sensitivity of a rock. A funeral dinner wasn't the place to discuss that. But with Nina's death, it was natural for him to consider outwitting mortality.

Humans who accepted the invitation to become a vampire's mate pondered the question at some point in their lives. The treaty communities prohibited turning anyone unless it would replace a vampire who was killed, and such a death was a rare event. With Kim Han's murder a few weeks ago, it wasn't abnormal for Dylan to ponder who would replace her—but he was rude to open his mouth about it here.

Jayden carried his plate, looking for a place to eat. In thirty minutes, he was back on duty. Tig had arranged the shifts so he could attend the funeral. He hadn't known Nina well, but felt bad for her family.

He found a group to sit with, and after greeting everyone at the table, he dug into the roast turkey and gravy. It was one of his favorite dinners, but so rare to have it—he would never cook a whole bird for himself.

"I'm glad I caught you," Haley said, taking the empty seat next to him.

"What can I do for you?"

Jayden regretted the question as soon as it left his mouth. She was leading the charge to get a mortal on the council. He didn't want to volunteer for committee work. He had enough to do investigating Nina's murder.

Haley pushed aside her long blonde hair, which curled at the ends, making her look like a teenager instead of a thirty-year-old. "I'm glad you asked. You should run for the open council seat."

Jayden glanced around guiltily. "This isn't a conversation we should hold here—out of respect for Nina." He took another bite of turkey. He didn't want to return to work hungry. "Aren't you going to eat?"

"Already did, thanks," she said. "Look, I don't mean to be insensitive, but I doubt our vamps are over there exchanging fond memories of the departed." She fluttered her fingers at the cluster across the room. "Knowing them, they're talking about business. Or are you afraid of being seen with me?"

"You know that's not it."

"Then why don't you consider running?"

"Because the council hasn't agreed to let one of us run for the seat," he said, and rapidly shoveled in a bite of green bean casserole. At this rate, he'd never finish eating in time.

"Our committee figured if we proposed a good candidate, we'd cut down on their reasons to resist the change." Haley's blue eyes pleaded with him. "So, what do you say?"

He swallowed. "No, thank you. I don't need the headache."

"But you're perfect for the job. The council respects you, the guest residents"—the current euphemism for mortals who lived on the Hill—"respect you; we couldn't ask for a better combination."

Nope. Not only did it violate the golden rule his father taught him—a police officer should never become involved in politics—but it would piss off Tig. If he won, he'd be her boss. No thank you—he didn't need the grief.

"I appreciate being considered," he said. "But I'm not interested. Why don't you run for the seat?"

Haley sighed. "I would, but I've been leading the charge. There are a lot of permanent residents who don't like me because of my campaign on the issue. We need someone with no baggage."

"Hmm," Jayden said, scooping up the last bite of gravy-drenched stuffing.

She batted her baby blues at him. "Please? Don't say no so fast."

"All right, fine, I'll think about your suggestion." It wouldn't hurt to consider the idea, and it would get her off his back. "Well, my break's over. I'm going to grab some coffee and report for duty."

He stood and started to gather his empty plate and silverware.

"Here, let me take those," she said. "Go grab some dessert. Enjoy life a little. You work too hard."

"Yeah, but I like it that way."

When Cerissa finished eating, she offered Luis a business card and said, "If you need anything, here's my phone number. Don't hesitate to call."

"Thanks, I appreciate it."

She took her plate back to the country club's kitchen, where volunteers were loading the industrial-sized dishwasher. Karen brought in hers, weaving as she walked in designer stilettos.

"Are you all right?" Cerissa asked.

"Would you quit asking me?"

Karen pouted, scrunching her slightly smeared auburn eyebrows. Normally she darkened them with precision. Tonight, they looked like she'd colored outside the lines.

"It's just, well…" Cerissa paused, trying to figure out how to say what bothered her. "Ah, you look a bit tipsy."

"Not so much." Karen waved her wine glass in the air. "Only my third."

Three? We've been here less than an hour.

Karen laughed. "You should see your face," she said, patting Cerissa's back. "Hey, relax—in my family, it wasn't a good funeral until someone got drunk and started a fistfight." She wobbled, and Cerissa caught her arm to steady her. "I'll grab a bottle of water and go take a siesta. There's a lounge down the hall."

"Do you want me to go with you?"

"Nah, I'm good."

They returned to the main ballroom, and Karen snagged water from the beverage table—and another glass of wine.

Funerals weren't a place where normal behavior reigned. Still, was this a one-off or a new habit developing?

I need to keep an eye on her. How will I do that from San Diego?

Cerissa hugged her arms. No easy answer came to her. She couldn't abandon her mission, not with so much at stake.

There must be a way to do both.

She scanned the ballroom. The founders were involved in an intense conversation. Henry would tell her afterward what they were talking about, but with her new orders from the Protectors to pass along videos of everything, it would be easier if she recorded the group herself.

She headed across the ballroom.

Zeke stepped in front of her. "Where do you think you're going, little lady?"

What's his problem now? She pursed her lips, holding back her desire to tell him off. She didn't want to cause a scene, and instead said, "To join Henry."

Zeke's face took on a mean, pinched look. "No, you aren't, ma'am. Ya need to go back with the other mates."

She tried to go around him, but he *whooshed* in front of her, blocking her path and grabbing her wrist.

"Hey, let go of me," she said, tugging her arm back. He didn't let go. "What do I have to do to convince you I'm not interested in you? I'm Henry's mate."

"This isn't about you bein' his. I'm just policin' the rules here, protecting your interests. You're not safe on this side yet."

"What are you talking about?"

Henry appeared next to her, and the crystal communicated his embarrassment. "I'm afraid the fault is mine. I forgot to tell her. Release her and I'll take her back to the other mates."

Zeke stared with disdain. "Shirkin' your duty to school her will get her killed, *Founder*. Good thing I'm protecting her even if you aren't."

What the hell did that mean? She glared at Zeke, and the pressure from his fingers started to ease off her wrist, but it was too little, too late. She was tired of him and his barbs. "If I need protecting, it's from the likes of you."

His gaze cut to her, his grip tightening again. "From me? You don't know—"

"I know all I need to know," she said, her fury spiking. "I chose the better man. Now, let go."

Zeke sneered at her and squeezed harder, crushing her bracelet against her skin. Pain shot through her wrist, but she didn't give him the satisfaction of flinching. He pulled her closer to him. "You have no idea what Bautista's done—"

Henry wedged himself between them and pushed Zeke's shoulder. "Release her. *Now.*"

Zeke let go and stepped back, a look of disgust on his face.

Henry put his arm around her and walked her back to where the mortals were gathered.

She stopped him. "Give me a moment."

"Are you all right?"

"I will be." She rubbed the red marks from Zeke's assault, tempted to turn on her heels and slap the cowboy. "What made him so crazy?"

"I'm sorry. It's my fault for not telling you, but I know how you feel about these rules. Still, I should have said something."

"Rule?"

He stroked her shoulder. "Mortals are supposed to stay away from the bereaved vampire. When the Covenant was written, we were less, well, civilized. The founders feared the bereaved wouldn't be able to contain their grief and would attack any mortal who came near. You would be safe around Abigale, but the rule is still in place. For now, it is best if you stay with the other mates."

So much for her efforts at spying. "All right."

"Thank you. When you see Abigale leave, it will no longer matter. Mortals and vampires will mingle then, and we can be together."

A wave of embarrassment washed through her. As much as she hated admitting it, she had to be more open to hearing the rules from Henry. There were landmines buried in this secret society. She needed to be…more understanding.

"Okay, I'll go check on Karen."

She stopped rubbing her wrist. The jewels had been ground into her skin, and she moved the bracelet further along her arm so the gold links wouldn't ride on the abraded flesh. Doing so uncovered the large marks.

Henry's gaze followed the motion. His eyes became solid black, and his anger chilled her. "Did Zeke do that?"

"Yes, but I'll be fine. Give me a moment to morph the skin—"

He spun around, not waiting for her to finish.

"Henry, no," she said in a loud whisper, and ran to catch him.

Chapter 17

Sierra Escondida Country Club Ballroom—moments later

Rage coursed through Henry. Cerissa was his mate. No one would ever hurt her.

He stalked to Zeke and grabbed the cowboy by the collar. With his fangs showing, Henry growled. "You ever touch her again and you won't live long enough to regret it."

Zeke pushed with both hands. "You think I want your leftovers? I didn't touch your whore when Nathaniel offered her to me, and I ain't gonna touch Cerissa, either."

"Don't say one more word." Henry couldn't let Cerissa learn the truth about what happened with Sarah. Not this way. "I have over fifty years on you. Be foolish enough to start something and I will surely finish it."

"You're the fool here. I figure if Cerissa's with you, she's got to be a whore like all the other women you take up with. And I ain't interested in no whore."

Heat ran through Henry's neck. The insult to her couldn't go unpunished. Still holding Zeke by his collar, Henry raised his other arm back, his hand curled into a fist.

Before he could jackhammer Zeke's face, Cerissa's emotions touched his mind. Her concern entwined around his anger and momentarily froze him in place.

He shook off the connection. Zeke had hurt the woman he loved. It had consequences, even if she wasn't comfortable with his lesson plan. Zeke had to be taught.

And then someone else grabbed his arm—someone very strong. It wasn't Cerissa—she was on his other side.

"Boys, boys," Gaea said, stepping between them. "This is no place for a fight. We must remember why we're here: to support Abigale."

Gaea put a hand on Zeke's shoulder as well, tightening her fingers until the cowboy flinched and stepped back. Henry held on to Zeke's shirt and moved with him, clenching his fist tighter. One punch and that smug face would be smashed to pulp.

"Now, Henry," Gaea said, pulling on his arm, trying to get him to lower it. "This isn't the way we resolve our differences. You don't want to face the whipping post, do you?"

Avenging Cerissa would be worth the pain.

Gaea gave a condescending sniff. "Well, if a whipping doesn't deter you, perhaps Cerissa's feelings might. Do you really want to embarrass your mate this way?"

Out of the corner of his eye, Henry saw Cerissa. Her eyes pleaded with him, silently asking him not to escalate things.

He exhaled loudly. As much as he wanted to use his fists to express his anger, he had to consider her feelings. He lowered his arm and released Zeke's collar with a shove. "This is a solemn event. My apologies, Gaea, for the disruption."

He patted Zeke's shirt forcefully, flattening the wrinkle his grip had caused. It didn't slake his desire to drive a fist into the cowboy's nose.

Zeke backed up before Henry could slap his chest again. "You better make sure Cerissa understands the rules," Zeke said with a sneer. "Or I'll report ya to Tig."

Henry started to lunge at him, but Gaea and Rolf stepped together to form a barrier between them.

"I expect better from one of our founders," Gaea said.

Henry narrowed his eyes. Gaea may be *much* older than him, but she had no right to chastise him.

"And I expect better from one of Tig's officers. Did you see what Zeke did to Cerissa's arm?" He carefully raised her wrist to display the red imprint of Zeke's fingers and the gouges where the jewels had been ground into her skin.

Gaea's gaze followed the motion. "Oh my goodness. Dear, are you all right?" Gaea reached out for Cerissa and *tsked* over her. "We should put some ice on your wrist."

Henry slipped an arm around Cerissa's shoulders. "I'll take care of her."

"No, you go apologize to Abigale," Gaea said. "Cerissa and I will be in the kitchen. I'm sure there must be a first-aid kit there. And afterward, I'll speak with Zeke. This should never have happened."

Henry started to argue, but Cerissa said, "I'll go with Gaea. My arm will be fine."

"Very well." He gave a slight bow and then threw a dark look in Zeke's direction. There would be time to punish the cowboy's impudence later.

Rolf leaned in close and said quietly, "I warned you Cerissa didn't understand."

Henry scowled at his business partner.

Rolf then pointed at Zeke and raised his voice. "Gaea can give you a piece of her mind after Tig gets through with you. You're coming with me back to Abigale's. We don't need any more *policing* here."

"It wasn't my fault she broke the rules," Zeke shot back. "Just doing my job."

Rolf grabbed Zeke's arm and marched him across the room to the exit. The meaning wouldn't be lost on the crowd.

That would have to do for now. Henry contained his anger and strode over to Abigale. With one more glance over his shoulder, he saw Cerissa was almost to the kitchen. She looked his way. Her emerald eyes brightened, and her love touched him.

Good.

His chest filled with pride. He'd made the right choice.

Turning back, he said, "My apologies, Abigale. I'm sorry we caused a disruption at Nina's funeral dinner."

She waved a delicate hand. "I'm just disappointed you and Zeke didn't battle it out. I wagered a thousand dollars on you to win."

"Abigale!" he said, shocked.

"I'm tired of all these rituals. They won't bring back my Nina," she said, dabbing at her eyes with a handkerchief. "You two were about to provide some much-needed entertainment until Gaea interfered."

"I see." Henry guided her over to a chair and sat next to her. "If you were betting a thousand dollars on me, who bet against me?"

"Méi, of course."

"I will have to thank my sister for her lack of confidence in me."

"Don't be offended." She laid a pale hand on his arm. "Méi did it to make me happy."

He folded his hand over hers. "We would all like to make you happy, if we could."

"Find the cretin who did this to my Nina. And I don't mean the killer who is chained in my basement. I mean the vampire behind these attacks.

None of us will have any peace until that devil is caught and staked."

"I am afraid you're correct. Do you have any thoughts about who the culprit might be?"

"Tig asked me the same question." Abigale looked away from him. "Who would want me dead?"

"The chief told me she has ruled out Kyle."

"My offspring?" Her graceful, pale eyebrows elevated ever so slightly. "The restraining order against Kyle is to keep him from bothering my other mates. He has never threatened *me*."

"He was on our list because the homeowners' board had recently denied him residency here." Henry patted her hand one more time and let go. "Since Yacov and I are on the board, we listed all residency applications we have denied. Tig investigated Kyle and learned he hasn't left New York in the past three months. He appears to have found a new object for his obsessions."

"I see."

He paused, looking past her. Cerissa had returned to the ballroom and was by the bar, talking to Karen. Seeing Rolf's mate reminded him. "You have heard about the Carlyle Cutter being involved?"

"It rules out a mortal do-gooder, doesn't it?" Abigale's eyes took on a contemplative mien. "Mortals would never use a serial killer to do their work. So, it can't be someone who's discovered we exist and believes the world would be better off without us."

Henry waited, not sure what else to say. Abigale's gaze drifted to her fingernails. They'd transformed into claws.

"When Tig captures the culprit, I want a night alone with the reprobate." She turned her hand over and splayed her fingers, emphasizing her claws' sharpness. "I daresay that sinner will regret killing my Nina by the time I'm through with him."

He understood how she felt. If anyone ever truly harmed Cerissa, they'd die a very painful death. Covenant or no Covenant, whipping post or no whipping post—he'd see to it.

Hmm. Whipping post...

He crossed his arms and let his gaze wander to the windows facing the town hall and council chambers. Zeke's insult to Cerissa deserved punishment. And since the council seemed so willing to dish out archaic sanctions, perhaps a complaint filed with them would be the best action. Then Zeke would be the one in line for a whipping.

Chapter 18

Abigale's House—Same Night

Tig attended the funeral but didn't stay long at the reception. She returned to Abigale's basement room, where Pascala was shackled and chained to the wall, but sitting in a chair—a concession to Jayden. A cot had been brought in, and the prisoner had been allowed to sleep lying down.

If she'd had her way, Pascala would have been left standing the entire time.

A door on the other side of the room led to an opulent bathroom with a hot tub big enough for seven people. During the day, Pascala had showered and put on a jail jumpsuit. No more half-naked prisoner.

She could have moved him to the town's jail. Even considered it. But she liked the latent threat the room held.

Lieutenant Bailey snapped to attention when she walked in. While she and Jayden attended the funeral, Bailey had been watching the prisoner.

"Guard the door," she ordered him.

"Yes, ma'am."

"And don't let anyone disturb me."

She closed the door behind Bailey and then gave Pascala a once-over before pulling up a chair across from him. He appeared in better shape—he was healing fast from the beating Abigale had given him. Tig started the video camera recording and picked up a notepad and pen from the table.

"How many times did you meet with Charlie?" she asked, balancing the notepad on her knee.

He stared back at her, uncertainty in his eyes. Was he trying to decide whether to tell the truth?

"Ah, three times," he finally said. "The first time in San Diego was a look-over. You know, sizing me up. He asked me about my past and what

I'd done. How I knew Tony. That sort of shit. He didn't tell me nothin' about his plan."

"What did he talk about?"

"He asked me if I ever thought someone needed killing. I said yes. He asked me if I was good with a rifle. I told him I was. He said he'd be in touch and left."

"And the second time you met with him?"

"He wired me money with a message to drive to Mordida and get a hotel room. Then he laid out the plan."

"Tell me exactly what Charlie told you," she said, sitting back.

"Look, lady, I'll try. Really, I'll try. But he didn't say a lot. He dropped off fifty thousand at the motel's front desk—the cash wrapped tight in a box—and called me to set up the meeting. That's how I knew he was serious. As soon as he sat down at the bar—"

"What bar?"

"Ah, I don't remember the name." He scratched at his chin. "I really don't. I think it had something to do with the army. There's a string of them on Third Street; the names all sound alike. I was so bored waiting, I spent time in each."

"Go on."

"Anyway, when I sat down in the bar, he says, 'I got a job for you.' 'What's that?' I say. 'There's a woman who lives in Sierra Escondida,' he says. 'She picks up her girlfriend after work.' He gave me their names, and the name of the winery. He described her. I snooped around and found out the girlfriend worked in the gift shop."

"What else did Charlie say to you?"

"Ah, can I have something to eat first? The cop who watched me didn't give me dinner."

Tig was prepared for this. Offering a suspect an act of kindness could break through their last bit of resistance. She unwrapped a sandwich from the funeral reception and handed him half. Pascala devoured the turkey on rye.

"Now finish telling me what Charlie told you. If I'm satisfied, you can have the other half," she said, returning it to the nearby table.

"He told me I had to use special ammo. 'To send a message,' he said. And he told me what kind of rifle to buy. 'I'll have the ammo delivered to you.' Those were his words."

"Where's the box the ammunition came in?"

"Back at the room I'm staying in."

The first break they'd had. "And where were you staying?"

"Mordida Motel. Off I-5 at Third Street."

Tig knew the area. A dive motel—the type a lowlife like Pascala would stay at. "What room number?"

"Can I eat the other half of the sandwich first?"

"No. What room number?"

"Two-oh-five. Second floor. I'm paid through the end of next week."

She wrote the details on the pad. "Where's the key?"

"In my wallet. A white card." Tig reached over the table where the contents of Pascala's pockets were spread out. She held up the card. "That's the one," he said.

He deserved a reward, and she gave him the rest of the sandwich. "What else did Charlie say to you when he told you to buy the Nam 900?"

The prisoner chewed and swallowed, rushing to answer her question. "He told me to try for a head shot, but it wouldn't matter where I hit her, as long as the bullet went in. I thought maybe they were dusted with poison, so I handled them with gloves."

In four bites, he finished the sandwich and then downed a bottle of water.

"Keep talking," she said, taking the trash from him and disposing of it.

"Ah, he described her car and gave me the license plate number. He told me Epsilon always drove, so aim for the driver of the car."

"Epsilon?"

"Yeah, he called her Epsilon a couple of times. He said her real name once in a whisper. He leaned in close so no one would overhear him in the bar."

An odd code name—the fifth letter in the Greek alphabet. But then, Frédéric had been infatuated with Greek gods. Had the plan been his? Was the Cutter pursuing it even with Frédéric dead?

"I see," she said. "What else did he tell you?"

"Nothin'. We met a third time, and he showed me a photo of Epsilon. He said he'd drive me to the best location and wait for me afterwards. He said he had some special reward in mind for me when I was done. It was kind of creepy, but I would be armed, so I didn't care."

A chill crept along Tig's back. Was Chuck disposing of operatives by indulging his Cutter persona, saving him the cost of paying them off?

"Anything else?" she asked.

"When he drove me here, he said something weird."

"What?"

"Something about if I did a good job, if the head guy was happy, there would be other opportunities on the Hill. That's what he said—'other opportunities on the Hill.'"

So maybe Frédéric hadn't been the ringleader. "We're going to go over your story again. If I'm satisfied you're telling the truth, we might even arrange for a second sandwich."

Someone knocked at the door. Her jaw tensed.

I told Lieutenant Bailey I didn't want to be disturbed.

Nothing was important enough to interrupt her now. She cracked the door.

Rolf.

She caught a bitter scent in the air. He smelled of anger. Why?

He pushed open the door, marched past her to the shackled man, and scanned him from head to toe. "Hmm. Let's step outside."

She grabbed her iPad and followed him to the hallway. "Timing is everything during interrogations. You know better than to interrupt."

"The mayor wants an update. He sent me."

Politics. *Shit.* She wanted to turn on her heels, slam the door, and return to what was *really* important. But then they'd just interrupt her again. "Tell the *mayor* the man who hired Pascala called himself Charlie." She displayed the Carlyle Cutter sketch. "And he identified this man as Charlie, except his hair was black."

"So, the Carlyle Cutter is using an alias similar to the one he gave Karen?"

"My thought exactly." The Cutter had told Karen his name was Chuck. Tig paused, looking away as she considered whether to voice her concern.

Better to mention it.

"When I first saw the sketch, I thought your mate might have gotten confused."

"Why?" Rolf took the tablet from her.

"The sketch bears a close resemblance to Marcus."

He stared at the screen. "So?"

"Karen was horribly tortured. Pain can play havoc with memory. It's not unheard of for a victim to describe someone she saw in her mind's eye while the torture was taking place."

"That's not the case here," Rolf said adamantly, and returned the tablet to her.

Why was he so convinced? Sure, the perps she'd captured had identified the sketch as the Director, but they could have been blowing smoke, telling her what they *thought* she wanted to hear.

She put the tablet in sleep mode. "With Pascala's identification, we have independent confirmation. The question remains: Since Frédéric is dead, who's giving Charlie his marching orders?"

Rolf opened a calendar app on his phone. "Not much time to find out. You'll have to hand him over for arraignment in two days."

Tell me something I don't already know.

If a vampire was killed, the town held a jury trial, with the council or an arbitrator presiding. They couldn't go into mortal courts and say: *See this dried mummy? It used to be a vampire.*

But if no vampire was killed, the offender was prosecuted by the county's district attorney.

"My interrogation is going well," she said, hoping he'd leave after receiving reassurance.

"If you need help—"

She raised her hand, stopping him. "I'll report to the council if I learn anything new."

"See that you do."

She ground her molars. "You don't give me orders."

"I—"

"You take care of your business, and I take care of mine." She narrowed her eyes and stepped closer to him. "That's our deal. Now shut up and get out of here."

"But we need to discuss Zeke first. I left him upstairs cooling his heels. He overstepped his bounds at the country club and got a bit handsy when Cerissa crossed the line to our side."

Tig snatched open the door. "I'll talk to him later. I have real work to do."

She was barely through the door when her phone rang. She read the caller ID.

Henry. Damn.

She couldn't ignore a founder.

"What?" she answered.

"Zeke laid his hands on Cerissa."

"Now, Henry, I know you're old school, but really, just because he touched her—"

"Zeke did more than touch her."

"Rolf told me Zeke stopped her when she crossed the line. He was doing his job. He was there at my request, keeping the peace."

"He squeezed her wrist hard enough to leave a mark. Is this how you keep the peace? By manhandling our mates?"

"Can you send me a photo of the injury?"

"I will check with Cerissa to see if she's willing. By now, the mark may have faded. But even if it has, he shouldn't have touched her at all. What are you going to do to punish Zeke?"

Henry really was old school, acting like his property had been damaged. A modern woman, a professional like Cerissa, well, if she was upset, she would be the one lodging the complaint. But damn it, Henry was a founder and higher on the food chain than Tig would ever be. "I'll speak to Zeke. It won't happen again."

"I want him brought before the council. His treatment of Cerissa is intolerable."

She rolled her eyes even though Henry wouldn't see. The paperwork alone would waste hours she didn't have. "If you make this a formal complaint, then the council may fine Cerissa for crossing the line."

"You can't be serious."

"I am. You're better off dropping this."

Henry huffed so loudly that Pascala probably heard the sound halfway across the room. "You'll have to find someone else to go with us to San Diego. We can't take Zeke. Not after this."

"Look, you want to know how I'll punish Zeke? Forcing him to go with you as your guard, making him responsible for your safety, that's how. He wanted out of the assignment. I'll tell him he has to go, and nothing better happen to either of you, or I'll fire him from the police force—at the very least."

"You should fire him now. He called Cerissa a whore."

"She's a big girl, I'm sure she can survive it."

"As you say, he was on duty at the time. Is that how you want your police officers to be perceived by our community?"

She let out a snort. "I'll speak with him about it. It won't happen again while he's on duty."

"And what's to stop him from harassing her when we're in San Diego?"

"Simple. If I receive any complaints from Cerissa—not you, but her—then I'll fire him from the force and take any other steps I deem appropriate. Henry, as I told you before, I don't have time for this. Get over it—it's Zeke or no trip."

Chapter 19

Driving Along Robles Road—Later That Night

Cerissa forced herself to relax once she was in the Viper. If she had interfered between Zeke and Henry, she would have made the situation worse.

No one liked to be told what to do, particularly when they were angry. And in Henry, the "don't tell me what to do" vein ran deep. He had shared the story early on, how his maker, Anne-Louise, had tried to control him most of his vampire life. It left him sensitive to being told what he could and couldn't do.

One hand on the stirring wheel, he put the Viper into gear, his jaw muscle working in and out. He seemed too wound up to talk. His anger drifted through her mind like an arctic breeze, the chill running down her back. At least it cooled her off a bit. The pre-summer hot spell was getting worse.

As much as she wanted to ease his agitation, if she used her aura to flood him with peaceful feelings, he'd resent it and be angrier after her influence waned, so she kept her hands to herself and looked out the window. She focused on the lush, leafy grapevines as they drove up the driveway in front of his—no, *their* house.

Zeke's comment had made her curious—and concerned. The "whore" Zeke referred to wasn't Anne-Louise. Not if the "whore" had something to do with Nathaniel, the vampire Henry killed in a duel in the late 1800s. The timing was off. Then who was she?

Cerissa glanced over at Henry again. His expression still radiated anger. Now was not the moment to ask.

It also hadn't been the moment to ask Karen about her drinking. After the kerfuffle with Zeke, Cerissa had found her friend at the bar, picking up another drink. Karen's so-called nap hadn't lasted very long. Something about the way Karen was drinking felt like more than a one-off. Cerissa couldn't put her finger on what was wrong.

Henry parked the Viper in the garage and escorted her back to the house. They stopped in the foyer, standing under the wrought-iron chandelier.

She faced him, and he took in a deep breath. His jaw seemed to relax—the bulging muscle had flattened out.

"How are you feeling?" she asked.

"I'm fine. But would you mind if I went out riding alone? The motorcycle came back from the shop today."

He had wrecked the bike during Karen's rescue, and it had taken the mechanic weeks to repair the damage.

Suspicion whispered through her. "You're not going to confront Zeke, are you?"

He shook his head. "I need to talk with Rolf, to brief him about some winery matters before we leave for San Diego. Do you mind?"

"Not at all."

She touched his cheek, his slight stubble rough, and gently pressed her lips to his.

His fingers entwined around hers. "I want to test the bike on the freeway at full speed. I would not take such a risk with you on the back."

Some speed therapy might work out his remaining tension. But would he be safe riding beyond the community's walls? "Perhaps I should fly along with you to make sure nothing happens."

"Nothing will happen. I'm a skilled rider."

"I don't doubt your ability." She tried to keep herself from sounding critical. "I was thinking about what happened to Nina. If there are other snipers outside the wall, you would be recognizable on the bike."

And if the VDM hurt *him*, the grief—and the guilt—would be crushing. It was bad enough her failure had allowed the VDM to kill others. But Henry? No, she couldn't let anything happen to him.

A sigh escaped his lips. "If you decide you wanted to watch from the sky, I would not object. But when I stop at Rolf's house, please return home. My conversation with him will go faster if I'm alone."

"If that's what you want."

"It is." He kissed her forehead and then hugged her. "The last couple of nights have been stressful. When I get back, perhaps we may relax together."

"I'll look forward to it."

She dashed upstairs and changed into a flower-covered silk robe. It would be easier to slip out of the robe before morphing.

She returned to find Henry rolling the bike from the garage. He stopped by the large fountain in the center of his circular driveway, water falling from an urn held by a nymph. Floodlights illuminated the dark night—tendrils of clouds floated above them, obscuring the moon, which was low in the horizon and ready to set.

He wore a black helmet and leather jacket. How would other drivers be able to see him in all black? She bit her lip.

Nope, not going to say anything. He knows what he's doing.

Instead, she asked, "May I borrow the Viper?" Her car had been bombed by Karen's kidnappers. Henry didn't want her driving his car, but it made no sense to waste money on a taxi. "I'm going into Mordida tomorrow to shop for a new car."

He smiled smugly. "There is no need. I've already ordered you a new one."

Indignation flashed through her. How dare he presume to know what she wanted? She planted her hands on her hips. "I'll choose my own car."

He swung his leg over the bike to straddle the seat and took his phone out of its holder. "Come see," he said, punching and sliding through screens.

She walked over to him. When she saw the sports car he'd chosen, frustration ruffled down her throat, joining her anger. "It's nice, but I don't want a roadster. Two seats are not enough. I'd prefer a sedan. Besides, the insurance settlement will cover a replacement—you don't have to buy me a car."

He looked disappointed. "But this one has a six-cylinder, three-hundred-horsepower engine, with a seven-speed transmission, and can do zero to sixty in *five* seconds."

"I know you like fast sports cars," she said, handing the phone back. "We need a car we can use when we go out with other couples. I was going to get another hybrid sedan."

"But that's what you had before."

"And I'd still have my car if it hadn't been blown to bits."

"I thought you might like something a little less—"

"Fuel-efficient?"

"No, ah, mundane. Your car looked like all the other cars on the road. If you want a fuel-efficient car, allow me to buy you a Tesla. Even better, the Ludicrous mode goes from zero to sixty in *two point five* seconds."

Raising her eyebrows, she asked, "Do you memorize the acceleration rate of all vehicles?"

"Only the ones I've considered buying."

She snickered. She couldn't help herself. In some ways, he was such a stereotypical male. "Well, I'll pay for my own car. Just because I'm living with you, doesn't mean I'm financially dependent on you."

The expression on his face said he had more to say on the subject, but his lips stayed sealed.

"So," she said, "can I borrow the Viper?"

"I have a better idea. I'll order a car service to come for you tomorrow morning at ten. One vetted to enter the Hill."

She threw up her hands. Someday, he'd trust her with his car. "Fine."

"If that is settled, is there anything else?" he asked.

"Tell Rolf I've revised the formula for adrenaline-enhanced blood. I'll give Karen a supply for him. He can try it while we're gone."

"Thank you. I'm sure he'll appreciate your thoughtfulness." Henry pressed the button to start the bike's engine and leaned over to kiss her. "I will see you later."

She let the robe slide off her shoulders and tossed it on the cedar bench near the front door. Within seconds, she morphed into a jabiru, a large stork native to Central America. She'd fallen in love with the form when she stayed in Belize for a year. The black head, bill, and neck graced a body of white, sleek feathers, supported with long, spindly legs.

So long as she flew at night, people didn't notice her unusual size. A large beetle skittered across the grass. She cocked her head and scooped up the insect. Her gizzard would make short work of the little guy.

Henry raised an eyebrow at her idea of a snack. Sure, she had admitted she hunted, but a beetle?

At least she wasn't squeamish about what she ate. She stretched her long wings and, with a little jump, gracefully took flight. He watched her circle, waiting for him. He put the bike in gear and took off down the driveway, weakly sensing her presence above him through the crystal's connection.

It was after midnight, and the freeway was almost empty. Provided he didn't leave the interstate to drive into Mordida, he wasn't violating the Rule of Two. He opened the throttle, letting his speed climb to ninety.

The bike didn't wobble, and the steering remained stable. The mechanic had done a good job repairing it.

After riding ten miles, he returned to the Hill, parked on Rolf's driveway, and dismounted. The rustle of wings and the creak of an oak tree branch told him Cerissa was watching from above.

He spied her through the thick branches and waved for her to leave. She stayed put.

Stubborn woman.

He knocked on the door. The porch light came on, and he removed his helmet, tucking it under his arm.

When Rolf opened the door, Henry asked, "Do you have time to discuss our plans for the Wine Expo? I'll be gone for at least a week. We should go over them."

"Karen is asleep." Rolf's eyes focused past Henry to the bike parked in the driveway. "I'll get my helmet. We can ride first. Wait for me by the garage door."

Henry hesitated. He wanted to complete their business and leave. He was still displeased with Rolf, both for his insistence that Cerissa be kept in the dark over her initiation ceremony and for saying she didn't "understand" their community.

"Go on. I'll be out in a moment." The front door closed.

Harrumph. He had no choice if he wanted to discuss the expo. He waited by the garage entrance. Cerissa landed on the lawn and morphed, the stork melting into a *puma*. She loped over and head-butted his leg.

Had she sensed his irritation?

"Don't worry. I'll be fine." He scratched behind her black-tipped ears and stroked her back. Her thick, tawny fur felt coarse as he ran his fingers over her coat. "Rolf has been edgy since Karen's kidnapping and his commitment to stop hunting. I may need to help him through this time."

Purring, she head-butted his leg again. She usually rubbed against him when she wanted his attention. Why was she doing it now?

He heard the garage door start to rise, so he gently grabbed her by the scruff of her neck and pointed her in the direction of his house.

"Go home, Cerissa."

She didn't move. He wasn't sure if her *puma* understood English.

"Now," he said in a firm but commanding voice. She got the point and moved off at a slow lope.

Rolf ran out of the garage with his helmet in hand. "Did you see the mountain lion?" His face was filled with excitement. "I'll get my rifle and we can track it."

"That's not a good idea."

"Why not? A lion brave enough to approach our homes might be dangerous. I can't believe the dogs aren't howling."

"That *puma* will not hurt anyone," Henry replied, "unless they attempted to hurt her. Or Karen."

Rolf's eyes got wide. "Cerissa was the mountain lion?"

"I tried to tell her to go home before you came out here, but she can be stubborn at times."

"I just can't believe you would…with an animal…"

"Rolf, don't start."

The younger vampire continued to stare in the direction she'd disappeared and ran one hand through his hair, sweeping the straight bangs away from his eyes. "Okay, I know you've picked her for your mate."

"Then what is the problem?"

"I don't trust her or her people."

"I do," Henry replied. "You usually rely on my judgment."

"In business. With women, your decision-making hasn't been so good."

I'm getting damn tired of being told that.

He wrinkled his brow. "Her people are no threat to us."

But how much to explain? Ari and his superiors had agreed—Rolf could be told anything Henry knew, so long as the information went no further.

He straightened his spine. "The Lux want to keep their presence here a secret, as much as we want to protect our privacy."

"Then why did Cerissa come to the Hill? To spy on us?"

"Perhaps, but not in the way you think. The Lux are here to watch over humans, to ensure evil does not destroy this world."

"You're serious?" Rolf said, his jaw dropping open.

"They take small actions to redirect the course of history. They stopped a third atomic bomb from being dropped on Japan during World War II. They were divided whether to prevent humans from developing the bomb. When they cannot reach consensus, they do nothing."

"How do you know this? They could be lying to you."

"Ari gave me video access to their archives, and I viewed the Protectors' debate from World War II. They wouldn't show me anything more recent. I saw videos of Cerissa from the same era."

"How old is she?"

"Slightly older than I am." Henry shifted his helmet to his other hand. "She is not a threat to us, and she is very important to me."

"You still need to school her about our way of life here."

Henry gritted his teeth. Cerissa had convinced him—many of the Covenant's restrictions regarding mortals were wrong. But perhaps Rolf was partially right. For Cerissa's protection, she had to learn the ground rules, at least, until they were changed.

"I will try to educate her better," he finally said. "But I should warn you—I now believe mortals must have more rights than they currently do, including the right to know about the initiation ceremony in advance."

"But you won't tell her until *after* the rule is changed."

Disappointment sat like a rock in his gut. Rolf knew a rule change was unlikely to occur before Cerissa's ceremony. "I don't understand why you couldn't make an exception for her—"

"And how would I explain it to the council?"

"I—" Henry began and stopped. What was his basis for an exception? He'd need one he could share with the entire council. Saying she was "smart" wasn't enough—they'd had other smart mates who weren't told, and it had worked out all right.

"So, we agree?"

"Fine. I concede the current rules apply. Satisfied?"

"*Ja*," Rolf said with a sharp nod. He slapped Henry on the shoulder. "Let's go riding. We're starting to sound like one of your *novellas*."

"After you."

Henry waited for Rolf to start his bike and followed him down the driveway. At Robles Road, Henry zoomed past his partner, taking the first curve on the inside. As he rode faster, the tension of the night sloughed off him.

Rolf tried to maneuver around him, but Henry refused to give way. He sometimes let the younger vampire have his way to keep the peace, but when it came to racing, he cut no slack.

An hour or so later, Henry was the first to arrive back at Rolf's home. They remained outside to discuss the Wine Expo so their voices wouldn't disturb Karen's sleep.

As they wrapped up their plans, Rolf also promised to check with the winery's gift shop supervisor to see how their employees were reacting to Nina's death. "If necessary, I'll hire a grief counselor while you're gone," Rolf said.

"Thank you," Henry said with a slight nod. *Hmm.* Perhaps Rolf could help with one more thing. "I spoke with Tig. She insists Zeke accompany me and Cerissa to San Diego."

"She's right about one thing. You can't go alone."

"I would rather have you at my back."

"I'll give the chief a call—see if I can persuade her to let me go instead."

Henry rested his hand on Rolf's shoulder. "Thank you. I appreciate it."

"It's what friends do for one another." Rolf gripped Henry's shoulder in return.

He said goodnight and raced home. He was anxious to spend time with Cerissa before going to sleep for the day.

He drove up the steep driveway and stopped near the front door, removing his helmet and letting the motor die. Her robe was still draped across the bench. Moments later, a *puma* appeared from the edge of the vineyard. He got off the bike and placed his helmet next to her robe.

She came loping across the lawn and jumped on him with both front paws, her claws sheathed. Caught off balance, he fell backward on the grass. She landed on top of him and licked his face.

"Yes, you are glad to see me," he said, trying to deflect her sloppy kisses. He rolled her off him and climbed to his feet. "Time to change back."

She ignored him and attacked, playfully biting his arm. He tugged, pretending to struggle, his leather jacket protecting his skin from her teeth. She growled deep in her throat and refused to let go.

After roughhousing for a while, he patted her on the head and said, "Enough. Come with me." He freed himself and held her robe out for her. "Change."

The transition from cougar to human took less than two seconds. Her body elongated, her fur receded, and her hair grew dark and wavy. She was now naked and on all fours, her ample breasts pointed toward the grass. He enjoyed the view.

She stood and slipped into the robe. "I'm glad you're home," she said, wrapping her arms around his waist.

A pungent smell greeted him. He pulled back. "What have you been eating?"

"Oh, a snack or two. We won't be bothered by the skunk that's been spraying the pool house. I'll go brush my teeth and shower. Why don't you come upstairs in a few minutes?"

"I have to put the bike away first. Everything appears to be working fine."

"How's Rolf doing?"

"He seems well. Now head inside." With his hands on her shoulders, he turned her around and gave her a gentle swat to get her moving.

"Yes, master." She laughed and tilted her head to catch his eye.

"And we will discuss your failure to return home when I went to Rolf's," he said, raising one eyebrow. "I do believe you broke your promise."

"Only a little. I wanted to make sure you were all right. I left when you wanted me to."

"We will talk about it later. Now go, so I can put the bike away."

Chapter 20

ABIGALE CHERRILL'S BASEMENT—THE NEXT EVENING, SHORTLY BEFORE DUSK

Jayden set his book aside and checked his watch. It was a few minutes before sunset. Tig should be awake soon.

He had taken the afternoon shift. The prisoner was shackled to the cot in Abigale's basement, but at least the man could lie down or stand when he wanted to.

Throughout the day, Pascala had tried to engage him in conversation. Jayden had pressed the video camera's "on" button whenever the guy got talkative. Unfortunately, his rants didn't include any new useable information.

"Hey, man, what are they?"

Jayden reached over to trigger the camera and sat back. This was going to be interesting.

"Come on, turn it off and tell me."

"Tell you what?"

"That bitch, the one I was supposed to kill—I never seen a woman move as fast or slap as hard as she did. She ain't normal."

"I don't know what you're talking about."

"Yeah, like you don't. And your boss. Why isn't she around in the daytime?"

Jayden chuckled. "She's busy."

"Come on. What is this, some group of Amazon women? I bet they're damn good in bed."

Jayden hooked his thumb toward the camera. "You may want to consider showing some respect."

"I'm right, aren't I? A bunch of Amazons. It's why I had to use special ammo."

Jayden picked up his book. It didn't matter what Pascala guessed. Tig would wipe his memory of his time in Abigale's basement before handing him over to the district attorney.

Pascala rattled his chains. "Come on, you can tell me."

"If you don't have anything to say about who you're working for, I'm going back to reading."

"Shit, dude. You're not one of them. How can you work for a bunch of women? Come on, let me go."

Jayden opened his book to the dog-eared page. The science fiction novel he'd been reading—the latest in the Expanse series—was more interesting than this conversation.

"I'll give you a cut of my two million."

He narrowed his eyes at the prisoner. "You could offer me the whole thing and it wouldn't interest me. You killed Nina. For money. You're going to prison, maybe death row."

"Come on, man. Think. Whatever they are, they aren't going to let me go. The blonde, she'll kill me. How can you let her?"

"As much as you deserve it, the chief won't let anything happen to you. You're going to get a fair trial."

"Yeah, right. You can't let them kill one of your own kind."

Pascala was completely off track. Tig would never let a prisoner be summarily executed, and neither would the council. But if Jayden was elected to the vacant seat, he would have a say—make sure it never happened.

The door swung open. "Let's go," Tig said. "Bailey will guard him while we're gone."

Tig parked the police van on the side street next to the Mordida Motel. The gray stucco building faced Rosecrans Boulevard. An alley buffered the motel from the residences behind it. Small details told her what she needed to know about the area: cracked sidewalks, dead grass in the parkway, and homes with bars on the windows.

"Wait here," she told Jayden. She slipped out of the van and circled the perimeter to see if anyone was watching Pascala's door. A good thing she had worn jeans and a maroon tunic—might as well write "cop" on her back whenever she wore a pantsuit.

When she finished inspecting the area, she radioed Jayden.

"All clear."

He joined her at the motel room door. She swiped the card key across the lock and cautiously pushed the door open, gun in hand.

"Police," she announced loud enough to be heard, but not enough to disturb nearby lodgers. She didn't want an audience. Jayden reached around the doorframe and flipped on the light switch.

They did a quick search—no one hiding inside. It was a typical motel room, right down to the distinct smell, a combination created by carpet deodorizer, illegal indoor smoking, and latent mold.

The bed had been made, but the rest of the room was a mess. Pascala had left clothing and other personal debris scattered around the room.

"This shouldn't take long," Jayden said, putting away his gun and pulling on nitrile gloves.

"Find the box of ammo first. Pascala said it would be on the table." Tig pulled on a pair of leather gloves. She would need them to handle silver ammunition.

Jayden strode over to a round laminate table. He gripped the carton by the edges and examined the label. "It must have been hand-delivered. No address." He handed the plastic box to her.

Tig lifted the lid. There were a lot of bullets left. "It's not the type of box Chet uses."

Chet Brundige was her silver ammo supplier. He lived with his wife, Pauline, a vampire who preferred the backwoods of Montana. His custom-made ammo was sold to all the treaty communities—or, at least, to their security chiefs. Silver ammo was strictly regulated, and Chet charged a pretty penny for it, but as required by the treaty, he never made rifle ammunition.

And what she was looking at was clearly made for a rifle.

Tig placed the open box back down. "Chet might recognize it. He knows the other licensed manufacturers."

Jayden aimed his camera, and the flash reflected off the ammunition. When he was done taking photographs, she closed the lid and dropped it into an evidence bag—box and all.

She searched the bedside drawers. A matchbook caught her eye. "Sarge's Bar" was printed on the cover. Not many bars offered matchbooks anymore—in a bad economy, freebies were the first to go.

Handling it by the edges, she slipped it into another evidence bag. Was this the bar Pascala had met Charlie at? He thought the name had to do with the army. Tig had looked up the bars on Third Street, and the other two were Last Call and The Mug. "Sarge's" might be a military or cop reference and fit the bill—worth checking out first.

Jayden pulled shirts and pants from the closet and rummaged through their pockets. Nothing much, except for a crumpled piece of paper he handed to her. "Abigale Cherrill" was written on it. They would dust the note for fingerprints later.

"Hey Tig," he called from inside the closet. "Found the money."

She snorted a laugh when she saw Pascala had thrown his dirty clothes over the box. Maybe that was why the maids hadn't discovered it.

Jayden bagged the money, the clothing, and other debris, even the trash. A tissue with dried blood on it had been left on the nightstand. He bagged it as well. When they were done, they carried the evidence with them to the police van.

"Let's swing by the bar," Tig said. "See what we can find out."

She drove a few blocks to Sarge's. The bar was a typical neighborhood watering hole—not too rundown, but not trendy either. She led the way to the shiny wood counter, where they took a seat and ordered drinks.

She surveyed the room. A noisy game of darts in the opposite corner was underway. A few customers sat at the scattered tables. The place wasn't a quarter full. No one there looked like the Carlyle Cutter to her.

When Tig paid for the drinks, she gave the bartender a big tip.

"Don't you want your change?" he asked.

"Keep it," she said. "I was hoping you might help us out." She showed him a photo of Pascala. "Has this man been in here?"

"Can't say for sure."

"His name is Angelo Pascala."

"Doesn't ring any bells."

She slid the sketch of the Carlyle Cutter across the bar. "What about this man? His hair might be darker."

The bartender studied the picture. "Yeah, he looks familiar, but he's been here only a few times."

He started to hand it back. She waved him off and flipped open her wallet to display her badge. "Keep the sketch. Show it to the other bartenders. If you see him, call us. There's a big reward for whoever calls it in."

"Sure. Ah, what did he do?"

"Let's just say he's dangerous. Don't approach him. Don't tip him off." She handed the bartender her business card after writing Jayden's number under hers. "Phone this number. Night or day."

"Sure."

She glanced at their watch—plenty of time to check the other bars—and started to say goodbye, then thought of something else. "Do you remember if he paid by credit card?"

"Memory's not what it used to be." The bartender frowned. "What's his name?"

"He might use Charlie or Chuck or Charles. We don't know if it's his legal name."

"When was he here? If I had the date, I could check our receipts for that night."

"Let me see what I can find out," she said, and took a business card from a stand on the counter.

The bartender extended his hand to her. "I'm Sarge. I own the place."

"Tig Anderson, chief of police for Sierra Escondida." She shook his hand. "Were you police or military?"

He laughed. "Army. I was a sergeant when we fought Iraq the first time—Desert Storm. You may not remember our defense of Kuwait; you're too young."

She tried not to smile. "I recall it. A difficult war."

"Not as much as the most recent one. See, H.W., God rest his soul, understood what he was doing. We halted Saddam Hussein's invasion, pushed him back, and then we stopped. He knew we couldn't hold Iraq together if we took over. Bush Junior didn't understand what Pops had done. He was all about those oil fields, you know? Now the whole area is screwed up even worse." Sarge paused, looking a little sheepish. "Sorry. Ya pushed one of my buttons."

"No problem," she replied. "Thank you for your service."

Leaving the bar, Tig leaned in close to Jayden and said, "Let's see if we can't stimulate Pascala's memory about his meetings with Charlie." She snapped the business card between her fingers. "The Carlyle Cutter may have finally slipped up."

Chapter 21

Sierra Escondida Municipal Airport—Same Night

That evening, Cerissa drove to the Sierra Escondida Municipal Airport, with Henry in the passenger seat. Unlike the Viper, her brand-new Chevy Malibu hybrid—purchased earlier in the afternoon—had space for their luggage, and he preferred to leave his baby garaged at home.

He takes better care of his car than he does of himself.

She bit her lip. With all the attempts on his life, he should have stayed in the garage with his Viper rather than accompanying her to San Diego. But she couldn't persuade him otherwise.

He'd drunk extra blood and aged himself for the trip. His hair had strands of gray, his face appeared more mature, and while he was still broad of shoulders, a little extra padding sat at his waist.

"Why didn't you wait until we were in San Diego to age yourself?" she asked.

"The ground crew that cares for my plane has known me for ten years, and the wine distributors in San Diego have likewise seen me this way. Is something wrong with it?"

"It makes me feel like you robbed the cradle."

He laughed. "You're one to talk."

Yeah, she was older than him. But judging by his looks, people would think he was the senior one—by at least thirty years. "When will you go to Costa Rica and return as young Enrique?"

"When it becomes too inconvenient to maintain Henry's life."

It was fortunate vampires could age themselves. Keeping up the appearance of being older was just one of the ways he blended in with mortals. And after each day's sleep, he automatically returned to the age he was at the time of his death.

"And what am I supposed to do when you change identities?" she asked. "Start dating your heir? That's going to look tacky."

"I usually stretch out the time, because assuming a new identity is getting more difficult, but perhaps you are right. I should make the change sooner rather than later."

She signaled and turned onto the road leading to the small municipal airport. It lay near the town's southern border on the public side of the wall and was dedicated to general aviation—no commercial flights. Corrugated metal hangars in two neat rows stood on each side of the runway. A tall tower with a business office completed the layout.

She spotted Henry's hangar with his last name "Bautista" painted prominently over the door and lights angled to illuminate the letters. On the tarmac, a two-man crew worked to ready a white Eclipse 550 twin-engine jet. Black and gray racing stripes curved along the plane's length.

The jet was small compared to the others he owned. He'd shown her photos of his collection, which included a corporate jet and an acrobatic plane.

"We're not taking the Cessna?" She stopped the car and eyed the size of the Eclipse again. She'd never flown in an aircraft that small before.

Henry stroked her arm. "For three people, the Eclipse will be better. It leaves the Cessna for Tig and Rolf in case they need to fly a large group on police business." He gestured to the open bay. "Please park your car in the hangar."

"Wait? Three people?" Another vehicle was already in the tall, barnlike structure: Zeke's pickup truck. Her eyes widened and her hackles rose. "Tell me he's not going with us."

"I'm sorry. Tig is forcing us to take him along."

She pulled in next to the truck. "Why didn't you tell me before this?"

"I was hoping Rolf would convince the chief to let us take him instead—"

"That's why you didn't want me there when you spoke with Rolf."

Henry took in a breath and let the air out in a noisy rush. "On the contrary—I had business to discuss with him, which I wanted to swiftly finish."

"Then why didn't you tell me—"

"Until I saw Zeke's truck, I wasn't sure Rolf had failed. Tig doesn't want a founder and a council member traveling out of town together without her. For some godforsaken reason, she trusts Zeke to guard us, but under the circumstances, I don't want you to be alone with him at any time. He doesn't respect boundaries."

"You're telling me." She rubbed her wrist where Zeke had grabbed her. The skin was still raw and tender. She'd spent the afternoon in the Enclave lab in Lux form. But when she morphed back to human, she had to re-create the gouges. Too many people had seen them.

A real pain in the butt.

Henry raised her wrist to his lips and kissed the spot. "It's not just Zeke," he said, his soulful brown eyes capturing her gaze. "You're my mate—you should never be alone with another vampire."

She snatched her arm back, starting to bristle. "How am I supposed to be an envoy and a spy if I can't meet with other vampires? I'm not your property."

"But you are my mate. Under the Covenant—"

"Are we having the same argument again? I told you, the Covenant is wrongheaded, and I won't be kept in some sort of plastic bubble. Either you trust me, or—"

"I do trust you." He took her hand, unwinding her crossed arms, and brought her palm to his lips. His deep brown eyes looked up at her over her fingertips, and he added, "But I don't trust Zeke."

Can't argue there.

The Lux didn't trust vampires at all, especially cold-blooded killers like Zeke. So far, the Protectors were taking a "wait and watch" approach to his work as a government assassin.

"And until the Covenant is changed," Henry continued, "you risk the council's censure if you violate it. I'm only looking out for your best interests." He squeezed her hand. "You're part of our community now. For your protection and mine, we must attempt to follow the rules."

Those stupid rules should be changed!

Maybe she needed to throw some support behind Haley's movement for mortal rights.

"Fine," she said. "I'll keep in mind your concerns about Zeke and the council. But I won't be hobbled by the Covenant. I'm Leopold's envoy.

My work for him puts me outside the Hill's rules in certain respects. Agreed?"

"Cerissa—"

"Agreed?"

"I would prefer if you didn't allow yourself to be alone with Zeke. As to others, I will try to understand and defend your right before the council if it comes to a showdown."

She could handle anything Zeke or the council dished out. She and Henry had gotten through a mandatory separation, house arrest, and a trial that nearly led to the whipping post. If it was important—and catching the VDM and building her lab were both crucial to her mission—they'd fend off whatever else the council threw at them. "Let's go," she said. "I want to be on time for our eleven o'clock meeting with San Diego's CEO."

As soon as they left the hangar, the ground crew leader—according to the patch on his coveralls—joined them. "Your plane's fueled and the preflight inspection is completed."

"Thanks, Joel," Henry said with a wave.

The gull-wing door was open, the top half up, the bottom part down. Zeke stood inside, hunched over at the door, waiting. While the bags were loaded into the small luggage compartment, Cerissa handed her briefcase to Zeke along with a box containing clone blood. Those items would be stored in the cabin.

Once everything was onboard, Zeke offered his hand to her.

Henry frowned at him. "Stay back. I'll help Cerissa."

And the pissing match begins.

"After you," Henry said, holding her arm. "Watch your head."

The steps were built into the door's lower half, and he steadied her as she climbed them.

Whoa. Small.

The plane had seats for four people. She hunched over to avoid hitting her head on the ceiling.

Henry followed her and waved to the ground crew from the opening. The lead gave the okay signal and folded in the bottom door, while Henry pulled down the top half and locked it.

"You can hang your jacket there." He gestured to a hook between the side windows. "Take the copilot seat on the right and buckle in. I want to get us airborne quickly."

She squeezed past Zeke and took off her suit jacket, leaving her wearing a white silk blouse and black skirt.

Zeke tipped his cowboy hat at her. "Evening, ma'am."

"Evening, Zeke," she replied coolly.

"Ah, before we get goin', I'm sorry 'bout what happened last night. I shouldn't have laid hands on you. I swear it won't happen again."

She backed into her seat, brushing her knee-length skirt down at the sides as she sat. Should she accept his apology? Or tell him off? If they were going to spend the week together, perhaps keeping the peace was best.

"Thank you, Zeke. If you have something to say about our safety, speak up, but keep your hands to yourself."

"Yes, ma'am."

Maybe he would behave himself.

Yeah, when crocodiles become vegetarians.

Henry helped her latch into the four-way harness. Her camel-colored seat was next to his in the cockpit, the leather covered in soft sheepskin fur. Zeke sat behind them in one of two passenger seats with her briefcase stored behind his seat. No barrier separated the passenger area from the cockpit.

Henry took the pilot's chair and fastened his harness. He flipped a switch on the instrument panel. The jets started. Five screens displayed various readings, including navigation, fuel gauge, and wind speed.

He finished readying the craft and radioed the tower to obtain clearance. His slight Castilian accent showed through when he spoke, the R's rolling lightly in his throat.

The tower responded, "Eclipse Bravo Alpha Tango One, wind is northwest at nine knots, runway one is cleared for takeoff."

"Cleared for takeoff runway one, Eclipse Bravo Alpha Tango One."

The first word was the plane manufacturer, followed by his call sign.

BAT One? What is Rolf, BAT Two?

He must have glimpsed the look on her face. "*Bat* as in baseball."

"Oh," she said. He was a rabid baseball fan.

The radio clicked. "Good flight, Henry. We'll see you when you get back."

"Wilco." He pushed the metal handle of the throttle forward, steering the plane along the runway, his gaze focused intensely on their path as the plane's speed increased.

Easing back into her seat, she let the tension from their earlier disagreement go and watched through the plane's window. The scenery sped past and their wheels left the tarmac with a slight bump, the plane bucking as they gained altitude.

She focused on the vista below them. Smog seemed to hang over California's central valley, the late twilight revealing the haze. A cut in the mountains bordering Sierra Escondida allowed ocean breezes through, keeping the bad air from settling over the Hill, but the flatlands of neighboring Mordida clearly suffered from it.

Once Henry had the plane level and on course, he said, "I hope the takeoff wasn't too rough for you."

"Not at all. I enjoyed the ride."

"What would you like to talk about while we fly?"

"I won't distract you?"

His smile twitched. "Not in the least. I put the controls on autopilot."

She glanced over her shoulder at Zeke. Whatever they discussed would be overheard by him.

"Tell me how the San Diego community is organized," she said.

Leopold had provided her with insider information on the key players he wanted her to meet with—vampires he believed would make good investors in their lab project. With everything happening around Nina's murder, she hadn't had time to ask Henry for his perspective.

"They call themselves the Mariners Lodge."

She laughed. "Did seafaring vampires found the community?"

"No. They bought the building when the original Mariners Lodge went bankrupt, and kept the name. They are governed by a lodge master and board. The lodge allows humane grazing—"

She raised one eyebrow. "Grazing?"

"Live feeding on a stranger. One take per night, by permit."

"You're serious?" she asked, her voice rising.

"Yes, ma'am," Zeke piped up from behind her. "I'll get my permit when we arrive."

Cerissa glanced his way, eyes narrowed. Her opinion of him couldn't go any lower.

"Ain't nothing wrong with grazin'." He lifted his hat and ran his hand through his hair. "No one gets scared; no one gets hurt. I got a vial of Tig's blood with me to heal the bite. Won't be no evidence of my feedin', or memory, either. I'm really lookin' forward to it."

"Why?" She scrunched her brow, puzzled. Did Zeke have the same problem as Rolf? "Bagged blood should satisfy you."

"Well, you gotta understand, the bags from the blood bank are missin' somethin'—alcohol. Plenty of tourists get soused to the gills at the conventions in San Diego. It's fun to imbibe some oh-be-joyful juice secondhand, if you get my drift. Mary Jane is good to relax—but I miss the feel of whiskey in my veins."

She raised a finger to her lip and tapped it. It didn't sound like Zeke was an adrenaline junkie—just the opposite. But she'd never heard of someone intentionally feeding on a drunk.

A vampire wouldn't stay inebriated for long after *directly* ingesting alcohol or painkillers—the vampire ability to heal neutralized the substance too rapidly. But once a drug or alcohol was processed by the human body, it had a longer effect.

Why did that make a difference? She didn't even have a SWAG—a scientific wild-ass guess. And what was Zeke using to relax? She'd heard the term somewhere...

"Mary Jane?" she asked.

"Yeah, you know, marijuana."

"You feed off someone who smokes?"

"No, ma'am, don't have to. Pot is one of the few things we can use to get high. Smoked only. Edibles do nothing for us."

Cerissa turned to Henry. "Seriously?"

"Yes, the fields in Sierra Escondida are older than our vineyards. If you drive all the way up Robles Road into the foothills, you'll find them."

This was news to her. Why were vampires affected by an inhaled substance? Another question for which she lacked a SWAG.

Then she recalled seeing Zeke smoke a cigar.

"Tobacco too?" she asked.

"Yes, ma'am. I enjoy a good smoke on occasion."

Her mind whirled with this new information. At the time, she'd thought his cigar was just an affect, a prop.

"But you can't get drunk while in San Diego—you're on guard duty."

"Not the whole time. A man's got to have a little fun. The Hill's a mite backwards in these things."

Henry glared over his shoulder at Zeke. "The Hill is not backwards. We are too concentrated in a small area to risk discovery; we cannot allow live feeding on strangers." He stabbed his finger in the air at the cowboy. "And you are not part of this conversation."

Cerissa crossed her arms and *tsked*. No one asked mortals how they felt about being dinner. At least Zeke had thought ahead. The biter's blood wouldn't heal a bite—it took the blood of another vampire to overcome the biter's fang serum. She added the information to her mental list—one more thing for her to research when she studied the relationship between fang serum and vampire blood.

"Most communities live off banked blood," she said. "Why doesn't San Diego?"

"They do supplement with banked blood." Henry checked something on the navigation screen and then looked at her again. "But given their high tourism numbers, they don't need to ban live feeding. One convention can feed the entire community for a week, without fear of discovery."

"Being able to hide the fact doesn't make it right."

Then an uneasy feeling invaded her chest. How could Henry sanction such an inhumane practice when an alternative was available? She had abandoned a vegetarian diet when she began regularly morphing—she needed the higher protein that came from meat to stay healthy—and had battled pangs of conscience ever since, especially when she morphed into a mountain lion and enjoyed the hunt.

Her *pita* had taught her his belief: the trauma suffered by a slaughtered animal entered the body of the person who consumed its flesh—one reason her human family had practiced vegetarianism—which was why she still carried guilt over her choices.

So, yes, she understood the need to live feed—graze, as Henry called it—before refrigeration made blood storage possible. But mortals weren't animals. Unconsented feeding when an alternative was available seemed wrong.

And then there were those vampires who hunted. When she hunted as a mountain lion, she never played with her meals to cause them intentional distress.

Henry and her "hunt" had been a voluntary thrill game.

And then she recalled—he had gone hunting with Rolf. She'd felt empathy when Henry first mentioned missing the chase.

How did she feel now? Were vampires more like her mountain lion counterpart than her human one?

Henry reached over and gave her leg a reassuring touch. "There is a difference between grazing and hunting. Properly done, live feeding does not terrorize the mortal."

"And hunting does?"

"Precisely. Don't conflate the two. I have fed live in the recent past—but I have not hunted since shortly after I was turned."

Had he sensed her emotions? She met his gaze. So, the last time he hunted was when he was a young vampire. But why indulge in "grazing" now? Blood banks provided enough to feed all U.S. vampires—and had, for decades, so long as their numbers didn't increase.

Hmm. She ate meat—and he sometimes grazed. Were they morally the same? As much as she wanted to give him the benefit of the doubt, she wasn't so sure.

CHAPTER 22

MORDIDA—SAME NIGHT

Chuck paced. He wanted to stab a knife into something. Many somethings. He'd been cooped up monitoring video feeds from his hidden cameras, waiting to find out what fallout came from Pascala's capture.

The cameras were set up near the Hill's gates, concealed in shrubbery along Robles Road. The video feed had caught "Beta" leaving last night to ride his motorcycle, but Beta wasn't gone long enough for Chuck to do anything.

And then Tig hightailed it off the Hill tonight—probably headed to Pascala's motel room. But why had it taken her so long to go there?

Shit. She must be taking her time, peeling Pascala like a grape.

Chuck had stayed away from the motel. Too much risk to go looking for the fifty thousand, and for all he knew, Pascala had stashed the money somewhere else. He didn't want to run into that bitch there, either—and he knew she would come.

He continued pacing—three steps, turn; three steps, turn. Maybe he should have searched the motel room. Nothing there would point to him, but the custom-made bullets could lead back to the President.

Fuck.

Why had he hesitated? He should have broken into the motel room on the night Pascala was captured and packed everything away.

Boy, was his fearless leader going to be pissed. It would be best if he gave the asshole a wide berth for the time being.

He made a note of Tig's departure in his log. The President loved reading the notes. A short while later, Beta left—his girlfriend driving the car. Chuck would wait to see when they returned. If a pattern developed, Beta might be the next target.

Chuck sent a brief text report to the President. *There.* That should hold the idiot.

Bored, he logged on to a video game and shot a machine gun at civilian bystanders in a war zone. Not as good as the real thing, but the pretend violence was better than watching the gate cameras. Besides, the camera feeds would buzz whenever a car sped by, which wasn't often.

The computer monitor hung on the wall, plugged into his laptop. He focused on his screen avatar and thumbed a button, whacking a machete into another hapless civilian.

Not satisfying.

He got up from the cheap desk, which sat against the wall straddling the line between his living room and his kitchen. The refrigerator was five steps from his desk. He took out a prepared meal he'd picked up at Trader Joe's and shoved the chicken marsala with broccolini into the microwave.

A cold beer would help him wait. He twisted off the bottle cap and chugged the whole thing.

The alcohol from one beer didn't take the edge off, but he didn't want to get hammered, either. He wrapped his fingers around another bottle and took a swig. Three was his limit. One more to go. The computer buzzed, and he strode back to the laptop to call up the monitoring program and rewind the video.

No one important drove by. He set the beer down on a napkin.

A few minutes later, he removed his dinner from the microwave. He placed the hot container on a plate and carefully peeled back the plastic cover to avoid burning his fingers in the steam. He didn't bother dishing the food out. He wolfed down the chicken straight out of the carton—less cleanup.

Finished, he brought up the video game, but he couldn't stay focused. The on-screen violence was like bubblegum—chew all you want, but you're still hungry.

The first cut was always his favorite. A special mental zone descended on him when he made the first slice over the right breast—the same place he'd stabbed his asshole grandfather. No matter how much his victim struggled, or tried to scream against their gag, he took his time carving his message on their torso.

Never.

He'd never be the victim—not ever again. And by the time he finished hacking off fingers, well, the sexual excitement overwhelmed him. He wore a condom in case he came. No chance of his DNA dribbling down his pants and leaving something for the cops to find.

His ritual hadn't changed in years, at least, not until he met the President. After Chuck went to work for the old guy, he had started bleeding them out at the end. A two-fer. He got the kill, and the President got the adrenaline-spiked blood.

And boy, was that blood potent by the time Chuck tapped a vein.

He smiled to himself at the memory. His creepy-ass smile. He knew it was scary, because seeing his smile always made his vics shit themselves.

He went back to the kitchen and dumped the empty dinner container into a plastic bag. He would take the trash to a public dumpster later. He never left his DNA lying around the apartment or in the rubbish bins out back.

And he never video-recorded his kills—too much risk of discovery if he did. He could always play it over in his mind anytime he wanted, but his imagination wasn't good enough to sustain him for long.

He glanced at the computer—an electronic ball and chain tying him to the apartment. Watching the Hill's gate all night was a waste. Not until a pattern developed.

Should he take some time off and satisfy his lust for *real* blood? Yeah, killing another vic sounded like a better idea. Two nights ago, he'd been rushed. But so far, the police hadn't found *that* body—at least, no word in the news feeds. It gave him confidence to cull another one from the herd, even if it was a bit soon.

Tonight, he would go slow. He changed into tight jeans and an expensive shirt to fit in at a singles bar. Like a chameleon, he transformed himself to attract his prey. Well groomed. Professional. Sexy.

He ran through his mental checklist. A stop at a hardware store for supplies was first up. He never used the same roll of duct tape twice—same with ropes and plastic sheeting. He protected himself and confused the cops by using different brands each time.

His special tools were never stored in his apartment. Even his supply of "roofies" was hidden throughout the city in safe locations—places where no one would accidentally dig them up. The nearest was sealed in an envelope stashed at a PO box he rented. He would grab the mail and the drugs at the same time.

He checked his watch. Nine o'clock—an excellent time to go hunting. Among his many rules: always use a different stalking ground. On his phone he searched for a hotel with a singles bar close by and found many to choose from.

Perfect.

He cautiously stepped out through the back door into his carport, looking for anyone who might observe his departure. No one was out at this hour. He'd tape over the license plate later. He started the engine and grinned to himself. Tonight was going to be fun.

Chapter 23

Sierra Escondida—same night

As Tig opened the door to Abigale's basement room, chaos met her.

Pascala, chained to the bed, was a bloody mess. Abigale was on the floor, fangs bared and fury on her face. Her knuckles were shredded.

Bailey was holding an electroshock gun pointed at Abigale.

"What is going on here?" Tig stepped into the room, with Jayden following her. "Lieutenant Bailey, report."

"She got past me and was hitting the prisoner, ma'am. I had to shock her."

"And how did she get by you long enough to beat him?"

The officer averted his eyes, looking anywhere but at her. "Ah, I went to use the bathroom. When I came back, she was hitting him, ma'am."

Tig pursed her lips and wrinkled her brow in disgust. Bailey should have called Liza to come over before taking a break. It was a gross violation of duty to leave the prisoner unguarded. Training the mates of other vampires to serve as police officers on the Hill didn't always produce the best candidates, but she had no other options.

She tossed the deli bag onto the table next to the video camera, strode over to Bailey, and snatched the electroshock gun out of his hand. "You're dismissed. Go home. We'll talk about this tomorrow night."

He hung his head and slumped out the door.

Jayden examined the prisoner. "He'll be okay. None of the injuries are too serious."

"Please stay with him. Call Dr. Clarke if his condition worsens." She locked eyes with Abigale and motioned with the electroshock gun toward the door. "Stand slowly and back out of here. You and I are going to discuss this now."

Reaching for the table's edge, Abigale pulled herself up and looked daggers at Pascala before leaving the room.

"Up the stairs," Tig said, prodding the angry blonde, "while I try to fix this."

Abigale snarled but cooperated, leading the way down the hall, rubbing her arm where the electroshock gun had zapped her. The two pinpoint marks would disappear soon enough. Once in the kitchen, the widow collapsed onto a chair like a wilted flower and rested her forehead on her arms.

Tig went through the same routine she had on the first night—filling a coffee cup halfway and slicing her wrist to pour in her own blood. She cued up a few choice things she wanted to say but bit back the words. Abigale was a founder. Just like Henry, the widow was higher up on the food chain.

"You're not going to heal him, are you?" Abigale asked shrilly.

Tig let out a cross between a grunt and a sigh. "We have to hand him over to the mortal authorities in Mordida tomorrow. Unexplained injuries will create more paperwork."

"I should have the right to kill him. I would, if Henry hadn't bullied those weaklings into rewriting the Covenant." The founder rubbed her arm. "Henry and his guilt keep us all in bondage."

Tig had heard the story. After Henry killed Nathaniel in a duel over a woman in the late 1800s, he'd pushed for changes. Dueling was made forbidden and a long list of protections for mortals instituted—including the rules that made Pascala's punishment a matter for mortal courts. The other four founders—Abigale among them—approved the amendments at the time.

"I understand how you feel. I do." Tig grabbed the seat across the table and tried to sound compassionate. "I know I said you'd get to avenge

Nina, and you will when we catch the vampire behind this, but we must follow the Covenant when it comes to Pascala. I'm sorry."

Abigale took a tissue from her pocket and dabbed at her tear-filled eyes. "I should have drained him the first moment I got my hands on him, but I wanted him to *suffer*."

"You told me you weren't interested in exacting vengeance against Pascala anymore. You wanted us to nail the person who hired him. What changed?"

The founder looked away and sighed. "Tonight was Carrie's night. She's so distraught—I can't do anything to console her. I hold her and listen to her cry. Luis looks like he's aged ten years overnight. The others—Stephen and Kyan may leave rather than deal with the loss we've suffered. Travis has shut down, his feelings walled off. Emily never stops raging. That man has destroyed my family, and I want to crush him, make him know the pain we're feeling."

"I'm truly sorry for what you're going through, but I can't let you hurt my prisoner. We found a witness who may have seen him talk with the Carlyle Cutter. We need Pascala's cooperation to nail the Cutter and catch the real person behind this."

Abigale buried her face in her hands. "I just thought, if I beat him enough, he'd tell me who hired him."

"And how did that work?"

"Not very well." The founder rose from her chair. "I won't do anything else to him, but before you turn him over to the mortal authorities, I want to say something to him."

"Which is?"

"It's better you don't know."

Tig nodded and took the coffee cup with her. She could guess what Abigale would say. If anyone ever hurt Jayden, someday, when the perp wasn't expecting her, she would hunt him down and kill him—her job notwithstanding.

Pascala was beginning to stir when she entered the room. She held the coffee under his nose. He pushed himself upright on his cot and, between battered lips, sipped the doctored drink. She examined his face as the superficial wounds began to heal.

"Tell me about Sarge's Bar," she said, standing over him, holding the cup.

He raised his chin, his bruised face hard with anger. "And then what? You gonna let her kill me?"

"No." All the work Tig had done to gain his cooperation was up in smoke, and she slumped into her chair across from him, putting them at eye level. "No one is going to kill you while you're in my custody."

He didn't look convinced. His trust had to be won again. The deli bag was on the table where she'd dropped it. She unwrapped a meatball sandwich.

"Hungry?"

She didn't wait for an answer. She handed the whole thing to Pascala. He devoured the sandwich like an animal afraid the food would be snatched away.

"Now, tell me about Sarge's Bar," she said softly.

He leaned against the wall, his knees bent, his feet on the cot's edge, and licked the marinara sauce off his fingers. "Why should I?"

She gave him a napkin and eased back in her chair. "Because we have everything we need to convict you. The rifle, the testimony of eyewitnesses, but I'm surprised you want to take the rap all by yourself."

"Huh?"

"This isn't the first attack on one of our residents. This is the fifth. The other assassins were captured or killed in the act. Charlie has viewed each of you as expendable."

"You're lying."

She leaned forward, bracing her forearms on her knees. "He knew how easily we'd capture you. I bet he even told you how close to the road to set up."

"You're—" Pascala stopped, his eyes unfocused as he fit the pieces together.

"Ever wonder why your friend DeLuca disappeared? Or Giordano? Both dead. Both died trying to carry out Charlie's mission. But you…I should be able to keep you alive—presuming you cooperate fully."

He cocked his head, studying her.

She switched on the video camera. "Did you meet Charlie at Sarge's Bar?"

"Yeah, the bar's name sounds right. I knew it had something to do with the army."

"You met there both times?"

His mouth thinned into a straight, skeptical line. "How do I know you aren't going to milk me dry and then kill me?"

Tig locked eyes with him. "Because that's not how I work. Trust me—you'll get a fair trial. I'll even put in a good word for you, if you cooperate."

Pascala didn't reply. "This is your last chance to answer my question. Did you meet Charlie at Sarge's Bar both times?"

He looked at his hands, resignation on his bruised face. "Yeah."

"When?"

"One week before I shot the lady."

She took a notepad and pen from the table. "That was the second time you met at the bar?"

"Yeah. The first time was a week before."

"And each meeting was at night?"

"Yeah."

She wrote the dates. "Did he buy a drink or anything to eat?"

"He ordered a drink."

"Did he pay?"

"I didn't, so he must've."

"Did he use a credit card?"

He scratched his head, the chains clinking with the movement. "Hell if I remember. I wasn't paying close attention."

"I'll be back." She left the room and found Jayden, who was in a chair outside the door. "Go in and keep an eye on him. Don't let Abigale in."

Tig fished out the business card from her pocket and punched in the number. "May I speak to Sarge?" she asked.

"Speaking."

"This is Chief Anderson. We spoke earlier."

"Sure."

"Remember the man I mentioned, the one called Charlie?" She told him the two dates Charlie was in the bar.

"I can check my records for those nights," he said. "I'll call you if I find anything."

She returned to the dungeon and dismissed Jayden.

Pascala continued to eye Tig warily. Her second-in-command had been right. Beating the truth out of a suspect may not be the smartest interrogation tool. Winning Pascala's trust had proven the better route.

From the deli sack, she offered him a chocolate-chunk-espresso brownie and a Coke—the perfect bribe and guaranteed to keep Pascala awake for a while. Tonight was her last night to question him.

He popped the can's top, and his eyes closed as he slurped the Coke. He then let out a satisfied burp.

"Okay," she said. "Let's talk some more about Charlie."

A fast knock interrupted them. Jayden's knock. "I'll be back."

Jayden stepped aside so she could join him in the hall. He was holding his iPad and looking grim.

She closed the door. "What's wrong?"

"The Cutter struck again, two nights ago."

"Shit. The night Nina was shot. Where?"

"East Mordida." He showed her the report on his tablet.

She scanned through it. "They're sure?"

"Same MO—fingers hacked off, the word 'NEVER' carved into the victim's torso, body drained of blood."

"Do they know time of death?"

"They think before midnight, but they aren't certain, because the body's been there for two days—dumped in a trash bin, like most of the others."

"Where was ground zero?"

"The actual kill location is still a mystery."

Tig closed her eyes, trying to figure out what to do. "Tomorrow, touch base with the detective in charge. Ask if they found anything they haven't released to the media and put in a request to examine the evidence collected. You might be able to piece together something to lead us to the Cutter."

"You got it, chief." He motioned with his thumb at the wall behind which Pascala sat. "I'll make the calls after I drop him off at Mordida Jail."

Her phone rang. The number for Sarge's Bar was displayed. "You have something?" she asked once they made it through pleasantries.

"No credit card slips for anyone named Charlie."

Tig gripped her phone tighter in frustration. "Anything close? Charles or Chuck?"

"No, but I found two receipts for C. Roberts—one for each night you asked about."

"Can you scan or fax them over?"

"I'll take a photo of them and send them to the email address on your business card."

"Perfect. Thank you."

While waiting for Sarge's email to arrive, Tig watched over Jayden's shoulder as he searched for C. Roberts on his iPad. The DMV listed over a hundred men who had similar names, a few Charles or Chucks, but none lived within fifty miles of the Hill. He culled them out for later research. Same with the criminal registries—none in the area—and V-Trak produced zilch. No vampire or mate in the treaty database matched the name.

Tig's phone *dinged*, and she opened the email from Sarge—the receipt was legible, and they could use the transaction number to trace the charge. She forwarded the photo to Jayden.

"Super," he said. "I'll start with the credit card company, and I'll contact Marcus if we need a warrant, then I'm going to catch some shuteye—tomorrow will be a long day."

"I have more to do here. I need to see if 'Roberts' triggers anything for Pascala. I'll see you tomorrow night." She paused, placing a hand on his shoulder and looking into his eyes. "Thank you, Jayden, for all your hard work on this."

"No problem. That's what I'm here for."

"You're here for so much more than that."

She glanced around to make sure they were alone—including no one on the stairs—and pressed her lips to his. His masculine musk and blood scent awakened a deep desire. She wished she had the time to satisfy the urge.

"I'll be glad when this is over," she said. "I've missed being with you."

"Right back at you," Jayden said.

She watched his ass as he jogged up the stairs and sighed. Yup, this case couldn't close soon enough for her—for more reasons than one.

Chapter 24

San Diego Mariners Lodge—Eleven p.m.

Henry parked in the visitors' lot next to the old Mariners Lodge. The familiar twelve-story building was constructed from tan brick. The architecture always struck him as an old-fashioned anomaly—only a few similar structures had survived the earthquakes plaguing California. Years ago, the lodge had retrofitted the place with steel-reinforced framing. The engineers had managed to preserve the edifice.

In the arch that spanned the tall double doors, a brigantine ship was carved in marble. The building's name was spelled out in sepia granite below the carving and created a pleasing façade behind which the community hid.

This wasn't his first visit. He'd spent a lot of time there over the years, including a particularly long stretch in the 1960s. The conference room on the sixth floor had hosted treaty negotiations.

They would check into their hotel later. First, they had to meet with the San Diego lodge master. Henry held the heavy door open for Cerissa, a gift bag in his other hand. Zeke followed close on her heels rather than taking the door.

Annoyed, Henry restrained himself from growling at the cowboy. Zeke had butted into their conversation way too often during the plane ride. When they picked up the rental car, Zeke had asked Cerissa to sit in the back seat with him—which she refused to do. Now, he was pushing the boundaries again, almost stalking her through the doorway.

They were long overdue for a talk.

When Henry stepped into the lobby and released the door, Zeke moved aside—at least he knew his place enough to do that.

"We're here to see Lodge Master Wagner," Henry told the reception guard, and gave their names. "We have an appointment."

"I'll let her know you're here."

Zeke plopped onto the lobby's couch, and Cerissa gracefully sat next to him, tucking her skirt around her shapely legs and crossing them at the ankles. Henry scowled. "Please take the chair, Cerissa. You'll be more comfortable."

She shot him a look. Her displeasure leaked through the crystal, souring his mouth.

"I'm fine where I am," she said.

"No, I insist." He stood by the chair across from the couch, waiting for her to move. She had no business being close to Zeke. He thought he'd made his preference clear before they got on the plane.

She fired off a furious look—the crystal made her meaning unmistakable—and rose to her feet. But instead of taking the chair, she walked over to a literature rack. He took the space on the couch so she couldn't return to it.

What was she looking for? She had flipped through the various community announcements and stopped at one, staring at the page. He joined her. "What have you found, *cariña*?"

"Ari told us to keep an eye out for anything about New Path Church," she whispered, handing him the piece of paper, her anger at him apparently forgotten.

Henry read the flyer:

A NEW PATH FOR YOU

> Welcome, friend.
> Are you bored with life?
> Do you long for greater freedom?
> Has hiding your true self become a burden?
> Have you ever wondered if you're on the right path?
> We've asked the same questions.
> We've found the answers.
> Curious?
> Email us.

An email address and PO box for New Path Church were at the bottom of the handbill.

"This flyer isn't the same one Tig had," he said. "It's similar, but different." He opened the document on his phone and showed her the copy Ari had sent them:

A NEW PATH FOR YOU

> Are you hiding who you are?
> Pretending to be something you aren't?
> Ashamed of what you've become?
> We want to help.
> Just like you, we were pushed into hiding. Told our survival meant living in the shadows. Told we must pretend to be like the sheep who walk the streets of every city. Told to shut up, sit down, and sign a document none of us agreed with.

But we aren't sheep. We're wolves.

And wolves were meant to hunt.

You have no reason to be ashamed. You have no reason to pretend. You have no reason to hide.

A strong wind is blowing, and it will clear a new path for our kind. Be the wolf you were meant to be.

Cerissa ran her finger along the PO box. "It may be a different message, but it's the same address. Should we send it to Tig?"

"If we did, she would demand we return immediately. Let me take this." Henry set down the gift bag, folded the page, and put it in his back pocket. "I'll ask the lodge master if she knows anything about the flyer. The question would be better coming from me."

"I'll take a copy for Ari." She picked up the remaining one and slipped it into her purse.

The phone on the guard's desk rang. A short moment later, he said, "Will do." He looked in their direction. "The lodge master is ready for you now. The elevator is this way."

Henry swept up the gift bag, and the three of them followed the guard, who tapped a plastic card key against a lit panel and punched the button for the tenth floor. "Don't get off before then."

Once the elevator doors closed, Henry positioned himself between Cerissa and Zeke. She rolled her eyes at him but said nothing.

An assistant met them at the door and ushered them in. Nothing had changed since the last time he had visited. Wilhelmina Wagner's office conveyed a message of utilitarian elegance. A hardwood desk, with matching bookshelves, occupied the office's back half. The front half included a sofa and two occasional chairs. All the furniture had hard lines; no soft curves, no plushness.

He strode forward to shake hands with the lodge master. "Wilma, it's a pleasure to see you. How is Hans?"

"Doing well." A gracious smile curved her thin lips. Her brown hair was braided and pinned in a circle on the top of her head. "And who is your entourage?"

He made the introductions and handed Wilma the gift bag. She slid out the bottle and examined the label—one of Vasquez Müller Winery's best reserve wines. Acting appropriately impressed, she set the bottle on her desk. Her mortal mate, Hans, would be the gift's real beneficiary.

"Thank you," Wilma said. "Now, how may I help you?"

"I'm in town on winery business. Cerissa was hoping to meet with your community members about investing in the lab she and Leopold are building in Sierra Escondida."

Wilma looked interested. "Barney Morrison told us about your project. He was impressed with your presentation. I'm pleased you've made our lodge the first stop on your tour."

"Thank you, lodge master," Cerissa said.

"Please, call me Wilma. We aren't as formal here as your mayor is." Wilma's gaze traveled to the cowboy. "And what about you? Are you here on business, too?"

"Zeke is along as our bodyguard," Henry said. "Because of some problems we've had on the Hill."

Wilma raised an eyebrow. "I heard about those problems. I hope you aren't bringing them with you."

"We have no reason to believe they would follow us here," Henry said, crossing his fingers behind his back. He disliked stretching the truth when speaking to someone he'd known as long as he'd known Wilma.

"Well, if there is anything I can do to make your stay more pleasant, don't hesitate to ask."

He nodded. "There is something. May I speak with you for a moment in private?"

"Of course. Why don't I have my assistant show your *Fraulein* our meeting room? Zeke can go with them."

Zeke alone with Cerissa?

I should have dismissed him and kept her here.

He started to voice his objection, but Cerissa beat him to it. "That sounds great," she said. "What night are we scheduled?"

"I'm working on the date," Wilma said. "We need to shuffle a few things scheduled for our larger room. I'll text you once I'm sure."

After Cerissa and Zeke left, Henry took the couch, and Wilma grabbed the chair across from him.

"So, what did you want to discuss?" she asked.

"This." He unfolded the page and, leaning across the small coffee table, handed the flyer to her. "What can you tell me about New Path Church?"

She appeared to scan down the page. "This is the first I've heard of them."

"They may be connected to the attacks on the Hill. New Path is run by Jim Jones. Do you know him?"

"Hmm. We have at least three Joneses on our roster, but none with the first name Jim or James. I could ask around."

"We would appreciate the help."

"Aside from the San Diego address, why do you think I should recognize him?"

"This flyer was from the lobby literature stand downstairs." Henry reached for it.

She didn't release the paper. "Do you mind leaving it with me? Our security chief should read it."

"May I take a photo of the flyer first? I want to send a copy to Tig."

Wilma flattened the flyer on the coffee table.

He took out his phone and snapped a shot. "Please let me know what you find out."

"Consider it done." Wilma escorted him to the door. She stopped at her assistant's desk in the outer office. "Ach, where did she hide them? Ah, there they are." She pulled out two pink slips of paper from a folder. "Your permits, for you and Zeke. You're familiar with the rules; nothing has changed. One take per night, one pint only, heal the bite, no permanent harm, no hunting within city limits, no sex without permission, and erase their memories."

"I'll make sure Zeke understands."

The policy was reasonable: one person and no terrorizing them. But a one-pint limit meant supplementing with bagged blood. Of all the rules San Diego imposed, he suspected the one-pint limit got fudged the most. After all, no one stood by to measure the donor's remaining blood volume.

And for those who wanted to hunt, well, Rolf had always gone to the unincorporated county areas not covered by the treaty.

Henry handed his permit back to her. "I won't need one. I brought my own supply with me."

Wilma laughed and slapped him on the shoulder. "I doubt your girlfriend can satisfy a hearty fellow like you."

"I didn't mean it that way. Cerissa is not my supply. I'll be drinking bagged blood."

"Of course," she said with a gentle smirk. "But a little fresh blood never hurt anyone. All our mates here understand the need."

But not Cerissa.

Wilma wouldn't let him give the document back. "Hang on to your permit, in case you change your mind."

"I sincerely doubt I will."

Cerissa had made her viewpoint clear during the plane ride—she didn't approve of grazing on strangers. With the clone blood she provided, Henry had no real need. Still, San Diego's system didn't strike him as wrong. He'd fed live for most of his vampire life because donor blood wasn't readily available until after World War II.

But he didn't want to sour the trip. He'd already bickered with her over Zeke's presence, and he didn't want to fight over anything else. They could discuss the issue some other time. For now, he'd refrain from grazing.

Chapter 25

Tuscany Bay Resort, San Diego—Thirty Minutes Later

The bellhop deposited their luggage in the suite's larger bedroom. Henry tipped the young man a twenty and closed the door.

The Tuscany Bay Resort was one of the massive luxury hotels near the convention center. He had chosen the place to impress Cerissa—it was their first trip as a couple—and as an added benefit, their accommodations weren't far from the Mariners Lodge.

"Lovely," she said, looking around the suite.

Her reaction pleased him. "Why don't you unpack? I need to speak with Zeke."

"Is something wrong?"

"Nothing for you to worry about. I want to make sure he understands our arrangement."

"Henry—"

He cupped her shoulders and pulled her close to kiss. "I appreciate your concern, but nothing will happen. I'll be right back."

Zeke had the room next to their suite. Henry headed down the hall, centering himself and suppressing the crystal's connection. This conversation required privacy.

He knocked. A short moment later, the door opened. "May I come in?"

Zeke stood in the doorway, his arms extended, blocking the way. He was still wearing his cowboy hat. "You're not gonna hit me, are ya? I promised Tig I wouldn't fight ya."

"I will not start any violence."

He pursed his lips as he seemed to consider it. Then his expression lightened, and he took a step away. "I reckon you can come in."

"This is for you." Henry closed the door and handed him the grazing permit. "Same rules—you've been here before."

"Yup." Zeke folded the paper and slipped it into his shirt pocket. "Is that all?"

"We didn't have an opportunity to discuss the terms of our arrangement before leaving the Hill. Tig insisted I take you as a guard, but I don't want you here and I don't need you here."

"Yeah, I didn't want to come either. But as you say, the chief insisted, and I gotta stay on her good side. So, I'm here whether you want my help or not."

Henry's gut tightened. The cowboy was missing his point. "Just keep out of my way and I'll make sure Cerissa's safe. We don't need your protection."

"Now there's where you're wrong." Zeke tipped his hat back. "I gotta make sure nothin' happens to you, seein' as you're a founder and all, though personally, I don't care if you wind up as ashes with a stake through your heart. But Cerissa? I definitely won't let no one hurt her. By my reckonin', she made the wrong choice, but the girl don't deserve to die 'cause she's with you—especially since I've been rethinkin' my position."

That didn't sound good. "I am going to say this only once. Stay away from her. She doesn't need your kind of protection. Her arm is still injured from where you grabbed her."

Zeke looked at his feet. "Look, I was outta line hurtin' her before. I let my anger get the best of me and I wasn't seein' the situation clearly. Won't happen again."

"Good, because if you do—"

"But a woman has a right to change her mind. So, don't be so certain it's all said and done."

Henry gave a short laugh. "Cerissa will never leave me for you."

"Really? You sound like a little boy, all bravado. You haven't told her what you did, have ya?"

Henry swiped at the air, dismissing the question. "She already knows about Nathaniel."

"But what 'bout Sarah? Your gal did a disappearing act right after you killed Nathaniel. I mean, I always wondered how you got rid of Sarah's body so quick like."

"How dare you." Henry fisted his hands at his sides. "If you repeat—"

"Now just hold on there." Zeke backed up, his open palms raised. "I got no reason to tell Cerissa anything. If'n I do, she'll blame me."

Zeke lowered his hands and examined his fingernails. "But see, like I said, I've been rethinkin' my point of view. I don't think she's a whore like Sarah was. I just think she doesn't know what *you* really are, Bautista. You got her all bamboozled with your suave founder bullshit. But once she catches on to the truth about you, I might not look so bad. So sooner or later, when you tell her, the two of you are over." A smirk slid across his face. "So I'm gonna sit back, be on my best behavior, and let you fall down the mine shaft all on your own."

"Don't hold your breath."

Henry grabbed the handle and slammed the door shut behind him. He braced himself against the hallway wall, his heart pumping faster than normal. Where could he go to calm down? He didn't want Cerissa to see him like this.

The desk clerk had mentioned a concierge lounge. He strode past his suite and found the common room. No one was inside—a good place for a private phone call.

Yacov answered on the second ring. "I didn't expect to hear from you. Is everything all right in San Diego?"

Henry scrubbed his face. No, it wasn't all right. "Tig made us take Zeke along."

"After what happened at Nina's funeral?" Yacov asked, his voice rising with disbelief.

"Tig refused to let two founders travel together, or I would have asked you." Henry collapsed onto the couch, watching the door. He didn't want this conversation overheard. "Is there any possibility Zeke learned what happened to Sarah?"

"I don't see how, my friend. I've told no one. Have you shared the story with anyone?"

"No, never."

"Then I don't understand how he can. What brought all this up?"

"Zeke. He continues to believe he can win Cerissa from me. He goaded me—he's convinced telling her about Sarah would help his goal."

"Cerissa is not a prize to be won," Yacov said. "She is an adult woman who can make her own decisions."

"I'm aware of that," Henry snapped, and regretted it immediately. "I'm sorry. I didn't mean to speak sharply."

"It's understandable. You're upset."

"Zeke believes Cerissa will leave me when she learns about Sarah, but how could *he* know what really happened?"

"A wild guess, I'm sure. Rumors flew when she disappeared so quickly."

Most current Hill residents had never heard those rumors, thank God. But Zeke had lived on the Hill with his maker—Nathaniel—when the terrible events occurred.

Henry rubbed his eyes with one hand. "What should I do?" His voice carried the strain he felt. "What if Zeke tells Cerissa what he suspects?"

"He has nothing to tell. The more important question is whether you should tell her before her initiation ceremony."

Henry shook his head even though his friend couldn't see it. "The whole thing is eating at me, but I can't tell her the truth. And I won't lie to her."

"What part is eating at you? That she might find out and leave? Or that you're wrong to hide your past from her?"

How did Yacov drill right into his soul? "That she might find out and leave."

"Hmm." Yacov paused. "Here is how I see it, my friend. You aren't putting your love for Cerissa first. You are putting your fear first—your fear she will find out, your fear of the consequences. You should put your love for her first. Then you will know the answer to your question."

"I— Thank you, Yacov. I will think about what you've said."

"Don't think too long. In this, Zeke is right. The story would be better coming from you than him. Good sleep, my friend."

"Good sleep."

Henry sat there after the call ended, his head in his hands. Was Yacov right?

I should tell her.

But not tonight, not here in San Diego. He needed the right moment. After things were settled with the VDM and they returned home, there would be plenty of time to tell her. She would understand, wouldn't she?

He pinched the bridge of his nose. Or was Zeke right? Would she leave if Henry told her what happened to Sarah?

On the plane, she'd been very judgmental about grazing. Would she judge him just as harshly if she learned about Sarah?

I can't take that risk.

He had worked so hard to push the past from his mind. There had been dark moments when he thought he'd never move beyond what happened—that his jealousy would once again drive him to violence.

In his heart, he knew the problem lay with him, the result of the bad choices he'd made. The women *he* had chosen in the past had never given him a reason to trust them—his relationships with Anne-Louise and Sarah both attested to his tendency to choose badly.

But I've changed. Cerissa is proof of that.

His regular confession sessions with Father Matt had helped him to make better choices. He'd learned to control his jealously and his distrust. Even Yacov had encouraged him to fall in love.

What if they are wrong? What if the problem is me? What if I can't change?

He dug his palms into his eyes, scrubbing them to block out the vision of Sarah cheating on him.

Cerissa wasn't like Sarah. He could believe Cerissa. He could trust her. But he didn't trust Zeke, or others of their kind, to act honorably. It was why Cerissa's demand scared him. Yet he had to let her meet unchaperoned with other vampires to fulfill her envoy role.

If he didn't, he knew deep in his gut he would push her away.

Henry sighed. Yacov was right. He had to put his love for Cerissa first. When he had tried to confess his sins before they mated, when he'd told her he wasn't a modern man, no matter what he may seem like, she'd told him she accepted him for what he was.

Zeke was wrong—she would understand.

Henry opened his eyes. He had to tell her about Sarah.

But not right now.

Chapter 26

Tuscany Bay Resort, San Diego—thirty minutes earlier

While Henry was gone, Cerissa divided the luggage between the two bedrooms in their suite. He insisted on sleeping alone. No amount of reassurance would calm his silly fear about hurting her when he woke. Even without the crystal protecting her, he had better control than he gave himself credit for, but she respected his wishes and moved her luggage to the other bedroom.

At least she wouldn't disturb him when she showered in the morning. Or would noise wake him? She'd have to ask. The one and only time she'd ever slept with him—as in literal sleeping—he had seemed dead to the world for the entire day.

She decided to use the living room to work and hummed a tune to herself as she laid the flyer on the desk, photographed it, and emailed the diatribe to Ari. She then removed her contact lenses, dropped them into a tray in the back of her phone, and downloaded the videos she'd recorded to the Lux server.

The *click* of the door lock told her Henry was back.

"How did your talk go with Zeke?" she asked.

He sank onto the couch. "Uneventful."

Really? Hard to believe, considering how long he'd been gone, but the crystal hadn't alerted her to anything, so she would accept it for now.

"I had a call to make," he added. "I used the lounge down the hall."

Aha. He must have noticed the look on her face. "Do you mind if I go to the lab? I want to run some tests on the samples I took of Rolf's blood. I haven't had time to analyze them."

He looked at something on his phone. "There is a soccer game I wanted to catch. It starts in a few minutes. Take your time."

"Soccer? I thought you were a dedicated baseball fan."

"I can like more than one sport."

She smiled. "How is it we've moved in together, and I'm still learning so much about you?"

"Come back early, and you'll learn even more," he said with a sexy leer. He wrapped his hands around her hips and pulled her close.

"We'll see about that."

She gave him a quick kiss and flashed back to the Enclave. After morphing to her true form and donning a white lab sarong, she removed Henry's blood sample from the lab's refrigerator, prepared the dimpled slide, placed it in the chemical analysis machine, and punched the control buttons to run a dozen tests.

She would examine Rolf's blood next and compare the results. Later, she'd work on the fang serum Henry had provided.

Hmm. Should I stay here or go back?

She ran a quick computer search using her neural link and discovered soccer games lasted at least two hours. He wouldn't mind if she worked while he relaxed. She would return before the game ended.

Tuscany Bay Resort—an hour later

Henry checked his phone for the sixth time. No messages. It was after one in the morning and the game was in its second half.

Where is Cerissa?

He pressed his palms against his temples. Yes, he had said he was going to watch soccer, but she didn't have to stay away for the entire game. He wanted to spend time with her before he had to leave for his appointment with Quentin Brown, the lodge's security chief. That meeting was scheduled for four in the morning.

He tried to focus on the television, but her upcoming initiation ceremony niggled at the back of his mind. She didn't like surprises. He wanted to talk with her about the ritual but couldn't figure out how without facing a hundred lashes. If he told her, and someone asked her—well, he couldn't ask her to lie for him. He just couldn't.

Why did Rolf have such a stick up his ass? Of anyone, he should understand why an exception must be made for Cerissa. She was an envoy—maybe that could be the excuse for telling her?

Henry rubbed the back of his neck. He was doing his best, trying to help Rolf with *his* problem—why wasn't his friend helping him out?

Then his mind flipped the question: was Rolf okay on his own?

What if the adrenaline-enhanced clone blood doesn't work? What if he can't stop hunting?

Henry picked up his phone again, and his finger hovered over Rolf's number. He wanted to check on Rolf—badly. But his partner would resent being checked on.

Bad idea.

With a toss, the phone landed on the coffee table, making a *thunk*. When would Cerissa return? The anxiety was like bees buzzing in his mind.

An incoming message chimed, and he snatched up the phone. Was it her?

No, the text was from Wilma: *Cerissa's presentation is scheduled for Tuesday at 10 pm. Earliest time the room is open.*

Two nights from now. He tapped out a reply: *That will be fine, thank you.*

He added the date to his phone's calendar, and the reminder for his appointment with Quentin popped up. Tig had arranged the meeting to give him a feel for the current San Diego community.

He'd leave Cerissa here so she could rest.

Hmm. Should I take Zeke with me? I don't want him disturbing her while she sleeps.

Moments later, he knocked on the cowboy's hotel door. No answer. He pounded louder. Still no response.

Returning to his suite, he phoned Zeke. The call went to voicemail. He'd wait another hour and try again.

Zeke's disappearance bothered him. And why wasn't Cerissa back yet? Henry dropped onto the couch with a grunt. He couldn't shake off his growing anxiety.

What if they are together?

Where did that thought come from? He gave his head a shake, rejecting the insidious idea. He refused to consider it.

She is in her lab, not with Zeke.

The cheering on the television suddenly got louder—a goal by the other team. He scowled at the screen. Mexico was losing, and the game no longer held his interest. His leg tapped with restless energy, making it impossible to sit still or calm his thoughts. He had to do something to distract himself—unpacking his suitcase might work.

He left the game playing in the living room and strode into the master bedroom. He pushed the remote's button, the bedroom TV snapped on, and the cheering echoed between the two rooms as Mexico drove forward.

Cerissa had removed her bags. Now that he considered it, she should take this larger room, and he could use the smaller one to sleep in during the day. He started to swap the luggage when he discovered she'd already unpacked, so he returned to the master bedroom and opened his bag.

As he worked, his unease churned faster. He ground his teeth, fighting to ignore the turmoil welling inside him, and lifted his clothes out of the garment bag to hang them in the small hotel closet.

The light reflected off the polished tungsten bracelet he wore. He couldn't sense Cerissa's emotions at this distance with the bracelet on. If he took off the dampener, he'd know with certainty what she was feeling and doing.

In one quick moment, he could silence his anxiety.

He fingered the bracelet's latch.

So tempting...

But it worked both ways. If he removed the bracelet, she'd sense his worry and his insecurity. What reason would he give for those emotions?

He fisted his hands, refusing to unfasten it.

He had been just fine until Zeke's comments, until his threats.

Is Zeke with her right now, sharing his suspicions, convincing her to leave?

Sure, Zeke said he wouldn't say anything. But it would be like him to lie, to try to lull Henry into a false sense of security, only to stab him in the back later. The man had no honor.

Everyone on the Hill knew the story, how Zeke became vampire. He was a highway robber who tried to rob Nathaniel. Nathaniel had turned the cowboy as payback.

Henry scrunched his eyes closed. He hadn't felt this insecure since Sarah cheated on him.

What will stop these thoughts?

He muted the soccer game and reached for the phone on his belt. He should call Yacov again—or Father Matt. Henry had never been able to confess the whole story to the priest, but he needed his doubts to end, and maybe if he finally did talk with Matt...

Staring at the phone, he punched the shortcut for Zeke's number instead.

"Yeah?" Zeke answered.

"I'm meeting with Quentin in a few hours. I'll need you to go with me. Where are you?"

"Out havin' my dinner. I'll be back in time to go with ya."

The sounds of a busy bar filtered through the background. Zeke wasn't with Cerissa—he wasn't spilling any secrets or trying to win her over.

The television in the living room suddenly went silent.

He let out a sigh. She was back. Relief settled in his belly.

"I'll meet you at three thirty in the lobby," he said, and disconnected the call.

"Henry?" She tapped at his bedroom door.

"*Cariña*." He wrapped his arms around her and took in her seductive scent.

Guilt flooded through him—he'd had no reason to imagine she had been with Zeke. Why did the thought keep coming back again and again? He needed to make an appointment with Father Matt the moment he returned to the Hill. He was being ridiculous, and his anxiety was causing his mind to go *loco*.

Against his shoulder, she said, "If you want to watch TV, I can read."

"The game is unimportant." He released her. "How did your research go?"

"I compared Rolf's blood to your sample. There are a few differences. I'm running a full genome mapping and sequencing now."

He furrowed his brow. "Aren't vampire genes rejected by DNA machines?"

"Because of the way they are programed, human DNA sequencers mistake vampire blood for a contaminated specimen. But Lux technology is way ahead—I'm conducting a series of tests. They'll take about a week to complete."

"Very good. I heard from Wilma. Your investor meeting is in two nights. And I have an appointment with Quentin at four."

Her gaze moved to the bedside clock. She took his hand and pulled him toward her room. "We have time before you leave." When they got to her room, she touched his bracelet. "Do you want to take this off?"

Would she be able to sense his doubts if he did?

I can't take that chance.

"Another time," he said. "I'm a bit out of sorts, traveling and all."

"It's okay," she said with a coy smile. "I have an idea for getting you relaxed."

She stroked his fly. He stopped her, his fingers over hers. "Ah, before we do, I— There is something I need to ask you. Rolf reminded me there is, well, an *obligation*, and I can't tell you about it. If I do, I'd violate the Covenant, and if it becomes known, I'd face the whipping post."

Her eyes showed her concern. "Henry, I don't want you at risk because of me."

"But I don't like keeping things from you."

"Could it cause us harm?"

"No. And the confidential matter has nothing to do with the VDM."

She ran her hands over his chest. "It's all right. Some things in a secret society are, well, secret. Will you ever be able to tell me?"

"Eventually, yes."

"And you're sure—you're in no danger from it?"

"Neither of us is."

She shrugged. "I don't like you keeping secrets from me, but I understand. Perhaps it's one of those things in the Covenant we need to change?"

"Perhaps," he said with a smile, and then it occurred to him. There was one possible threat to her. "How often do you use the stabilizing hormone?"

"If I won't have a chance to morph during the day, I inject the stabilizer when I first wake, and again before we make love."

"Do you mind experimenting to see how long a shot lasts?"

"What do you suggest?"

"Don't take it this time."

"Sure." She kissed him. "But I call 'top'—it's uncomfortable morphing when I'm on my back."

He instantly understood. Her wings would have no room to expand. "Of course, *cariña*."

"Now, where was I?" she asked.

He held still as she unzipped his pants, pulled them down, and, kneeling before him, took him into her mouth. The pleasure zinged through him as her sucking hardened him.

He threaded his fingers through her hair. She loved him; she was his, and nothing—not even Zeke's threats—would change that.

All will be fine.

He just had to remember it.

After they made love, Cerissa dozed off, waking when Henry slid off the bed and tiptoed to the bathroom. He closed the door soundlessly, and the shower turned on.

Their experiment with the bite proved she didn't need a second dose. The last dose she'd had was at two in the afternoon, and she hadn't morphed spontaneously when he bit. Taking the stabilizing hormone twelve hours in advance would still fight the effects of fang serum.

But the chemical compounds in fang serum had left her antsy, so she morphed to her native form and went back to sleep. Next thing she knew, Henry was leaning over to kiss her cheek, smelling of his cologne—cloves and other exotic spices.

It was nice to be awakened that way. She lay on her stomach with her long wings folded in and her silky hair spread out on the pillow to the side. He moved her wing before the mattress dipped with his weight. She twisted to look up at him and smiled when he stroked her feathers, stopping to toy with one.

A quick kiss and he eased off the bed to stand by her. Naked, he resumed drying his long hair with a towel.

She morphed back to her human form, stretched, and yawned. Rolling over, she sat up against the high-backed headboard, and her gaze traveled to the area below his waist. The vigor with which he dried his hair was causing things to bounce.

"It does sort of look like an anteater," she said.

He draped the towel over his shoulder. "I beg your pardon?"

"Some mates were gossiping at the funeral—they said most of the older male vampires aren't circumcised. They referred to it as looking like an anteater. Yours does sort of look like one, but for the anteater, it's their nose."

"I see."

"He's cute, that's all," she said, smiling at him.

Henry sat down on the bed and ran his index finger along her ribcage, a silent threat to tickle her if she continued. "Didn't we reach an understanding?"

"I know. I'm not supposed to call you cute. But *he* is."

"Cerissa..."

"All right, all right. What if I called him 'sexy' or 'manly' instead?"

"That would be fine."

"He is sexy, the way he huddles underneath the foreskin."

He ran his fingers down her arm, took her hand, and kissed it. Then he gave her a teasing smile. "Have I not been paying enough attention to you?

You seem rather focused on a singular part of my anatomy."

She blushed, the heat flowing all the way to her breasts. "That's not it."

"If I haven't satisfied you, I am willing to try again."

She looked at where he held the towel over his lap. "Quite satisfied, thank you." Then she looked into his eyes and smiled coyly. "For now."

"You are sure?"

She smirked at him. "Go on and get dressed. I'm going back to sleep. I have a long day ahead of me."

"Of course, *mi amor*. I will see you tomorrow night." He stood and gave her a little bow. His "anteater" bounced when he did. She suppressed a grin, trying hard not to stare, and giggled.

I'm going to need a better pet name than anteater.

He headed back to his room and her gaze followed his backside. She didn't get to see him walk around fully naked very often. She enjoyed the look of his sculpted back, his tight ass, his long legs and manly *cojones*.

She rolled over and sighed to herself, a contented sigh—she liked living with Henry. Feeling like a piece of cooked pasta, she closed her eyes and drifted off, grateful to be his mate.

Chapter 27

Mordida—The Next Afternoon

Jayden yawned. The subpoena had been faxed over to the credit card company's lawyers around nine that morning. But the legal department was still sitting on the billing address. After dropping off Pascala at Mordida's jail, he'd met with the detective in charge of the latest Cutter case. So far, nothing new—the same MO as the original three murders. He left the Mordida police station and needed a quick pick-me-up to keep going.

The Starbucks drive-through was fast, so he parked in their lot to call the credit card company for the umpteenth time to learn what he could about C. Roberts.

He took a sip of his double espresso macchiato, and the customer service representative came back on the line. She started reading out an address.

He almost sprayed the coffee over his car's dashboard. Instead, he forced himself to swallow the hot liquid and said, "Give me a chance to write this down." He slid the cup into a holder and grabbed the pen from his pocket. "Go ahead."

She read out, "Eight-oh-five East Rampart Street, Unit B, Mordida, California."

He repeated the address back to her. Thank God for credit card companies. They required a real street address, not a PO box. "And the first name—do you have anything other than an initial?"

"Charlie."

"Place of work?"

"The card was issued to On the Vine, Inc., based on the company's credit. Charlie Roberts doesn't have much of a credit history. He or she— no sex listed; that's strange—works for On the Vine. Looks like a Swiss corporation. The company's deposit of ten thousand dollars guaranteed the card."

He added the company's contact information to his notes. He thanked her and plugged the Mordida address into his navigation system. Fifteen minutes later, he cruised by the apartment, a one-story duplex, which shared a common wall with its neighbor. The carport in the back was empty.

It took him an hour to obtain the warrant. He asked the judge for more than a standard search. He half expected her honor to take out a bright red pen and strike out his "sneak and peek" and "electronic surveillance" requests. Instead, she signed the whole thing, and he let out a long breath.

If "Charlie Roberts" wasn't home, Jayden could enter surreptitiously without notifying Roberts of the search and install surveillance cameras in the apartment.

He phoned the officer on duty at the Sierra Escondida police annex and requested backup. Located in the business district, the annex was outside the community's walls and staffed by mortals who were unaware vampires existed.

He had to do whatever it took to protect the Hill's secret. If a vampire was asleep in the Cutter's apartment, Jayden would tell the other officers the vampire was a dead body and slap on the silver handcuffs when they weren't looking.

The sergeant agreed to pull two officers from patrol and bring in two more on overtime. It would put them over budget for the week, but neither Tig nor the council would object to the cost—not when they were so close to a real break.

When the extra help arrived, Jayden deployed two policemen to guard the back door, and he took two with him to the front.

He knocked in case the Cutter had returned while he put the plan in motion. No answer.

"Okay, cover me," Jayden told the two at his back. He squatted and, using a lock pick kit, had the door open in a snap.

"Police," he called out as he led the way, gun drawn.

No one was in the living room or kitchen. Both rooms were visible from the front door. The bedroom and adjoining bathroom were empty as well.

The place was spotless. Wearing nitrile gloves, he carefully searched through the bureau drawers and clothes closet. No paper, no mail, no bullets—nothing to tell them whether they had the right person.

It felt *wrong*. He had the sense no one lived there. Even the paper shredder bin next to the computer desk was empty. But the air wasn't stale. Someone had been there recently.

Should he put a team on surveillance? Watch the place twenty-four seven?

The street out front was narrow and filled with parked cars on both sides. If the Cutter was as careful as this apartment indicated, an observation van—even one camouflaged as "Ready Plumbers"—might tip him off.

And that was assuming they'd find a place close-by to park the van.

No, remote surveillance would work better. He called the station annex again and found out the department's electronics specialist was on vacation.

Damn.

Then it hit him. He phoned Ari. "Your résumé listed an expertise in electronic surveillance. Ever do any covert work?"

"Why do you ask?"

"We've found the Carlyle Cutter's apartment in Mordida. I want to put cameras inside."

"Ooh, sounds like fun. Yeah, I'm up for the job."

Jayden read off the address. "How long until you can be here?"

"I need to grab a few supplies."

"There's a kit ready for you at the police annex. Can you swing by there to get it?"

"Done deal. I'll bring along a few toys of my own, too."

Twenty minutes later, Ari walked into the apartment. "This is so cool—a serial killer's home. Who'd-a thought." He dropped two bags on the living room floor. "So, video, audio?"

"Both." Jayden handed him gloves to put on. "But we need to be fast and get out of here quickly. I've got officers posted at the street corners—they'll radio if they see anyone coming. There's no car registered to this apartment with the DMV, so we don't have a license plate number yet."

"Call me the speed demon," Ari said with a laugh. "We'll be out of here in ten minutes tops."

Jayden was impressed—Ari did fast work. He set a contact alarm on each door. Then he hid four cameras: one aimed at the living room front door, another at the desk near the back door, the third in the bedroom, and the fourth one outside under the carport.

"No electricity out here." Ari fastened the camera to a beam. "You'll need to change the brick every two days."

"Brick?"

Ari handed him a black cylinder. "An extended battery. Camera plugs into this here." He took back the battery and strapped it to the beam. "It transmits to a Wi-Fi dongle I connected to the modem. The dongle bypasses the modem's password. We can watch over the internet."

"Great. As soon as you test the transmission, we can go."

"Done." Ari held out his phone and slid through a view from each camera. "And if you leave the browser open to this page, the program will transmit an alarm when he opens the door. What about the landline? Want to bug it too?"

"There isn't one. We should go."

"Super. Anytime you need help, give me a ring. This was a blast." Ari waved goodbye and left.

Jayden locked the back door and worked his way carefully through each room, making sure everything was as they found it, the tiny cameras hidden, the lenses not blocked.

Satisfied, he shut the front door and, using the lockpicks, turned the deadbolt. He tried the door.

Locked.

He waved the other officers back to their cars and instructed one pair to establish a rotation. They'd wait at the coffee shop about three blocks away. If the door alarm triggered, the team could return in under two minutes.

His chest filled with pride. Tig was going to be so happy.

As he drove back, he pondered how the rest of the Hill would react if they captured the Cutter because of his work today. Haley's suggestion threaded through his mind. He wasn't interested in running for the council seat. But on the other hand, if he accepted the nomination, he could use the capture in his campaign literature. That would impress them. Hard to argue he was unqualified if he pulled off that coup.

Chapter 28

Tuscany Bay Resort, San Diego—at dusk

Henry opened his eyes and reached for the knives at his hip, curling his fingers around the handles. Darkness. Where was he?

"Henry, are you awake?" Cerissa asked excitedly.

The hotel. San Diego. He was in his sleep protector: a lightproof full-body suit. He uncurled his fingers from around the knife handles at his side.

The bed moved. "Henry?"

He grabbed the zipper and rose, peeling off the protective suit from his arms. It zipped over his head like a body bag, but the similarities ended there, as it had sleeves, sewn-in gloves, and knife sheathes attached to the outside.

Cerissa was kneeling on the bed next to him, wearing a tank top and shorts. What was she doing in his room?

"*Cariña*, I've asked you not to sleep with me."

"I wasn't sleeping. I've got news."

He accepted the pouch of warm blood she handed him and took a sip. "Still, please wait until I wake."

"But with the crystal in your arm, you can't injure me. When are you going to get over your fear?"

"Never." He had every reason to be afraid. He knew what he was capable of when startled awake. He'd never forgive himself if he ever *tried* to hurt Cerissa—even if the crystal stopped him from doing so.

He took another sip from the pouch. "Now what was so important you disregarded my request?"

"We found where Jim Jones preaches."

He raised one eyebrow. "That is good news. How did you find him?"

"I stationed two Lux colleagues at the PO box. The church's secretary came by to collect the mail, and they followed her to the location."

"Where?"

"A small church not too far from here. He's a guest preacher this week. His sermon is at nine."

Henry ran a hand through his loose hair, trying to figure out what to do. "I'm booked to meet with the owner of Fine Fabulous Wines tonight. She's our biggest distributor in the region." He couldn't let Cerissa go alone to New Path. "I'll come up with an excuse to cancel."

"Don't call off your dinner." She squeezed his hand, her alluring eyes looking at him intently. "I can go by myself."

"No, you will not."

"Then I'll take Zeke."

"I would prefer you didn't," he said, a little too strongly, and regretted it immediately. To cover up his reaction, he finished his drink in two gulps, rolled off the bed, and stepped out of his sleep protector, leaving him wearing a pair of black boxer shorts.

She took the empty pouch from him. "You have no reason to be concerned. He's just here as a bodyguard."

"But he doesn't view it the same way. He believes he has a chance with you. He told me so last night." Zeke had said more than that, but now was not the time to share what happened with Sarah. Henry suppressed the crystal, cutting off the fear rising in him. "I don't want him alone with you. I don't want you to have to rebuff his advances."

He folded his sleepwear into a neat square and slipped it into the dresser drawer.

"Zeke's not going to do anything," she said from behind him. "We'll be fine."

Henry's throat tightened. He couldn't tell her about his conversation with Zeke, and he couldn't risk the cowboy telling her about Sarah. No matter what Zeke promised, he had no scruples—he'd say one thing and do another.

"I forbid it," Henry said, his fear spiking. "You are never to be alone with Zeke." He strode to the bathroom to shower and get ready to go with her.

"Forbid?" she repeated, her voice rising. "Stop right there. You don't get to give me orders and then walk away."

Her anger broke through the crystal, marked by a cold chill encasing his spine. He halted by the bathroom door and counted to ten. His fear had led him astray.

He turned to face her. "I'm sorry, *cariña*. When it comes to Zeke, I'm not rational."

She sighed and crossed to where he stood, resting her hands on his naked chest. "If you don't want Zeke to go with me, I can go by myself. All I'm going to do is record the service. Once we have video of Jim Jones, we should be able to identify what community he's affiliated with, so we can figure out if he's connected to the VDM's assassination attempts."

"I don't like the idea of you going alone. Can you take one of your colleagues instead?"

"I'll arrange to have one watch from outside the church." She swept her hands down his chest and stopped at his waist. "Don't worry. I'll be okay. I'll be armed. And if there's a problem, I can flash back to the Enclave."

He gazed into her beautiful eyes. Would she really be safe on her own? He wanted to believe her. "And how would you explain your sudden disappearance?"

"I wouldn't need to. Trust me. I know what I'm doing."

"Still..." He wrapped his arms around her and pulled her close. She smelled so good that all he wanted to do was drag her to bed and devour her.

"Henry, we promised the Protectors. I can't waste this opportunity."

"Then I'll postpone my business dinner."

It was the only way. They would go together, and he would rebook with Fine Fabulous Wines at a later date.

She stepped back, breaking their embrace, and shook a finger at him. "Now you're doing that vampire overprotective thing. There is no need for you to cancel tonight. I'll be fine. I'm just going there to observe."

He looked down at the floor.

She's right. She isn't mortal; she doesn't need me to protect her.

He sighed. "If you insist."

"I do."

He took her in his arms again and held her tight. "All right. Please be careful."

"I will, but you have nothing to worry about."

Henry took a quick shower, letting the hot water pelt his face to rinse off the shaving cream. He'd died with a full beard and had to plane it off each night. After shaving, he had aged himself. An inconvenience, but one he had to tolerate if he was going to blend in with mortals.

He turned off the water, grabbed a towel and caught a glimpse of himself in the mirror.

Merde, am I acting like the way I look? An insecure old man?

Cerissa was right. He was being both overly protective and overly possessive. It was time to let go of his need to control everything and trust her.

Trust.

He finished toweling himself dry. But what about Rolf? Could he count on Rolf to abstain from hunting? Henry only wanted what was best for his friend.

Should I check on him before I leave?

The bedside clock read twenty minutes to eight—plenty of time to make a call to Rolf. Henry parked himself on the bed's edge and hit speed dial.

"So how is your trip?" Rolf answered.

"I'm having dinner with Danielle tonight."

"Good. Pitch her on my idea."

"Will do."

"Anything else? Karen is waiting for me."

"I wanted to ask how you are doing. Are you feeling all right?"

"Feeling?"

"Yes, did the blood Cerissa give you help?"

"So that's why you called." There was a beat of silence. "*Scheiße*, Henry. I'm not hunting."

"I know. I just—"

"Damn it, it's not your problem. If I tell you I'm not hunting, I'm not. Leave it alone."

Henry cleared his throat, feeling like he was trying to drink blood from a shattered glass. "All right. But I wasn't doubting you, and I'm sorry I upset you. I only meant to see if you needed anything."

"I am *fine*, as I said. But I'm growing tired of your holier-than-thou attitude. I'm not the ticking time bomb you think I am."

"Now, Rolf, you're not being fair."

"I'm not? Talk about fair. You're treating me like you don't trust me."

Trust. Was the problem his and not Rolf's?

Henry rubbed his eyes, resisting the thought. He couldn't be the problem. This wasn't all about him.

No. With Rolf, there is a reason I'm worried.

"I do trust you," he finally said. "But you must remember, I covered for you for years. It's not an easy habit to break."

"And whose fault is that? No one asked you to cover for me. You stuck your nose into my business because you didn't believe I could keep my hunting legal. Well, I did. I only hunted outside treaty areas. And don't forget you went hunting with me sometimes. So, don't get all condescending with me. You may not have the problem I do, but you still partook in it."

He hadn't meant to sound disapproving. And while he'd done a little grazing, he hadn't *hunted*. There was a difference. "Rolf—"

"There's a word for you, too, you know. It's *codependent*. An enabler. I've been learning more about this, and that's what you are. You're no better than I am—you've always been attracted to addicts."

The arrow hit too close to the mark. A deep unease settled in Henry's belly. "I know you're struggling with this, but you have no right to be nasty with me."

"Nasty? Well, just chalk it up to my withdrawal. Because, despite your fears, *I am not hunting.*"

The Tuscany Bay Resort's steakhouse had a five-star rating. The restaurant had the added benefit of carrying Vasquez Müller Winery's premium Cabernet. Ten minutes after his conversation with Rolf, Henry met Danielle Foster at the maître' d's desk, and they were seated in a private, glass-enclosed room with a view of the pool on one side and the elegant lobby on the other.

He offered Danielle the chair facing the pool; he took the seat across from her. She chose the filet mignon, and he did likewise, ordering his *very* rare.

He could eat food if he wanted to, but it tasted like cardboard—or something worse, depending upon what he ate—and his body couldn't digest anything except blood. He'd regurgitate his meal later—not a pleasant process. But a few times a year he made the sacrifice for business dinners like this one.

His stomach churned uncomfortably in anticipation. Or was the churning caused by his argument with Rolf? Their harsh exchange had left him uneasy.

Stop it. I need to focus.

Shaking himself out of his malaise, he poured the wine.

Danielle made a show of swirling and sniffing her glass. "Excellent," she said, after taking a sip. "Dark cherry and blackberry notes with a hint of spice—nice finish, very smooth. You've done well with this one."

"Thank you." His own glass held only an inch of wine—wasting a good vintage on him was a sin. "We hope to expand distribution next year to more restaurants."

"You'll need to reduce the wholesale price to entice them." She raised her glass and took another sip.

They discussed his ideas on how to accomplish his goal. The waiter interrupted, serving the meal. As they began eating, Henry told Danielle about their plan to expand internet distribution—hoping to partner with her company. Consumers would order through Fine Fabulous Wines' website and Vasquez Müller would ship the product.

"Rolf thought if we could take advantage of direct shipping to the public, we could improve our market share."

"Interesting. And how is Rolf?"

"He is well."

At least, Henry hoped that was true. He cut into his steak, speared a repulsive bite, and raised the almost-raw meat to his lips.

Over Danielle's shoulder, he looked out to the lobby. Cerissa's beautiful profile caught his eye. She hurried from the elevators, lovely in casual pants and a lacey, long-sleeved blouse, her high heels tapping across the hotel's marble floor. He glanced at his Patek Philippe watch. Eight thirty. She was on her way to the church to record Jim Jones preaching.

The steak sat in his mouth like spoiled blood, and he resisted the urge to retch. He said a short prayer for Cerissa's safety while he sucked juices from the disgusting meat.

Cerissa had almost reached the door when Zeke joined her, grabbing her arm.

Hot flames crawled across Henry's skin, and his teeth ground the steak to a pulp. What was Zeke doing touching her? The two of them discussed something, but they were too far away for Henry to hear. Through the crystal's connection, he caught a sense of her nervousness and something else—he thought the emotion was…impatience?

A moment later, she pulled away from the cowboy, who followed her outside to the rental car parked at the valet curb. Zeke got into the driver's seat, and she took the passenger's side.

Henry forced himself to swallow. Despite his wishes, she was going with Zeke.

Why?

The voice in his head offered only one reason: she had *asked* Zeke to go with her, and she was impatient with the cowboy because he met her inside, where Henry could see.

Whether because her colleague couldn't watch her or because she'd felt less safe after all, she had turned to Zeke rather than Henry. At the thought, acidlike jealousy shot through his veins.

Chapter 29

New Path Church, San Diego—twenty minutes later

Cerissa took a seat in the church's back pew. Zeke removed his black cowboy hat and motioned with it for her to scoot over, to make room for him to sit. She frowned angrily at him.

Why didn't I rip the key fob out of his hand?

He had stood there in the hotel lobby, dangling it from his finger, refusing to relinquish the car key, leaving her with no choice but to take him along.

She was getting tired of bossy vampires. The way he'd blindsided her in the lobby ground at her. Had Henry seen them together? Probably. She had sensed anger and jealousy through their connection.

Well, she'd deal with that when she returned to the hotel. Right now, completing her mission mattered the most. She couldn't abandon her plan—too much was at risk, and her guilt over her past delay wouldn't let her.

Zeke waved his hat in a "shoo" motion again. She slid over to let him in and scanned the room, pointedly ignoring him.

The church was a humble rectangle with an open-beamed pitched ceiling. Dark walnut pews in two sections filled the room but were half-empty. Raised choir stands sat behind a matching pulpit.

Her lenses confirmed which parishioners were vampires by measuring their lower body temperatures and pulse rates. The few mortals sprinkled through the audience sat close to a vampire—probably their mates.

Above the entry door at the back, someone had covered the word "Methodist" with white paint, but a ghost image bled through and rust marks stained the ceiling. The roof had seen better days.

Based on the sign out front, multiple congregations, along with New Path, now shared the old building. The shabbiness jarred with Cerissa's mental picture of the VDM. Whoever was behind the movement had a lot of money—enough to pay assassin fees. Nothing about the run-down house of worship made her think its inhabitants were wealthy, let alone that vampires determined to dominate the world ran the church.

She read the half-page program. Entitled *A New Path for You, Reverend Jim Jones, Guest Speaker*, it repeated the message from the lobby flyer.

A tall, lanky man—a vampire—strolled to the pulpit, wearing a crimson vestment robe. His light red hair was trimmed short and his freckles stood out on his pale white skin. He adjusted the microphone. The holder made an amplified squeak.

"Howdy, y'all, I'm Jim Jones."

He looked like England's Prince Harry, except Reverend Jones had a handlebar mustache and a distinct Texas drawl, stretching out each syllable as he spoke. Her lenses didn't identify him—his dossier must not be in her database.

He turned to a cluster of vampires in the audience. "Paul, it's great to see your group here tonight. Everything goin' well out in your territory?"

"Good for now, reverend. But we're having trouble getting fresh supplies. The local council won't let us hunt, or even graze."

"I understand, my friends." Jones looked to another section. "And how about you folks?"

There were nods in the audience. "Same story, reverend."

"That's just pitiful. I've heard the same thing across this great country of ours." He looked in Zeke's direction. "To the newcomers, welcome to our meetin'."

Zeke swiveled toward Cerissa, an expression of "what do I do?" on his face. She elbowed him.

"Ah, thanks mightily, reverend," he called out, his Midwestern twang less rolling than the Texan's. He held up his hat, acknowledging Jones. "Glad to be here, to see what you got to say."

"Well, my friends, here's my message for tonight. I've been traveling across our country, even dipped my toes into Canada and Mexico, and I hear the same questions over and over again. Why are we eatin' stale leftovers? Why are we scrounging for supplies? Why are we hiding? Why aren't we in charge of this rodeo? And the answer I get isn't good enough: we might *scare* them if they find out what we are."

Laughter rippled through the room.

"It's high time we scared them." He gripped the podium's sides. "Back when I was *mortal*, well, I learned a few hard lessons early. I was eight when my pappy came back from the War Between the States missing both legs."

Cerissa cringed. Having his father return from the war crippled must have been rough on Jones as a young child.

Pity began to color her view, but then she tamped down her feelings—this may be the man behind Nina's and Kim's murders, the man who tried to kill Henry.

He would receive no sympathy from her.

"I had to step up and be the man of the family," he continued. "We moved to Texas, and I went to work on a cattle ranch, sending money home to my ma and pa. And that's why I saw firsthand the range wars. Men putting barbed-wire fences where they didn't belong, stealing the choicest grazin' and waterin' pastures. Them big ranchers were as greasy as fried lard. I tell ya, how's a man supposed to care for his cattle if the best pastures are cut off? The land's supposed to be for everyone to share."

Had he never heard of the *tragedy of the commons*? Ranchers would enlarge their herds and graze their livestock in common areas—fields shared by the entire community—until nothing was left but dirt. Without regulation, greed would run wild until shared public resources were destroyed, leaving nothing for anyone.

Jones leaned his forearms against the podium, moving closer to the mic like he was having an intimate conversation.

"I learned an important lesson," he said, lowering his voice. "Those who try to take our God-given rights, the right to graze freely, to do a little hunting, well, them there men are so low they'd steal the nickels off a dead man's eyes."

He chuckled and smiled, like he'd made a joke. "Yup, you ever wake up and have to peel off those coins? Strangest sensation I ever did feel."

The congregation laughed with him. Then his face took on a serious look and he stood straighter. "As I was sayin', they'd steal the nickels off a dead man's eyes. Just like those boys who wrote the treaty. They're so crooked you couldn't find a straight edge among the lot of them." He stuck a finger in the air. "But that's the past. I'm a lookin' to the future."

He scanned the crowd again. "Now, how many of you good people don't belong to a *treaty community*?"

He spat out the last two words like they tasted bad in his mouth. Hands shot up in the audience—most of the vampires present.

"And how many of you have saved up the buy-in price?"

All the hands dropped.

"Yup, just what I thought. They've made it so only the *rich* can join and hogtied all y'all so you can't make enough money to buy in. *They* may've stolen, cheated, and lied in the past, but no, you can't."

Cerissa shook her head. From what she'd learned, the treaty communities hadn't been founded on theft. The communities had been founded on hard work and preservation of capital.

"So," Jones continued, "with the deadline looming, what're ya gonna do? Wait for them to come after you, put a bounty on your heads? Or are you going to resist? 'Cause if you're willin' to stand up for yourselves, I may have a way to solve your problem."

He opened his hands and swept them across the congregation. "I'm here to bring God's vision to earth. A new way of living where all your needs are taken care of, where we take back our right to graze the land. No fear of hunger, or of surviving on meager, stale…*rations*."

A guy in the front row pumped his fist. "You preach it, brother."

"A vision of life where we don't have to join no *treaty community*. Where we've come out of the shadows and taken our rightful place. Where we get to *convert* more people, make them like us, without worrying about those doomsayers."

A shiver ran along Cerissa's spine. Didn't he understand what would happen? If they made more vampires, they'd soon outnumber their food supply. The tragedy of the commons all over again.

"Now," Jones said, waving his hand dismissively. "I've heard all the reasons to keep us in hidin'. They'll hunt us down and kill us if they find out. There'll be chaos. There'll be famine. It'll all go to hell in a handbasket."

He raised a finger. "Now let me take those one at a time. Done right, we'll be in charge before they know what hit 'em. And chaos is good, my friends. Chaos will keep them in their homes, out of our way, afraid of us. There'll be plenty of time to calm them later and show how the new world order is to their benefit. What we can *offer* 'em."

An "amen" was shouted by the congregation.

"And famine? That's a bunch of hooey to keep those rich boys in power, the ones who wrote the treaty.

"So tonight, I bring the good news: you're not alone. Others like us want what we want. And you are the missionaries who will make our vision happen, the chosen who first saw the light. And to those who see the light first, well, there will be rewards aplenty.

"Now, you keep doin' your mission, talkin' up our cause, findin' those who might be of a mind to agree with us and bring 'em here. I'll be back in a month with another message. So keep the faith and spread the word!"

The audience started applauding. Cerissa joined in politely, while cringing internally. With his old-boy charisma, Jones could charm the venom from a cobra.

A vampire stopped in the aisle by Zeke. She wore jeans and a t-shirt—a little less formal than most of the vampires in the room. The woman laid a hand on his shoulder and leaned in close to whisper. "Jim would like to speak with you after the service. Would you come with me?"

Cerissa stood when Zeke did.

"Not her," the woman added with a derisive sniff. "She can wait here."

"Well, now, she goes where I go," Zeke said. "I'm not leavin' her here alone."

The woman eyeballed Cerissa and looked back at Zeke. "What's the problem? You henpecked or something?"

He kept his hat in one hand and dragged his fingers through his honey-blonde hair. "It's like this, ma'am. I don't know no one here. I don't trust no one here." He motioned with his hat to the rest of the room. "So, I'm not leavin' her alone with the lot of them. If the reverend wants to speak with me, she's a-comin' with me."

The woman pursed her lips, like she was considering something. Finally, she said, "All right. Your mate can join us."

Cerissa didn't correct her. As much as the woman's bad assumption irritated her, Zeke had played the situation right. She followed the woman to a shabby office. The square wooden desk had to be sixty years old, and the folding chairs for guests weren't much newer.

New Path didn't waste its money on furniture.

But it didn't make sense. Most vampires had multiple lifetimes to build a fortune and wouldn't be impressed by this show of poverty.

A side door opened, and Jones strode in, shucking his robe. "Land's sake, it sure is nice to see a new face in the crowd." He stopped in front of Zeke, offering his hand. "Reverend Jim Jones. Call me Jim."

"Zeke Cannon. And this here is Dr. Cerissa Patel."

She offered her hand, and the reverend swept his gaze over her, his hazel eyes becoming black, and a leer formed on his lips.

Disgust slithered down her spine.

What a pig.

Ignoring the offered handshake, Jones looked back at Zeke. She dropped her arm to her side. *Damn.* So much for using a light touch of aura to influence Jones. With Zeke in the room, she couldn't let her aura out—he tended to overreact to it.

"I can see why you want to show her off," Jones said. "You must be happy as a clam at high tide. But I'm sure she'd be more comfortable waiting outside while you and I palaver."

Cerissa ground her teeth but said nothing.

Zeke rolled his hat's brim. "She's not my mate."

Great. There goes my plan.

Jones sniffed in her direction. "But she's mated to someone. Hmm. Someone with a higher rank than you got?"

"We don't got rank on the Hill, we're all equals."

Cerissa narrowed her eyes. *Yeah, unless you're mortal.*

Jones took the chair behind the desk and waved for Zeke to sit. "So, you're from that fine community. I haven't been to visit you folks yet." He settled back and crossed his hands behind his head. "So, who's the little gal hooked up with?"

"You'll have to ask her. She's the one you need to talk with. She wanted to come here, not me."

Really, Zeke?

She wanted to throttle him, but instead swiftly ticked through ways to avoid Jones's question.

Lie? Doing so might not go over well. He'd eventually find out.

Pivot? Jones seemed pretty determined to get an answer. How could she distract him?

The flyer.

She removed the handout from her purse, held up the page, and kept her face friendly. "I wanted to ask you about this." She pointed to the sentence: *We've found the answers.* "I'm curious what answers you're offering."

Jones ignored her. He came forward in his chair, placing his hands on the desk, and directed a puzzled look at Zeke. "You let a mortal do your talking? Her mate must be a big muckety-muck."

"If you don't stop saying that, I'm going to knock your teeth into the back of your throat."

Jones laughed a good-old-boy laugh. "Well then, who's she mated to?"

Cerissa sat up straight. So much for being incognito. "I'm Leopold Leidecker's envoy, and Enrique Bautista Vasquez's mate."

"Well, howdy do. We got royalty in the house. I'm cooking on a front burner today." He looked at her. "What can I do for you, missy?"

"Please call me Dr. Patel." She flattened the flyer on his desk. "Like I said, I'm curious. What changes to the treaty are you proposing?"

He grinned. "Changes? We ain't gonna change the damn thing—we're gonna throw it out."

"An interesting proposition," she said, smiling at him. If she pretended to go along, she might have better luck than challenging him. "What's in it for mortals if you do? I mean, will you lift the ban on making new vampires?"

He laughed deeply. "Now, if you weren't mated to Mr. Bautista, well, I might just tell you. You'd probably be interested in what we plan to offer, but your mate won't be."

"Why not?"

"'Cause the treaty was his idea. So I don't think he'll cotton to our plans."

"Then you're preparing to go to war?"

"Well, *Doc-tor Pay-tell*," he said, mispronouncing her name, "let me set something straight. I'm not a violent man. I've seen enough violence in my life. I don't need to lead anyone who wants to use his fists. We're all about a peaceful change to the treaty, a *voluntary* transfer of power. Not like the man you're mated to. He started a war between our people to keep things his way. To keep folks starved and our numbers small—so he could stay in control."

She crossed her arms. "And if you throw out the treaty, what will replace it?"

"Now that's between me and others like me." He relaxed back in his chair. "Mortals don't got a say in what we do, but there'll be a special place for those who follow us."

"And those who don't?" she asked. "What happens to them?"

He shrugged. "Why, nothin'. Why should anything happen to them?" He raised his hand like he was taking an oath. "As God is my witness, since becoming what I am, I've never killed any mortal, and I never will." He paused. "Can your mate say the same?"

Yeah, right. Jones's claim rang false. Almost all vampires had killed after they were turned, unless their makers kept tight reins on them. Henry had admitted to taking human life early in his existence when the lust for blood overwhelmed reason. But how would Jones know that? It sounded like something more.

"What's that supposed to mean?" she asked.

"I hear things. And from the look on ole Zeke's face, he's heard the same."

"What things?"

"You should ask that mate of yours. Now, if y'all would excuse me, moonlight's burning and I have others to meet with. The door's this way."

CHAPTER 30

SIERRA ESCONDIDA POLICE STATION—SAME NIGHT

Tig stared at the video feeds from the Carlyle Cutter's apartment. Jayden had sent her the link, and she had monitored the four cameras since rising. Nothing so far. She checked the "alerts" screen—no entry, no motion detected.

She had burst with pride upon seeing Jayden's report when she woke for the night. He'd done a great job marshaling resources and putting his plan into action. They were close to a break—she could feel it in her bones.

But I can't sit here all night staring at the Cutter's digs.

Too bad the apartment's lease agreement was a dead end. A company registered in Switzerland had rented it—the same one on the credit card—and no DMV records were associated with the address.

No mail was delivered during the day, either. The Cutter probably received paperless bills, but there was no computer in the apartment. Cables lay across the desk, disconnected from a wall-mounted monitor and a modem. Maybe he used a laptop to connect to the screen and took it with him.

Jayden had tried finding information on the Swiss company, but so far, no luck. Aside from its address and corporate registration, On the Vine, Inc. didn't exist.

She took one more glance at the monitor. No change. The Cutter still hadn't returned home.

Back to work.

Tig spread the bagged evidence from the motel on the squad room worktable and stacked the reports in a neat pile next to it. The fingerprints on the stuff they'd found matched Pascala's. No trace evidence on the box of silver bullets, and the note with Abigale's name was clean too.

The only exception: the wadded tissue with blood. She had taken the tissue to Mordida's police lab, and they were running it for DNA. Pascala may have cut himself shaving, so she gave them a sample of Pascala's blood for a comparison. They already had the Cutter's DNA on file.

Jayden had dusted the doors and other hard surfaces, hoping to find fingerprints. Plenty of prints, but none leading them to a suspect. Motel rooms were notoriously difficult to clear. The prints he found could belong to people unrelated to the crime, like prior guests and the maids who serviced the room.

Tig ran the fingerprints through V-Trak as well as all the major criminal registries. No new hits.

She tapped her fingers on the worktable's laminate surface.

Last night had been her final interview with Pascala. The district attorney in Mordida would prosecute him for Nina's murder.

Of course, Tig had had a free feed at Pascala's expense—she had to take his blood in order to control his memory and make him forget "Amazons" existed.

Amazons, indeed.

She had laughed so hard when she came across his theory in the videos that Jayden had rushed to her side, concerned she was having a fit. She smiled at the memory—she now understood what mortals meant by ROFL and LMAO.

Before Pascala was taken away, Abigale was given an opportunity to speak to him. Whatever the founder said had left him looking panicked.

Tig shook her head.

Not my problem.

Ari wasn't able to do much with Pascala's phone. The text messages were interesting. There were two separate queues of texts, each denoted as private caller, suggesting two masked phones. A few incoming calls from one private number matched the dates Pascala met with the Cutter. Was the Cutter using two phones for a reason? It seemed strange.

Jayden had already sent a subpoena to the phone company to track down the private numbers. Probably burner phones. She was getting antsy about Ari's unsanctioned searches, concerned his work would be traced back to the Hill, and had instructed him not to hack the phone company. Safer to subpoena the info.

The serial number on the rifle was a dead end. Pascala probably paid for the Nam Hunter 900 in cash—three thousand dollars was missing from the fifty thousand he had in the closet.

The registry of stolen guns listed the rifle. The theft took place two years ago. She assigned a detective from the police annex to research it, but she suspected the rifle had changed hands many times and been sold through an unlicensed gun show. Tracking it wouldn't be worth the effort.

Next step on her checklist: identify the source of the silver bullets used. She changed screens on her laptop and browsed through the photos Jayden had downloaded, finding the ammunition box.

She emailed the photos to her bullet manufacturer. Even with the time zone difference in Montana, Chet would likely be awake. Her phone rang moments later.

"Hey, Tig. What are these photos about?"

"Do you recognize the packaging? Any of the other dealers use that kind of box?"

"Why?"

"We had another shooting."

"Anyone hurt?"

"One of Abigale's mates is dead."

"I'm real sorry to hear that. Please give her our condolences."

"I'll pass it along," Tig replied. "I was hoping you could help us track down who made the rifle ammo. We captured the shooter and recovered the box."

"Well, they used a standard plastic box, you can buy them from any online gun dealer." He sounded apologetic. "I don't recognize the ammo style, either, from the photo. Ship some my way and I'll take a closer look and let you know if I find anything."

"Will do."

"But I did learn something you might be interested in."

She had called him weeks ago after the first attack on Yacov. The perps had used handguns filled with silver bullets, and Chet hadn't recognized who made those either. But he'd volunteered to keep his eyes open for anything leading to the person who manufactured them.

"Go on," she said.

"Remember I mentioned there was a bulletin board for writers?"

"Sure." His wife wrote dragon romances. Tig enjoyed them—not that she'd ever admit to it in public.

"Pauline got me access. There was this one thread between three posters who were trying to figure out how to create silver ammo for rifles. I contacted one of the folks who posted. He was a writer who was researching the issue for a friend of his—another writer."

"Go on."

"The second poster wrote werewolf novels. Pauline has met both writers—they go way back." Chet paused. "But the third guy, no one knew him. He was the one who started the chain about three months ago."

"Shortly before the shootings on the Hill began."

"I thought you'd make the connection."

"Were you able to find out a name or location for the third poster?"

"Nope. Dead end. Pauline registered under her pseudonym to get us on the bulletin board, but the moderator wouldn't give me the time of day. You might have better luck getting the website to cough up the real name."

"Please email me the login information and links to the posts."

"Consider it done," Chet agreed, and said goodbye.

The station door buzzed. "Jayden," Tig called out. "I'm back here."

He had texted her earlier—he'd gone out on a dinner run. Entering the squad room, he carried a white bag from his favorite diner in one hand and a large coffee in the other.

Tig kissed him. "Great job on the Cutter's apartment—smart idea to put in surveillance gear. And here I thought I couldn't love you any more than I already do."

He spread his arms and puffed out his chest. "Hey, you're supposed to love me for my ripped body, not my mind."

"It will have to be both."

He hugged her despite his hands being encumbered with a coffee cup and bag. It felt good.

After another kiss, he sat down and unwrapped his French dip sandwich. "One other thing," Tig said. "Who knows about the surveillance?"

"Ari and the officers at the substation. I didn't file a report with the council. Figured you'd want to do it. And no reason to loop in Liza unless we need her to pull a surveillance shift tonight."

"Agreed. Let's keep this a tight secret for now, and I'll wait until we have something definite to report to the council. Thanks."

He went back to eating, and she resumed reviewing the evidence. Her mind wandered to something Liza had reported. Certain community members wanted the council to either increase the height of the wall or put concertina wire along the top. Why didn't people understand that a wall only kept out honest people? Bad guys would always find a way around it. They'd use a tall ladder to get over, or a tunnel to go under.

And who wanted to live behind a wall that made their community look like a prison? The wall trapped them in as much as it kept anyone out.

Still, as soon as she had time, she'd go over the contractor proposals to install surveillance cameras along the wall. That was one security measure worth doing.

A short time later, an email *dinged* into her inbox. She opened Chet's message and clicked on the link to the discussion thread. He had included Pauline's password.

"Got something?" Jayden asked.

"Chet thinks 'SilverSmith' could be the source of ammo for the shooters."

He set his French dip aside, wiped his hands on a napkin, and came over to her. His warm presence hovered near her shoulder as she scrolled through the online conversation.

"What about the other two?" he asked.

"They're legit. We can always run them later, but I thought we'd start with the obvious one first."

"Works for me," he agreed. "Let me see what I can find out about the website." He swapped places with her and conducted a few searches, swiftly finding the website's owner. "We're in luck. They're in California, which will make serving a warrant easier."

"I'll call Marcus and ask him to get one signed," Tig said.

"Let's try the easy way first. I'll email the owner of the website and ask for the registration and IP address of the 'SilverSmith.' See if that leads us to a brick and mortar address." Jayden sent the email. "Anything else you need before I finish my dinner?"

"Go ahead. I'll read through the blotter. Can I have my computer back?"

He slid the laptop over in her direction and moved back to his seat at the other end of the squad room table, away from the evidence she had spread out, and picked up his sloppy sandwich, the *au jus* dripping on the wrapper as he focused on his iPad.

She returned to looking through the reports and was halfway through when Jayden interrupted her. "Hey, Tig, look at this."

"Got something?"

He took the last bite of his sandwich and wiped his fingers. "Yeah," he said, tapping the screen. "The website owner gave us everything without a warrant."

"Great. What do you have?"

"The name 'SilverSmith' registered under, as well as his IP address. That's all the moderator collects."

"At least it's more than we had."

"Yeah. The name's Darby Dennis."

"Can you trace the IP address?"

"Already on it."

She used her own computer to run the name in the system—no hits in V-Trak, and the criminal database located a few men by the same name, but they were all out of state. The IP address was the best way to find the Darby Dennis they wanted.

After a few minutes, Jayden grumbled, "Good news, bad news."

"What?"

"Darby accessed the bulletin board over a commercial internet provider, so we have to obtain the name and address of the registered user from them." He wadded up the bag his sandwich had come in and tossed the paper ball to the trash can across the room. Three points. "The bad news—they're notorious for fighting requests from police agencies."

She shrugged. "Where are they based?"

"Florida."

"Shit." The location made serving the warrant more difficult. The internet provider would argue a California warrant wasn't good there. She would need a local police department to write one. "I'll ask Marcus to start on it."

She hit autodial for his number and explained the situation.

"Understood," Marcus said. "I have a few friends in Florida. They may be able to help us."

"Not too late to call them?"

"They're night owls, like us," he said with a laugh.

"Super."

"And if they can't help out, I'll put Nicholas on the matter first thing tomorrow and we'll go through official channels."

"Thanks, Marcus. I appreciate the quick response."

"That's what your friendly town attorney is here for."

"Appreciated." Then something else occurred to her, something she had considered the night Nina was killed. "Hey, one more thing while we're talking. Why haven't you been targeted yet?"

He laughed. "The night is young."

The same cynical thought she had. "Four out of five founders—"

"Have been attacked, yes, I know. I keep thinking about why and watching over my shoulder. But I don't have an answer for you."

"If you come up with anything, call me."

"You may count on it."

"In the meantime, be careful."

She clicked off the call. Things had been tense between her and Marcus during her salary negotiations. He had represented the town council, and his game of hardball had backfired on them. Now that she had her *sizeable* raise, she was glad their working relationship was on an even keel. She made a note of their conversation.

There had to be a reason why Marcus hadn't been attacked yet. She wrote down the order they were attacked in: Yacov, Henry, Méi, and then Abigale.

By age? No, it couldn't be that, Abigale was slightly older than Méi. Or was it the men, and then the women? Again, no—Marcus had been omitted from the men. Was there a reason behind the order aside from opportunity?

The outer door to the station buzzed. She wasn't expecting anyone. "Keep working," she said to Jayden, and went out to determine who had arrived.

Ari was standing in the lobby. He spread his arms wide. "Hey, my favorite police chief. Just the person I wanted to talk to."

She stopped a few feet from him. "You have something to report?"

"I've hit a snag at the winery. A lot of people had admin privileges to the winery's server at the time the Trojan was installed, so I've got a program running to identify which one."

"Can't you tell who was logged in?"

"If only." He looked at the ceiling like he was asking the ancestors to change reality. "Those logs were overwritten years ago. I have to do it the hard way."

"Which is?"

"I'm glad you asked that question," he said, and rolled his shoulders, clearly pleased.

Tig crossed her arms. "The short version."

"Hey, you can't rush genius."

She glared at him. Why did he have to make everything a production?

"Okay. I'll keep it as simple as I can." He brushed his curly hair off his forehead. "Every programmer has coding tells. Not as certain as fingerprints, but they tend to code the same way, the way they sequence, the expressions they use, the way they approach the problem. I'm running a program to compare and categorize all lines of code from the original custom software installation, to put them into 'buckets,' so to speak, to identify lines written by the same coder."

This wasn't good news. "How long will it take?"

"A few days. Fifteen people had access. After my program finishes, I'll be able to winnow down whether one of them wrote the Trojan—based on coding similarities—but I won't have their name. Or I'll be able to conclude someone unknown wrote the code and inserted the back door using a hack or stole an admin user's login. But let's not get ahead of ourselves."

"If you can tell the Trojan was written by someone who had administration access, why won't that give you their identity?"

"No logs to connect a name to. So, I'll have to examine the programmer's level of sophistication, frequency of use of certain coding terms, a lot of things I know to look for, and it would take days to explain—and then I'll check the personnel files to determine who is a likely match."

"Okay, anything else?"

"Yup. I've done everything I can to make your email more secure. Until your council hires a contractor to build your server room, I can't start installing the new hardware. The room needs to be access-restricted and environmentally controlled."

She'd have to write another report to get the expense approved. At least the town had a building contractor pre-vetted. "We could add a room to the police station. Constructing it here would provide the best physical security."

Ari nodded. "Works for me. Anyway, I'm going back to Florida. What I need to do can be done remotely for now. I'll be in touch if I get anything."

Tig saw him out. Frustrating, to have to rely on other people. At least Ari seemed proficient at what he was doing. He'd certainly been handy when Jayden needed help to plant surveillance at the Cutter's apartment.

Hmm. Would he be willing to move to the West Coast? It would be easier when they needed onsite help.

She returned to the squad room. Jayden was looking through the reports. She took her seat, and her phone rang.

"Hi, chief," the caller said.

It was Ynez, the tech from the Mordida crime lab, who'd promised to test the motel blood right away.

"DNA results already?" Tig asked.

"Not anything you can use. Our tests keep coming back as non-human. Not animal, either. We suspected something corrupted the sample, so we recalibrated the machine, but nothing worked. You might send the sample to another lab, just to be sure."

She eyeballed Jayden and shook her head. "Thanks, Ynez. Captain Johnson will pick up the tissue in the morning. Goodnight." She tapped the end button.

"Bad news?" he asked.

"Well, now we know for sure a vampire was in Pascala's motel room."

"But Pascala didn't mention it."

She leaned back in her chair. "He spilled everything else. I doubt he omitted it on purpose. He was likely compelled to forget."

"Too bad we don't have a way to do a DNA match with vampire blood." Jayden flipped the keyboard cover closed on his iPad. "You know, Cerissa offered to help before. Why not let her take a shot at analyzing the sample, see if she can find a way to create a matching system?"

"No way. I won't allow her to take vampire blood to a lab we have no control over."

"She's Henry's mate. She can be trusted."

"I'm not worried about her. What if some uninitiated mortal stumbles across the blood or her results?" Tig shivered at the thought. "I won't be the one responsible for letting news of our kind slip out."

It was bad enough she had to trust the Mordida police lab to run their DNA test. But a research lab filled with inquisitive scientists? No, she couldn't risk going any further. They'd have to find another way to solve this.

Her computer started a high-pitched beeping. *What's that?* She didn't recognize the sound. Then she remembered the surveillance monitor.

She banged on the key, switching the screen. "Jayden, get over here," she said, motioning for him to hurry.

The Cutter had opened the rear door and entered the apartment. He raised his chin and sniffed. His lips turned down at the corners for the briefest of moments, and then he sprang into action, tearing through the place.

Shit. A vampire had been feeding him blood—it was the only way to explain his reaction.

Tig grabbed the nearby radio and keyed the mic. "Unit 2. Suspect is in the apartment. Repeat. Suspect is in the apartment. He entered through the back door. Assume armed and dangerous. Use a silent approach."

"Roger, chief," Unit 2 responded.

On the video feed, the Cutter snatched a bag from the bedroom closet, hurried into the kitchen, and, wearing gloves, opened the cabinet under the sink. He picked up a whiskey bottle—which went into the bag—peeled back the shelf paper, and then lifted out a board and started pulling out documents and what appeared to be bundled money. He stuffed everything into the bag, along with a couple of guns, grabbed the bag's handles, and headed to the rear door.

"Unit 2, what's your status?"

"A block away."

Stopping, the Cutter looked right at the camera lens. He raised his gloved middle finger, flipping Tig the bird, and dodged out the back door.

"Fuck," she said, slamming her fist on the table, bouncing the laptop. "Unit 2, he's going out the rear exit. Repeat—rear exit. He is armed."

Tires squealed over the radio. "Ten-four, chief. Rear exit. Armed."

The carport camera showed a nondescript SUV. The Cutter jumped in and backed out. The license plate was missing from the front and the manufacturer's identification had been pried off. Could be a Ford or a Chevy—they might be able to identify the make based on the grille. As the SUV swung around, the rear plate came in view for a split second, and then he peeled rubber.

"Unit 2, he's eastbound down the alley."

"Ten-four. We're turning in the west entrance now."

Thirty seconds later, Unit 2 sped past.

"Unit 2, report."

"We lost him. We didn't see which way he turned. Do you want to put a chopper in the air?"

"You've lost visual?"

"Ten-four."

"Pick a direction and go. He's driving a black SUV. If you find one in the area, pull it over. He's wearing gloves. Black hair, repeat, black—he's dyed his hair. Hazel-brown eyes, Caucasian, six feet, one-eighty pounds."

Jayden swung the laptop computer around and rewound the video, freezing the screen on the license plate. He captured a still image and enlarged the partial number—it looked like: N8R.

Tig radioed Unit 2 with the information and then phoned Mordida dispatch.

"We are in pursuit of a suspect," she told the dispatch person. "Is your chopper airborne?"

"Negative."

"Any patrol officers in the area of 805 East Rampart Street?"

"Give me a moment, chief."

Tig continued to watch the empty carport.

The dispatch operator came back on the line. "We have an A unit in the area."

A two-person car. "Tell them we're looking for a black SUV, partial California license Nora-Eight-Robert."

"Ten-four."

"Perp is armed and dangerous. Call me back if they find him." She hung up and looked at Jayden. "This close," she said, her fingers inches apart. "We were this close."

"I'm sorry, Tig," he said. "I should have used a surveillance van. I thought the cameras wouldn't tip him off, but I figured he'd notice a van."

"You couldn't have known he's been drinking vampire blood. He sniffed the air and smelled your presence. It's how he knew we were on to him."

Whoever the Cutter was working for had been stupid to let it go that far—most Hill vamps were cautious about feeding mortals their blood except in medical emergencies.

The amount needed to enhance senses came with a high risk of triggering the turn—accidents happened—and with the treaty ban on creating new vampires, the penalty was harsh but necessary: either the maker was put down or the fledgling was.

Tig keyed the radio. "Unit 2, report."

"No sign of the suspect."

"Keep patrolling. He may have gone to ground and will make his move when he thinks our search has cooled down."

"Ten-four."

Jayden rested a hand on her shoulder. "What do you want me to do?"

"Run the partial plate. Cross-check against variations on the Cutter's known aliases. If the SUV isn't registered to the apartment, it has to be registered somewhere." She looked up at him. "Find it."

Chapter 31

City of Mordida—Moments Later

Chuck drove two blocks, turned right, drove two more blocks, and turned right again. No police car in his rearview mirror. He pulled into the carport of another apartment—one he knew was empty because On the Vine had rented it as a backup.

He jumped out, grabbed the car cover, and spread the stiff fabric over the SUV, camouflaging the vehicle, then crawled under the flap, cracked the door enough to slide into the driver's seat, and yanked the door shut.

His heart thumped in his chest as he lifted the handle to recline the seat back, panting in the dark, trying to catch his breath.

That was close.

He would spend the night sleeping here. Odds were the police would give up. Even a door-to-door canvass wouldn't find him.

As much as he hated filth, he had allowed the cover to become dirty and encrusted with all sorts of bird shit. To a clueless cop searching for a killer on the run, his vehicle would look like it had been sitting there a long time.

A glance at his phone—he was overdue to call the President. He slammed the phone down on the console. Their conversation could wait. The asshole never liked bad news.

Resting in the seat, Chuck felt his heart rate begin to slow, and desire crawled under his skin. Last night, he hadn't succeeded in finding a perfect victim. First rule of being a *successful* serial killer: discretion is the better part of wisdom. He never let his craving for a playmate force his hand into doing something stupid.

And last night, none of the potential victims were worth the risk. He had called off the hunt when his phone vibrated—an alarm telling him the police had found his last victim from two nights ago. It would be in the news and his prey would be alert. Better to let them go back to being oblivious to his existence before culling another from the herd.

The duct tape, rope, and plastic sheeting were still in the back of his SUV. If the police caught him with those things, they proved nothing. He hadn't used them in any prior killing. Cops could match the torn end of duct tape to prove it came from a certain roll. Spending extra money for new supplies each time was worthwhile.

But should he get rid of his tools now?

No, at most the stuff was *modus operandi*—a weak link to the prior killings. The police had better evidence of his involvement, if they put it all together. His supplies were meaningless and could stay in the back.

Besides, he just might be able to use them soon.

He clenched and unclenched his whole body, trying to force it to relax. In the past, he had spread out his kills by date and location. But all this stress was ramping up his need. The image of making the first cut kept drifting through his brain, again and again.

He wouldn't let the urge control him. It was just too soon to take the risk, at least not here in Mordida.

Hmm. Now there was a thought. How far away would he have to travel before his potential victims stopped being alert for him?

His phone rang. He jumped, grabbed the phone, and swiped accept.

"What happened?" the President asked. "You missed your call-in time."

Shit. Just whom Chuck didn't want to talk to. "Ah, the Hill figured out where I live. I got out of there before they caught me."

No response. He could almost hear the asshole's anger in his silence. Chuck hadn't bothered to use their business code either, and that probably added to *the President* being pissed.

Fuck him.

"But I got away," Chuck continued. "I'm hidden behind the other apartment. I'll sleep in the car tonight. I figure it'll be safe to move tomorrow."

"How did you slip up?"

It wasn't me.

Chuck gripped his knife in its sheath on his belt, the action soothing. He hadn't made any errors. He was careful to the point of absurdity. "I don't know what happened," he said. "They must have tracked the apartment through the corporation somehow. That's the only way I can think of."

"You better not lie to me, Mr. Director."

"Never. But what do I do now?" He regretted the words as soon as they left his mouth. The last thing he wanted was to be ordered back to the asshole's headquarters.

The President cleared his throat. "As soon as it's safe to move, I want you to go to San Diego."

Chuck sighed with relief. "Who's the target?"

"Beta's there with his girlfriend. The doctor bitch could destroy my plans. She claims she can produce clone blood that's as satisfying as blood from the vein. I thought she'd never get it off the ground, but the grapevine is buzzing about her next presentation."

"Shit." If the President's followers were happy with her product, they might decide to abandon the scheme. "With an increase in supply, they might lift the ban on creating new, ah—"

"Exactly. And they'd quit caring that they can't source the product directly. Both would undermine the shareholders' motives for supporting our hostile takeover."

The asshole was back to using code again. Chuck paused, running his fingers through his hair, and took a moment to translate the jargon. Okay, the "shareholders" had to be vampires who were part of the movement to destroy the treaty and take control.

"So, what's the plan?" They had to do something. Chuck wasn't willing to abandon his year-end bonus. If things went south, the President wouldn't turn him vampire.

"Drive to San Diego, find a place to stay—and for now, keep using the Charlie Roberts identity."

"But our competition figured it out. They might find me if I keep using the name."

"We can take the risk for a few more days."

Yeah, no risk for you, but it's my ass on the line.

"Are you sure?" Chuck asked. "I could use cash. I cleared out the stash before leaving."

"No. Park your SUV in long-term parking and rent a car using the Roberts credit card and ID. Not the abbreviated C. Roberts—the one with the full name."

"But the hotel room? If they find me…"

"Fine. Use a different credit card for the hotel room. But you must use the Charlie Roberts's card for the rental car. This will be the last time. And don't mask the license plate number."

Now that sounded suspicious. Chuck always altered the number. Was the asshole planning to sacrifice him? "Why not?"

"I'll fill you in on my plan when I'm ready for you to know it," the President snapped. "I'll talk with you tomorrow night."

The line went dead. Chuck didn't like that part about using the Charlie card, but at least he didn't have to go back to the asshole's compound. He hated when the President bit him. He hated the sexual rush, the loss of control, the humiliation that always followed the bite.

He pushed the anxiety away and closed his eyes. The image of the first cut floated into his mind's eye again, and he played out the last kill, reliving every knife stroke, breathing faster as the scene neared the end.

Hmm. San Diego. Perhaps a change of location would give him the opportunity to use his tools. A good thing they were still in the back of the SUV. He caressed the knife handle at his waist, anticipating the hunt, envisioning the ease of finding a tourist traveling alone.

By tomorrow night, he might find a new playmate.

CHAPTER 32

TUSCANY BAY RESORT, SAN DIEGO—THIRTY MINUTES LATER

Dessert had been served. Henry declined the waiter's offer and made small talk as Danielle cut into a chocolate bourbon soufflé. Through the glass wall, he saw Cerissa hurry past the hotel check-in desk. Zeke was nowhere in sight.

Henry's chest clutched. He had to find out why she'd gone with Zeke and whether the cowboy had said anything. He rose to his feet, setting his napkin aside.

"If you'll excuse me a moment," he said, and left Danielle behind. The bathrooms were beyond the elevator, so she wouldn't find his absence odd. He intercepted Cerissa at the elevator. "Where have you been?"

"At New Path Church. I need to get upstairs to report to Ari."

He gripped her arm, turning her to face him. "Why was Zeke with you? You promised to go alone."

"Henry, let go of me and take a step back." She pulled away and he let go. "And watch your tone."

"Where is Zeke?"

She pointed to the lobby. "He's giving the car to the valet. Or he was. Look behind you. He's coming through the doors now."

Henry turned in the entryway's direction. She touched his sleeve, and peace began to fill him.

"No." He brushed her hand away. "You don't get to control me with your aura."

"And you don't get to control me with your anger."

He glanced over at Danielle, who was staring at them. "I'll see you upstairs when I'm done with my meeting."

Cerissa tilted her chin in the same direction. "You mean your dinner with the pretty blonde?"

"It's business."

"So was my going with Zeke—I couldn't pass up the opportunity to spy on Jones. But you refuse to consider *that*."

Henry opened his mouth to reply, but Cerissa continued. "Don't you dare say you were worried about me, that you thought Zeke would make a move on me. There's something more going on in your head."

His gut churned with fear.

What did Zeke tell her?

"You're being so possessive. Why don't you trust me around other vampires?"

His anxiety waned. If the cowboy had told her, she'd know the answer to her question. "It's the men I don't trust, Zeke in particular," he said with a growl, and glanced back in the direction of the restaurant.

He couldn't afford a scene with Danielle watching them. "We will talk of this later," he said, and pivoted on his heels.

Cerissa marched into the elevator when the door opened. If she stayed there in the lobby, she'd likely scream. She repeatedly stabbed the button for her floor and stared at the lit number.

Yeah, they'd talk about his behavior later—he could count on it.

Possessive fucking vampires.

And Jones's crack about Henry killing a mortal.

Should I ask Zeke?

No, that sounded like a very bad idea. He would use the question to stir up trouble. Besides, Jones was probably just throwing shade over Henry's early kills as a young vampire, when he was learning to feed. She'd warn Henry about the rumor and let him explain it.

But only after they both calmed down.

Zeke dodged into the elevator before the doors closed. She crossed her arms and ignored him. When they arrived on their floor, she took her card key from her purse and exited. He dogged her steps.

Damn. What does it take to get rid of him?

She stopped at her suite. "Goodnight, Zeke."

"Cerissa—"

"I said, *goodnight, Zeke.*"

Her plan was to open the door, scoot inside, and slam it in his face. Before she could, his hand shot out. He pushed against the door and charged past her into the room.

She glared at him. How dare he? She couldn't believe the lack of respect. But then, after the way he acted at Nina's funeral dinner, what did she expect? His apologies on the plane had meant nothing.

"You're not welcome here."

He tipped his cowboy hat back with one finger. "Got to make sure you're okay, ma'am."

"I'm far from okay. And I won't be okay until your butt is out the door. Please leave me alone!"

Ignoring her, he lumbered into Henry's bedroom and came back out. "No one's a-hiding in there."

Then he strolled into her room. She gritted her teeth. He was taking this whole bodyguard thing much too seriously.

When he returned to the living room, she said, "As you can see, everything's fine. Now please go."

Instead, he plopped down on the couch. "We need to talk."

"Absolutely not." She wanted him gone before Henry appeared and had a bigger fit at finding them alone, but Zeke kept right on talking. Left with no choice, she sat down in the chair across from him, and five minutes later, he was still there, spewing nonsense about Henry.

She tapped her foot anxiously. She had important information about Jim Jones to tell Ari and couldn't call him until she was alone. "Stop. I don't want to hear any more. I want you to leave."

The door clicked. Henry was back.

Damn. Double damn.

Zeke jumped to his feet. "Cerissa, think about what I said. Don't stay here. Please, for your sake."

"Zeke—"

Henry barreled past her and shoved the cowboy back. "I told you to keep away from her."

"I was just leavin'."

"We're going to settle this now." Henry peeled off his suit coat, tossed it on a chair, and started rolling up his cuffs.

His anger flooded her mind. The last thing she wanted to do was referee a battle, and she couldn't use her aura on both—her charm was likely to cause Zeke to cling harder to his fantasy.

She gestured at the door. "Just let him leave."

"Not until he and I resolve this."

"That isn't necessary. He didn't do anything."

"You're defending him?" Henry asked loudly. He marched over to her.

Her mouth hung open. How dare he raise his voice in anger? She held her breath for a moment, unable to rub two words together, and then shot him a withering look.

"What did Zeke tell you?" he demanded.

"Nothing of importance."

Zeke edged toward the exit, concern on his face. "Consider what I told you, ma'am. Please."

It was the worst thing he could have said. Was he trying to make a liar out of her?

Henry gripped her arm. "Cerissa, you can't believe him. I—"

Zeke dashed out the door and pulled it shut, stopping Henry mid-sentence.

He turned to chase the cowboy, but she grabbed his shirt, holding him back. "Please, don't."

He didn't listen. "Let go of me."

She did with a disgusted shrug. He ran after Zeke but lost time getting the door open. Moments later, she could hear Henry pounding on Zeke's door down the hallway and bellowing, "Let me in."

Enough!

She stomped to her bedroom and slammed the door shut behind her.

She clutched her head in her hands, trying to ignore his anger. First Zeke talked trash about Henry, and then Henry acted like a jerk. What was happening?

She glanced at her watch. It was twenty-four hours since she'd last morphed into another form. She could use the stabilizer to remain human longer, but she had no intent of staying confined to these four walls just because Henry was being pissy.

She popped out her contact lenses, slid them into her phone's compartment to upload the video of Jim Jones, and texted Ari: *I need direction.*

The preacher hadn't admitted to any wrongdoing—still, his message aligned with the VDM's purpose. Would the Protectors take him into custody based on a mere suspicion?

Finished, she left the phone on the nightstand and slid open the balcony doors. The private area overlooked the swimming pool and had ornate wrought-iron railings bolted to stucco pillars. At this hour, the pool was closed, and the other balconies were dark and empty.

She unbuttoned her blouse and unzipped her pants. Her transition to a white-feathered jabiru was fairly fast. Her clothes dropped to the floor, covering her black claws, and she lifted one spindly leg to step out and shake them off.

She stretched her wings and used her long beak to preen. It was like scratching an itch she hadn't been able to reach in human form. She hopped onto the railing, leaned forward, and swooped off the balcony.

She flew past the pool, skimmed over a restaurant's roof, soared higher toward the ocean, and caught an updraft, riding the current to the top.

Henry stopped pounding on Zeke's door. Tempting as it was to bust it down, hotel guests were starting to stick their heads into the hallway to see what the noise was all about, so he returned to his own suite.

Cerissa's door was closed. He stormed off to his room. There, he fisted his hands, pressing them against his eyelids, trying to block the memories that kept surfacing.

Cerissa is not Sarah.

Doubt grew in his gut. Zeke had pleaded with her to come with him. *But she didn't say yes.*

Henry slumped onto the bed. What had he done? She was going to be furious with him. He should never have let the cowboy get under his skin.

His stomach roiled. The food he'd eaten was sitting like a brick, and the bloodlike juices from the rare meat were making him a touch crazy—in the days before blood banks, he'd developed a tolerance for animal blood, but now he lived exclusively off human blood and had lost his immunity. Consuming a small amount threatened to magnify his obsessive thoughts all out of proportion.

He went into the bathroom and threw it up.

After rinsing out his mouth, he swallowed hard. He'd overreacted. Cerissa hadn't learned anything of importance from the cowboy—Zeke had kept his lips sealed about Sarah.

The only way to fix this with his mate was to make amends, to throw himself on her mercy and hope he hadn't screwed up everything between them.

He knocked on her door. When there was no answer, he twisted the knob. Not locked. He cracked the door and peered in. She wasn't in the room. He pulled it wider. The bathroom light was off. She wasn't there either.

The balcony light was on. He strode over and opened the sliding glass door. Cerissa's clothes were outside, and he brought them in. She must have decided to morph and go flying.

He was two strides toward the living room when it hit him. He'd seen Zeke beg her and now she was gone.

No, that couldn't be.

It was almost meditative to fly. Cerissa emptied her mind and flew downward to pick up speed, looking for an updraft to ride again. She found one and soared into the night sky.

After a while, her stomach rumbled. Diving into the ocean to fish was an option, but she didn't want to remain a jabiru long enough to digest a whole sea bass.

At some point she had to go back and deal with Henry, but she would do so with a clear head. Why was he so controlling? She understood her first attempt at a relationship might not work out, but she never guessed how much freedom would vanish overnight. Perhaps she had allowed her life to become entwined with this strange being without learning enough about him.

Her heart broke just a little at the thought.

She flew close to the white caps, riding the spray, allowing her long wings to glide steady, only flapping when necessary to stay aloft. Finally, she had come full circle. The hotel came into view, the suite's lights out.

Where had Henry gone? Out grazing?

She pulled up and landed on the balcony rail, wrapping her claws around the cold metal. Her clothes were gone. Craning her neck, she peered one-eyed through the tinted glass.

No one visible.

She hopped down and slid the door aside with her beak, tentatively setting a clawed foot inside. Henry sat in the dark, one leg draped over the chair arm, lounging back at an angle, his eyebrows drawn together.

A frigid blast of his anger invaded her mind. It left a bitter taste in her mouth and was followed by the acid feeling of jealousy. Another emotion came in rapid succession, harder to decipher, and she focused on it: betrayal.

Not good.

The leather string he normally used to bind his ponytail was in his hand. He kept winding and unwinding it around one finger. His eyes were solid black.

She morphed back to human form, the cool night air causing goose bumps to crawl on her naked flesh, her long hair hanging in waves to her waist. She closed the balcony door and took a silk robe from the closet, slipping into it. Only then did she flip on the lights and open her small suitcase to grab a protein snack bar—a private stash for when she needed energy fast.

His gaze followed her, but he had yet to move. She sat cross-legged at the foot of the bed, bit into the protein bar, and waited.

It didn't take long for him to start. "Where did you go?"

"I flew across the bay and back."

"Alone?" His jaw muscle bulged out.

What did he think? That Zeke went flying with her? She stared right back at Henry, her own jaw tightening. "Yes, I was alone, unless you count the school of sharks I saw in the water, and they were a hell of a lot friendlier than you are right now."

"Zeke asked you to meet him."

"He did not."

She took another few bites, disliking both the snack bar's taste and Henry's attitude. His anger felt like ice in her lungs.

He swung his leg off the chair arm and planted his feet on the floor, leaning forward, his hair hanging in his face. "Zeke begged you. I heard him with my own ears."

She took the last bite of the snack bar and tossed the empty wrapper into a nearby trash basket. "You don't understand what you heard."

"On the contrary. It makes perfect sense now." He continued to wrap and unwrap the leather string around his finger, his eyes still focused on her. "You asked him to go with you to the church. You wanted him with you. I saw the two of you meet in the lobby."

"Wrong—Zeke had the car keys and wouldn't let me go alone."

"You couldn't take a taxi? Or call an Uber?"

"I wanted to leave before you saw us and had the fit you're having now. I couldn't let your irrational possessiveness stop me from tracking down Jim Jones. Tonight was our only opportunity to find him at the church."

As much as she wanted to add, *and catching the VDM is more important than your feelings*, she didn't. Guilt had weighed on her ever since Nina's death—the same guilt she'd experienced as a child when she learned that Lux medicines could have saved her father. She wouldn't let her relationship interfere with her mission again.

He narrowed his eyes, the pupils still blown to solid black with anger. It was clear he didn't believe her. What had come over him? This was not the Henry she knew.

As he continued to stare at her in silence, she curled her fingers in frustration. She'd had enough. "It's time for you to leave."

He *whooshed*. But instead of leaving, he lunged toward her, stopping short of touching her. His face was contorted with rage, his hair hung wildly to his shoulders, and his fist clutched the leather string.

Really? He thinks he can intimidate me?

He looked dark and dangerous. Father Matt had questioned whether she liked playing with bad boys. Maybe the illusion of danger excited her, but this certainly didn't.

"Tell me the truth," Henry demanded, his voice low and threatening. "You left here to go to him. Why? Why would you choose him over me?"

"I told you the truth already. Now, step away from me."

He hovered over her with his fists clenched so tight that his arms trembled. Then he moved back a foot from the bed. He inhaled a deep, ragged breath, his chest rising and falling as he let the air out. Slowly, his eyes returned to normal.

But the chill of his anger continued to blast down her spine. She was fed up with being subjected to his rage and was ready to hit the app on her phone to completely suppress the emotional connection between them.

She bit her lip. Activating the app might make her feel better, but doing so would just piss him off more. She had another way to fix this, to show him how wrong he was, and perhaps get to the bottom of his behavior at the same time. She swung off the bed to dig into her suitcase. Rather than grabbing her phone, she pulled out a heavy velvet bag and tossed it to him.

"Open it."

He caught the black pouch and looked like he wanted to throw it through the window. Instead, he dropped it on the bed. She untied the drawstrings, allowing the touchstone to fall into her hand. Perfectly round, the polished jasper was four inches in diameter and solid black.

She grabbed his wrist, pulled him to the bed, and placed his hand over the stone. "Unclench your fist."

He frowned at her, but he wrapped his hand over the stone's top half, squeezing the rock tightly. His knuckles turned white with the effort.

He'd ease up soon enough.

"Sit down," she said, resuming her seat on the bed and sitting cross-legged. "And ask me the question you want answered."

He sat down and stared at her. "Tell me the truth."

"Be *precise*." She tightened her own grip on the stone's bottom half. "A specific thing you want to know. Humor me on this."

She could have shown him the recordings her lenses made, but she wanted to demonstrate how the touchstone worked.

Henry glowered at her. "Did you meet with Zeke after he left our suite? What did he tell you about me tonight?"

Two questions, but the same answer. That would work. And the next question would be hers.

She didn't warn him what would happen. The shock of their memories connecting would be disorienting, like having an icepick shoved through your forehead.

He deserved it.

Henry shut his eyes and fought the sharp pain flooding his mind. When he could see again, he wasn't seeing the bedroom—he saw and heard Cerissa talking with Zeke at the hotel room's door, all from her perspective.

"Goodnight, Zeke."

"Cerissa—"

"I said, *goodnight, Zeke.*"

The moment she cracked the door, Zeke shouldered past her into the suite.

"You're not welcome here," she said.

"Got to make sure you're okay."

"I'm far from okay. And I won't be okay until your butt is out that door. Please leave me alone!"

Zeke went into Henry's bedroom and came back out. "No one's a-hiding in there."

Anger surged through Henry's chest. The cowboy had no business in his room, violating his privacy.

When Zeke came out of Cerissa's room, she said, "Okay, as you can see, everything's fine. Now please go."

But he didn't. He sat down on the living room couch. "We need to talk."

"Absolutely not."

"There's no one hidin' here, but ma'am, it may not be safe for you to stay. We should get you another room. Tig'll never forgive me if I let sumthin' happen to ya."

Henry could almost hear her thoughts in the moment: she didn't want the cowboy to be there when Henry got back.

She continued to hold the door open. "I'll be all right. Now leave."

"I couldn't help but notice that Henry was upset."

"My relationship is none of your business."

Zeke held his hat in his hands. He rolled the brim, turning it nervously. "I mean, I know he's had your blood now, but maybe you shouldn't stay here tonight. He looked pretty angry. I wouldn't want him to hurt you."

She released the door. She didn't want anyone in the hall hearing his stupid ideas. "Henry would never harm me."

"I wouldn't be too sure about that. It might be safer if you get another room."

She took the chair across from him. "Do you know how crazy you sound? I don't like what you're implying."

"I'm not implin' it, ma'am. I'm saying it. You'll be safer in a different room tonight."

"That's a terrible thing to say."

"It's not terrible when it's the truth." He raised his hat, rocking it on his head. "If things get bad, you can pound on the wall. I'll be over here in a jiffy."

"Listen," she said, leaning forward and clasping her hands. "I'm sorry I hurt you, but I could never be with you. Now please, stop all this, and leave me alone."

He dropped his gaze to the floor. "You don't know the history, ma'am. I'm not the bad one. I know you think I am, but I'm not."

"Zeke—"

"The men I kill. They're evil men. They've killed innocent people. Drug lords, ya know? I don't do no political assassination."

"It doesn't matter."

He raised his head, his gaze meeting her eyes. "Sure it does. I don't want nothin' to happen to you. Henry, well, he's—"

Henry held his breath. Would Zeke say it?

"Stop." Cerissa turned at the sound of the key card. "I don't want to hear any more. I want you to leave."

In the vision, Henry opened the door and strode into view, his face rigid with rage. Seeing himself in her memory, seeing the monster he turned into when angry, caused him to flinch.

Madre de Dios. He would *never* hurt Cerissa. He worked too hard to protect her from what he was. And yet facing himself so angry—he loathed what he saw. This was what his jealousy and suspicion had done to him.

He'd been so afraid she'd leave if Zeke told her the truth, so scared she'd run to Zeke, and instead he had become the monster to flee from.

In the vision, the cowboy stood. "Cerissa, think about what I said. Don't stay here. Please, for your sake."

Henry cringed. He pulled back as if he could escape from what he'd seen, and the memory faded to black.

When his eyesight cleared, he realized he was seeing her in the present. She didn't look happy.

"Now you *really* know what we were discussing," she said. "Are you satisfied?"

"You didn't go to him afterward?"

"Do you see that blank wall?"

"Y-yes." In his mind's eye, he did.

"It means there's nothing further to show in answer your question."

He looked at the ball, still clutched between their hands. "How—how did you do that?" he asked, the hesitation in his voice betraying his uncertainty.

"It's a touchstone. A real one." She released his hand, leaving him holding the black stone. He ran his fingers over the smooth crystal. He found no seal, no opening.

"What magic is this?"

"We've had this conversation already. You call it magic; I call it technology."

"How does the touchstone work?" He scratched the surface with his fingernail. The stone continued to shine unmarred.

She took the orb from him. "The brain stores memories chemically. The touchstone reads those chemical changes. I used a similar device when I read Karen's memories of the Cutter's attack." She placed it back in his hand and wrapped hers around his. "Now it's my turn to ask you a question."

The hair on the back of his neck stood. "You can do this in reverse?"

"If you give me permission, I can use the touchstone to view your memories, those arising when I ask *you* a specific question. Are you willing?"

Henry's stomach sank. He closed his eyes, guilt crawling through his veins.

Cerissa had told Zeke to leave her alone. How had he so misread the situation? Seeing the two of them together tonight—his jealousy and insecurity had hijacked his reason.

He opened his eyes. "Before I say yes, I have something to say."

She sat there, her face a mask.

He cleared his throat. "I had no right to distrust you or to treat you the way I did. I'm sorry."

She showed no reaction. "May I ask my question now?"

Shame rushed through him. His first impulse was to crawl away and hide. He dreaded letting her see what he really was, but he was stronger than that. And if he didn't let her in, he knew his refusal *would* end them. If he had any chance of keeping her with him, the answer had to be—

"Yes."

CHAPTER 33

Tuscany Bay Resort, San Diego—moments later

Henry didn't hesitate—Cerissa had to give him that. He placed his hand back over the touchstone, and she considered how to frame her request. She needed to ask the surgical question to drill down to the key point in his history—*something* in his past had triggered all this.

Before tonight, she'd stayed out of his past, not asking questions, letting him disclose those life events when he was ready. She hadn't asked about Abigale or anyone else. But his behavior had pushed them beyond her natural inclination to give him privacy, and she couldn't stay blind any longer to what came before her.

She bit her lips together. What did Henry think Zeke had told her? She wanted to know, but even more so, she wanted to find out what was at the heart of his anger and mistrust. Then she recalled the emotion she'd sensed behind the anger—betrayal.

Her question crystalized. "What single experience has made you so convinced your mate will betray you?"

As the touchstone connected, she let the pain wash through her mind, his memories racing by like paintings frozen on a moving wall, until one folded out in front of her.

She closed her eyes to see his memory more clearly, the movie playing itself on the back of her eyelids. A young woman appeared: blonde, buxom, and dressed in a low-cut scarlet jacket, with a short, frilly skirt revealing white batiste bloomers and black stockings. Ruffled silk garters matched her red slippers.

The young woman danced a rather botched cancan on a wooden stage with two other dancers, lit by gas lamps. The audience—all men—sat around rustic tables. Most of the men wore walrus mustaches. Based on the clothing styles and the dance, Cerissa guessed the year was around 1890.

Like a badly edited film—Henry's memory had degraded over the years—Cerissa saw the old concert saloon from his perspective and heard his thoughts. He had come in hoping to find a mortal to lure outside after the show. For too many nights, he'd fed on cattle blood. He needed to feed on human blood. Badly.

He stood by a bar at the back, scanning the audience for a potential victim. His gaze stopped at the stage.

The scantily clad blonde who was singing caught his eye. She was curvy, the corset-like jacket showing off her large chest and ample hips. His predator's vision zeroed in on her blue-gray eyes. They sparkled as she flirted with the audience.

Beautiful.

He lost all interest in feeding on anyone except her.

When the show ended, she scooted off the stage, her short skirt rising to reveal a few inches of bare flesh, and his *pene* stirred. The singer picked up a tray with glasses and a bottle, and she began working her way through the audience.

His groin pulsed again, his desire for her growing stronger.

Cerissa fidgeted a little. Experiencing Henry's attraction to the singer made her own jealousy rise, but she pushed the feeling away. This had occurred in his past, long before they met. She had no reason to be jealous.

In the vision, Henry leaned against the bar. "What is her name?"

The bartender picked up a glass and wiped it. "Which one?"

Henry cast his gaze sideways in the woman's direction and slid a coin across the counter. "The blonde."

"That's Sarah."

"How long has she been with you?"

The bartender pocketed the coin and continued to work his way through drying a row of glasses. "Been here 'bout three months."

Surprise shot through Henry. "She looks too young to do what she does."

The bartender shook his head. "Her? Nah. Seventeen at least. She's been touring the saloon stages for a few years now."

"Where is she from?"

"South of here. Ran away from her family, from what I hear."

"Why did she do that?"

The bartender laughed. "Who cares? She has what the men want to see."

Henry smiled—Sarah did indeed have an unmistakable charm. He leaned with his back against the bar, watching as she carried a whiskey bottle and offered drinks for sale. Any man who bought her a drink could enjoy her company until she finished it. He'd seen women like her before.

But she wasn't like all the others. Something about her was different.

He pushed away from the bar and strode across the room, taking a seat in the section she worked. His gaze continued to follow her.

It had been years since he and his maker had separated and gone their own ways. During all that time, he'd avoided entanglements with women. So why change course?

Sarah leaned over to pour a drink at another table. Doing so emphasized her bosom, which was mounded and outlined by frilly lace. Now here was a woman with Anne-Louise's allure, but who would *never* be able to control him the way his maker had.

Was that what drew him? No. Something else about Sarah ignited him in a way he hadn't felt in a long, long time.

She sashayed to his table, rolling her hips suggestively so the short skirt rode up her leg. "Care for a drink, mister?"

"If I buy a drink from you, would you sit with me?"

"I might."

He stood and pulled out a chair for her. When he bent to move the chair, his gray tweed suit came into view and the high collar tightened at his neck.

"Ain't you a dandy," she said, smiling at him as she sat. She placed the bottle and glasses on the table. "I'm Sarah. What's your name?"

"Enrique Bautista."

"What's a Spanish gentleman like you doing in here?" She poured a shot and slid the glass to him across the marred wooden table.

He didn't correct her. He was from Mexico, not Spain, but old West bars were rigidly segregated by race—best not to call attention to his true parentage. He accepted the drink and touched his lips to the liquid.

"I'm in Stockton on business," he said, returning the glass to the table in front of him. The whiskey was watered down—way watered down—but he didn't care. "May I buy you a drink?"

"Sure—if you're buying, I'm drinking." She leaned forward, letting him see a little more cleavage, and poured her own shot. "That's fifty cents for both."

He removed the silver coins from his pocket with leather-gloved hands. He paid her, adding a dollar, an extravagant tip. "You are quite lovely."

She preened at the compliment, twining her finger around a lock of hair. "I imagine a fine man like you has his pick of the ladies."

"Not really. I'm from Sierra Escondida. Few single women live there."

"But the ones who do, I bet they know you well." She belted back her whiskey.

He shrugged. "I have not found anyone I want to settle down with." He looked at her empty glass and placed more coins next to it. "Would you like another?"

"Don't mind if I do." She poured from the bottle. "Aren't you going to finish yours?"

He raised the drink to his lips. The watered-down liquor smelled foul, and the small sip he took burned his throat. "What time do they close the saloon?"

"Oh, in an hour or so, or whenever the last cowboy leaves."

"Would you like to go for a stroll with me?"

She belted the second shot and daintily wiped the corners of her mouth with her fingers. As he waited for her answer, his usually slow heart beat faster.

She gave him a flirty smile. "I figured you'd want to come up to my room."

"No, thank you."

He wasn't ready for sex. As much as he wanted her, he wanted more than one night. He'd move slowly to ensure she was suitable for Sierra Escondida before making her his mate. His immediate need for blood would wait.

He stood. "Please meet me out front when the bar closes." He took her hand and kissed the soft skin of her fingers. Her face registered surprise. "Until then."

The memory abruptly jumped forward, parts missing. Henry's stroll with Sarah ended, bringing them back to the saloon.

"May I kiss you?" he asked under the moonlight.

She giggled. "No one's watchin' at this hour. I guess it's okay."

He took Sarah in his arms and met her lips chastely. His *pene* hardened, twitching against his pants, and his fangs extended. All he wanted was to part Sarah's lips and taste her mouth.

Would one deep kiss really hurt?

Yes, it would.

He wouldn't be able to stop there. His desire for blood and sex rose until the craving threatened to overpower him. He stepped back and, bowing to her, hid his fangs as he spoke. "Goodnight."

"Goodnight," Sara echoed, and climbed the stairs behind the saloon to a room above it.

From the boardwalk below, he watched her light the kerosene lamp near her room's curtained window. Seeing her naked silhouette as she got undressed tortured him. He turned away to seek other sources to slake his hunger.

Over the course of a month, Henry continued to court her. His memories were disjointed, fragmented, providing a little of this evening, a little of that, which sped up the viewing process.

His thoughts told Cerissa she was now seeing his last night in Stockton. He strolled with Sarah along the boardwalk. "I have to return to Sierra Escondida," he told her.

She cast her gaze at the ground, looking disappointed, and he thrilled at her reaction.

"When?" she asked.

"Tomorrow night. I hoped you would come with me."

Her face lit up. "Really?"

"Yes, really. How long will it take for you to pack?"

"Ah, I don't own a trunk or anything to put my clothes in."

"I'll have one delivered to you in the morning." He held her hand to his heart and gazed into her blue-gray eyes. "May I come to your room? There is something I must show you before you make your decision."

Sarah looked away shyly and then lowered her gaze in his groin's direction. "You injured or something?"

"Not in the way you are thinking. If you lie with me, you won't be disappointed."

She led him up the wooden stairs to her room, inviting him in.

Dread filled Cerissa. Should she break her contact with the touchstone? She didn't want to watch Henry making love to Sarah.

He must have had the same thought. He released her hand, breaking the connection, and the images in her mind receded back to hang on a black wall. "There is no reason for you to see that. It isn't what you seek the answer to."

"Okay," she said, trusting him. He hadn't lied to her before; he'd only withheld information. "What happened next?"

"She and I made love. Then I bit her. She didn't react well."

"All right. Focus on the bite to take us past the sex."

He nodded and wrapped his hand back around the touchstone. The image swung out from the wall and filled her mind.

She saw two puncture wounds on Sarah's neck. When Henry backed further away in the vision, Sarah looked at him frightened.

"You bit me."

She covered the bite with her hand. When she removed her hand, she looked at the trail of blood on her fingers. He lost control and licked the ambrosia off them.

She recoiled in horror. "You're one of those perverted fellas!"

He got on his knees so they were at eye level to each other. "I'm sorry," he said. "It's better this way. I couldn't tell you what I am before I took your blood."

Trust slipped from her eyes, a shadow of fear joining the hardness he had seen when he first met her. She pulled away from him, drawing her knees up for protection. "What are you?"

"I'm a vampire," he said solemnly. "Do not be afraid. I will never hurt you."

She scrambled away from him and pressed against the headboard. "Stay back or I'll scream. The barkeep's room is right next door. Come any closer and I'll scream. Truly I will."

She held one hand tight against her neck.

He took her other hand between both of his—she was shaking so much. How could he comfort her?

"Sarah, I love you. I want you to come with me. You deserve better than this life—let me take care of you."

"Why did ya bite me?" She removed her hand from her neck again and stared at the blood dotting her fingers.

"I live off blood. Human blood when I can get it. Animal blood if I must."

"The cowboys, they been talkin' about strange attacks on cattle. Someone's been draining their blood, makin' them weak."

"That was me."

She pulled her hand from his and crossed herself. "You're in league with the devil."

"I am not." He looked away from her, ashamed. "I cannot help what I am, but I swear by all that is holy—you will never have anything to fear from me. Please," he said, drawing her to him, "please let me hold you."

She tried to resist, but he held her gaze with his, mesmerizing her, draining her repulsion, until she yielded to him. He wrapped his arms around her.

"I had to do it." He stroked her wheat-blonde hair. "I couldn't tell you what I was without first ensuring your loyalty."

"Hmm," she said drowsily, relaxing against him.

Good. He'd be able to control her until she fully accepted his truth.

He let her go and got off the bed. His coat was hanging on a chair. He drew an envelope from its pocket. "Here is your ticket. The train leaves at three in the afternoon. Can you remember the time?"

She rubbed her eyes. "I guess so."

He put the ticket in her hand and began dressing. He had a few arrangements to make at the train depot in order to travel safely.

"I'll see you tomorrow night on the train," he said, and glanced around the small room.

One trunk was all she'd need to pack her pitifully few belongings. Then he noticed it: a blue glass medicine vial on her dresser, with a small pearl-drop cork sealing the narrow top.

Laudanum.

Putas sometimes used the opium-based medication, hooked by the men who pimped them out. She wasn't under anyone's control—how did she come to use the noxious fluid?

"You will not need this," he said, snatching the bottle and pocketing it. "Promise me you will never use it, or you cannot come with me."

"But I need my medicine to sleep..." Then she slowly nodded.

He finished dressing and left.

Henry's memories jumped to the next evening. At dusk, he opened the lid to the wooden coffin he had slept in during the day. He made his way forward from the cargo section to join Sarah in the train's passenger compartment.

She seemed subdued when he joined her. She was anxious and her hands shook—the effects of withdrawal from the laudanum. Pity swayed him. It wasn't fair to make her stop so suddenly. He would wean her off the drug slowly so she wouldn't suffer.

After asking how many drops she took each night, he poured half that quantity into a glass of wine and gave it to her. She drank the opiate and seemed better.

Another jump in memories—Sarah was living in his Sierra Escondida home and no longer taking any laudanum. She appeared healthier than she had working at the saloon. She even stopped being afraid of the bite and welcomed him to her bed.

When he didn't have to work, they played card games. Sarah knew all the popular ones and preferred playing cards to reading. Her education had ceased after three years, and while she could print and read basic messages, most books were beyond her.

He had bought her a child's primer, hoping she'd improve so they could read to each other. So far, her progress was slow.

Most nights, she went to bed around four in the morning. He accompanied her to her room. He didn't enter unless she invited him. Not because he was a vampire, but because he wanted the choice to be hers.

At the door, she gave a little tug on his hand, her signal for him to join her. He took her in his arms and kissed her deeply.

"Enrique," she said when the kiss ended, "I'm having a powerful hard time goin' to sleep. Could I have my medicine back?"

He stroked her hair. "It's not good for you." The laudanum wasn't good for him either. "Try to go a little longer without it. You'll start sleeping again. I promise."

She crawled under the cover, and instead of joining her, he stared deep into her eyes and said, "Sleep."

She closed her eyes and her breathing became relaxed and regular.

With his help, she'd get through this. She'd chosen him and he would show her—he was more powerful than any drug. He was sure of it.

Chapter 34

Henry's Memory—Moments Later

The night-shrouded vineyards had gone from dormant to full leaf. The next jump in Henry's memory had taken them to a few months later. He was saddling a horse, and Sarah stood by wearing a high-collared muslin blouse with embroidered lace. Her black skirt was full-length, covered by a blue-striped apron—much more conservative clothing than she'd worn when working for the saloon.

She twisted her apron nervously. "Can't I come with you?"

"I'm sorry." He tightened the saddle's bellyband. "I must focus on the negotiations. I would have no time for you."

"But I'm so bored here."

He faced her. "Why don't you visit the other mortals?"

"Not at night. They're busy with their mates."

"Don't you have work to keep you occupied? My socks need darning."

"I can fix 'em during the day. But I can't be with you."

He kissed her. "Sarah, I'm sorry, but I must go."

Another flash past broken memories.

He woke suddenly in his basement crypt. The room was pitch-black, but it was neither a sunset nor moonrise that had roused him—daytime lethargy still weighed too heavily on his bones.

So, what woke him? The sound of shoes on the stone floor—someone was in the room. He forced his body to move, to lunge at the intruder, his fangs ripping into the intruder's neck, tearing the soft flesh, the blood gushing into his mouth—

A taste he knew all too well.

"Sarah," he gurgled as he swallowed. "Oh, Sarah, no."

"Enrique," she said weakly. Her head lolled to the side as her life force pumped out the gashes.

He picked her up and struggled up the basement stairs. With the sun still high in the sky—and no moon out—each step was like lifting bricks tied to his feet. But he had to reach the icebox to help her. His blood wouldn't heal a bite he inflicted.

The door at the top was open, and he stumbled into the windowless kitchen. Dropping to the floor, he laid her down and pushed himself up to unlatch the icebox. Inside, a Mason jar held some of Yacov's blood. Kneeling next to her, he unscrewed the lid and drizzled it along the two large gashes.

The skin began to knit, and the flow of her blood slowed.

He slid a hand behind her head to raise it. "Drink this," he said, holding the jar to her mouth.

She wrinkled her nose and turned her head, struggling to avoid the red liquid.

He held her firmly. "You must. The blood will heal you. Please."

She took a small sip. As her eyes focused on him, he saw her fear. "Oh, Sarah, I told you never to come down there when I slept."

"You didn't leave your clothes in the kitchen for me to clean 'em.

I didn't think it would cause any harm if I went in and got 'em." She blinked, tears running down her face. "You said you'd never hurt me."

"I'm so sorry. It will never happen again, I promise." He'd never forget to lock his door after this. "Just please, don't come to me while I'm asleep. I—I will attack anyone who wakes me. It's part of what I am."

The shame he felt at having attacked his mate overwhelmed him.

Cerissa shuddered. So this explained why Henry was afraid to have her wake him. But there was more—something he feared, something... darker.

His memory skipped forward suddenly.

He rose at dusk, and Sarah met him with the mail. She'd gone into town to collect it. He gave her a quick hug and then perused the letters.

"When are you leaving?" she asked.

"Soon." One message was disturbing. A land purchase deal was in jeopardy. He needed to meet with his agent tonight.

She checked her watch and then tucked the timepiece back into her waistband. He caught the action out of the corner of his eye, and then turned to focus on her. She was wearing her "fancy Sunday-go-to-meeting dress"—her term for the outfit, not his. It had a fitted bodice, a long tulip skirt, and a small bustle puffed out behind her. The pale turquoise flowers looked good with her blonde hair and blue-gray eyes. A little rouge smudged her cheeks.

"Why are you dressed up?"

"Just felt like it." She held out a hanger. "I pressed your shirt. Here, let me help you."

She untied his bathrobe and helped him on with his starched shirt.

"If I didn't know better," he said, as she buttoned the tall collar, "I would think you are trying to get rid of me."

She laughed a high, girlish laugh. "Now why would I want to do that? I just know how important business is to you."

She scurried about, getting everything ready for him. He narrowed his eyes, and suspicion swirled in his chest. Something about her behavior struck him as off.

The land deal be damned. He had to find out what she was up to.

He rode toward Mordida on horseback but doubled back and followed her as she drove her carriage to Jose's Cantina. He hung back, waiting while she went into the bar, then he tied up his horse and looked through the window. His gut sank as she flirted with those who had gathered there to play poker, drinking the drink someone had bought her.

When she accompanied Nathaniel to a private room, Henry had seen enough. He flew into the saloon, banging through the short swinging doors, and strode across the room to where she had disappeared.

Cerissa gripped the touchstone harder. *Nathaniel.* Henry had told her about a duel with a vampire by that name. Was she about to see their combat?

Méi *whooshed* in front of Henry. Cerissa had met her once and immediately recognized his vampire sister. The petite woman from China blocked his path, one hand grasping his arm, the other holding poker cards. "Don't go in there."

He swept her aside. "I must and I will."

She was instantly in front of him again with her hand pressed flat to his chest. "This is not the way. Take it to the council."

"Damn the council. I will defend what's mine."

Henry moved around Méi and kept going. When the door to the room flew open, he froze, betrayal gripping him. Sarah leaned against a small table in the room, balanced on her pillowlike bustle, a trickle of blood flowing from her neck. Her long skirt and petticoat were raised over her hips—her drawers missing—and Nathaniel continued to thrust into her.

"Get off her." Henry grabbed the man by the coat and collar, hauled him back, and threw him across the room.

Nathaniel landed with a thud but was back on his feet swiftly. He began buttoning his trousers. "Your turn," he said with a laugh.

Henry rushed the other vampire and punched him with all his strength, sending him flying across the room. Closing in on where he lay, Henry swung, punch after punch, each one feeding his fury until *el bastardo*'s face was a bloody mess.

Cerissa felt lost in the rage, her brain believing it was her fists flailing at Nathaniel, her knuckles being battered on his cheekbones, the skin of her hands being shredded.

Méi grabbed Henry's arm as he raised his fist to punch again. "Enrique, stop. That is enough."

He whipped around and snarled at Méi. "Not when he steals from me. He deserves so much more."

Then he focused on Sarah. She had snatched a goblet off the table and was guzzling the liquid down. He flew to her and ripped the drink from her hand. He sniffed the wine, the bitter scent present.

Laudanum.

Nathaniel had been providing her with laudanum.

El bastardo had sabotaged everything Henry had done to help Sarah. Rage filled him. He dumped the contents of the glass on the floor, took her by the arm, and pulled her out of the room. The *thief* didn't follow—he was on the ground where he belonged, holding a handkerchief to his bleeding face.

Henry propelled Sarah outside to the gig-style carriage and thrust her up onto the seat. He tied his horse's reins to the back rail so it would follow them home.

Méi stood at his elbow. "What are you going to do?"

He climbed into the gig. "What I must."

He lifted the whip and urged the draft horse forward.

When they reached his house, he pulled Sarah from her seat.

"Go inside," he ordered her.

She stumbled but managed to stagger into the house without his help. He put the horses and gig in the barn. Despite his fury, he couldn't leave the horses untended and took out the brush to groom them.

While he worked, his anger went from flaming hot to a cold fire, a fire consuming his soul. When he returned to the house, Sarah was upstairs, the door closed, and he collapsed into his drawing room chair.

He rubbed his eyelids, trying to rid himself of the ghostlike image. No matter how hard he pressed, the sight of Nathaniel fucking her remained.

The thief. It is all his fault she's hooked again.

And Sarah—how could she do this?

She loves the drug more than me.

He didn't bother going upstairs to confront her. By now, she was probably sleeping off the opium.

The next night, his vision remained clouded by what he'd seen. No matter how hard he tried, he couldn't force himself to forget. He got dressed and climbed the stairs, determined to end their relationship, once and for all.

She was still passed out on the bed. Nathaniel had given her so much of the drug that she'd slept through the day. Henry's anger boiled over. He lunged at her, grabbing her and pulling her from the bed.

"How could you do this to me?" he demanded.

She struggled to stay on her feet, looking sleep-dazed. "Let me go," she whined. She twisted her arm to break his grip and stumbled as she pulled away. "I—I'm leaving. I don't want ya no more."

"And just where will you go?"

"Nathaniel asked me to live with him."

Henry's stomach spasmed. If he let her go to *el bastardo*, everyone would know *she* left *him*.

He clutched his belly to keep from doubling over. He should let her leave. It was what he'd come to tell her. In his heart, he knew they were wrong for each other.

But being abandoned in such a public way, being *rejected*, was like taking a knife to the gut. She didn't deserve his love—she had betrayed him. But he couldn't let her walk out, not if she was running to Nathaniel's arms. He just couldn't take the humiliation in addition to the hurt.

"Sarah." His heart tightened painfully, and he stared into her eyes. "You belong to me. You can't leave."

He continued to hold her gaze, mesmerizing and freezing her until she calmed. Shame engulfed him. He shouldn't need to use his powers on his *mate*.

Except she'd stopped being his mate when the thief bit and fucked her. The knife in his gut turned again at the realization.

He ignored the pain. "I can help you. You don't need Nathaniel."

Her eyes took on a dulled look. She sniffed back her tears, and he took her into his arms, holding her until she finally leaned into his embrace.

She exposed her neck to him with a sigh.

His fangs lowered. He slid them in and took a few big swallows before lowering her to the bed. The pain in his gut lessened as her blood warmed him.

Cerissa's throat tightened, and she wanted to release the touchstone to stop watching. Seeing Henry manipulate the woman's feelings appalled her.

Cerissa flexed her fingers on the touchstone. As much as she wanted to stop the process, she had to see his memories through to the end. She had asked the question. She owed it to Henry to watch what was revealed.

His memories continued to play in a fragmented fashion. By the change in seasons, months must have passed.

He saddled a horse and trotted down Robles Road toward the burgeoning Mordida. Once again, he suspected Sarah was trading herself for more of the drug she craved, but he didn't turn back. There had been no evidence of any new bites. If she was returning to Nathaniel, then *el bastardo* was healing the bites using the blood of another vampire. So long as she was home by ten, Henry would pretend to live in ignorance. It was simpler than fighting it.

He returned home from a business trip one summer night, the vineyards heavy with purple grapes. The night air was stifling with the heat of the day.

His grandfather clock read eleven twenty. He searched the house and didn't find her. Then he checked the barn. Sarah's horse was gone, and rage shot through him. It was an insult for *el bastardo* to keep her this late.

Henry could ignore the situation no longer.

The memory flashed forward, and he stood outside Nathaniel's clapboard house.

"Nathaniel," he called out. "You have something that belongs to me."

The door flew open, and the thief stepped out onto the porch, tucking his shirttail into his pants. "If you can't keep her in your bed, that's not my problem."

Henry held a wooden stake. "We will end this. Here. Now."

A small group of onlookers had already gathered. From their chatter, word had spread through the small community—a duel was imminent. Others soon filtered in, arriving in ones and twos to watch the challenge.

"Don't be melodramatic, Enrique." Nathaniel adjusted his shirt cuffs and ignored Henry's gaze. "She's just a stupid mortal. No one need die over the likes of her."

"You should have considered that before you lay with her again," Henry said, clutching the stake and pointing it in Nathaniel's direction.

He would take no more disrespect. He knelt and shoved the stake into the ground. Stepping back, he drew a circle in the dirt with his boot heel, a twenty-foot radius from the instrument of death.

"Choose your position," Henry said.

"And if I refuse this nonsense?"

Méi stepped forward. "Your life is forfeit. You trespassed. Fight the duel or die."

From out of the crowd, Yacov appeared, waving his hand. "Friends, one moment, please."

The older vampire didn't look much different from the way he did today: his face was that of a man in his early thirties, his beard long and frizzy, and his brown hair curly and covered by a kippah.

He pulled Henry aside and turned him around until they were face to face. "Enrique, my friend, you don't have to do this. We can ban Nathaniel from the community—send him and Sarah away."

Henry glanced over his shoulder to see where *el bastardo* stood with the others. The sight steeled his resolve. "I am sorry. This is something I must do."

"No, it's not." Yacov cupped Henry's face and turned him again, staring into his eyes with concern. "Once you put this in motion, you won't be able to stop it. Think. You don't have to succumb to your anger."

"My honor demands it."

"There is no honor in this, my friend."

Henry wrenched his arm away. "If you are not on my side, leave."

"I will always be on your side." Sadness filled Yacov's eyes. "But I won't stand silent when you're wrong. You can't make Sarah into what you need her to be. Forgive her for what she is and let her go."

"Enough talking. This is something I must do." Henry started to march back to Nathaniel.

"When this is over, my friend, I hope you'll be able to forgive yourself." Yacov left the clearing, walking off in the direction of his homestead.

Henry stopped for a moment. The truth of Yacov's words penetrated the stone barrier his rage had erected, letting doubt filter in. But when he saw Sarah half-dressed and supporting herself against the doorframe, his rage blasted the doubt away.

"What—what are y'all doing here?" She swayed like she was drunk. The bite on her neck was clotted and drying. From what Henry had heard on the grapevine, Nathaniel never gave her laudanum until after feeding on her. Her appearance gave truth to the rumor.

A man stepped into the doorway behind her—Zeke, Nathaniel's fledgling.

Had both men been using Sarah?

I should have put a stop to this months ago.

Henry ran to Sarah and grabbed her arm. "Come out here and see what your infidelity has caused." He pulled her from the porch and thrust her toward Méi, who caught the mortal. "Watch as your lover dies."

He then chose his position on the circle. For the one who picked second, there was strategy involved. Stand opposite your opponent and hope to reach the stake first? Start near them and engage in hand-to-hand battle instead? Nathaniel was slightly older, but not by much. He probably had better strength and stamina, but in speed, they were evenly matched. Henry waited for the thief to choose.

With disdain in his strut, Nathaniel stopped at the circle's edge, and then positioned himself opposite Henry. "Who will call the start?"

"I'll count to three," Méi said. "On three, begin. One...two..."

The honorless *bastardo* didn't wait for three. He lunged for the stake.

Henry launched himself a split second after the cheater and didn't go for the stake—he dove for Nathaniel. They collided in the middle, the spiked wood left in the dirt.

Henry landed the first punch. The pain in his hand didn't even register as he sent Nathaniel flying, a sense of righteous power fueling his anger. He ignored the stake and ran to where Nathaniel fell.

The thief deserves punishment before he dies.

But Nathaniel didn't stay down long enough. He *whooshed* to his feet and dodged out of the way. Henry's speed carried him forward until he collided with a thick tree. Rage filled him. His head throbbed and his reasoning clouded over.

A sharp elbow drove into his kidney, magnifying the pain. He dropped to his knees and rolled onto his back. As Nathaniel lunged at him, Henry kicked up, propelling *el bastardo* through the air to land hard on the same tree. A branch stub pierced Nathaniel's side, holding him upright.

As much as Henry wanted to punish the man who stole his woman, he couldn't risk losing. He lunged for the stake. He grabbed the weapon from the circle and flew at his opponent, the stake pointed outward.

Nathaniel struggled to free himself from the tree branch. Henry didn't pause—in one fluid move, he charged, using his momentum to drive the stake in.

The sharp point pushed through soft tissue, meeting resistance when the tip hit bone. Then the rib cracked, and the stake drilled through Nathaniel's heart, coming to a jarring stop as it met his spine.

Cerissa's hand flew to her mouth. Experiencing the deathblow as if her own hands had held the stake shocked her.

Sarah screamed. Henry glanced over at her—would she have screamed if the loser had been him? Warm blood burbled from around the wood, coating his hands and running between his fingers to drip on the ground.

Nathaniel writhed. As the thief's skin dried and shrank, his body dissolved into a mixture of mummified remains and dust. The dust scattered in the night breeze.

Soon, nothing was left but a dried-out carcass wearing Nathaniel's clothes, hanging from the tree branch. Guilt flooded Henry's heart.

I should have done something sooner to stop this.

Cerissa blinked, seeing a double image of Henry in the present and Nathaniel's corpse in the past. As terrible as it was to experience him killing a man, she hadn't been surprised by the duel.

What had surprised her was the reason: his toxic relationship had been the driving force. He had treated his mate as a possession to be fought over, and his current-day possessiveness had been a reaction to his misbelief that if he'd controlled Sarah better, if he'd done something sooner, Nathaniel's death could have been prevented.

With that insight, she expected the replay of his memory to end. But in the present, Henry's fear washed over her through their connection. Why?

Then she realized the vision was continuing.

There's more?

Henry turned to the crowd. They stood there, staring at him, eerily quiet. One of their own had been killed, and they seemed unmoved. He strode to Sarah to claim her as his.

Méi blocked him from reaching his mate, holding the mortal to the side. "Enrique, end this."

"Nathaniel got what he deserved." The other Hill residents started closing in on him. He stepped back as they surrounded him. "I was within my rights."

Another vampire moved to the front. "We've given you time to fix the problem yourself," Aaron said. "You haven't. You can't control her."

Henry *whooshed* around them and grabbed Sarah from Méi. "What do you expect me to do? Her family doesn't want her. I cannot send her back to the saloon she was in. Her return will raise too many questions."

"Do it anyway," Aaron said. "A man must be willing to shoot his own dog."

Henry drove her back to his house. Taking her by the arm, he pulled her from the carriage and through the front door into the foyer.

It was over between them. His community mattered more than she did. He pointed upstairs. "Go to your room and pack your things."

She stumbled, stopping at the sweeping staircase, leaning on the wooden banister. "What—what...what's gonna happen to me?"

"That's not my problem anymore."

Tears streamed down her face, but her despair didn't change anything. His own heart had become stone again when he drove the stake through Nathaniel's.

She swiped at her tears. "I got nowhere to go. No money."

"You should have considered that before you went back to Nathaniel."

"Please, don't..."

"Don't what? Leave you? You left me."

She sniffed. "I— You—you wouldn't— He gave me my medicine."

"I gave you *me*." He pounded his fist on his chest. Failure had roosted there like a turkey vulture, its beak picking him apart. "I gave you my heart. I gave you my home. Why wasn't I enough?"

"I know ya gave me all that," Sarah said with another sniff. "But I also needed my medicine."

Cerissa's stomach knotted tighter. Sarah's actions had little to do with Henry or Nathaniel. The woman was driven by her addiction—an addiction that soothed a greater pain. Cerissa hadn't missed the bartender's comments about Sarah running away from home at a young age—a typical symptom of abuse or violation.

Henry didn't understand addiction then and likely still didn't. He couldn't substitute himself for the drug or fill the hole in Sarah's soul. The woman needed proper treatment and the correct medications, which didn't exist back then.

In the vision, he stared at Sarah and anger seethed through his body. "So, you betrayed me for your drug. Well, you can find someone else to give your *medicine* to you."

"But Enrique—"

"Leave. You are not trustworthy." He turned his back on her. And it wasn't just Sarah. Images of Anne-Louise flashed through his mind. He would never let his guard down for any woman again.

From behind him, Sarah mumbled, "Nathaniel was going to make me like you."

Henry swung around and closed the distance between them, flashing his fangs at her. "You want to be like this?"

"Better than being like this," she said, slurring her words, and falling backward to sit on the staircase.

He glared at her. If he turned her, he'd be able to control her, keep her with him, and punish her for cuckolding him. But did he want her in his life forever?

His rage said it was a small price for revenge. He'd make her regret betraying him. And if he couldn't have her, no one would—he'd keep her bound to him and never release her. Then she'd learn the true extent of the pain and death she so carelessly caused.

Cerissa gasped. Yacov's words echoed in her mind: *There is no honor in this.*

Taking Sarah in his arms, Henry bit her neck, sinking his fangs in deeply, tearing the tender skin. He both wanted her and hated her, all the emotions rolling together at once.

The more he drank, the more he tasted the fear in her blood. She struggled to stop him, but she was too far gone—if he didn't finish turning her, she'd die. Her breathing became labored and her heart beat faster, trying to compensate for the loss.

He eased her onto the stairs and stood. He needed to feed her his blood to complete the turn. Raising his wrist to open a vein, his head suddenly spun. He lost his balance and grabbed the banister rail, collapsing next to where she lay.

The world went black.

When he opened his eyes, he saw two rivulets of blood trailing down her throat, pooling on the wooden stair, dried a sticky dark red.

He rose, still dizzy.

The laudanum.

He touched her, feeling for her pulse. He found none. Her body was cold. How long had he been out? He bit his wrist, pried her jaws open, and dripped his blood over her tongue.

She didn't swallow.

He stroked her throat, trying to force her to drink.

The muscles stayed slack.

Horror shot through him, the guilt clawing at his gut, surrounding him like a shroud.

I killed her.

He rose to his knees and gathered her in his arms. The keening sound he made was loud enough to be heard throughout the hillside valley.

He cried when he buried her on top of the mountain behind his homestead. Yacov was the only one to join him by her graveside. Henry let everyone else in the small community believe Sarah had left.

He placed a stone bench next to her grave. He carried the heavy stone up the steep terrain himself, refusing any help, even though the weight broke something in his back when he lifted the bench. His back would heal; his soul wouldn't.

The memory flashed—a quick transition to San Francisco two months later—and a woman asked, "Is this what you need?"

A whip cracked. Cerissa flinched as the searing pain ran across Henry's shoulder blades. Tightly blindfolded, Henry saw darkness—the darkness in his soul. His hands were bound in rough rope, his arms stretched above his head. He stood almost on tiptoe. In his mind's eye, he could see the braided horsewhip flip back.

"Again," he said, his voice hoarse with pain.

The sharp sting glided across his skin, lighting his muscles beneath on fire.

"Again."

Another crack sounded; more pain exploded across his back.

"Again."

Another crack and his balance wavered.

"My fee is higher for drawing blood."

Abigale's voice. It was Abigale who wielded the whip. This was how he knew her—she was his penance.

"Do it," Henry said through gritted teeth.

The next strike split open his skin, the pain sharper as flesh ripped from his bones. Warm blood trickled a path along his back. The agony did nothing to alleviate the guilt and remorse he felt.

Guilt and remorse he still felt.

Cerissa dropped the touchstone, breaking the memory, unable to share his pain any longer, and opened her eyes to see him in the present.

She tried desperately to clear the vision of Sarah's death from her mind. Henry's remorse had not been faked. His anguish still issued from him, with an intensity she had never experienced before. Tears streamed down his face.

"I'm sorry I made you relive that," she said. She had ripped the scab off this memory, and he was bleeding right in front of her.

But she didn't know what to think. She wasn't naïve when she began dating him; he'd told her about his accidental kills during his early years as a vampire when he was still learning to feed without harm. But his own mate? Henry—the moral compass of his community, the defender of the Covenant—had killed the woman he was mated to?

When he bit Sarah and imbibed her drugged blood, he had to understand the risk. But his judgment, clouded by anger and shame, had left no room for rational thought.

Cerissa gave her head a shake to clear it.

Why am I making excuses for him?

As she tried to process her reaction, Henry pulled away and fled the room. She didn't follow him. She needed space and stretched out on the hotel bed. Her head throbbed from the strain of using the touchstone, and she used the remote to turn off the lights.

It didn't help, it didn't allay the horror she felt.

Rubbing her palms against her eyelids, she wondered if anything ever would.

CHAPTER 35

TUSCANY BAY RESORT, SAN DIEGO—LATER THAT NIGHT

Cerissa spent a restless hour trying to sleep. Her head hurt and there was a sharp pain behind her eyes. She rolled on her side and focused on emptying her mind, but the image of Henry killing Sarah kept playing out whenever she closed her eyes.

The instruction manual for the touchstone had warned of this. Sharing memories was dangerous and should only be done with extreme caution.

She'd been wrong to read his. The vision of Sarah's death wouldn't leave her.

At the sound of him returning, she opened her eyes. His were red-rimmed. "Are you all right?" he asked.

"I need to rest. The touchstone has given me a fierce headache and upset stomach. The pain will pass."

At least, the physical pain would.

"Do you want me to leave?"

Did she? She didn't know. She needed time to clear her head.

"I— No, Henry. You can stay." She wasn't ready to push him away just yet. "But don't touch me. Not for a few minutes at least. It's like all my nerves are on fire. I have no defenses; I wouldn't be able to keep you out of my mind."

He stretched out on the bed next to her. After a while, Cerissa fell asleep. The soft, rhythmic sound of her breathing was a welcome relief. As she slept, the crystal grew silent. Her horror at what he'd done faded from his consciousness.

He stared at the ceiling. The light from the hotel living room illuminated the spot he focused on. Not that he needed the light. He didn't need it to see the ceiling, and he didn't need it to see what he was.

Broken. Irredeemable. A monster.

The touchstone had cleared away the cobwebs and made the nightmare of his past fresh in his mind. He would never forgive himself for being so lost in his anger that he ignored the risk the laudanum presented. In his rush to punish Sarah, he'd killed her. It was an unforgivable act.

He didn't deserve to have Cerissa as his mate. It wasn't just his past—it was how quickly he turned on her. He had no reason to believe she'd gone to meet Zeke. He'd allowed his fear, rage, and distrust to run away with him once again.

He would never *hurt* Cerissa—he was certain of it. But he'd lost himself to his anger, treating her like she was his possession to order around. He'd broken her trust. He'd caused her pain simply because he was afraid of his own.

He wasn't free from his past. Perhaps he never would be.

He rolled over on his side and, facing her, propped himself on his elbow. So beautiful, so peaceful, to watch her sleep. If only he could freeze this moment. Then he would never have to witness disappointment in her eyes again.

She woke and abruptly rose, rubbing her temples. He started to reach out to comfort her and pulled back. He would only make her feel worse.

"It was just a nightmare," she said, fluffing the pillow. She lay back on the bed, facing him. "When I experience another person's memories, I'll dream about what I've seen."

He looked into her eyes. "I don't know how to say this. I've wronged you and I'm truly sorry."

He didn't want to ask the next question. But while he might be a monster, he wasn't a coward.

"After seeing what I have done"—he swallowed—"do you still want to be with me?"

He watched her face and waited.

She blinked, sadness pulling down her eyes. "Henry—"

"How can I even ask? You know. You know what I am." He buried his face in his hands. "You know the real reason I accepted the crystal. To protect you. So in my anger, I never forget the vampire in me and hurt you."

"That's why you agreed?"

The truth sat like a bitter herb on the back of his tongue. "I worked so hard to bury what happened to Sarah. Sometimes, I believe it was all a bad dream." He swept his hand in front of himself as if he were pushing the memory aside. "Then I would climb the mountain, see the stone bench and know Sarah's death at my hands was very real."

Too real. But he had to explain, to get her to understand.

"Afterwards, I would shove the recollections back down. I could either go on with my life or resign myself to die. So, I worked on forgetting. Zeke dredged up the memories when he challenged me over you, and I could no longer forget. It's why I accepted the crystal."

She rubbed her eyes. "Henry—"

"I will release you if you want me to," he said, his heart rending with each word. But he would. He'd not make the same mistake again that he made with Sarah.

"I don't know what I want." She wrapped her arms around herself. "I'm on overload. Give me time to process it all."

"I'm so sorry, Cerissa. I'm sorry I withheld the truth. I'm sorry I let the past drive my actions in the present. But most of all, I'm sorry for not trusting you."

She sat there staring at him, cradling her arms across her chest.

There were too many thoughts flying through her mind, and the pain still throbbing behind her eyes made it difficult to focus on any one of them. She'd seen the worst moment of his life. Or was it?

She picked up the touchstone from the nightstand. It was dangerous to use the stone again so soon, but she had to.

"Will you answer one more question?"

He looked at her warily, his long, silky hair wildly fanned across his shoulders. His anxiety weaved through her body, but she wouldn't let his reaction deter her. After a moment, he nodded, and his hand joined hers on the touchstone.

I have to phrase the question carefully.

She mulled over a few versions before asking, "Since Sarah, have you killed or attempted to kill someone who was not trying to physically hurt you or the people you cared about?"

"No," he said adamantly.

She waited, watching, to see what memories might form.

Nothing.

He shook his head forcefully. "After Nathaniel, I vowed I'd never duel again. And after Sarah, I vowed never to harm anyone I took as my mate. I have kept my vows. I will never let my anger drive me to do to another person what I did to them."

He stopped, the anguish on his face becoming more intense. "And I—I forced the other founders to accept amendments to the Covenant, a ban on dueling along with other revisions to protect mortals. Turning a mortal vampire became a decision and process the entire community shared, so what happened to Sarah would never happen again. Those rules are still in place in the event we decide to turn someone to fill the position left vacant by Kim Han's murder."

He averted his gaze. "But even with those changes, I still didn't trust myself. For the first half of the past century, I lived mateless. It has only been since Father Matt's arrival—and with the memory fading—that I believed I could risk taking a mate again."

She sighed and unwound her hand from his, relieved. The most pressing question had been answered.

If it had gone the other way, if he had killed someone else in anger, she would have immediately left him. But there still lay between them a chasm opened by his failure to be forthright about his past and his controlling possessiveness in the present.

She needed time—time to consider how she felt about everything, including how she felt about him.

A thought flitted across her mind. "I have something else to ask of you," she said. "Without the touchstone."

"Anything."

"Wait until you hear what I want. You talk with Father Matt, right?"

"He is my confessor," Henry replied, caution in his eyes.

"Then I would ask you to speak to him about the memories you've shared with me tonight."

"As penance for mistrusting you?"

"If that's how you need to view it, then yes, as a penance for mistrusting me."

"I'll do it for you."

You'll actually be doing it for yourself.

He reached out, like he wanted to touch her, and then pulled back, his fingers hanging between them, and he curled them in. She froze, unable to decide whether to meet him in the middle or pull away.

"I'll do anything you need me to in order to make this right," he said. "Please, believe me."

He lowered his hand and grasped the bracelet on his arm.

"No, Henry, don't—"

He flipped the catch before she could stop him. His remorse flooded through her, knocking her back, with his fear following it—fear of being unworthy of love, fear of being alone forever, fear of losing her.

She clamped down on her own emotions, but not fast enough. Her anguish, her horror, her disappointment—the crystal sucked them out like a wave receding from the shoreline, an undertow dragging them from her mind and into his.

"Please," she begged, "put the bracelet back on. It's too soon. I need time."

He nodded, his heartache written in the lines on his face, and clicked the latch back in place.

As their emotions disconnected, panic seared her. She felt turned inside out, raw and confused. She needed space to breathe.

"I can't deal with this right now. I just can't." She rolled off the bed. "I'm going to the Enclave. I'll come back here tomorrow night. We...we should go to the Mariners Lodge together for the presentation."

"Cerissa, please, don't lea—"

She flashed to her room, unwilling to hear any more, and morphed into her true form. All the reminders were there: the black rock walls, the thin air of high altitude, the empty space where the charcoal drawing of *pita* had hung for close to two hundred years.

Home.

Was this her real home? Would the Enclave always be? The moment she needed to escape Henry, she'd returned here.

He had been afraid that having this room would make it too easy for her to leave. Had he foreseen this moment? If he had, he had been right to be afraid.

She sat on the bed, sadness weighing her down.

Pita had died young.

Her *dadi ma* had never returned for her.

Her *amma* had disowned her.

And Henry...she wasn't sure what would happen with him.

A sinking realization hit her. Eventually, in one way or another, the people she'd loved the most had left her, had failed her, had abandoned her.

Now, she was alone. Again.

She dropped her face in her hands. Maybe it was for the best.

Chapter 36

THE ENCLAVE—THE NEXT DAY

The sky reddened and faded to a light blue-gray before turning black. Cerissa had spent the day harvesting and packaging clone blood. From the Enclave, she flashed back to Henry's hotel room. She couldn't give her presentation to investors without him. People would question it if she arrived at the Mariners Lodge alone.

She waited in the living room for Henry to finish getting dressed. At her side sat the sample case filled with clone blood pouches.

Pain coiled in her chest like a cobra, ready to strike out without warning. She didn't want to deal with the snake.

When she arrived at the Enclave last night, she had left her emotions frozen and worked in the lab until she collapsed into bed for a few hours of restless sleep. She had important work to do tonight. She didn't have time to thaw her feelings. If she started defrosting everything, she feared she'd collapse in a puddle of tears and never rise.

The door from Henry's room opened. His gaze swept over her and his eyes filled with hope. "*Cariña*, you look lovely."

She'd worn a black dress. Tied at her neck was a scarf with splashes of vermilion on a field of royal blue. Perhaps she was sending the wrong message to Henry by wearing the Hill's color, but they needed to present a united front to strangers.

"I'll wait in the bedroom," she said, her throat tight, her voice strained.

"A moment, please." He took her hands in his, raising one to his lips. The light tingle from his kiss warmed her sadness, and she struggled to keep her feelings on ice. "I will give you the space you need, I promise.

But I hope with all my heart you'll return to our home so I can make this right between us."

"Your home."

"No, our home. No matter what happens, it will always be our home." He paused, like he was struggling to find the right words. "I love you, Cerissa, and I will do whatever I need to become the man you deserve. I am sorry I wasn't honest with you about Sarah earlier. I'm sorry I hid the truth. I am sorry I didn't trust you. I am sorry for my behavior toward you—"

"Henry—"

"Please let me finish." He looked down at his feet. "I'm sorry I still struggle to control my...my irrational possessiveness. The first night we were here, when I confronted Zeke, what he said to me, I thought he was going to tell you about Sarah before I had a chance to. I wanted to wait until we returned to the Hill, had a little more time together, the right moment..."

"You were going to tell me?"

"The touchstone—I'm willing to show you if you don't believe me."

"It's not necessary."

He lifted his chin, and his chestnut-brown eyes gazed into hers again. "I—I'm sorry I'm not a better man."

Tears formed in her eyes, the skin stretching to contain them, until one overflowed from the corner. He caught the tear with his thumb, stroking her cheek.

She pulled away, fishing for a tissue in her purse then dabbing at her eyes. "I'm going to ruin my makeup if we keep talking."

Her phone rang. She slipped it out of her pocket.

Karen.

She wiped her nose—why did it run whenever she cried?—and swiped her phone to accept the call.

"Can you talk?"

Cerissa glanced at her watch. "I have ten minutes before we have to leave. Let me go in the bedroom." When the door was closed behind her, she asked, "What's up?"

"You erased my memories of what the Cutter did, right?"

"Your emotional memories." She'd used a touchstone to read Karen's emotions and desensitize the worst ones. "Is something wrong?"

"I keep having the same nightmare, over and over."

Cerissa perched on the end of the bed. "Can you describe your dream to me?"

"Ah, I'm in a box, and I can't get out, and I try pounding, but they won't open the lid. When I wake, my heart's racing and I'm all sweaty. What's wrong with me?"

"I don't know." Cerissa pinched the bridge of her nose. Had something gone amiss with the process? The touchstone hadn't been used before to treat a human. "I only erased the emotional memories of your injuries. I didn't wipe what you felt when you were first kidnapped. You could be suffering from post-traumatic stress disorder—PTSD—from the kidnapping itself."

"What should I do?" Karen sounded desperate. "These nightmares are wreaking havoc with my work schedule. I'm afraid to go to sleep, and when I do, I wake with my heart racing and lie there awake for hours. I'm exhausted. I thought maybe a sleeping pill—"

"Did you try talking with Father Matt? He may be able to help."

"I'd prefer a pill. Something to make it all stop."

A headache began forming behind Cerissa's ears. She rubbed at the painful spot. How could she help? This was so far outside her expertise.

And then an idea hit her. "I'll tell you what. If you'll see Matt first, I'll discuss possible medications with him."

"But I can't talk with him. I can't tell him you erased my emotions from what the Cutter did."

Karen had a point. A good one. "But you could talk to him about the nightmares."

"Nuh-uh. I don't want him knowing my business."

"All right. What if I found another therapist for you? Someone who knows about the Lux—maybe one of my Lux colleagues. Would you be willing? Then you wouldn't have to worry about revealing something you shouldn't. Working together, we could find something to help you."

"I don't want to talk to a stranger either."

"Karen—"

"Why won't you help me? Just do whatever you did before, but take all my memories of what happened. Or give me a pill. Just make it stop."

"I don't know how to," Cerissa said, rubbing the tense spot behind her ear again.

"But you saw what the Cutter did. You understand what I went through better than anyone."

"I saw, but I don't know how to fix this for you. Let me find someone who can—"

"I thought we were friends."

"We are." She squeezed her eyes shut. "I just can't help you on my own."

"Yes, you can."

She sighed. Everything was crashing down on her. "Karen, give me some time to figure this out."

"I don't have time. The nightmares are getting worse."

"Then please, let me find someone to assist on this."

Silence fell on the line.

"You don't really *want* to help me, do you?" Karen said after a few moments. She sounded stiff and angry.

"Of course I want to help you, but we have to leave right now. Once my presentation is over, I'll call you—"

"Don't worry about me. Your work is more important. Everything is more important. Clearly."

"Karen, no—"

The line went dead.

Cerissa stared at the now-silent phone. So much pain, so much hurt in this world. She felt like she was drowning in misery.

As soon as the presentation is over, I'll arrange for someone to help her.

But if Karen didn't want therapy, what next? As a medical doctor, there was nothing more Cerissa could offer.

She checked her makeup in the bathroom mirror and saw there was no major damage from her earlier tears. She returned to the living room. Henry watched her with sad eyes, waiting for her to make a move.

Through their connection, she sensed him struggle with his emotions, as if he was fighting against the urge to ask her who had called.

She wasn't going to tell him. He'd have to learn to trust her, to give her space.

She took a deep breath and let it out. "We should leave now."

He gave a slight bow and opened the door.

Cerissa grabbed the sample case's handle and led the way to the elevator, rolling the case at her side.

"I emailed Tig," he said.

"About us?" Was he rushing to tell others they were breaking up? Her stomach dipped. She wasn't ready. Not yet. She hadn't agreed to that decision.

His hand gently brushed her shoulder. "The flyer. I sent her the flyer. I'm going to call her after your presentation to tell her about Jim Jones. We've waited too long."

"Oh," she said, fighting to control her emotions. "I spoke with the Protectors. They don't want to take Reverend Jones into custody. They want more evidence."

"I promised to work with you—"

"Henry—"

"I keep my word."

He stopped to knock on Zeke's door. The cowboy joined them in the hallway.

Cerissa stared at the lit elevator button. How was she going to give an investors presentation feeling like this? Her whole world, the world she'd carefully crafted when she claimed her free will, was falling apart, and with it, her heart.

Henry watched from the back of the lodge's meeting room. He ignored the other vampires gathered there. A gray fog seemed to surround him, his focus solely on Cerissa. She stood by a whiteboard at the front, clicking through her slide presentation. She'd done a brilliant job. Investors would be throwing money at her afterward.

As she spoke to the crowd, she never looked his way.

His chest felt heavy, sadness weighting his shoulders, desperation clawing at his gut. Had he lost her for good?

I should never have hidden the truth.

If he had told Cerissa about Sarah from the beginning, he could have spared himself this heartache. She would have rejected him before he gave his heart to her, and he would have faced a much smaller hurt than the one currently pounding through his veins.

Perhaps I deserve it.

No one should love him. Not after what he did. The pain of their separation was just one more penance he had to pay.

She brought the presentation to a close and began passing out blood pouches to the group, samples of her product for them to try.

From behind him he felt a tap on his shoulder, and he spun around to see a redheaded man with a handlebar mustache.

Jim Jones.

The description Cerissa had provided during their drive from the hotel matched this man.

"Henry Bautista?"

"Yes."

"Isaiah Jones," the man said, sticking out his hand.

Out of reflex, Henry shook it. "I thought your name was Jim Jones."

"Shush," Jones said, pulling back his hand to raise a finger to his lips. "I don't use that name here."

"Why not?"

"No one here knows me by it."

"My mate does—she told me about you."

"So, the little gal is yours after all? Wasn't sure she was telling the truth."

Henry gave him a nasty look. "Cerissa does not lie."

"She's cute as a Coke bottle," Jones said with a sly wink. "But pardner, how do you stand it? A brainy chick, I mean."

"Don't speak about my mate that way." Was she still his mate? Or was that another falsehood?

The reverend patted Henry's arm. "Take it easy. No need to get your dander up. You two married?"

"My relationship is none of your business."

He chuckled. "I get it. So, you're hitched but not churched. I'm happy to do the honors when you're ready."

Henry clenched his teeth even harder. "Was there something you wanted?"

"Let's step out here where we can talk without disturbin' everyone."

He followed Jones into the hallway. Here was an opportunity to pump information from the man who may be behind the attacks, and he was blowing the moment by getting defensive about Cerissa.

Henry glanced around. Others had started to leave the presentation and were milling about. "Is there somewhere we can speak more privately?"

"Ah, sure—through here." Jones opened the door to a smaller meeting room containing chairs but no table. "That blood thing, it ain't real, right? I mean, her mouth's talking but her ass can't deliver."

"I assure you the blood is real," Henry said stiffly, bristling at the crude reference. "I live off it. You should try some. What she produces in her lab is quite good."

"Well, you look like a healthy fellow. Hasn't done you any harm. Here, y'all take a seat." Jones closed the door and moved two chairs to face each other. He took one and scraped his hands through his short red hair. "I wanted to talk to y'all 'cause not everyone knows I'm a preacher.

It's why I go by my middle name when I preach. I'd rather you kept my volunteer work to yourself."

"It's a little late for that. A few others are already aware of your conversation with Cerissa and Zeke." Henry settled onto the offered chair. "I'm surprised you think you can keep your preaching a secret, considering you left your flyer in the lodge's lobby."

"Someone else preaches if anyone from the Mariners Lodge shows up."

Why did Jones think that was all the protection he needed? On the nights Jones preached, someone in the audience, someone who was not a lodge member, could still recognize him as being from San Diego. "Cerissa told me what you said from the pulpit. But your intent is, well, vague. What are you trying to accomplish?"

"Same thing I told your mate. I'm fixin' to get rid of the treaty."

Didn't Jones understand the peril they were all in if the restriction on creating new vampires was lifted? After all the work Henry had put into drafting the pact, the long nights negotiating a deal to save his people, a few upstarts wanted to trash their compromise?

Over my truly dead body.

"And how do you plan on eliminating the treaty? Are you going to war against us?"

"Ya know, this ain't my first rodeo. I've been through wars before. I'm not fixin' to start one."

Henry crossed his ankle over his knee. "Then what are you planning on doing?"

"Support's tricklin' in, not plum but pert near. I'm not the only one who thinks we've gotten the short end of the stick."

"Did you not read the committee's report?" Henry snapped. "The treaty was passed to prevent a Malthusian disaster. If we allow our numbers to increase, we will soon outnumber the mortal population."

Jones held up his hands, patting the air. "Hey, settle down there. No need to throw a hissy fit."

Had Henry spoken too sharply? The situation with Cerissa had left him edgy. He needed more finesse if he was going to trap Jones into incriminating himself. "My apologies. I would like to hear more about your ideas."

"You pullin' my leg?"

"Not at all. We would both benefit by talking about this." During treaty negotiations, he'd learned that listening was as important as talking—maybe more so.

"Then why don't we meet up tomorrow night?"

"Cerissa and I are staying at the Tuscany Bay Resort. We could discuss the matter there."

"A hotel? Nah. Come on over to my apartment. My place may not be as roomy as the grand mansions you Hill folk are used to, but we can relax and jaw a bit."

Henry took his phone off his belt and tapped his calendar. "Would midnight work?"

"Yup. Give me your email address and I'll send you directions. And bring your purty little girl along. I wouldn't want to be on her wrong side in this. I bet she's meaner than a skillet full of rattlesnakes when she's angry."

Chapter 37

Sierra Escondida Police Station—Same Night

"She what?" Tig demanded into her desk phone. Henry had called her at the station with some disturbing news. "Cerissa met with Jim Jones?"

"His real name is Isaiah Jones."

Jayden came running into her office. He must have heard her yell.

"Close the door," she mouthed to him, covering the receiver with her hand, and punched the speaker so Jayden could hear.

"I'm sorry, Tig," Henry continued. "She was only going to observe. Zeke went with her. Isaiah spotted him and—"

"And where were you?"

"I had a business meeting. I didn't like the idea of her going, but she insisted."

Why didn't he control his mate?

Tig looked at Jayden and rubbed her forehead. She would never try to control him that way. Why did she expect it of Henry?

She didn't. But she could expect him to keep her better informed.

"And this was last night?" She stared at her desk blotter. "Why am I hearing about it now?"

"We had, I mean, Cerissa and I, well, we had a disagreement afterwards." He sighed heavily. "The reason isn't important. What I'm trying to say is I saw Isaiah tonight at the lodge and confirmed what he told her. He's invited us to his apartment to tell us about his plans. He claims he's involved in a nonviolent movement and knows nothing about the recent attacks."

Tig ran her hand over her short hair, not believing what she heard. Could Henry be that naïve? Or was there something else driving this? "You are not permitted to kill him. No revenge. We have to convict him first."

"I'm not going there to kill him," he said sharply. "I'm going there to listen. Zeke will be with us."

She tapped her fingers on her desk. "You could be walking into a trap."

"Which is why I'm calling you. I'll email you the location we're going to. We're meeting him at midnight tomorrow night. I'll call you when we're done."

"This is the most insane plan—"

"Tig, I'm convinced we will not be in danger there. Trust me on this."

If he'd been standing in front of her, she would have throttled him. Instead, she focused on calming her breathing. "I can't let your group go in alone." She glanced at the time—ten thirty. "I'll fly a team there tonight, and we'll have your back tomorrow night."

Silence on the other end of the line. She was coming whether he liked it or not. The choice wasn't his.

"Very well," he said. "I'll reserve rooms for you at the Tuscany Bay Resort. Text me the names. Goodbye."

The call disconnected, his voice replaced by a dial tone. She punched the speaker button to turn off the obnoxious sound.

She had no option but to go. Last night's drama with the Cutter hadn't produced any solid leads. The partial license plate number didn't belong to anyone named Charles—or any variation—and it didn't match up with the Swiss company renting the Cutter's apartment.

Thousands of license plates contained N8R. She'd assigned officers at the annex to analyze the data. Maybe they would narrow down the possibilities. The crime scene investigators were still crawling all over the duplex, looking for fingerprints or any other clues.

She eased back in her chair. "Well, that's a mess," she said to Jayden. "Call the airport and tell them to prep Rolf's plane for a quick departure. If his plane isn't available, rent another one. Preferably one I've flown before."

"Roger, chief."

"And there's time for you to run home and pack an overnight bag. My kit is already here." She always kept a suitcase packed for emergencies. "While you're at home, please grab an ice chest and throw in some bagged blood. I'll refill in San Diego if I need to."

He gave a nod and headed out the door.

"Oh, and call Liza," she shouted after him. "I want her with us."

"Will do," he yelled back, and the exit door buzzed.

Tig lifted the receiver and hit speed dial for the town attorney. "We need some movement on the Florida warrant," she told him.

Marcus harrumphed. "The district attorney there hasn't helped, and none of our brethren have enough sway with local law enforcement."

"We need to consider other options."

"Hmm. This will require delicate handling." She heard tapping over the phone, like Marcus was typing. "I can catch a commercial flight to Miami before sunrise."

"Going to hire one of our own to break into the ISP's offices?"

"Not quite. A little more finesse, but just as risky. It's better if you aren't aware of the details."

What was this clandestine stuff all about? She chewed her lip as she considered the implications. No, it wasn't worth asking.

"Be careful," she said, standing to leave. "Do you want me to send Jayden with you?"

"I'll be fine. I have the utmost confidence in the mortuary service. They've never tried to tamper with a body shipped through them; no reason to start worrying now."

"Are you sure? I could send Jayden with you. It wouldn't be a problem." Actually, it would put her at a terrible disadvantage to go to San Diego without Jayden, but she had to make the offer.

"Your concern is appreciated, but I bought the most recent style of security casket; the box locks from the inside. Nicholas will ride with me to the airport and see me loaded on. Trust me," Marcus said. "I'll be fine on my own."

She hung up and punched Rolf's number. She got his approval to use his company plane. The town would pay him for the use—there were no free rides.

The vice mayor would be in charge as the interim chief in her absence, with councilwoman Carolyn Cubbedge backing him up. Given what happened to Karen, Tig could count on Rolf to take swift action if another attack happened in her absence. And Carolyn wouldn't take shit from anyone.

The two of them couldn't cause too much trouble while Tig was gone—they both had received training and knew to call the crime investigators at the police annex if they needed help.

Mortal memories could always be wiped later.

She then emailed Quentin, notifying him she'd be in the lodge's jurisdiction overnight. She hated giving advance notice—anyone could be behind the attacks—but violating the treaty would only hamper her investigation.

Abigale was right. Tig would be able to get her job done faster without all these picayune rules and procedures.

Then she thought about Jayden. He valued those operational limits because it meant the rights of the innocent were protected.

She understood the reason even if it frustrated her. Some days she longed to be back in the field, doing work for her maker, Phat. Those were freewheeling missions where no one questioned the techniques they used so long as they got results.

But their world had changed, and she had to change too. She slid on her coat, grabbed her go bag along with extra ammunition, and headed out the door for the airport.

Chapter 38

THE ENCLAVE—TWO HOURS BEFORE DAWN

A trill roused Cerissa from a troubled sleep at the Enclave. She raised her head, and the clock read four in the morning. The phone trilled again. She shifted her wings to be able to reach the bedside table, her two thumbs wrapping around the device.

Rolf.

Anxiety constricted her stomach. Why was he calling? Had something happened with Henry?

She morphed back to human form, her long hair braided back, and swiped the accept button.

"How soon can you be here?" he asked, sounding panicked.

Not Henry, then. She rubbed her tired eyes. "Do you need more adrenaline-enhanced blood?"

"I'm not calling about me. Karen tried to kill herself."

"What?" Cerissa shot to her feet. She had arranged for a colleague to visit Karen later today. She knew about the nightmares, but this…

Why didn't I do more before going to sleep? Maybe visited her myself?

"She needs your help right now."

Cerissa pulled on a pair of jeans. "Are you at the emergency room?"

"No, we're at home. Karen's bedroom."

"Why didn't you take her—"

"I used my blood to heal the cuts on her wrist. But she hasn't woken up—I can't feed her my blood until she does."

"I'll be right there."

She threw on a t-shirt, grabbed her medical kit from the Enclave lab, and flashed to Karen's room.

Rolf sat on the bed next to an unconscious and naked Karen, holding her hand. He moved aside as Cerissa rushed in to check her pulse and breath rate, both of which were way too fast. The sheets were wet, but not with blood, and her auburn hair was damp.

"I found her in the bathtub," he said. "The smell of blood—"

"Understood. Was she submersed?"

"No—she was breathing."

"Where did she cut herself?"

He lifted Karen's left wrist. Vampire blood had closed the gash and stopped the bleeding, leaving an angry red line. From there, the skin would heal on its own. No stitches were needed.

As horrible as this was, Karen's attempt while Rolf was awake was a good sign—a scream for help.

How had I misread the crisis so badly?

Karen had insisted—repeatedly—that she was fine until yesterday's call. What Cerissa heard on the phone was worrisome, but not overly so.

Nothing suggested Karen would attempt to harm herself. "Did she take anything? Pills? Poison?"

"I don't think so." Rolf rushed into the adjoining bathroom and returned quickly. "No empty bottles on the counter or in the trash can."

Cerissa wrapped the blood pressure cuff around Karen's uninjured arm. Ninety over fifty. "Her pressure is critically low. I'm going to transfuse her. Are you okay being in the room if I do?"

Rolf looked paler than normal but nodded.

From her medical bag, she removed a pouch of clone blood—O-negative, the universal donor—and a short time later had the transfusion started. She then drew a blood sample from Karen and used a Lux device to test for drugs.

The reading came out negative, and Cerissa breathed a sigh of relief. Satisfied, she took her phone from her pocket.

"Who are you calling?" Rolf asked.

"Someone who can help. I can't leave Karen alone during the day, and taking her to a conventional inpatient facility isn't an option, not with all the secrets she's carrying."

Fidelia answered. "Hello?"

"The patient I mentioned to you—she tried to comment suicide. How soon can you be in Sierra Escondida?"

"A few minutes. Same place you're phoning from?"

"Yes, thank you." Cerissa clicked off the call and looked at Rolf. "Fidelia is trained in psychology and medicine."

"How can we trust her?"

"She's Ari's sister."

A pixyish blonde flashed into the room, her fine hair short and spiked. She pointed a finger at Cerissa. "I told you it was stupid to use the touchstone on a human."

"What choice did I have? You saw what the Cutter did to her."

Desensitizing Karen's emotional memory had seemed the best way to help her process the trauma of having five fingers hacked off and a message carved into her stomach by the serial killer.

"Yeah, well, see what happens when you don't process the PTSD properly? This—" Fidelia waved a hand at Karen's unconscious form. Her voice was high-pitched and always reminded Cerissa of the good witch, Glinda, except she wasn't always as nice. "This is what happens when you play with things you're not supposed to."

"I don't understand," Rolf said. "She seemed fine. She told me she doesn't feel—"

"Your girlfriend feels enough." Fidelia glared at him. "She tried to finish what the Cutter started."

"What can we do to help her?" Cerissa asked.

"Well, I can't do anything until she wakes."

The clone blood was almost gone. Cerissa checked Karen's vitals. "Her pulse and pressure are returning to a normal range. I'm going to give her one more liter."

She hung another bag. Moments later, Karen's eyelids fluttered, and she moaned. "What…"

Rolf pushed his way in and took Karen's hand. "*Liebling*, I'm here."

"What happened?"

"You tried to hurt yourself," Cerissa said.

Karen thrust her chin in Cerissa's direction. "What is she doing here?"

"I called her," he said. "I had to do something."

Karen ran her hand over the sheets, the IV tube following the movement. "The bed's wet."

"Rolf," Cerissa said, taking a plush cotton bathrobe from Karen's closet. "Go find dry sheets. Here"—she helped Karen stand—"put this on for now."

Karen resisted. "I don't need your help."

Rolf took the robe. He got Karen to her feet so she could slip into one sleeve and draped the robe over the side with the IV. Her balance wavered.

Cerissa grabbed her arm. "Are you dizzy?"

"A little." Karen shook her loose. "But I don't need your help."

"Karen—"

"No, you don't want to give me the help I need."

Fidelia stepped closer and offered a hand. "Then perhaps you might accept my help while your boyfriend changes the sheets."

The psychologist introduced herself and helped Karen to a chair. In a whirlwind of motion, Rolf remade the bed. Cerissa stood by, her chest constricting, helplessness engulfing her.

Karen pointed in Cerissa's direction. "I want her to leave."

"But the transfusion—"

Fidelia checked the IV line. "I can handle it from here."

Cerissa's throat tightened even more. She loved her friend. She'd sacrificed so much to save Karen and would forever carry the scars of punishment on her own back—in part for using Lux technology to heal her.

Except I didn't really help her.

And now Karen no longer wanted her as a friend. Fidelia gave a little shooing motion.

My feelings aren't important. This is about what Karen needs most.

Cerissa nodded to Fidelia, sniffed back a tear, and flashed to her room at the Enclave. Landing on the bed, she mashed her face into the pillow.

How could I be so wrong?

She'd sworn never to let a loved one suffer again. If it had been within her power, she would have saved *pita*. And when faced with the choice—heal Karen or let her suffer—she thought she'd made the right one. But were the Protectors right? Was it misguided to use Lux technology to save a mortal's life?

She pounded on the bed, trying to block the pain.

The matter was out of her hands. She'd have to let go and trust Fidelia with the delicate task of healing Karen—even if it meant sucking up more hurt than she could handle.

Chapter 39

FLORIDA—SHORTLY AFTER SUNSET

Marcus rang the doorbell of a flamingo-pink home in South Beach. He brushed his fingers over his mustache to smooth the bristles. After rising, he'd taken the time to trim off the handlebars, but he could feel a few stiff bristles sticking out wildly. It was a pain in the ass that the facial hair he died with grew back during his day sleep, but he refused to show up at Ari's looking like a reject from the 1800s.

The door opened. "May I come in?"

The pleased look on Ari's face was worth all the indignities Marcus had tolerated to travel there. Despite what he'd told Tig, he hated waking up at dusk in a locked coffin, waiting for the mortuary service to deliver him to a safe place where he could unlock and rise.

Ari glanced around as if he expected to see other people accompanying Marcus. "Are you alone?"

"Outside our jurisdiction, the Rule of Two doesn't apply."

"All right, come on in."

Marcus brushed past him, intentionally sweeping his hand across Ari's Guayabera shirt. His other hand carried a briefcase.

"You have a beautiful home." The living room was predominately decorated in white leather and chrome. "That's a nice Andy Warhol. An original?"

"Why didn't you call? I'd have met you at the airport."

"The funeral home takes care of everything, even the rental car. I didn't want to be a bother."

"It wouldn't have been any trouble," Ari said.

He looked damn hot with that cute curl gracing his forehead. Marcus raised his hand to brush the errant lock back. "Are you alone? Anyone else in the house?"

"Nope."

"In that case," he said, tossing his briefcase on the couch, "I deserve a proper welcome."

He swept the young man into his arms and kissed him. The kiss progressed from a greeting to a ravenous hunger in under ten seconds.

So tasty, so good.

While Marcus lost himself exploring every inch of Ari's mouth, he felt a hand clutch his butt.

When they broke, panting, Ari asked wickedly, "How about a *very* proper welcome?"

I'll give you proper.

Marcus ripped open Ari's shirt, running his hands down Ari's sculpted chest, stroking his washboard abs, before stopping at his belt. Curling his fingers over the leather strap, he pulled the mortal closer.

"Which way is the bedroom?" he whispered, half an inch from Ari's lips. Although the living room was nicely furnished, the couch didn't look comfortable for what he had in mind.

Ari pointed to a hallway. Keeping his grip on Ari's belt, Marcus towed the young man toward an open doorway.

Play first, business after.

"Give me a minute." Ari broke away and disappeared into an adjoining bathroom.

A short time later, he popped out of the bathroom naked and bounced on to the bed, tackling Marcus in the process. "Now, what did you have in mind?"

A short while later, Ari lay back in bed and said, "You are just what I needed."

"My pleasure." Marcus felt a grin curl his lips. Yes indeed, mixing business with sex was paying off.

The mortal propped himself up on an elbow and gave a little frown. "Though I did like that shirt you ruined."

"It's not ruined." Marcus chuckled and gave a dismissive wave of his hand. "I'll happily pay for the button repair."

"Deal," Ari said with a laugh. "But as much fun as you are in bed, you didn't come all this way just for a reprise." He suddenly sat up, looking panicked. "Or did you?"

Marcus rolled toward him. "Now, dear boy, I'm not trying to trap you. As much as I'd like to say yes, the truth is I need a favor."

"Good, 'cause this horn dog doesn't do relationships, *capisce*?"

"Of course." Disappointment lodged in Marcus's chest. After two couplings, was he attached to this new blood? Or was it the excitement of a new paramour? And what about Nicholas? He pushed the uncomfortable feelings away. "What I need couldn't be asked over the phone."

"Oh? Do tell." Ari crossed his legs yoga-style, looking down at Marcus.

Marcus raised his head and rested his cheek on the mortal's lap. The warmth felt nice. "We might have a way to find out who is behind the Carlyle Cutter."

Ari's eyes lit up. "Cloak-and-dagger stuff? I'm all ears."

Excellent. With any luck, his curiosity would outweigh his scruples. "We discovered an IP address for the person we think manufactured the silver bullets used in the attack."

"And you want me to track down said ammo maker?"

"We've tried more conventional means." Marcus sat up. The musky scent of their recent sex was distracting him. "The internet service provider has been throwing all sorts of legal roadblocks in our way, and the Florida authorities have been ineffectual in serving our warrant."

"I get it," Ari said with a nod. "You want me to hack into the ISP and pilfer the information. That's why you came here—you didn't want to discuss a highly illegal venture over the phone."

Marcus leered and pushed him back on the pillow. "It wasn't the only reason."

Ari laughed. "Okay. You're just lucky I don't give a rat's ass about the law."

"Whereas I have great respect for our legal process, but sometimes one must bend the rules."

"Particularly when you don't care whether the evidence stands up in court."

"You understand." Marcus stretched out on the mattress and cuddled in close. "It won't matter to the council how we got the information, as long as it isn't fabricated. I do have ethics—I won't put on falsified evidence. Never have, never will."

"Great." Ari kissed him and then rolled out of bed. He pulled two robes from the closet. "Put this on and we'll see what I can do for you, and later," he added with a smirk, "we'll see what you can do for me."

Marcus slipped on the robe, tied the belt, and followed Ari to a large room off the kitchen. In most homes, the area would be decorated as a family room. Not Ari. He had converted the space into a tech center.

"Impressive," Marcus said, as he surveyed the tall racks of computer gear lining one wall.

Ari walked over to a workstation, plopped into a captain's chair, and motioned to the kitchen table across the room. "Pull over a seat."

The workstation sat on a walnut desk with three high-definition monitors and three keyboards. One screen swung out on an arm attached to the wall. The arrangement looked like command central in a Star Wars movie.

Marcus remained standing and pointed at the computer racks. "What are all those?"

"Part of my server farm." Ari stared at the main monitor as he tapped at the keyboard. "I have lots of different projects running. My servers overflow into the next room, kept cool and dry from Florida's steam bath."

Even more tech. Interesting. Why did he need all this? Marcus walked behind Ari and looked over his shoulder. "That's not what I see on my PC."

"I'm using Linux, not Microshit. Can't do anything worthwhile with a closed system."

"Linux?"

"Open-source. No one owns the rights, so I can work with the source code. I made my name in the geek world this way—I've tested and debugged so much open-source software that 'Ari-improved' is almost a status symbol for a program."

Marcus chuckled to himself. *Ego goeth before a fall.*

Getting Ari to brag might lead to new information about him—and his cousin. Oscar's betrayal had honed Marcus's sixth sense to a sharp point. It told him those two were hiding something, and he was determined to learn their secrets.

Marcus ran his fingers through Ari's hair. "How do you make a living if your programming isn't copyrighted?"

"Because I've collected so much bug bounty I don't care—"

"Bug bounty?" He pictured a bright green beetle sitting on a stack of money.

"Yeah, companies pay a bounty when you find a bug—a vulnerability—in their system and report it to them. Going rate is five thousand a bug."

"And how many have you found?"

"About one a week."

Marcus raised his eyebrows. "Two hundred and fifty thousand a year?"

"More or less. Not to mention when someone wants something programmed, they'll pay for the best. Just as your community did."

Marcus sat in the chair he'd pulled over. "What programming language do you use?"

"Whichever one works for what I'm doing."

"A name, please. I may be almost a hundred and fifty years old, but I've kept up."

"You didn't know what open-source was."

"Don't quibble."

"All right." Ari snickered and continued to type. "C++, Perl, Python—like I said, whatever serves my purpose. I'm fluent in about ten languages, and I keep adding new ones as needed. But you've read my CV."

Indeed, the young man had an extensive curriculum vitae for his age. But Marcus wanted Ari in the habit of answering even the smallest question. He'd learned the technique watching Tig work.

A strange-looking web browser opened on the computer screen.

"What are you doing now?"

Ari stopped and looked over. "You keep asking questions and I'm going to double my fee."

Marcus swept his fingers over Ari's thigh. "I might have a way to compensate you. So answer my question."

Ari grinned smugly. "I've written a crawler program to surf the web for me. I'm looking for known vulnerabilities of Orange Tree Internet—the ISP of your bullet maker. There's a whole hacker world out there tracking that sort of thing."

"Now what are you doing?"

"Another web crawler program. It's set to search for postings of Orange Tree employees."

"Come again?"

"In due time," Ari said with a belly laugh.

Marcus rolled his eyes.

"Don't give me that look. You invited it. And to answer your question, sometimes a company's peons will do stupid stuff. They'll go on a web board and post questions about the software their company runs—something like 'I work for Orange Tree and we use Stopper for a firewall. We've been having problems with it reverting to manufacturer setup.' They give away the program name and the problem, making it easy for yours truly to exploit the vulnerability to hack their system."

"Ingenious."

"I'd like to think so, but it's nothing I invented. Hackers have known this for years. IT types think they're invincible, so they do incredibly stupid things. It's only a matter of finding their errors in judgment." Ari typed a few more lines. "I'm using a script I wrote for another purpose and made minor modifications to the keyword search. There. Those two programs will need time to run."

"What would you like to do while we wait?"

"You have to ask?"

Marcus ran his hand along Ari's thigh. Dropping to his knees, he moved the robe away and leaned in to press his lips over a bright blue vein in the mortal's quad. The sharp scent was intoxicating.

Ari picked up a metal cylinder—it looked like the calibrating tool that had fallen out of his pocket the first night they were together—and wrapped his arms around Marcus, pulling him up close for a deep kiss while he did something with the stubby wand out of sight. A light *hiss* emanated from the device.

Marcus sat back, breaking from their embrace. "What was that noise?"

Ari tossed the tool back on the desk. "Nothing for you to worry about."

What was he calibrating while they had kissed? Marcus took a deep breath. The scent of blood and masculine musk stirred him, and a strong sense of peace invaded his body, overcoming his suspicions. He would find out later what Ari was doing with the tool—he had his ways.

Leaning in, he kissed the luscious vein in Ari's leg again. "Do you mind?"

Ari laughed, a deep bass sound. "Not at all. It would be my pleasure—literally," he said, as Marcus's fangs sank into his skin.

Chapter 40

Tuscany Bay Resort, San Diego—three hours later

Tig stared out the hotel suite's window at the muted orange glow. A layer of fog had rolled in, masking the sun as it disappeared into the Pacific Ocean. They'd arrived last night with enough time to check in and bed down for the day.

Jayden sat across from her at the dining table. He had ordered room service, and she'd finished a mug of blood and was working through her email, but she couldn't concentrate.

"Damn it," she said. "I should have sent a team weeks ago to stake out New Path's mailbox."

"Don't beat yourself up," he said, rising from his chair. "We don't have the resources for that kind of stakeout."

"How could an amateur like Cerissa find Jones?"

"Come on, Tig. You had to deal with Kim's murder, Karen's kidnapping, and Nina's death." Jayden moved behind her and rubbed her shoulders. His thumbs were a welcome chisel into her rock-hard trapezius muscles. "You can't do it all."

"Yeah, but—"

"And don't forget—Jones returned to town this week. Henry and Cerissa got lucky. If we had staked out the mailbox for a month, it wouldn't have made a difference. Jones wasn't here to be found."

Tig's mobile phone rang. Ari's number. She punched accept, and Jayden stopped massaging her shoulders, taking his seat at the table.

"Yes?" she answered.

"Marcus asked me to call you."

"Regarding?"

"Who made the silver bullets."

Tig paused. So, this was the illegal maneuver. Computer hacking. She didn't like it, they kept sliding down the slippery slope Jayden was concerned about. But then, that was why Marcus hadn't told her anything.

She glanced at her tactical watch. The town attorney had arrived in Florida during the day. Even with the time zone difference... "This fast?"

"Now I'm hurt."

"Look, do you have something to tell me?"

"I don't know. Maybe I should go back and check my results..."

She rubbed her forehead. High-maintenance consultants would be the death of her. "I have the utmost faith in you. Now, what did you learn?"

"Guy's real name is Lance Griffin." She could hear the prideful smile in his voice. "The name he registered under in the chat room—Darby Dennis—appears to be an alias."

That explained why she couldn't find anything about him under Dennis.

"He makes custom ammunition," Ari continued. "Sells blanks to movie studios and bullets to hunters who want a special load."

Bingo. "Where does Lance Griffin live?"

"San Diego." He started dictating the address. Tig grabbed a pen and took notes. She had suspected San Diego was the focal point all along—this was more evidence confirming her suspicion.

"Got it," she said, throwing down her pen. "Thank you. I'll call you if I have any questions later."

"Wait. You're going to need me with you when you interview him."

"This is a police matter. I appreciate your offer, but—"

"Are you going to search his computer?"

"Probably."

"Then you'll need me along."

Tig snorted. "Even if I consent to taking a civilian with us, you're in Florida."

"I can be in San Diego by tomorrow evening. Of course, you'll have to pay for first-class airfare. It's in my contract."

Tig tapped her fingers. She didn't care about the cost, and it would be easier if she had a computer expert with her.

"Is it a deal?" Ari asked.

"My deputies and I will serve the warrant. Once Mr. Griffin is under our control, you may join us to search his computer."

"Works for me," Ari replied. "I'll see you at his house at nine tomorrow night."

"The time is fine, but we won't meet at his house. I don't want to tip him off." She looked for nearby coffee shops on her tablet. "I'll email you the details on where to find us. Thank you for your help."

"I'll say adieu for now."

Tig clicked off and then called Marcus's number. She asked him to get a warrant for Lance Griffin's house. A quick check of V-Trak revealed no vampire or mortal mate with that name. Still, the man might be an unregistered mate or a thrall—a mortal under a vampire's control but not their mate.

She'd have to be careful.

A short while later, Jayden opened the hotel room door to let Liza in, and the three of them discussed the plan for protecting Henry and Cerissa during their meeting with Jones.

When Tig got on the phone again, Jayden saw his chance.

Ever since Nina's funeral dinner, when Haley had asked him about running for the council, he had chewed on the idea. He wasn't thrilled about throwing his name in the hat, but he hadn't exactly pulled himself from consideration, either.

His father had drilled into him the police code, or at least his father's version: police officers didn't get involved in politics. But his father's code wasn't enough of a reason anymore. Not when he lived in a small community unlike anything his father had any experience with.

And the way mortals were treated on the Hill had grown from irritating to downright insulting. Those flyers the dead councilman had stuck under his windshield wiper—*Fuck and suck—that's all a mortal's good for. No council seat.*—had been the last straw. He didn't want all the headaches the position came with, but the lack of representation was like a grain of sand under a contact lens.

He hadn't planned on being an active part of the much-needed change, but when Haley asked him, it'd triggered something.

As a kid, he had never been picked first to join any sports team. Too short, too much of a runt. A late growth spurt and dedicated weight training had gotten him into the police academy, but the sting of being the last selected had never gone away.

Which was why being asked to run for the council seat *had* felt good, even if he hadn't admitted it. His initial success in finding the Cutter's apartment had made the idea grow.

And then he'd fumbled the Cutter's capture. That wouldn't bode well for an election campaign. Tig didn't blame him for the failure, but he blamed himself.

In any case, he kept mulling over running for council—more often than he expected.

But sitting on the fence wasn't a comfortable position. He would consider the proposition, which meant analyzing it to make a rational—not emotional—decision, and included methodically examining his strengths and weaknesses, as well as the job's positives and negatives.

And his research started with gathering as much information as he could about what a council member did. From the outside, he'd seen the council function. But he needed an insider's view.

"Hey, Liza." He stood and rubbed his leg where he'd been shot. Damn thing was hurting again. "Do you have a minute for a question?"

"Sure, what's up?"

He took her into the suite's small kitchen, so they wouldn't disturb Tig's phone call, and rested against the tile counter. "What's it like being on the council?"

She laughed. "A real pain in the ass. We get two hundred pages of reports and contracts to review before each meeting." She ran a hand into her short, dark brown hair, fluffing the back. "Everyone always wants something—and for free. We make unpopular decisions and listen to people gripe about them. And then there are all those phone calls from constituents. The whole thing is a real time suck."

"Sounds like it isn't much fun."

"Oh, the job has its moments." She gave a catlike grin. "Why do you ask? Is Tig considering running?"

"No, I was thinking—"

"*You* want to run?" She laughed. "Really?"

Why didn't she take the idea seriously? His stubbornness perked up. "I've been thinking about it."

"Don't take this the wrong way. You don't want this job. Yeah, you get a say in how things work, but you're one of five. You need at least two others to agree with you, or you're sitting there with your butt hanging in the breeze, know what I mean?"

"I guess." He'd seen it happen often enough. "But who says I'd never convince some of you to vote with me?"

Liza looked him up and down, a little more respect shining in her eyes. So, their minds *could* be changed. "You'd make a great choice, I'll give you that. But you wouldn't enjoy it—trust me."

Wouldn't he?

She slapped him on the shoulder. "Come on, let's see if Tig's off the phone."

"I'll join you in a minute," he said, watching her saunter out to the living room. He opened the fridge, took out an iced tea he'd squirreled away earlier, and returned to leaning against the counter.

Public service appealed to him, which was why he enjoyed being a cop. What Liza had said hadn't dissuaded him from the idea. But he wasn't sure he was fully committed to it either.

Hmm. Maybe I should talk with Tig?

Later. Tig had too much going on right now. And he wanted to make up his own mind first. If he didn't want the job, there was no reason to hash it out with her. But if he started to lean in the direction of running for the seat, well, then it was a decision for them to work through together.

He'd do the preliminary research and then approach her with his findings.

An hour later, Tig took the elevator at the Mariners Lodge to meet with Henry and the lodge master on the tenth floor. The meeting was the sort of official formality that grated on her nerves.

"I'm here to provide extra security because of the recent threats on Henry's life," she told the lodge master, downplaying the real reason.

Wilma looked suspicious, but accepted Tig's assertion without questioning it, and issued the necessary permits to allow her to do her job.

Afterward, Tig spoke with Henry alone to go over her plan for his meeting with Jones. He agreed to everything except the wire—he refused to let anyone in his party wear one. He *claimed* he wanted a frank conversation with the preacher without his own words being recorded for posterity.

What was he trying to prove, and why?

Reckless.

But in the end, she couldn't force him, so she gave him an emergency call switch to alert her if he was in trouble. All he had to do was push the button to trigger the device. He slid it onto his key ring. Zeke would accompany Henry and Cerissa inside, but Tig and her team would be outside, ready to move in. They finished their plan, and he returned to the hotel to wait there.

By eleven o'clock, she was on her way to Jones's apartment with Jayden and Liza. Using a mapping service, she had examined the residential complex, both satellite and street-level views. The apartment wasn't far from Pascala's—both were in areas dense with rentals.

The two-story building occupied an entire block. The units created a rectangle with a pool in the center courtyard. Her team would enter through the front double doors, which led into a lobby. Interior hallways ran left and right, and there was a doorway to the courtyard from which they could reach the apartment's patio.

Jones's apartment wasn't far from the lobby.

The parking lot was underground and card-controlled. She skipped it—no telling if they had security cameras—and parked a block away on a city street.

Liza would be first in. She'd check the lobby doors.

"If they're locked," Tig told her, "wait for someone to come by. Play helpless—you forgot your key. Can you do helpless?"

The councilwoman fluffed her pageboy hair and fluttered her eyelids. "How's this?"

"Helpless, not sultry."

"Don't worry. I'll get in, one way or another. After all, I have my grazing permit from Quentin."

Tig looked heavenward. Every job had its perks. Liza made the most of the ones that came with being a reserve officer. "I don't care how you do it. We have thirty minutes. Just get inside the building. Henry should arrive shortly before midnight, and I want everyone in position when he does. Now go."

Chapter 41

Tuscany Bay Resort, San Diego—Eleven Thirty p.m.

Cerissa waited by the main entryway to the hotel. The driveway was a ghost town—no one else was going anywhere at eleven thirty on a weeknight. Zeke remained a respectful four feet behind her.

Henry stood by the valet stand, giving her the space she'd requested. He asked the attendant to bring their car around, and the young man took off at a run along the sandstone walkway to the underground parking lot.

She tried to keep her gaze focused on anything but the man she loved. The driveway widened in front of her, three one-way lanes curving around a flowerbed of succulents, the xeriscape creating a hundred-yard buffer between the hotel's entrance and the main boulevard out front.

The emotional expanse separating her from Henry was as wide as the cactus patch and twice as thorny.

She sighed.

She had heard from Fidelia earlier in the day. Karen was doing okay but refused to see Cerissa. Fidelia said the rejection was a form of transference—the mortal's anger over what happened had been redirected at the person who saved her.

At least the PTSD treatment had begun, including an advanced desensitization using rapid eye movement, and Karen was responding well. Humans were just beginning to use this technique—they called it EMDR—and as a doctor, Cerissa was aware of EMDR, but had thought the touchstone would do the trick.

She was still kicking herself for that mistake.

Fidelia had also started Karen on medication, but it would be a while before the antidepressant did any good. In the meantime, someone from the Lux would stay with her twenty-four hours a day for the next week.

Cerissa pressed a hand against her chest. How was she going to get through their meeting with Isaiah Jones mired in all this pain?

Last night, when she had returned to the Enclave after saving Karen's life, Cerissa had collapsed on the bed and gave herself over to a good cry. Afterward, she began the process of examining her frozen feelings for Henry. Doing so hadn't been easy. It had taken an ice pick just to get started.

At bottom, she felt *wronged*. She couldn't come up with a better word. *Betrayed* came close; he'd betrayed their love by suspecting her of going behind his back to meet Zeke—and by withholding what he did to Sarah. He had guessed how horrified she would be over his part in Sarah's death, but he'd held back the truth when he told her about Nathaniel. He'd actively omitted something that *might* have changed everything between them—all the decisions she'd made.

Just like *amma* hid Cerissa's Lux origins from her as a child; just like *dadi ma* hid the truth that they'd never see each other again.

Did everyone who claimed to love her withhold the truth from her? Her heart clutched at the thought.

She'd given Henry a pass on the duel with Nathaniel. Yes, he had treated Sarah like property. And no man had a right to kill another man over his mate's infidelity. But it was a different era, a different ethic. He'd acted honorably under the standard of the time—he'd challenged Nathaniel to an open duel; he hadn't lain in wait, killing in cold blood. He'd followed the code then in place.

She wished he had been more evolved at the time, but she couldn't judge his actions in 1889 by today's standards.

Most importantly, he'd been upfront with her about killing Nathaniel.

And she might have accepted his history with Sarah, too, if he'd been honest. We all did things we regretted, and Sarah *had* agreed to the turn—although as drugged and emotionally fragile as she was, how could she truly consent?

Cerissa's vision blurred, her thoughts whirling. She was once again judging him by today's standard. Back then, the concept of "consent" was a rather foreign one. Sarah had asked to be turned—a decision she'd presumptively made when Nathaniel had offered to do it. Yes, Henry had acted in a rushed rage, but not without his mate's invitation.

And the situation—Henry and Sarah's relationship—was a mess. They were toxic to one another. He was acting out his codependency, not understanding the nature of addiction. If he'd told Cerissa from the start about what had happened, if he'd worked through the ramifications with her, she could have come to accept his past.

But Henry kept all his old shit hidden and let it interfere with seeing her for who she really was. *His* anger and possessiveness in the present had gotten them to this point; *his* anger and possessiveness in the past had killed Sarah.

Had he really changed?

Her gaze wandered back to where he stood tall by the valet desk. His perfectly tailored suit coat was tucked in at the waist, making his broad shoulders look even broader. The pants flowed over his muscular butt, the fabric hanging straight, his black dress shoes polished to a high sheen.

Damn.

She wanted him. She always would. But he had betrayed her when he lied by omission. He had forsaken their love by believing her capable of betraying him. He'd wronged her by treating her like she was his to control rather than his equal to respect. Yet all she wanted to do was go back to the happy couple they'd been.

Her thoughts were like an ouroboros: all one-big-snake-swallowing-tail circle. No matter how hurt and betrayed she felt, she still loved him. But would she ever be able to forgive him?

The valet pulled the rental car into the third lane, the farthest from the lobby entrance. The young man opened the passenger doors for her and Zeke. She followed Henry but looked over her shoulder at the sound of another car, a reflex glance. The driver's window rolled down, and she saw a glint of silver under the hotel's muted lights.

"Henry!" she screamed.

The gun pointed at her. Zeke jumped—a blur of vampire speed. The driver fired, the blast echoing under the stucco awning.

Zeke crumpled in front of her.

Just as quickly, Henry dove for the shooter.

The driver swung the gun.

"Henry, no," she yelled, her ears still ringing, her heart pounding, the bile traveling up her throat like a high-speed train.

I can't lose him this way.

He grabbed the gun's barrel and ripped the weapon from the driver's hands. The force flung the gun away, sending it skittering across the pavement.

The car accelerated and its wheels squealed against the asphalt. Rather than draw his own Glock, Henry hung on to the doorframe, holding the car back. The driver raised a knife and stabbed at Henry's hands, ripping the blade out and plunging it in again.

His hands a bloody mess, Henry struggled to hold on, his fingers curled around the doorframe, but the car broke lose, careening down the driveway and out to the main boulevard.

Cerissa's head felt like it was filled with cotton. For a moment, silence engulfed her, and she couldn't process what she had witnessed. Then Zeke moaned, doubled over on the ground, clutching his chest. Just as suddenly, her brain caught up with the surreal events.

The driver was the Carlyle Cutter.

She dropped to her knees by the cowboy and ran her hand under his leather jacket and over his back. His shirt was dry, no exit hole. She rolled him over, unzipped his jacket, and found blood blossoming.

She ripped open his shirt buttons, pulled off her scarf—the same one she'd worn last night—and pressed the silk over the wound. The edge of Zeke's heart shield was stiff under her palm. The square, made from layers of steel, leather, and Kevlar, was positioned directly over his sternum.

Damn. Vampires of all people should know the heart was off-center, closer to the left than the right.

The bullet had entered a half-inch to the left side.

"Zeke, talk to me."

His face scrunched with pain. "Silver, ma'am."

Cerissa glanced up when she heard Henry use voice command to call Tig. His palms cradled the phone, his bent fingers incapable of any movement. Blood trailed from them and dripped on the asphalt. When the chief picked up, he gave her the license plate number along with the make and model of the Cutter's car. Finished, he used his palm to drop the phone back into his pocket.

"How is Zeke?" Henry held his hands in front of him, his fingers curled like useless claws.

"One entry wound, no exit. We need to get him to the room."

"Let me take care of this first," he replied, and strode to the valet, who was standing frozen in place. Without preamble, he bit the young man's wrist and then did something she couldn't see. A moment later, he locked gazes with the valet and spoke so quietly that all she caught was "forget." He then told the valet to pick up the key ring from where it fell, and in a normal tone added, "Return the car to parking. We've decided not to go out."

She looked around. What else did they need to do to cover this up? The gun had landed close to her. She shoved the Beretta in her purse and then zipped up Zeke's jacket to keep the scarf in place. She pressed her hand over his chest. "Let's go."

Henry slid his arms under Zeke's, hooking his inner elbows under the cowboy's pits to help him to his feet. "The valet will think he cut himself. I used a fang to scratch between the bite marks." He looked up toward the portico's ceiling. "I can't do anything about the security cameras."

The whole incident happened so fast that, from the lack of response, the guard on duty must have missed the action. They'd deal with the recordings later.

Cerissa supported Zeke from the other side, and they made their way through the empty lobby. The clerk at the reception desk looked their way, and Henry said, "Too much to drink. We'll take him back to his room."

They swept by too fast for the clerk to guess anything was really wrong. Zeke's gunshot wound was hidden by his hanging head and hunched shoulders. He hadn't yet bled through his leather jacket. One of Henry's bloody hands was under the cowboy's arm and the other was stuffed into his pants pocket. Nothing to see here.

A few minutes later, they exited the elevator. Henry held Zeke while Cerissa opened the suite's door. "Lay him on the floor," she said. "I'll be right back."

The silver bullet had to come out. She ran into her bedroom, tapped her watch, and flashed to the Enclave lab. Zipping around, she packed a bag with surgical supplies and flashed back to the hotel.

Is this a good idea?

After what Cerissa had gone through with Karen, was using her skills—and Lux technology—to save Zeke the right thing to do? Would there be unintended consequences she didn't foresee, just as there had been with her friend?

Cerissa shook her head. She couldn't second-guess herself this way. She'd made a commitment to heal those under her care—and Zeke qualified.

She carried the bag to where he lay and unrolled a blue plastic tarp, and Henry helped her slide him onto the barrier. The cowboy's breath hitched with the movement.

They kneeled on opposite sides of him. She found her hypo, dialed in the stabilizer, and pressed it to her throat. Then she changed the combo and held her wrist to his mouth. "When I say bite, start feeding on me."

Henry frowned as her words sank in and fear spiked his heart rate. Zeke would bite her? "Why are you doing this?"

"I'm going to take a strong anesthetic and feed him. I may pass out—hold my wrist to his mouth and let him take as much as he can until he doesn't respond to a pain stimulus." She handed Henry the hypo. "Then you're going to give me the antidote. Dial in 2222. Can you do that?"

It was the last thing he wanted to do. He didn't want Zeke anywhere near her wrist. But it was Cerissa asking. She waited, focused on him, her emerald eyes repeating the question.

"I will try," Henry said.

He took the silver cylinder and struggled to rotate the dials. Pain shot through his fingers, sharp, electric spasms. The torn muscles were not yet healed, but he managed to dial in the number. He handed the hypo back to her.

Zeke moaned. "It's okay, ma'am. You don't got to do this."

"The bullet has to come out, and I'm not operating on you while you're awake. It's too cruel." She dialed in the anesthetic and shoved her wrist under his nose. "Bite."

His lips hovered over her pulse.

"What are you waiting for?"

Henry didn't like where this was leading. "Why not use a knife?"

"Zeke will benefit from the fang serum backwash, as well as the anesthetic in my blood." She focused in the cowboy's direction. "I said bite."

"I can't, ma'am," he said with a grimace.

Henry's gut twisted. "He won't, not without my permission."

"Then give it."

He looked at the two of them, at his rival so close to his love. If he was ever to crawl out of the hole he'd dug for himself, he had to show her his possessiveness wouldn't stop him from acting honorably.

He sighed. "Zeke, you may do whatever Cerissa says to do."

She lay down, her arm draped across Zeke's chest, her wrist at his lips.

"Don't worry about me," she said, pressing the hypo to her neck and injecting the anesthetic. "Let him drink as much as he can. I don't want to do this twice."

The way she pressed against Zeke, offering her wrist—jealousy burned through Henry's heart. Hard as it was, he struggled to push the words out. But his love for Cerissa gave him the strength to say, "I-I will. I promise."

Except Zeke didn't bite—instead, his eyelids drooped closed.

She ground her knuckle into his shoulder joint. "Come on, wake up."

He moaned and cracked his eyes open.

"Bite..." Her voice trailed off as her eyelids fluttered.

He gripped her arm and sank his fangs in. For a moment, his blue eyes widened in satisfaction before they drifted shut again.

Henry wanted to rip the cowboy's mouth off her wrist. Watching Zeke pierce Cerissa's skin was harder than watching Nathaniel fuck Sarah. If it was only about fang serum, why hadn't Cerissa asked him to bite her instead? He could have made the wound from which Zeke fed.

Henry furrowed his brow. Maybe the idea hadn't occurred to her. Or had he become so repellent she couldn't stomach his bite? The thought caused his heart to constrict even more.

Zeke stopped sucking and released her wrist. Henry clamped the hypo between his palms.

If I let them sleep, Zeke will die.

A chill passed through him. If he didn't act, Cerissa would wake to find Zeke's mummified body pressed against hers. She would blame herself. And the cowboy's death would haunt her, just as the memory of Sarah slumped on the stairs in his arms, her cold, dead flesh lying against his when he woke, haunted him.

I can't do that to Cerissa.

She was relying on him. She trusted him to carry out her request. He couldn't betray her, no matter how much saving the cowboy pained him.

He pinched the shiny cylinder between his palms, struggled through the pain to dial the numbers, and reached across Zeke's body to press the hypo to her neck. A moment later, she sprang upright. Her eyes crossed and her lips pressed together. She gave her head a shake, blinking rapidly.

"Damn, that feels awful," she said, rubbing her eyes with her palms. The antidote left her wired, like ants were crawling across her skin and hunger growled in her stomach. She ignored both sensations. "I don't know how long he'll stay under, so I have to operate fast."

She stripped off her blazer and skirt and pulled on surgical scrubs and gloves. Kneeling on the floor next to Zeke, she lifted a tray of instruments from the bag and then unzipped his jacket, removed the scarf, and cleared his shirt away from the bullet's entry point. With a pair of sharp shears, she snipped the leather straps holding on his heart shield so she had greater access.

Time was her enemy. She had no idea how swiftly the silver would poison him. Selecting a scalpel, she made a fast incision along his centerline, inserted a rib spreader, and cranked it open, revealing the thoracic cavity. The smell of iron and ground hamburger filled the air.

Zeke's heart wasn't beating. It didn't matter. A vampire's heart and breathing could stop without any permanent damage.

His thick blood oozed around the organ. She used a portable suction machine to remove the blood covering it. The silver bullet had clipped a rib and sat lodged in his left lung, pressing against the left heart ventricle. The lung and heart muscle were black at the point of contact with silver, the black spreading out in weblike veins.

"Why is it black?"

Henry peered into the cavity. "The silver is killing him."

Using forceps, she gripped the smashed bullet and pulled it out. Fortunately, the slug hadn't fragmented. But then, she'd yet to see one fragment. Was it because silver was a harder metal than lead? Almost twice as hard on the Mohs scale, with a shear modulus five times as much. She gave her head a little shake—it wasn't important right now.

Thick, dark blood filled the small hole where the bullet had sat. "Will he heal on his own if I close him?"

"He might."

"But his chances would be better with your blood?"

Henry looked like he was fighting with himself. His sadness invaded her mind, and then suddenly stopped—he had blocked his feelings from her.

He presented his wrist. "Vampire blood poured directly on the wound should heal the silver's damage."

"Do you want to make the incision, or should I?"

She offered him a scalpel, so he could select the vein he preferred to use.

"You should make the cut," he said. "You're his now. You can speak for him."

"What the fuck are you babbling about?" She rarely used the F-word out loud, but he was trying her last nerve.

"He bit you, with my permission. That makes you his now."

She gaped at him. *Unbelievable.* "I've had enough of you and your stupid vampire rules."

She wasn't anyone's *anything* unless she said so.

She took a deep breath, stilled her hand—her anger had made it tremble—and, using the scalpel, made the cut as painlessly as she could, turning Henry's wrist over to let the blood drip unto Zeke's heart and lung. The organs seemed to soak it up like a dry sponge.

"How much?"

"This is not an exact science—you'll have to watch for signs of healing."

She had to reopen the vein in his arm twice when it healed itself. In between cuts, she devoured a protein snack bar. Zeke had drunk more than a pint of her blood before passing out. The loss had left her weak and hungry.

Five minutes later, the black poison lines began to recede, and a faint blue bruise remained.

"A little more," Henry said.

"Are you sure? We won't risk putting him through the turn again?"

"I've never heard of the turn initiated by pouring blood on a wound—only ingested." He offered his arm to her again. "And if you feed him a pouch of human blood upon waking, it should counteract any risk."

That was new information. Her knowledge had holes in it—at some point, she'd have to plug them.

Still kneeling on the floor, she made another cut in Henry's wrist and watched the dark red liquid fall into Zeke's chest. The sight of Henry donating his life force to save the man he believed was his enemy—maybe something had changed in him.

Henry grunted and collapsed on his side, catching himself with his forearm. His eyes were unfocused, and fine wrinkles appeared in his skin. He had donated too much.

She took a pouch of regular clone blood from her kit and handed it to him.

He fumbled the blue bag. His damaged hands had trouble gripping it. She reached over and tore off the corner for him.

"Thank you," he said.

Pinching the bag between his palms, he raised it to his lips and took a long, deep drink.

She checked Zeke again. His heart had returned to a normal reddish-orange color and his skin was trying to grow together, but the rib spreader stopped the process. She removed the device. "How quickly will the chest wall knit? Does he need stitches?"

"More of my blood will close it cleanly."

She opened Henry's wrist wound once more and dripped it along the pleural lining, then shoved Zeke's ribs back in place and let more flow over the incision as the area slowly healed.

She sponged off the excess, cleaning his new skin. Now what? Zeke hadn't moved.

"Do I need to restart his heart?"

"I doubt it. Once the anesthesia wears off, he should start breathing on his own, and his heart will beat."

"You're sure?"

"All I know is what my experience tells me. My heart stops beating, I stop breathing, when I sleep during the day. I suspect your anesthesia has put him into day sleep."

"Damn." She stripped off her gloves and pressed her fingers to her temples, rubbing in small circles, tension sitting behind her ears. "I'm working in the dark ages, experimenting on live beings. We need more information on vampire physiology."

"I'm sure Zeke will appreciate your efforts when he wakes."

"He'll do more than be grateful. Whatever it means that he bit me, he'll undo it."

"That will be up to Zeke," Henry said, his eyes looking sad like a basset hound's. "Whether he releases you is up to him."

"Damn it, Henry. The choice is mine, not his." She started repacking the surgical tools into her bag and tried to suppress her frustration with the whole "vampire bite is like a dog marking its property" thing.

Finished packing, she reached for Henry's hands. "Let me see how your fingers are healing."

The surface cuts had healed. She flexed one of his fingers, checking the range of motion. He flinched when she did. "Are you in much pain?"

"Do not worry about me. I will be fine soon enough."

The tendons beneath his skin were still weak. "I should have brought Rolf's blood from the lab to help you. Do you want me to go back for it?"

"That isn't necessary."

A sharp inhale and sucking noise—she jerked her head in the sound's direction. Zeke was waking. She searched for his pulse. Beneath her fingertips, a slow rhythm had started. "How do you feel?"

"Ah," he said, his gaze slowly focusing on her. "Like I fell off my horse and got stomped on."

She handed him a pouch of clone blood. "The bullet is out. We used Henry's blood to heal the damage."

Zeke gripped her arm instead of taking the offered bag. "Thank you, ma'am. I wouldn't of made it without you."

"You took a bullet meant for me. I appreciate your sacrifice."

"My pleasure." He smiled weakly at her. "And ma'am?" He brought her hand to his lips, kissing the back. She didn't fight him. "If you want, I'll release you. You can go back to being Henry's."

She looked over at Henry. His eyes held pain, and a spike of sorrow leaked past his control. Did she want to go back to being his mate? He hadn't interfered with her plan to save Zeke's life. He'd shown honor and nobility, kept his promise to her, and chosen her desire over his. But was it enough? Could she trust him going forward?

She glanced back at Zeke. "Thank you. I accept your offer to release me."

Whether she became Henry's mate again, well, the decision was between her and Henry. Zeke would have nothing to do with it.

A loud bang on the hotel room door stopped any further discussion. "Open up."

Tig.

Cerissa jumped to her feet and unlocked the door. The chief rushed in, followed by Liza and Jayden.

"How is Zeke?" Tig asked.

"He should be okay." Cerissa showed them the silver bullet she'd removed. Jayden held out an evidence bag, and she dropped the slug in.

"The license came back to a rental car," Tig said. "We're running down who rented the car. Tell me what happened."

"There isn't much to tell." Henry slowly stood and leaned against a nearby table, steadying himself. "We were waiting for the valet to bring our car when a man drove up and tried to shoot Cerissa."

"Are you sure?" Tig looked skeptical. "He aimed at her and not you?"

"Henry's right." Cerissa crossed the room and picked up her purse. "The Carlyle Cutter was driving the car; he was alone. Zeke jumped in front of the bullet to protect me." She opened her purse and showed the chief. "Here's the gun the Cutter used."

Tig motioned to Jayden, who deposited the Beretta into an evidence bag.

"You're positive the driver was the Carlyle Cutter?"

"Absolutely." Cerissa would never forget his face. Not after seeing him in Karen's memories. "The hotel's guard didn't come out; he probably didn't see the attack. But there may be security video."

Tig turned to Liza. "Find out where the security cameras are monitored, get a copy of the recording, and erase the original off their system. If you have to—bite and mesmerize the guard on duty to forget."

"You got it, chief," Liza said, licking her lips before charging out the door.

Cerissa felt Tig's laser-like gaze land on her. "How did the Cutter know you'd be in front of the hotel when you were?"

"I—" Henry let go of the table and fell down hard on the couch with a groan. "I told Isaiah we were staying at the Tuscany Bay Resort. Originally, I invited him to meet us at the hotel. The drive to his apartment from here is half an hour."

Tig snorted in disgust. "It wasn't difficult for him to figure out where and when you'd leave." She headed to the door. "I'm going to the lodge, to talk with Wilma and Quentin. It's time to lay out the case and take Isaiah Jones into custody."

A few hours later, Henry helped Zeke return to his room. They still hadn't heard from Tig. Cerissa offered to sit with the cowboy, but Jayden said, "I'll take over—you've done enough."

Henry escorted her back to their suite, hoping she'd stay the night with him. Facing her, he eyed her neck. If she stayed, they could renew their bond. "Would you like me to order room service for you? You must be tired and hungry."

"It's okay. I'll go back to the Enclave." She swept her hair forward, adjusting the waves to conceal her neck from him. He didn't have to guess her meaning; she didn't want to be his again.

His stomach clenched. Hadn't he done enough to prove he'd changed?

"Don't look at me like that," she said.

He nodded and held out his hand. She took it, and he encased her in his arms. "I can't tell you how sorry I am or how much I know I was wrong. But I can tell you this. I love you, *cariña*. I always will."

She gave him a squeeze and stepped back. "I know," she said. "I just need time."

She tapped her watch and disappeared. He sank onto the couch and stared at his damaged hands. They would heal soon, but would his relationship with Cerissa?

Like a thorny vine, the pain wrapped around his throat and chest, piercing him. He took in a deep, shuddering breath.

He had to be patient. He had to wait for her. He had to let go. As painful as it was, as much as he hated being powerless, he had to suck it up. The decision was out of his control.

Chapter 42

San Diego—the next night

At eight thirty the following night, Tig and her crew arrived at the Beanlicious Coffee Shop near Lance Griffin's address. She tried not to let the frustration distract her.

Last night she had asked Quentin to take Isaiah Jones into custody.

"One of my officers was shot guarding Henry," she had told him. "Jones knew when they were leaving the hotel. It's enough to hold him on."

"Not in my jurisdiction, luv," Quentin said, his Australian accent thick, his voice rising.

She ground her teeth. She'd forgotten about Quentin's habit of calling all women "luv." A dominance gesture she didn't appreciate.

"You admitted Jones wasn't the bloke who shot the girl," he continued, looking at her down his aristocratic nose. "You have any evidence tying him to the drive-by?"

"A group called New Path Church picked up the assassins when they were paroled—the ones who tried to kill Yacov and Henry. Jones is in charge of New Path Church."

"But did *he* pick up the parolees?"

Damn. She knew where he was going. "No, they were released in the daytime."

"So you bloody well don't have anything. When you have hard evidence tying the crimes to Isaiah, come back to us, luv."

Quentin was lucky she didn't still carry a spear, or she'd have turned him into a pincushion. A moment's nostalgia wafted through her. The Maasai didn't decorate their spears, preferring plain and deadly over artistic.

Not that she wanted to kill him—just express her frustration the politically incorrect way.

At least Liza had been able to obtain the security video of Zeke being shot, and the guard's memory had been wiped. Tick that box as done.

Unfortunately, the video didn't show much. The camera angle missed the shooter's face. For now, Tig would rely on Cerissa's and Henry's identification of the shooter.

Tig looked over when movement caught her eye. Ari had walked into Beanlicious like he owned the place. "Where's Marcus?" he asked.

"We don't need a lawyer to serve a search warrant."

Ari shrugged. "I assumed he'd be here. He was shipped on the same plane I flew in on. We both reserved rooms at Tuscany Bay."

Why had Marcus come here rather than returning to the Hill? Didn't matter. His presence might be helpful.

She gestured to a chair. "Take a seat. We were going over the plan. Zeke will handle the battering ram if Griffin doesn't open the door. That is, if Zeke's feeling up to it—"

"Cerissa fixed me good as new," he said with a nod. "You can count on me, ma'am."

Ari raised an eyebrow. "A battering ram? Can we say overkill? All this guy did was ask questions in a chat room and make custom ammo."

Tig shot the evil eye at her consultant. It wasn't Ari's job to question her methods. In the military, no one questioned their superior. But in civilian life? Everyone had an opinion.

"Lance Griffin had no legitimate reason to ask those questions," she replied, containing her anger. "And he's located in San Diego, which gives him a nexus to the conspiracy. Plus we found this."

She held up her phone. A brand-new website on the dark web advertising custom silver ammo for both handguns and rifles. Griffin's silverbullets.onion site hadn't existed until a short time ago. Chet had alerted her last night. He was regularly checking for unlicensed dealers.

"Griffin may be hooked in with the conspiracy and is helping arm them."

Ari scrolled through the website. "What an idiot. He used the dark web but then posted his real name."

"Precisely. We'll start with the soft approach, but Zeke and Liza will be in position to assist if Griffin tries to run. And you will stay in the car until I send an officer for you."

Ari made a face. "You're a buzzkill."

"Yeah, I know. Let's get moving."

They left the coffee shop in a rental van and drove around the block before approaching the house. As they parked, Tig said, "Liza, you and Jayden will enter the backyard through the side yard. Once you're in place, Zeke and I will approach the door."

"Whatever you need, chief." Liza slipped out of the van and hopped the tall fence silently, then unlatched the gate from the other side for Jayden.

Tig waited, giving the two time to circle to the back of the house.

"Okay, go." At the front door, she knocked and called out, "Police, open up. We have a warrant."

Footsteps running—but no one opened the door.

She stepped aside. "Zeke, do it."

He hurled the ram into the door, and it flew off its hinges. Gun drawn, she led the way in. Following the scent of a mortal man, she ran down the hall to a bedroom office. He was halfway out a window.

"Police. Freeze, Mr. Griffin."

He froze bent over the windowsill, leaving him in the perfect position for her to handcuff him. Afterward, she grabbed the back of his shirt and lifted all two hundred pounds of him into the room. Looking around, she dumped him in a desk chair near his computer. That should save time.

She signaled for Jayden and Liza to join them inside and glanced at Zeke. "Officer Cannon, is anyone else here?"

"Nope, chief. He's the only one."

Tig stared down at the captive. "You're Lance Griffin?"

The man cowered. He had a deer-in-the-headlights expression. With a hand thrust under his armpit, she lifted him and took his wallet from his back pocket. "Lance Griffin" was the name on the driver's license. She held the photo next to his face—a good enough match.

She released Griffin, letting him plop back onto the chair. "Captain Johnson, please get Mr. Dumont."

"Roger that, chief."

"Officer Ehrgott, start the camera."

Liza fastened it to a small tripod. When the red recording light came on, Tig asked, "Mr. Griffin, who ordered silver bullets from you?"

"I want a lawyer," he croaked.

Tig growled. Where did mortals learn that? "You're not getting a lawyer. What you're getting is a chance to avoid being charged as part of a conspiracy to commit murder. Now, who ordered the silver bullets?"

"I don't know. I want a lawyer."

At least his answer confirmed he had indeed sold silver bullets to someone. She dropped a copy of the search warrant into his lap and turned to Liza. "You and Zeke tear the place apart. Look for anything to tell us who SilverSmith was working for."

Jayden and Ari arrived. Tig grabbed Griffin's chair and rolled the casters away from the desk with him in the seat. "Mr. Dumont, the computer is all yours."

Ari dumped a magazine stack on the floor, freeing another chair, and seated himself in front of the keyboard and monitor. "This shouldn't take long."

Ten minutes later, Liza handed Tig a box of rifle bullets identical to the ones found in Pascala's motel room.

Zeke discovered the second link: a cashier's check. The copy was stapled to an envelope postmarked out of San Diego, but no return address.

"Got 'em," Ari said.

"What do you have?"

She heard the printer spit out a page and grabbed it: an email order for forty rifle bullets, two boxes. The thirty-thousand-dollar fee covered both.

At the end, the email read, *John Doe will pick them up when you're finished.*

John Doe? These guys lacked imagination.

She held the order in front of Lance Griffin's eyes. "All right, Mr. Griffin. We have everything we need for a conviction."

He looked from Liza to her. "It's not a crime to make bullets."

"Why do you think the bullets had to be silver?"

"I—I don't know."

Tig crossed her arms. "Come on, take a guess."

"The guy who used them wanted someone to know who he was?"

"He's not as stupid as he looks," Zeke said.

"You didn't just make the bullets. In addition to murder, we can add a RICO charge for being part of an ongoing criminal enterprise."

Yeah, she was exaggerating—he'd never be convicted on this evidence in mortal courts—but he didn't know that. She wanted him worried. Violence may be out of the question, but nothing stopped her from lying to him to get the answers she needed.

Griffin's pasty skin paled even more. "I didn't know he was going to kill someone."

She leaned over him, planting one hand on each chair arm, inches from his face. "It's not too late to tell us what you do know. Help yourself out."

"I—I," he stammered. "I get this call from a guy. Can I make silver bullets?" A bead of sweat rolled down his cheek. "I tell him sure, but it'll cost him. I've never worked with silver before. Turns out to be a real pain in the butt. Needs a hot furnace. If you don't pour the melted metal fast enough, the stuff cools and doesn't form right. But this guy, he's willing to pay."

Griffin was cooperating, so Tig backed up to give him some space. "How did he contact you?"

"First time, by phone. After, by email."

"You didn't think it strange he called himself John Doe?"

"Nope."

"The caller—male or female?"

"Male."

"Tell me about the delivery arrangements."

His eyes slewed toward the computer. "Ah, once I had the bullets ready, I emailed him." When his eyes centered again, he avoided looking in hers. "When I got the cashier's check, the envelope included instructions. I wrapped the boxes and left them on my front porch, like they said to do."

"Do you have those directions?"

"Nah. I trashed those."

She stepped in closer, hovering over him. "Did you see the man who picked them up?"

"N-no. They paid me enough not to look."

"Then why did you keep a copy of the cashier's check?"

"Taxes. When you get thirty thousand dollars for a job, you need good records."

She stared at him. What an idiot. She began to back up and then stopped. "Wait." Tig held up the carton Liza had found. "If you delivered both boxes, who is this one for?"

"He placed another order—for the third box you got there. I finished packaging them yesterday, but he hasn't paid yet."

They had confiscated one ammo carton at Pascala's motel room. If she was holding the third box, that meant the second box was still out there and unaccounted for.

Not good.

Tig walked over to Ari. "Look for another email from the same address."

He hit the mouse, and the messages alphabetized themselves. He clicked on the most recent one. "The order was placed after you captured Pascala."

"Can you trace the emails back to the person who sent them?"

"Already tried," he said, shaking his head. "It's going to take time—they used a Gmail account. You don't need a real name or identification, and they routed through a server in Dubai. I copied the routing information. I'll take it home and try from there."

"Do that."

"But I've got something else." Ari reached for a page from the printer and handed it to her. "Looks like they ordered a couple of boxes of handgun bullets a few months before the rifle ammo order."

Tig turned to Zeke. "Go back through his files and see if you can find payment for around that date too."

"Yes, ma'am," he said, and left the room.

Jayden held his hand out. "Chief, I've got an idea. What bank is the cashier's check drawn on?"

She gave the copy to him. "Royal Beach Bank. No local address."

"Let's do a search on the routing number," he said, and read off the nine digits.

Ari typed the numbers into a web browser on Griffin's computer. A few seconds ticked by as the circle spun and stopped, the information appearing on screen.

"Bingo," Ari said, and clicked the address to map it.

The bank was right down the street from New Path Church. The evidence kept pointing to Jones. "Ari, please pack the computer," Tig said. "Take anything you need to track who sent those emails."

"Will do."

Zeke returned with a copy of an older cashier's check and handed it to Tig. Same bank. No new information.

"Looks like his workshop is in the garage," he added, hooking his thumb toward the other side of the house.

"Take the camera to video the whole thing. Confiscate all bullet molds and silver."

"Yes, ma'am. Then what are we going to do with this hombre?"

"We can't take the risk. He might contact the guy who ordered the ammo, and if he does, they might decide he's a liability and put a hit on him."

Griffin's eyes got big. "Take me with you. Please. Don't let them kill me."

"Done," she said with a smile. "You'll spend a nice vacation in our custody."

Zeke raked his fingers through his hair. "And how do we tie Jones to this?"

Jayden snapped the cashier's check copy he was holding. "Remember the financial crimes training I took? I have a way that just might work."

Chapter 43

Royal Beach Bank, San Diego—The Next Day

That afternoon, Jayden wore a suit and tie to visit Royal Beach Bank, trying to appear professional and nonthreatening. He'd pressed Ari into guarding Lance Griffin in his absence.

The computer expert was more than willing, provided he was paid his hourly consultant fee plus room service: a bottle of ten-year-old scotch and a Kobe beef burger. But he grumbled about the scotch. "And they call themselves a luxury resort. What kind of a luxury resort doesn't carry a twenty-year-old scotch?"

Jayden snickered as he left the room. The council was going to shit two loaves when they saw the bill. Maybe it was a good thing he wasn't part of their august group.

The neighborhood bank was a one-story stand-alone in the corner of a shopping center parking lot. The front doors were nested—the first door had to shut before the second door was unlocked.

Jayden waited in the small chamber while a security camera monitored him.

This should be easy.

When a buzzer sounded, he stepped through. A small sign on the first desk identified the woman as the receptionist.

He stopped in front of her. "May I please speak with your manager?"

"What about? Perhaps I can help you."

He showed her his identification badge. "It's a police matter."

"Ah, the manager's on a break," the receptionist said, still staring at his ID.

When she looked back up at him, he pocketed his wallet. "Is the assistant manager in?"

"Can I tell her what this is about?"

"A police matter."

The broken record—a technique they taught at the police academy. Keep saying the same thing over and over until you got the response you wanted.

The receptionist offered him a seat by her desk and then phoned someone. At least he didn't have to say it a third time.

Moments later, a woman wearing too much perfume approached him. "I'm Katie Temblar. What can I do for you, detective?"

"Captain Jayden Johnson." He stood and shook her hand, and then handed her his business card, followed by a copy of the warrant. "I'm here to serve this. Do you want to discuss it here or in your office?"

Katie gave a nervous little sideways glance at the security cameras. "I'd prefer to talk here."

Jayden didn't push it. It hadn't escaped his attention that he was the only black person in the room. He wasn't tall, but he worked out enough that his muscles had muscles, and he understood how a skinny white female might feel intimidated being alone with him.

He understood it—that didn't mean he liked it. And he was getting damn tired of it.

She flipped to the end of the warrant. "The judge who signed this is in Mordida County." She examined his business card. "You're from Sierra Escondida. You and your warrant are outside your jurisdiction. I'm sorry, but I can't help you."

"*People v. Fleming* says you must honor an out-of-county warrant."

She bit her lower lip. "Our corporate policy is to cooperate with a San Diego County or federal warrant. Our attorneys—"

"Are wrong."

He was fudging here. *Fleming* dealt with a search warrant served on the suspect, not a third party. Still, courts had upheld third-party warrants—but the bank had the option to challenge the search first, delaying his investigation.

She handed the paperwork back to him. "You have to serve this on our headquarters. They deal with all warrants."

"Where are they?"

"San Francisco."

He'd lose a day flying there. "You don't keep the records here?"

"Ah—"

"Lying to a police officer would be obstruction of justice. Think carefully."

"Well, we have remote access. But the computers are in San Francisco."

Serving search warrants on a third party required police to act reasonably. And he'd rather have her cooperation—it could take days to go through the bank's records to find what he wanted. Appealing to her sense of right and wrong might work faster.

He handed her a copy of the cashier's check. "This was drawn on your bank and paid for the ammunition used to kill two people. I only need the name and address of the purchaser."

She stared at the check. "Thirty thousand? Shit," she said. "Oh, sorry."

He smiled. "No problem."

"That's a lot of money. How many bullets did they buy?"

"I can't discuss the details. But as you can tell, this wasn't a normal ammunition purchase. And two people were murdered."

"Terrorists?"

"You could say that."

She looked at the warrant again, uncertainty in her eyes. "We really should wait for my manager to return."

More delay. And the manager might call the bank's lawyer. "How does this sound? Why don't you take a peek at the records—see if you can identify who paid for the check? Then you can decide what to do. If you find nothing, there's no reason to argue about it." She chewed on her lower lip. He almost had her. "You know, you could be a hero—help us break up a terrorist cell."

She stopped biting her lip. "All right. Wait here."

Five minutes later, Katie returned and handed him a photocopy. "They paid with cash."

"If the amount's above ten thousand, you have to file a currency transaction report with the Treasury Department, right?"

She was ready for his question and showed him the completed form.

He scanned for the purchaser's name: On the Vine, Inc.

Gotcha. The same corporation Charlie's credit card was issued to and that rented his apartment. When a company was listed on the currency transaction form, the individual representing it had to provide his or her name, except the individual's name was left blank and the box "conducted on own behalf" checked.

It wouldn't fly with the Treasury Department, but Jayden was shit out of luck. He flipped to the receipt: amount, date, time and a series of numbers.

He pointed at the numbers. "What's this?"

"It tells us which teller station completed the transaction."

Bulletproof glass separated the customers from the tellers, and cameras were bolted to the wall behind them.

"Which one was the purchaser at?"

Katie took the receipt back. "Number three. That's what the '003' means."

"Do you have access to the security video for station three on the purchase date?"

She looked at him like he'd asked her to sell her first born. "Ye-e-s," she said, "we do."

"Can I see the video?"

She bit her lip again. "If they fire me, I'm suing you."

He stayed silent. If she sued him personally, it'd get tossed out of court. But he didn't need to rub it in.

She huffed. "Follow me."

They walked beyond a locked door marked "private" and into a small room near the manager's office. Katie sat at a computer terminal and scrolled through a list until she came to the date the cashier's check was purchased. By clicking the arrow, she expanded the day into quarter hour segments.

"Seven fifty-three p.m.," he said, looking at the receipt.

She clicked on seven forty-five p.m. and hit play. The time code was embedded in the video, and the jumpy color images of people conducting bank transactions played on screen. At seven fifty-three p.m., she hit pause.

Jayden stared at the face. Tig was going to be *so* happy.

He smiled to himself. Sometimes he thought vampires had all the advantages, until moments like this one where he had the edge on them.

They couldn't match his superpower: the ability to go out in sunlight to track down criminals.

This was what he lived for: using his mind to get people to cooperate, to build an evidence pile to bury the perps, to outsmart them. Maybe he didn't need to be on the council to make a real difference or to prove his worth to the community after all. Succeeding at his job was all he needed.

CHAPTER 44

MARINERS LODGE—SAME DAY AFTER SUNSET

Tig strode into Wilma's office. Jayden followed a half step behind her with the proof. If the lodge didn't approve a treaty arrest warrant now, she would take the culprit into custody without their permission. She didn't care if her actions started a war.

But she'd start things politely. "Thank you for seeing us."

Wilma offered them the chairs across from her and Quentin. "I was surprised to hear from you," the lodge master said, with a side glance at the Aussie. "I thought we made ourselves clear two nights ago."

"Things have changed."

"Look, luv," Quentin said, "I don't see how anything could change so quickly."

Tig accepted the folder from Jayden. "Last night, we searched the house of this man." She laid the photo on the small coffee table in front of Wilma. "He made the silver ammunition used to kill Nina."

Quentin raised his long nose as he sat back. "So?"

"The ammo maker was paid with a cashier's check." She added a copy of the check to the stack. "It was purchased by Isaiah Jones."

"You can prove that, luv?"

She motioned to Jayden. "I visited Royal Beach Bank today—they're the ones who issued it," he said. "The branch is down the street from New Path Church, where Jones preaches."

"Circumstantial evidence," Wilma said, with a wave of her hand.

"I gave the bank the purchase date, and they checked their security footage. They stay open until eight on Wednesday nights."

Jayden pulled out the last photo—a grainy shot of Jones at a teller station.

"The bank was able to confirm it was this teller who handled the transaction"—Jayden tapped the woman's image—"and the time stamp on the internal receipt matches the security footage. Isaiah Jones paid for the cashier's check."

Wilma uncrossed her legs and edged forward to study the photo. "We will bring him to the lodge for questioning. Quentin will escort him here."

"Not enough," Tig said. "I want you to sign off on a treaty warrant to search his apartment. He may be the ringmaster behind two murders, along with a kidnapping and a slew of attempted killings. I want to find out who he's working with."

Wilma drummed her fingers on the arm of her chair. Tig held her breath, waiting for Wilma to convince herself.

The Aussie picked up the photos and shuffled through them. "I don't like admitting it, but fuck me dead, we can't ignore this kind of evidence."

It's about time he got with the program.

The lodge master strode to her desk and grabbed a pen. "Very well. I'll sign the warrant."

Quentin stood and locked eyes with Tig. "I'm going with you when it's served, luv. Got to make sure everything is on the up-and-up."

She shrugged at him.

What the hell—the more the merrier.

Wilma called Jones, asking him to remain at home for a blood delivery from the lodge, a pretext to keep him in place.

Tig phoned Liza and Zeke and told them to meet her at Jones's apartment. Quentin may insist on going, but her own crew would be at her back.

Jayden drove the rental car, Tig in the passenger seat. Quentin took a separate car.

Jayden hadn't had two seconds alone with his mate since Zeke was shot. And he didn't know when another opportunity to talk would present itself.

He smiled to himself. Yeah, for them, it was kind of normal to squeeze in a personal conversation while driving to a suspect's apartment.

"Ah, Tig," he said. "I've been meaning to tell you something."

"What's that?"

"At the funeral dinner, Haley approached me about running for council."

"Why didn't you mention it before this?"

He kept his focus on the road but caught the puzzled tilt of her head as she asked the question.

"I've been mulling over the idea," he said. "And I've made my decision."

She touched his leg. "Look, Jayden, if you want to run, I'm all for it. You'd make a great council member."

Well, knock him over with a feather. He'd expected her to argue against the idea.

"Thanks, but I've decided not to run. I like being a police captain. I don't want to be involved in all the political bullshit. I don't have the patience for it."

"If you change your mind—"

"Not likely." He squeezed her hand. "But I appreciate it. Knowing I have your support means the world to me. And I..."

"Go on."

"I'm going to volunteer for Haley's committee. She's right, we do need a mortal on the council."

Tig gave a quirky little smile. "How can I help?"

"If you'd run interference with the council, keep them from seeing my volunteer work as a conflict of interest, I'd really appreciate it."

"Consider it done."

Twenty minutes later, Tig pounded on Jones's apartment door. Could they really be this close to ending the attacks? Excitement fluttered through her veins and across her skin.

"Yes?" Jones answered, opening the door a crack.

Tig pushed the door open and grabbed him by the arm, pinning him to the wall. Although adrenaline flooded her system, her hands were rock steady. "Isaiah Jim Jones, you're under arrest for conspiracy to commit murder."

"What? What are you talkin' about?" he whined. "Quentin, they're makin' a mistake."

"Sorry, mate." Quentin said. "The evidence is pretty damning."

I'm "luv" and the suspect is "mate"?

She ignored her irritation and snapped the vampire-proof handcuffs on Jones. After shoving him onto the couch, she held up the search warrant for him to see.

"Do you have a mortal mate? We don't want to hurt anyone."

The prisoner looked at her with hate in his eyes. "Not here."

"Okay, Zeke and Jayden, search the place. Quentin, please keep an eye on Mr. Jones."

Tig opened the patio door for Liza. The councilwoman had slipped through the courtyard to guard the rear door in case the suspect tried to get away.

The apartment had two bedrooms. Jones used one as an office. Zeke pulled a sack from the desk drawer and opened it. "Well, what do we got here?"

The plastic bag contained six phones. "Don't touch them," Tig said. "We don't want to taint any evidence. We'll take them back and dust for prints. Ari can check them afterwards."

Zeke closed the sack. "So, these might be the burners used to talk to Pascala?"

She nodded. "Could be. Bag and tag them."

No guns were found in the apartment, but hidden at the back of Jones's closet was a major surprise.

In her gloved hands, Tig held out a small plastic carton for Jones to see and took off the lid. Silver bullets. "Do you have a carry permit?"

The prisoner sat there silent and sullen.

"The answer is no, luv," Quentin said. "I haven't issued him one."

"Doesn't matter," Tig said, taking a closer look at the ammo. "These aren't for a handgun. These were made for a rifle." Tig stared at Jones, watching for his tell. She'd need to recognize it once the interrogation started in earnest. "What are you doing with illegal ammo?"

He didn't blink. "They aren't mine, and I'm not sayin' anything more."

"Are you sure? It might go better for you if you explain having these in your possession."

"Yeah, right. Y'all are setting me up. After the little gal heard me preach, well, you don't like my politics, so all y'all came gunnin' after me."

"I don't give a damn about your politics, Mr. Jones," Tig said. "All I care about is whether you're behind the attacks on my community." Disgusted, she turned to Zeke and Liza. "Get him out of here."

Zeke grabbed Jones's arm and pulled him off the couch.

"Where are all y'all takin' me?" Jones let his body become dead weight, and fell to his knees, fear in his eyes. "Quentin, ya got to stop them. It's a frame job—they'll kill me the minute they get me alone."

The Aussie scratched his chin. "You're going to the lodge. The lodge master wants to talk with you first."

"But with all this evidence—" she started.

"Sorry, luv. I can't let him leave our jurisdiction yet. You can question him back at headquarters."

Tig sucked her teeth, keeping her mouth shut, trying to understand his resistance. Sure, she would protect someone under her authority from extradition, but with this evidence? She would have thrown in the towel by now. Why was Quentin still resisting?

"Wilma's orders," he added.

Jones looked daggers at Tig. "Y'all get me alone, you'll torture me. But torture won't work on me. I'll name everyone in your pisspot community. Startin' with your mayor."

His comment about the mayor was bullshit. "We don't need to torture you to learn the truth."

Tig avoided looking at Jayden when she said it. The way she had treated Pascala was still a touchy issue for her mate. And he'd been right in the end. It hadn't been pain or humiliation that cracked Pascala.

"Get this scum out of here," she said.

Chapter 45

Tuscany Bay Resort—later that night

Cerissa placed her two bags in the suite's living room. She could flash her luggage to the Enclave, but for appearance's sake, she had to leave the hotel the old-fashioned way.

Henry sat on the couch hunched over and dejected. His sadness invaded her mind despite his attempts to control it.

A knock at the hotel door startled her. Henry met her eyes and shrugged.

"It's Tig," came the voice from the other side of the door. "We took Jones into custody."

Finally, some good news. Opening the door, Cerissa asked, "Did he confess?"

"Unfortunately, no. We have circumstantial evidence he was involved, but he claims it was a setup—that the stuff we found in his apartment was planted."

"I wonder…" she began, recalling what she saw at New Path Church.

"Yes?"

"Something struck me as odd the night I met Isaiah. The church is shabby. If they have enough money to buy silver bullets and hire assassins, well, why aren't they spending some on the building, trying harder to impress converts?"

Tig shrugged. "Perhaps they are saving their bankroll to fund attacks. You're right, silver bullets aren't cheap. Right now, I must follow the evidence, and the signs all point at Jones. We even found vampire blood in Pascala's motel room. Jones paid for the ammo, so we suspect he delivered it to Pascala himself. If we could link the blood to Jones, the case would be a slam dunk."

"Ah," Cerissa said, and closed her mouth. The chief had forbidden her weeks ago from taking Blanche's blood samples off the Hill for analysis.

"Speak up. What is it?" Tig asked impatiently.

"Ah, well, I—"

Henry stood and squared his shoulders. "What Cerissa is trying to say is she has samples of my blood and Rolf's. She is looking for ways to help Rolf with his feeding problem. The lab she uses is very secure, and I was convinced the data would not be compromised, so I approved it."

Tig gave Cerissa a withering look. "Is this true?"

She gulped. He'd just thrown himself under the bus for her. What if the chief thought his actions violated the Covenant? He would be facing the whipping post. She couldn't let that happen—

"Well," Cerissa said, pausing to figure out how to persuade Tig. "I've begun working on decoding the vampire genome. I hoped to get enough samples to conduct a comparison, to see if there is some abnormality in Rolf's blood, some way to help him. Ultimately, I hope to develop a system to categorize vampire blood like human blood is categorized—"

"Can you do a match? If I gave you a sample of Jones's blood, and the dried blood from Pascala's room, would you be able to tell if they were from the same person?"

Bingo! Just what Cerissa had in mind. "I could try. I'm about to leave for Huntington Beach, to give another investor presentation. I can return to the lab the day after it's over. How soon can you provide the samples?"

Tig's scowl relaxed. "If you come with me now, you can draw Jones's blood before you leave."

"No problem. We'll need to pack the sample in ice so I can ship it to my lab."

"Understood. But the dried blood from the motel is back at the Hill."

"If you give it to Henry, he can get it to me."

"He's not going with you?"

Cerissa glanced in his direction. He looked so forlorn. "No, he's returning to the Hill."

"Who's going with you? Zeke?"

"Absolutely not." She'd cancel the presentations before she'd let the cowboy accompany her.

Tig seemed taken aback. "You shouldn't travel alone. You're a target—the Carlyle Cutter tried to shoot you."

"Don't worry about me. I'll be careful."

"But you are Henry's mate—"

Cerissa crossed her arms. "And I'm Leopold's envoy. As such, the Hill can't stop me from traveling on his behalf."

Tig's face clouded over. Then her expression changed to one of grudging respect. "I guess I have no choice in the matter. Are you sure you don't want a guard with you?"

"Positively certain." The last thing Cerissa wanted was someone from the Hill hamstringing her. She needed to be able to flash back to the Enclave without anyone guessing.

Tig moved toward the door. "Then I'll see you at the lodge."

Henry slipped an arm around Cerissa's shoulder. She had to fight the impulse to draw away. "I'll go with you," he said.

"You don't have to. I'll leave from there and see you when I get back to the Hill."

She gave him a peck on the cheek, and her heart clenched. She loved him but couldn't let go of feeling wronged. She stuffed down her emotions, grabbed her bags, and rolled them out the door, following Tig to the elevator.

CHAPTER 46

THE HILL CHAPEL—LATER THAT NIGHT

Henry pushed at the partially open door to Father Matt's office. He had made the appointment before returning to the Hill alone. Zeke had stayed behind with Tig's crew.

Flying the plane home without Cerissa's companionship had been the longest ninety minutes of his life.

He trudged into the empty office and stopped. Maybe he should leave. Nothing good could come of his confession.

But I promised Cerissa.

Noise emanated from the chapel's kitchen down the hall. Matt must have taken a break to feed.

Henry slumped onto the office couch and buried his face in his hands. The musty scent from old books lining one wall usually brought him comfort. He associated the familiar smell with clearing his conscience.

Tonight, nothing could comfort him.

Footsteps sounded, followed by the creak of Father Matt's chair.

Henry pressed his hands to his eyelids, too ashamed to look at the priest. "Bless me, father, for I have sinned," he managed to say around the boulder lodged in his throat. "It has been ten nights since my last confession."

He paused. How to give voice to his shame? He'd allowed his sins from the past to poison the present. Sins he'd buried deep in his soul until the rot spilled out, tainting his relationship with Cerissa.

"Go ahead, Henry. Whatever is on your mind."

He raised his head. It didn't matter how long he'd hidden from the truth. He would face his terrible sin now. "I—I killed my mate."

Empathy disappeared from Matt's face. He sat there frozen, like a man waiting for the stake to descend.

"Her name was Sarah."

The priest let out a relieved-sounding noise when he exhaled. "Cerissa is all right?"

"She is fine. But I need to confess my past to you. For her sake. Now please, let me tell you what happened. It is hard enough without questions."

"Certainly. Go ahead."

Henry knotted his fingers together and dropped his gaze to them. Keeping his eyes focused on his knuckles, he told Matt the story of Sarah and then launched into an edited version of what occurred in San Diego. Cerissa's Lux abilities had to remain a secret, even from his confessor.

When he finished, he looked up. "I am as evil now as I was then. No matter how long I live, I'll never change. I wanted to let Zeke die."

"But you helped save him."

"It is..." Henry began, the shame moving through him like worms under his skin. "It is only because of Cerissa. She made me see what I didn't want to face: my jealously and anger were responsible for Sarah's death."

"This happened in the 1800s?"

"Eighteen eighty-nine."

Matt clasped Henry's knotted fingers between his own. "You're not the same man. You didn't kill Zeke when he challenged you to a duel months ago, and you didn't let him die on the operating table. You did the right thing. You've learned better ways to deal with your fear of abandonment."

The hair on the back of Henry's neck stood up. "I am not afraid—"

"Your jealousy and distrust arise out of fear—fear you'll be abandoned."

"I—" he began, but stopped. Matt was right.

"You've mentioned your father before, how he rejected you because you looked like your mother's father."

Henry stared at his hands, still clasped between Matt's. His grandfather was *mestizo*—a derogatory term for mixed race. His ancestors included the indigenous people of Mexico as well as the Spanish colonialists. "I could do nothing to earn my father's love."

"And just as you were about to get married, Anne-Louise turned you, forcing you to abandon your mortal life. Add in Sarah's infidelity, her abandonment of you, and your fear became rooted in who you are. But you're reacting in a healthier manner today than when Sarah cheated on you."

"You're wrong. I haven't changed; I can never change."

"Henry, you already have. When Erin left you, you were very upset. You struggled with your feelings."

More shame crawled through him. His ex-girlfriend had seen Anne-Louise's bite on his neck and assumed he'd cheated because the bite was in such an *intimate* location. "No matter what I said, Erin would not believe I had been faithful."

"Yet you didn't react with violence. You didn't harm her even when she lashed out at you. You let her go."

Henry sat back, breaking contact with Matt's hands. "It is because I didn't care about her."

"You know that's not true. You cared about Erin."

He glanced up. Matt's face expressed only acceptance. Henry's own face shut down, becoming a mask, the frozen look he used to keep others out. He didn't deserve Matt's understanding. "But I haven't changed. When I thought Cerissa had gone to Zeke, I flew into a rage at her. No one is safe around me."

"Did you touch her?"

"No, I would never hurt Cerissa—"

"Then why isn't she safe around you?"

"Because of Sarah. You don't understand. I—I wanted to punish Sarah. I didn't mean to kill her. But I was so angry, I wasn't thinking straight, and she died because of my anger. If it could happen once, it could happen again."

"Henry, what do you get from believing that?"

"I must face the truth—"

"But is it the truth? It's been over a hundred years. You haven't harmed anyone, and it's not like you haven't had the opportunity. Why do you hold on to the belief you haven't changed?"

It was so hard to say out loud. "After what I did to Sarah, I—I don't deserve love."

"Now I think we're getting closer to the truth. That's the message your father gave you—because you're *mestizo*, you don't deserve love. And what happened with Sarah, well, you took that experience and used it to validate your father's message. But you arrived at a fallacious conclusion."

"I don't understand," Henry said, furrowing his brow.

"You *do* deserve love."

He hung his head. "No, I don't."

"So, what will you do? Keep your heart locked away forever? Never let anyone close to punish yourself?"

"It has worked so far."

"What about Cerissa? Are you going to keep her locked out of your heart?"

"Too late." He flexed his hands. They had fully healed. It was his heart that was eternally damaged. "I love her as I have never loved another."

"Henry, believing you haven't changed may be easier than risk being hurt, but believing you haven't changed doesn't make it true."

What did it matter? He couldn't undo what was done. "Cerissa has left. I don't see how she can forgive me."

"Her forgiveness isn't what you need," Matt said softly. "Accept your past for what it is and forgive yourself. Once you do, you'll begin a healing journey. You'll be able to love her the way you want to love her. And love yourself too."

Henry shook his head. Even if he learned to forgive himself, he had destroyed his relationship with Cerissa.

"I want to ask you a question." The priest stroked his short beard and looked thoughtful. "And I don't want you to take my question the wrong way. So please listen carefully."

Henry narrowed his eyes. "I will try," he said.

"You told me Cerissa keeps secrets. Does she have a drug problem? An eating disorder? Anything like an addiction?"

"Absolutely not."

"Addicts keep secrets. I wonder if you were attracted to her because of her secrets, if it felt familiar to you."

Had it? She'd hidden her true appearance from him. When he first learned she was keeping something secret, a suspicious twinge had risen in his chest, the same kind he'd felt from Sarah's attempts to deceive, but then the feeling vanished when he saw Cerissa's beautiful wings. "I learned her secret shortly after you and I discussed the situation."

"Does her secret have anything to do with an addiction?"

"No."

"Sarah's story made me think something else had triggered your reaction. You were doing well with Cerissa until you traveled to San Diego. The switch seems sudden."

"I don't understand."

"Is there anyone else in your life struggling with an addiction? My intuition tells me there was a catalyst."

Rolf.

Carrying the burden alone had been too much for Henry. He should have confessed the truth weeks ago. "I— What I tell you is confidential, yes?"

"Of course, Henry, it is."

He bowed his head. "Cerissa and I have been trying to help Rolf with his addiction to adrenaline-spiked blood. Even though she is providing clone blood enhanced with adrenaline for him, I suspect he continues to hunt live mortals. I have no evidence, but…"

"How does his hunting make you feel?"

Henry opened his palms. How did Rolf's problem make him feel? He sat there, unable to dig out the precise emotion. He'd worked so hard to control his environment, to make Sierra Escondida a safe place to live, and Rolf's hunting threatened his carefully crafted world.

"Helpless," he finally said.

"Or powerless?"

"Yes, powerless."

"Just as you were powerless to do anything about your father's rejection, Anne-Louise's theft of your mortality, or Sarah's addiction."

He wrinkled his brow. "I don't see how they are the same."

"Henry, feelings aren't logical. Your attempts to help Rolf may be raising those same feelings. You fear you won't be able to help him, just as you were unable to help Sarah. And when Zeke triggered your fear of abandonment, everything got thrown in the emotional blender. Cerissa became Sarah, even if Rolf is the one with the addiction problem. Trying to control Cerissa was the outlet for your feelings of powerlessness."

"What does it matter? She has left. Our relationship is hopeless—"

Father Matt leaned forward and wrapped his hands around Henry's again. "There is always hope. You don't have to go through this alone like you did when Sarah died. I'm here, and I have tools you can use to heal the past wounds and deal better with today's problem. Do you trust me?"

"I do."

"Then believe me—together, we've got this."

Chapter 47

The Enclave—Next Day

The black volcanic rock walls admitted no light. Cerissa had long suspected the Lux home world was not well lit. Her large, silvery eyes were meant to see in darkness, and her pale blue skin was unable to protect her from strong UV light.

The alarm on her phone buzzed. *Sunset.*

Last night, she'd met with the Huntington Beach community and then driven to Los Angeles to check into a hotel. From there, she'd flashed to the Enclave. In a few hours, she would return to meet with the Fairfax vampires.

Her heart ached, as it did each time the alarm announced sunset, regret and anger swirling together, her mind spinning like a carnival Tilt-A-Whirl. When would she find the courage to stop the ride and make a decision?

She ruffled her wings and grabbed a chunk of her long hair, twisting the fine strands back and around, using a beaker clamp to hold the mass away from her face.

Focus.

The test results were finished. She had completed a full DNA sequencing of Henry's blood during her free time—of which she had too much now.

What I wouldn't give to turn back time.

Would she use it to avoid falling in love with Henry? Or to avoid learning the truth about him?

No, there had been no way to evade either. Even if she had to do it all again, she couldn't stop herself from falling in love with him. And his possessiveness—his distrust—had guaranteed the truth would come out eventually, one way or another.

Images of Henry killing Sarah floated through her mind again. The angst caused her feathers to rise, and she shook her wings to release the sensation.

Even though she could rationalize the situation—given the time period and the complexity of what happened—the truth still haunted her. What was worse: that he was so blinded with rage he meant to tie Sarah to him for eternity so he could punish her, or that he was so blinded by rage he couldn't foresee the effect Sarah's laudanum-filled blood would have on him?

But he'd lived a long time—he had a complicated past, and there was no simple way to reconcile his history. Her only choice was to either accept it or reject it.

The more urgent and unknown variable was whether he was a different man in the present. His possessive behavior would suggest a lack of change, but despite his flaws, he tried to be an honorable man.

When push came to shove, he had helped her save Zeke. He'd given his consent to Zeke's bite, even though his face told how much it pained him to see the cowboy take her blood and, by some stupid vampire law, cause her to "become Zeke's." Henry had controlled his possessiveness and overcome his trust issues.

Was that enough?

Once again, her thoughts were running around in endless circles, ones she found impossible to resolve. A series of but, but, but, but, but... Her mind sounding like a motorcycle with a carburetor problem.

The phone rang, and she held it up to see the display. *Gaea.* Why was she calling?

Cerissa morphed back to human form and answered, "Hi, Gaea. What's up?"

"My dear girl, it's so good to hear your voice. I was very concerned when Henry returned alone."

Oh, damn. She didn't want to have this conversation. "He returned to attend to winery business, and I'm traveling to the other communities to pitch my project, so there's nothing to worry about."

"Now, don't lie to me, young lady. I understand as well as anyone how hard relationships can be in the early stages, and we all know how difficult and demanding Henry can be—"

"Henry's not difficult and demanding." In San Diego, they had kept up the pretense of being a happy couple. What had tipped off Gaea? "It's just... Look, it's not fair to him. I can't discuss what happened with you."

"Now, dear, whatever you tell me will stay private. You know that."

Gaea and Father Matt were both ombudsmen, appointed to look out for the welfare of the mortals in the community. "It wouldn't be right."

"Would you rather speak with Father Matt?"

"No."

"Then tell me this. Henry didn't hurt you, did he?"

"Gaea, how can you even ask?"

"You didn't answer me."

"No, he didn't physically hurt me."

Emotionally, maybe. But not physically. Never physically.

The phone buzzed. Another call coming in.

Fidelia.

"Ah, Gaea, I have to take this. We'll talk in a few days when I have time."

"Think about what I said. All couples go through rough patches."

"Thanks. I really have to run." She swiped the screen to switch calls.

"Are you available to meet with Karen?" Fidelia asked.

"If it would help, absolutely."

Anxiety clung to Cerissa as she dressed in slacks and a blouse. She flashed to Karen's house, and Fidelia escorted her to the living room. The extravagant room was twice the size as Henry's, with a gray-veined white marble floor, heavy white drapes, and formal furniture. A huge oil painting of a sixteenth-century Bavarian king in an ermine robe hung over the fireplace.

She felt underdressed for the room.

Karen sat on the silk couch, biting a hangnail, looking equally nervous, with Fidelia taking the seat next to her. Rolf's two German shepherds were curled at Karen's feet. Mort stood when Cerissa took the chair across from Karen but didn't come over to greet her. Sang remained with her head on her crossed paws, her black eyebrows dancing as her sad brown eyes tracked Cerissa's every move.

Dogs are so sensitive to their owner's moods.

Normally, Mort and Sang would be all over her, greeting her with doggie kisses. Their reticence raised her apprehension level.

Fidelia cleared her throat. "Karen has something she wants to tell you."

Karen stopped biting her hangnail, wrapped a strand of auburn hair around her finger, and tugged. "I'm sorry I got angry with you."

Cerissa let out a sigh of relief. "Everything's okay. I understand."

"It's just—I started blaming you. I mean, they meant to kidnap you."

"I blame myself too." Cerissa leaned forward, wanting to close the distance between them.

Fidelia raised her hand. "Let Karen finish, okay?"

"Of course," Cerissa said, cringing with mortification. She hadn't intended to say anything wrong. Guilt had taken control and was driving her mouth.

Karen released the twisted lock of hair and stared at her lap. "I started feeling like what happened was my fault too. I got angry with you and then with myself. The nightmares—it felt like they'd never end. I thought I deserved them." She looked up. "But Fidelia helped me see—it's the fault of the men who kidnapped me, only their fault. She's helped me to see my nightmares are the fear of being trapped. It's my traumatized brain replaying the trauma. And when you wouldn't help me—"

"I'm sorry." Cerissa clasped her hands, holding them tightly together, her whole body rigid with tension. "You have no idea how sorry I am."

"Cerissa, please," Fidelia said. "Put a lid on it."

Karen met Cerissa's gaze. "And when you wouldn't help me, I thought you didn't want to be my friend anymore. But I see now you were…trying to help. You did."

Cerissa opened her mouth to say she hadn't done enough, but Fidelia shot her a look. She waited.

Karen stared at her hands again, sadness in her eyes. "But I'm going to end up losing you anyway. Rolf is leaving me."

Cerissa furrowed her brow. "Did he tell you that?"

"He didn't need to. Since the Cut—" Karen paused, struggling to say the Cutter's name. "Since I was kidnapped, Rolf has been"—she waved her hand—"weird about everything."

Cerissa's heart ripped open, torn between two loyalties. She wasn't able to tell Karen the truth about him; he was her patient. But what could she say and not violate his trust? "His weirdness may have nothing to do with your relationship."

Karen looked at her sharply. "You know what it is, don't you?"

Cerissa hadn't told Karen the pouches for Rolf contained adrenaline-enhanced blood. "I can't say. The same way Fidelia isn't permitted to share anything you two have discussed."

Fidelia laid a hand on Karen's shoulder. "I think I understand. Cerissa might be bound by doctor-patient confidentiality. If she knew something, she wouldn't be able to tell you without getting Rolf's permission."

"Then get his ass in here." Karen jumped up and raced across the room to the door. The dogs, startled, scrambled to their feet, their claws clicking on the marble, and followed her. "Rolf, you get in here now."

Rolf *whooshed* into the room. Had he been listening nearby?

"*Liebling*—" he began.

"Don't *Liebling* me." Karen poked him in the chest. "You're going to tell me what's going on with you. I feel like I'm going crazy. You're keeping something from me, I just know it. I thought you were leaving me because of what happened with the Cutter, and it turns out there's a different reason."

Cerissa stood. "She's noticed your behavior. I didn't tell her anything, but you should."

Rolf ran his fingers through his hair, flipping the longer blonde strands back over the shaved sides. Instead of his usual arrogance, his icy blue eyes held fear as his gaze shifted from one woman to the other.

Finally, he stopped his vacillating and focused on Karen. "I have a feeding disorder," he said.

Cerissa raised an eyebrow. So that was what he was calling it—a good enough term as any.

Karen whipped around, looking at Cerissa. "A what?"

"You." Rolf pointed a finger at Cerissa. "You explain it to her."

She took a step closer to Karen. "I've been supplying him with adrenaline-enhanced blood to counter his disorder. He needs an abnormally high level of stress hormones to stay stable. I'm researching the matter—I was in my lab working on preliminary tests when Fidelia called."

Karen stared at Rolf and covered her mouth, which had become a big circle as she put the pieces together. "Oh my God. Your trips to San Diego. You hunt?"

"He used to." Cerissa crossed the room to her. "He's promised to stop, and you've probably noticed his withdrawal symptoms. I've been providing him with special blood. We're trying to find a maintenance dose to keep him satisfied."

Tears streamed from Karen's eyes.

Cerissa opened her arms. "I'm so sorry I haven't been here for you—that I didn't pay closer attention or insist on talking more."

"It's okay," Karen said with a sniff, going into Cerissa's open arms and hugging her. "I pushed you away, too, in the beginning. It's like I'm on an emotional seesaw since the kidnapping. One minute I'm raging and crying, the next I feel like if I finish what the Cutter started, I'll stop the pain."

Fidelia laid a hand on Karen's back. "That's the trauma brain talking. We're going to keep working on exercises to recognize when it's speaking. And I have a few techniques to help you reprogram and calm it. We'll keep working together until you have a handle on the nightmares and flashbacks."

"But I still don't understand," Karen said, blotting her eyes with a tissue. "Cerissa wiped my emotions of the torture. Why is this happening?"

I should never have used Karen as a guinea pig.

The disapproval in Fidelia's eyes was clear. "Cerissa desensitized your emotional reaction to the worst of what the Cutter did. But you were scared senseless by what happened. Anyone would be. Wiping your emotions wasn't a substitute for treatment. As a doctor, she should have known better."

Cerissa squeezed Karen's shoulder. "I'm so sorry. I thought I was helping, but I've only made a mess of things."

"I forgive you," Karen said, wrapping her arms around Cerissa again. "You did what you thought was best. You saved me, and now you brought me Fidelia, too. We're friends. Friends forgive."

Cerissa sighed and hugged Karen back, tears forming in her eyes.

I couldn't bear to lose her to the Cutter, and I almost lost her to my own actions.

Karen suddenly stiffened, breaking their embrace, and turned around to face Rolf. "Did you cheat on me?"

"No, never. Believe me. *Ich liebe dich!*"

Karen crossed her arms, looking unconvinced. Rolf edged closer, like he was afraid Karen would bolt, until he had his arms around her. Karen sighed and relaxed into his embrace. "If you're lying..."

"*Liebling,* I didn't cheat. I've never cheated on you. Only hunted."

A short while later, Cerissa flashed back to the Enclave. Fidelia wanted to work with Karen and Rolf to help them communicate about his problem and how it would impact their relationship. Cerissa wasn't needed for their discussion.

As soon as she morphed back to Lux form, her thoughts focused on Henry again. Would she ever be able to forgive him the way Karen had forgiven her?

She gripped the lab bench, her wings drooping behind her. What if he continued to fall prey to fits of distrust? Would she always have to worry how he'd react to her need for autonomy?

Then she pictured the night he took her blood for the first time, and her heart gave a little *ka-thub.*

He'd told her so much about himself as she ate the chocolate cake he had baked for her, the room lit by warm candlelight. He'd *tried* to tell her something—that he wasn't a modern man. She'd *known* that and had told him she accepted him unconditionally.

Yet she'd withheld something from him at the time—her Lux appearance. She had been afraid he'd reject her if he thought she was an angel.

Had she committed the same sin as him? Withholding important information? But he'd done so much more—

But, but, but, but, but...

She flapped her wings, forcing the endless cycle of thoughts to stop.

Enough. I need to get back to the lab report.

She retrieved the DNA analysis using her neural link. For now, she had two priorities: first, to find out what she could do for Rolf, because helping him would help Karen, and second, figuring out how to match vampire DNA to confirm or disprove Tig's suspicions about Jones.

Both required her to understand the genetic building blocks that made a vampire, well, a vampire. Later she would study the individual components of Henry's blood, maybe use them to create medicines to benefit humankind.

She tabbed the analysis open with her mind, and the computer displayed the DNA model created from Henry's white blood cells.

This can't be right.

She searched backward in the report to make sure the sequencer hadn't crossed its links. The date stamp and time were correct—this was the right one, the sample she'd put into the machine six nights ago.

She clicked back through to the twisted ladder image and flicked at the screen, causing the strands to float in midair above the monitor.

She touched the image, rotating the ladder, first horizontally, then vertically, spinning the projection around its axis. His double-stranded DNA had a third strand, coating the first two.

Just like the Lux had.

Impossible.

She opened another screen, retrieved a model of Lux DNA, and flicked it to float next to Henry's. The similarities were striking. Not identical, but close.

How can this be?

Then it dawned on her. The Lux morphing hormone was present in fang serum. It was why she had to inject a stabilizer before he bit her. And unlike mortals, who were healed by vampire blood, she was deathly allergic to it.

Suspicion slowly crept through her mind, walking on tiptoes.

She morphed back to human form and found her phone. She hadn't spoken to him since her last night in San Diego, but she needed an answer, and she didn't want to ask Leopold. Despite what happened, she trusted Henry more than her sponsor.

"Cariña," he said when he answered. "Are you coming home?"

"N-not yet," she said, her voice cracking.

His words had awakened the pain, and her uncertainty threatened to consume her again.

Focus.

"I, ah," she said, pressing the phone tight to her ear. "I need to ask you something."

"Anything."

"How far back can you trace vampire history?"

"You mean our origin?"

"Right. What year was the first vampire made?"

"We're—we're not sure. Our oral tradition places it around 600 BCE in Mesopotamia." His gentle Castilian accent stroked her ears, and she longed to be with him. "Some say genies—the Jinn—were responsible. But no one is alive to verify the date."

"The Jinn?" she repeated. Her world spun, and abruptly her legs went out from under her. She plopped onto the lab chair behind her.

No. It's not possible.

"Cerissa? Is something wrong?"

"I— Nothing. I'll be in touch."

"When are you coming home?"

"I still have six communities to visit."

"That isn't what I asked."

"Henry, I told you I need time." She closed her eyes, picturing him standing there, talking into the phone. The ache in her chest grew. "Please understand."

"I'm trying to be patient," he said, and his voice cracked. "I—I long to see you."

His sadness, his yearning, had wrapped around her lungs, squeezing until she felt choked by his emotion.

Had he taken off his bracelet?

"Henry, please—"

"Is there anything I can do to set this right?"

"Please put the bracelet back on. I can't think."

His love filtered through her mind before being suddenly cut off. He must have snapped the bracelet over the crystal.

"I have a midnight appointment with Father Matt," he said quickly. "My second one."

Why did that make her feel a little better?

"I love you," he said. "I know my feelings for you don't change what I did." He paused. "But please don't leave."

"Give me time." She pictured his intense brown eyes. Would she ever be able to look in them and not see the anger on his face when he accused her of being with Zeke? "I'll talk with you another night. Good sleep, Henry."

She disconnected before he could reply. Dropping the phone on the lab bench, she rubbed her chest hard, fighting the pain inside and trying to process the information he'd given her.

Jinn.

Had the Lux appeared to the ancient residents of Mesopotamia? The pre-Muslim people who lived there believed Jinn were creatures with free will who could be good, evil, or somewhere in between.

She had claimed her own right to free will. In doing so, had she inadvertently struck upon the truth? Were the Lux closer to Jinn than to angels?

She morphed and fanned out her wings, the soft ivory feathers ruffling with surprise. The transformation from mortal to vampire required fang serum as well as ingesting large quantities of vampire blood. The Lux morphing hormone must facilitate the change.

Did the Lux and vampires share a common ancestor?

No, that didn't make sense. This wasn't a recent evolutionary quirk; it would take millions of years for vampires to evolve naturally from the Lux—or vice versa, for the Lux to evolve from vampires.

Too many specialized compounds were involved—including the DNA third strand and the morphing hormone. But unlike the Lux, vampires could only morph into bat or wolf form, and age themselves.

Her gut said vampire physiology included those aspects by design, not accident.

If Henry's oral history was trustworthy, if the Jinn *had* created vampires, what did it mean?

Her feathers ruffled at the idea. No, she didn't believe it. The Lux couldn't have created them. It would go against all their codes.

She fanned out her wings and turned back to the computer to key in her search. It wouldn't take long to skim through the records from 600 BCE.

Another chill ran through her. Did she really want to know what happened? Look at what disclosure had done to her and Henry. Maybe she should leave well enough alone, let sleeping crocodiles lie and all that. She didn't want to get bit by the jaws of truth again.

Or did she? If she'd learned anything, it was this: she was better off knowing, no matter how much the truth may hurt. She pulled up a chair and started scanning the records. The answer had to be in there somewhere.

Chapter 48

Rancho Bautista del Murciélago—Twenty minutes earlier

Henry dropped the phone on the oak end table next to his leather chair. He buried his face in his hands.

What can I do to win her back?

Now that Father Matt had named the emotion, he felt the abandonment more acutely. A great big hole where his heart should be.

A flash of light. Was it Cerissa returning? He glanced up, a thin flame of hope warming his chest.

What he saw extinguished it. Ari stood by the empty fireplace.

"Okay, sitting here in the dark gives new meaning to *brooding vampire*."

Henry narrowed his eyes. Cerissa's cousin had flashed in without permission.

I will have to speak with her about Ari—

Except he didn't know if he'd ever see her again.

"Earth to Henry." Ari waved his hand in front of Henry's face. "You okay, old man?"

"Step back," Henry demanded, his fingers tightly gripping the chair's claw-like armrests. "You have no right to enter my house unannounced."

"Your phone went to voicemail."

"I was busy."

"Yeah, I can see." Ari scanned him. "A little early to be in your PJs, isn't it?"

"Ari, I have no patience for your impertinence tonight. Please leave."

"All right, grouchy, I'll get out of your hair. Just tell me where Cerissa is."

"I don't know."

"What do you mean you don't know?"

Henry scrubbed a hand across his face. "She—she wanted a break from me."

"Wait a minute." Ari dropped his briefcase. "After all I did to keep you two together, and now she wants to split?"

"This isn't about you."

"Everything's about me," Ari said, tapping his chest. "I'm her supervisor. She should have told me."

"That is between you and her. You have your answer from me. Now leave."

"Not so fast. As long as I'm here, I need the winery's personnel records. Suri wouldn't give me the hard files. I've been all through your computer system, but no, I can't see ten-year-old personnel files. She said she sent them over to you."

Henry gripped the chair's armrests and pushed himself up. The loss of Cerissa weighed so heavily that he felt like an old man as he stood. "The files are upstairs in my office."

Ari collected his briefcase and touched Henry's shoulder. Two blinks later, after being pulled and stretched through nothingness, his body snapped into place in his office, with him inhabiting it once again, and Ari standing next to him.

"Must you do that?"

"Hey, man, it's faster to flash. Where are the files? I'll leave, and you can return to sitting in the dark and brooding, which is *so* much more important than catching the bad guys."

Henry picked up the stack from his credenza and shoved them in Ari's direction. "Here. Take them and go."

But Ari didn't. He rifled through them using Henry's pristine desk to make piles. "Not him, not her, not him—oh, wait. Got a sticky flag?"

Why couldn't Ari just leave? The term "melodramatic" didn't begin to capture him. Henry sighed, opened a drawer, and took out a container of colorful tabs.

Ari slapped a flag on something he found in one file and kept flipping through the others. "No, nyet, nope. Whoa. Here's another possibility. And this one."

"What are you muttering about?"

"I'm talking about who had the right kind of access on May 13, 2009, the date the patch was installed. It contained the back door through which they inserted the Trojan. Their bug sat there humming along, collecting all your email and calendar entries." Ari ran his hand through his curly hair. "And only three people had the kind of access needed to do this. Don't you want to know who they were?"

Henry crossed his arms. The only thing he wanted was for Ari to leave, but the question caused him to pause. "Do your suspects still work for me?"

Ari flipped through the three files. "Doesn't look like they do."

"Then no, I don't care. Tig will be more interested than I am. Take your findings to her and let her handle the matter."

"Whoa, you *are* grumpy." Ari dumped the files into his briefcase. "Look, do you want me to talk with Cerissa?"

"I don't want you to make things worse." Henry wasn't sure it was possible, but he couldn't take the risk.

"You're hurting, aren't you?"

"How astute."

"Relax. They don't call me Cupid for nothing." Ari patted Henry's shoulder and then disappeared.

ENCLAVE LIBRARY—AFTER MIDNIGHT

Cerissa spent three hours giving presentations to the Fairfax community. Her feet ached from standing in dress heels all that time. Whichever advertising guy thought pantyhose could be energizing should be forced to wear them twenty-four seven.

On the positive side, six Fairfaxians had agreed to invest—progress was being made.

But her heart wasn't in it. As soon as she got back to her hotel, she flashed to Henry's to pick up the bloody tissue. The envelope was waiting for her in the basement lab. Seeing the empty room, starkly painted, ready for her lab equipment—a new beginning that might end before it started—sent a wave of pain right through her.

She quickly flashed to the Enclave. The blood analysis could wait. After placing the evidence envelope in a locked cabinet, she returned to searching the computer files for any clue that might explain the similarities between vampire and Lux DNA. What she found hinted at some experiment gone wrong, but the details were missing. She had a name, Ninevah, a doctor and scientist, but nothing more.

Frustrating.

She tapped her six fingers on the table. There was another way to track down the missing info. The Enclave had a small library of hardbound books. Most documents were in the Lux server system, backed up to ten locations to prevent any data loss. But the hermetically sealed library contained the sacred, historic records her people had compiled for four millennia.

It normally took librarian permission to enter, but the head librarian was out.

Better that they don't know.

Cerissa entered the code she had filched. The library door cracked open with a slight *pop* as the seal released, and she peered in, her heart pounding, her breath coming fast, her fear of being discovered tightening her throat.

The Protectors wouldn't want her suspicions confirmed.

She hastily slipped inside and closed the door behind her. The bookshelf for 600 BCE was halfway through the large room. Running her hand along the metal shelf, she slowed her progress to read the spine on each book and stopped at the one she wanted: *Ninevah's Journal*. She rested her finger on the old leather binding, frayed and fragile despite the room's inert atmosphere, and eased the tome from its resting spot. A faded red ribbon marked a place toward the end.

Contrary to a popular misconception, she didn't need cotton gloves to handle the ancient manuscript—clean, dry Lux hands would cause less damage.

Taking the book to a glass table, she opened the cover. *Journal of Experiment XIX* was handwritten on the title page, and underneath it, *Ninevah Sargon, reproductive researcher*.

Cerissa turned to the next page, being careful not to tear the fragile paper. It hadn't been exposed to light in over twenty-six hundred years, so the ink was legible. It read:

Goal: An experiment to create self-reproductive Lux.

Problem: Lux cannot procreate without mating with humans. With each generation, human traits are expressed more and Lux traits suppressed. Gene surgery on embryonic Lux to rectify the imbalance is not an ideal solution.

Hypothesis: Use gene surgery to create a Lux who can self-fertilize and replicate herself without mating with humans.

Results: FAILURE. Hypothesis abandoned, resulting genetic product destroyed.

Cerissa eased herself onto the kneeling chair by the table, her wings hanging free behind her, her pulse beating faster as she continued reading. Underneath the "Results" entry was stamped:

FOR PROTECTOR EYES ONLY.

And beneath was handwritten:

If you're reading this, we failed. Turn to the bookmark.

Even more carefully, Cerissa used the ribbon to slowly open to its marked place. A musty smell rose from the yellowed paper and the binding crackled as the book flexed.

> DAY 60: The subject is healthy and awake at night but falls into a deep sleep during the day. The introduction of bat and wolf DNA may have made the subject nocturnal, and the subject can only morph into either a bat or wolf. Use of vampire bat and rattlesnake DNA may have been an error. The subject cannot eat normal food, has snakelike fangs, and appears to hunger for human blood. Otherwise, the subject is smart and has mastered language and basic math skills.
>
> DAY 61: An attempt to introduce the subject to the world outside the Enclave was a failure. The subject attacked and drained the blood from a human, then attempted to feed the human the subject's blood. Guardians had to be called in to restrain the subject, and the dead human was abandoned.
>
> DAY 62: The subject was ordered destroyed by the Protectors.
>
> DAY 78: The nearby village has reported deaths from bites and resultant exsanguination. We believe the subject used the human it killed to reproduce itself. Guardians are being summoned from around the world to converge on the village, find the subject's spawn, and destroy it. Based on local reports, it appears the spawn has not reproduced.
>
> DAY 85: The subject's spawn has eluded us. Attempts to track it have failed. The Protectors have ordered a "wait and see" approach. All data has been stripped from the knowledge database.

What the hell?

Cerissa fluttered the tips of her wings, refusing to believe what she read. The Lux had created vampires? And then adopted a "wait and see" policy?

She stared at the page.

It can't be true.

Using a small device she brought with her, she tested the age of the book.

Damn.

This was no forgery. The paper was twenty-six hundred years old, the ink of a kind no longer used.

"What are you doing in here?" Ari demanded angrily from behind her.

She jumped out of her seat, raising the tops of her wings and fluffing them out. "I could ask you the same question. I'm working. What about you?"

Ari strode over to her, flapping his wings in annoyance. He flipped the manuscript closed—showing none of the reverence she'd felt handling the book—then opened to the title page and pointed at the "Protector eyes only" inscription. "Not wearing your lenses and reading a proscribed book," he sang angrily. "What the fuck do you think you're doing?"

"I can't wear my lenses in Lux form."

"Which raises the question. Why are you here and not back at Henry's? The last two nights, you returned to the Enclave after your investor meetings."

She averted her eyes. "I had stuff to do."

"Yeah, well, I stopped by your house and found him alone and all broody. Did you two have a fight?"

"It's none of your business."

"Ciss, everything about you is my business. I went to extreme lengths to keep you and Henry together. Want to see the scars?" He turned his back to her and spread his wings. Two dark blue lines paralleled his spine above his sarong. "You're not going to throw away my sacrifice over a minor lover's spat."

She fluttered her wing tips. "It wasn't minor. A hundred years ago, he killed his mate. He just got around to telling me."

Ari turned to face her again. "I know all about Sarah."

"How do you—" She stopped, her mouth hanging open. "Wait, I had my lenses out."

He gave her a sly grin. "I have a backdoor trap on your crystal ball."

Her eyes got bigger as rage pulsed through her. "You're monitoring my touchstone?"

"Hey, after what you did with Karen, I thought it a good idea. But that's not the issue—"

She fanned her wings. "It is indeed. How dare you invade my privacy?"

"Ciss, the Lux have little privacy. And the topic is you and Henry. You need to return to him."

"But he killed his mate and hid his history from me." She waved her fingers at him, rolling each individually, a gesture of disagreement among the Lux. "And then he accused me of meeting with Zeke behind his back. He didn't trust me not to betray him, and he didn't trust me with the truth."

"He was going to tell you about Sarah soon."

Damn her lenses and Ari's spying. "That doesn't magically fix it. He's still responsible for her death."

Ari crossed his arms, tapping his four thumbs against his skin. "What part of being a two-hundred-year-old vampire did you *not* understand when you fell in love with him?"

"Huh?"

"Jeez, Ciss, of course he's done things he's not proud of. Of course he has secrets. Of course he has issues."

"But—"

"Hold your thought," Ari said, waving his hand at her. "Reality check: to turn a mortal, he had to kill her. So, he botched the job. It wasn't a great situation, but why are you punishing him for it? Dude's been punishing himself for a hundred-plus years."

"'Botched it'? No, he doesn't get off that easy." She crossed her arms, matching his stance. "He killed her in anger."

"A little judgmental, aren't we? What happened to forgiveness?"

She fiddled with the moonstone bracelet. Despite everything, she couldn't bring herself to remove the symbol of being Henry's mate. "It's not my job to forgive. Besides, he learned nothing from it—he's still jealous and possessive."

Ari shrugged his wings. "Yeah, he has outdated attitudes."

"But—"

"But nothing. From what I can tell, he's worked hard to change his attitudes. He's created a whole community based on not harming mortals. He's put in place systems to make sure what happened with Sarah never happens again." Ari's silver irises swirled faster. "Now, if he were human,

I'd say get the hell out. Those attitudes in a human male spell trouble, and not the good kind. So, if he were human, I'd hold the door open for you."

Ari pantomimed twisting a knob with his six-fingered hand and swinging a door out.

"But he's *not* human. And he hasn't tried to hurt you. Intimidate you? Yes. Blown a gasket? Yes. But attack you? No. And he's accepted the crystal just to double down. Sure, it only prevents physical abuse, not emotional abuse, but Henry hasn't shown signs of being emotionally abusive. He's not critical of you; he doesn't insult or belittle you. I'll concede he's a little jealous, possessive, and overprotective—"

"A little?"

"The way I see it, the real issue is he's afraid of losing you. And he's willing to work on how he expresses his fears. Very willing. You, on the other hand, left at the first sign of conflict. One bad thing about his past and you're outta there. You say you love him—"

"I do love him. Why do you think I'm so upset"—she waved her arms in frustration—"about all this?"

"Well, from where I stand, you're not showing him much love or understanding."

"You're serious? The way he treated me is okay with you?"

Ari took in an intense breath and let it out with a whistle. "No, but he's trying to change—has been since the thing with Sarah happened. And when his fears got the better of him this time? He confronted you, asked if you went to see Zeke. He didn't follow you, he didn't try to catch you—he *asked*."

"That makes a difference?"

"Sure it does. His fears aren't going to go away overnight, especially not with Zeke poking the bear. But Henry talked with you about his suspicions—yeah, his approach had the finesse of an angry gorilla, I'll give you that, but it's still a far sight better than how he responded to Sarah."

Ari raised his wings and continued. "Besides, you're a Watcher, not an Avenger, not a Protector. Your rank isn't high enough to judge anyone—especially not your mate. Now get off your high horse and get back to the Hill and work it out."

Was Ari right? Had she been too quick to judge?

"And as far as distrust goes," Ari continued, "don't forget you did the same thing to him when you hid your Lux appearance 'cause you were afraid he'd reject you. You're just as guilty as he is."

"Don't you think I know that? But—"

He huffed out a breath and then cupped her chin. "Look, I get it, Ciss. You're grieving the loss of the fairytale."

She twisted and pulled away. "What are you prattling on about?"

"What you felt for Henry, your infatuation with him—and I don't mean it in a bad way—he's the first guy you've felt something for, right? And the image you fell in love with, well, it's gotten a little tarnished since then."

"More than a little."

"Exactly. But now you have a chance to grow some real love, one without blinders or pedestals. Look at it this way, kid. Love between two people—the kind you thought you had with Henry—is a garden. You get to decide what will grow there. One person's dandelion is another person's weed. Roses have thorns and all that jazz. You could choose to plant hemlock, it's a pretty flower, but do you want poison in your garden?"

Cerissa scrunched her face. "You're not making any sense."

"Not everyone wants the same thing in a mate. Set some boundaries. Tell him what you'll accept and what you won't." Ari's swirling silver irises held compassion—a rare thing to see. "The choice is yours. Can you pluck the weeds and nurture the kind of flowers you want with Henry?"

"You're not exactly one to lecture on love. You change partners more frequently than I change my bed sheets."

"Hey, I may not have fallen for all the sappy stuff you did, but it doesn't mean I don't understand relationships—or you." Ari tried rolling his large silver eyes. The move didn't work. "Now get your ass back to the Hill."

She stood completely still as Ari's advice reverberated in her mind. *Boundaries.* Relationships took work—and she had run off at the first sign of trouble. She needed to return and do the hard work of talking through their problems and setting boundaries.

"Well?" he asked.

"I'll think about it." The moment the words left her mouth, her guilt surfaced again. Didn't she have more important things to do than indulging in a relationship? Particularly one requiring so much of her attention?

Sure, a suspect was in custody. But did his arrest really end her mission? If more people were killed, it would be her fault—

"Come on, kid," Ari said, snapping his fingers in her face. "What's going on in that brain of yours? Why haven't you left yet?"

"If I return to Henry, I'll just get distracted again. Won't I? I did last time. It's my fault the VDM has killed so many people."

"Now you're being stupid." He grabbed her index finger, holding it up. "See this? Your ability to control anything ends here—at the tip of your finger. You're not responsible for what the bad guys do, *capisce*?"

Did she? Fidelia had said the same thing to Karen, and her words had sounded true then.

"I give up," Ari said, ruffling his feathers. "You're too stubborn."

"I said I'd think about it."

"You'll do more than *think*." He pointed at the glass table. "You'll put the book back where you found it—carefully—and ignore what you learned—"

"Do you know what's in here?"

"I suspected. The Protectors' 'hands off' vampires in the 1800s didn't pass the sniff test. They already had too much information about bloodsuckers when you saved Leopold."

"Why didn't you say anything to me back then?"

"Wasn't my place—and then you started poking into things. So, I monitored your research and read the book last night. I should have burned it."

"Then no one would find out we created them."

"Wouldn't that be best?" He reached over and shut the book. "And I'm surprised you didn't recognize the name."

She touched the leather. "Ninevah?"

"Is science all you know? Ninevah was our great-great-great-great-great-grandmother."

The gooseflesh traveled along her wings until all her feathers stood up.

My direct ancestor created vampires?

"Ya know, kid, looking back, when you saved Leopold's life, I think you recognized you were connected to vampires. Did you get to the part where Ninevah used her own morphing DNA strand? You and I are kissing cousins to bloodsuckers."

"Please quit using that term. It's highly offensive to them."

Ari blinked. "Whatever."

Cerissa strode over to the bookrack and carefully re-shelved the book. She stood there a moment, her back to Ari, her head bowed. His sledgehammer approach had been painful, but the wall around her heart began to crumble and something inside her shifted.

The Lux weren't any better than the creatures they created. How many deaths had they visited on humankind by releasing vampires into the wild?

Henry was responsible for Sarah's death, but the Lux were culpable for every mortal killed by a vampire, ever.

No one is perfect. Not even the Lux.

Her worldview shattered.

Ari was right. She thought herself above the kind of mistakes Henry had made, and she'd withheld her love and understanding because of it.

An image of *dadi ma* flashed through her mind. Her ten-year-old self would never have let go if *dadi ma* had laid out the whole truth to her.

Sometimes those who love us hold back the truth because we aren't ready to hear it.

Had Henry sensed how judgmental she was? She had never viewed herself as holier-than-thou. But if he had been forthcoming from the start, would she have stayed? Or to use Ari's words, would she have jumped on her high horse and ridden away?

Learning the truth about the Lux had knocked her off that horse.

She had fallen in love not only with Henry's handsome face and sexy body, but with his strong sense of right and wrong, his moral compass. His beliefs made it difficult for him to compromise and prompted the creation of the Covenant and its rigid rules designed to protect mortals.

Now she understood the events setting his moral compass, and his struggle to keep the needle pointed at true north, despite his fears and flaws.

Ari was right, damn it. Cerissa had no right to judge Henry. She had no right to give up at the first sign of difficulty.

She could forgive his lack of candor. She could forgive his role in Sarah's death. She could forgive his jumping to the wrong conclusion when it came to her and Zeke. And she could forgive the Lux for releasing vampires into the world—a mistake running completely counter to the Lux oath to protect humans.

She could even forgive herself for not being perfect, for straying from her mission, for wanting a life of her own.

Just like Karen forgave her. They were all trying their best to be good people.

The door cracked, and her heart opened.

She could love Henry, despite his fears and flaws and past transgressions. She returned to where Ari stood, amazed he had kept his mouth shut while she worked through it.

Her cousin nodded at her, as if he had been in her mind, following along with her.

She nodded back.

With forgiveness filling her chest, she was ready to return to Henry's home—to her home. It was where her heart belonged.

Chapter 49

RANCHO BAUTISTA DEL MURCIÉLAGO—NEXT DAY, SHORTLY BEFORE DUSK

Cerissa spent most of the day working in the lab. When her alarm rang, she flashed back to the master bedroom at Rancho Bautista and morphed into human form. A peek out the window told her the sun hadn't set yet over the rolling hills behind their home.

Between investor presentations and research on vampire genetics, she'd been awake for forty-eight hours and even managed to email Tig a report about Isaiah's blood sample. Not a perfect result—she needed a much larger donor pool to be certain—but the chief should be able to use the comparison to help convict Isaiah.

Emotional exhaustion weighed heavy on her shoulders. She crawled onto the bed to rest.

The sound of the basement door shutting woke her. She rubbed her tired eyes, threw on a summer dress, and brushed the tangles out of her hair.

Anxiety fluttered through her stomach. At the staircase rail, she stopped, afraid to go downstairs. Setting boundaries wouldn't be easy. But Henry had shown courage by letting her see his worst memory. Now, it was her turn to be courageous.

When she entered the kitchen, he was pouring heated blood into a mug. His hooded eyes were red-rimmed but brightened when they focused on her.

"*Cariña*," he said. He took a step toward her and stopped. "I am glad to see you home."

"I'm glad to be back." She sat at the mahogany kitchen table, not yet ready to rush into his arms. The awkwardness, the distance, was still too great. She needed time to bridge the gap. "Come join me and finish your drink. I've already had dinner."

He took the chair across from her. "I have another midnight appointment with Father Matt."

She smiled at his news. "What time do you think you'll be home?"

"It should not be later than a quarter after one."

"Maybe I can do my laundry while you're gone. I put a week's worth in the hamper."

"Indeed." He gulped down his drink faster than he normally did. "Now, how would you like to spend the next hour before I leave? We could go for a walk? Play chess? Whatever you'd like."

She'd come here to repair their relationship, to open her heart to him again. "I'd like to talk about boundaries."

Henry closed his eyes slowly and then opened them. "All right."

"I need you to trust me—trust I won't betray you, trust I love you and won't cheat on you, trust I can take care of myself, even around other vampires. I—I know you can't change how you feel overnight, but you can change your behavior. No more demands over who I can and can't be around."

He nodded. "Done."

She thought back to the funeral. Her attitude had been partly responsible for the altercation with Zeke. "If there is a Hill rule I should know about, I want you to be comfortable telling me. But I'll decide how to deal with it. Okay?"

"Done."

His agreement came too easy. Wait until he heard the next one. "And I can't live under all the paternalistic rules the Hill has adopted. I want you to take an active role in changing those rules that treat mortals as second-class citizens."

He paused, looking uncertain. "I will do so provided there is a better way to protect mortal interests. I can't let what happened with Sarah happen again."

Hmm. "All right, we'll work together to find a solution meeting both our needs. Are you willing to?"

"Yes, of course."

She stood and offered him her hand and led him upstairs to the bedroom, feeling relieved to have worked things out so easily. But what if he backslid? What would she do then?

He stopped her at the bedroom door. "You don't want to do this."

Damn that crystal.

"Take off your bracelet."

He did as she requested, and she wrapped her hand around his wrist. With a deep breath, she let go.

"You're uncertain—you're...you're grieving?" he said, surprise lighting his eyes.

She nodded. A single tear formed and fell.

He broke her grasp. "You're grieving the end of us?"

She gave a small, sad smile, and gently wrapped her fingers around his wrist again. "Dig deeper."

Henry dropped his barriers and let Cerissa's feelings invade his mind.

In the past, her love had wafted through his consciousness like the perfume of a new spring rose. This time he smelled an entire garden—from the night-blooming jasmine to the sweetness of a cut apple.

Then something changed. He didn't just smell the fragrances. He could see the garden. A sense of peace invaded him, and he knew—he just knew—he had been engulfed by her aura and joined her on the other side of it.

She stood in the middle, surrounded by lush trees and colorful blooms, a blue angel with ivory wings, and she beckoned to him. Her third eye glowed, forming a halo above her head. In the vision, she took his hand and leaned to him, touching her third eye against his forehead.

Warmth flowed through him, a powerful feeling of pure love—love and forgiveness, romance and passion, with just a tinge of grief. Grief for loss of their love's innocence, grief for the pain loving him had brought her, a slight whiff of fear he wouldn't be able to honor the boundaries she had set, but hope for building their love, stronger this time.

He wouldn't disappoint her—no matter what, he would never hide anything from her again, and she would always have his trust.

She released his wrist, and the scents and vision faded into the background. He slid his arms around her and brought her closer. "I am sorry, *cariña*. I didn't mean to hurt you."

She met his gaze. "It's all right, Henry. I understand. Everything will be all right."

He brushed her wavy hair away from her face. The love in her eyes shone like the stars in heaven. *How can I be worthy of her?* "I am—I will—try to be a better person."

"No matter what happened with Sarah, you're a good man. I, ah, I owe you an apology too. I judged you for the same thing I did—withholding information. I withheld my appearance, afraid you'd reject me for religious reasons."

Indeed she had. But it made no difference to him. He loved all versions of her.

She averted her eyes before continuing. "And I let the Lux worldview color my reaction. We tell ourselves we're more evolved—wiser, better. But I learned a few hours ago…" She paused, struggling with something. "The Lux created vampires."

The room spun, and he closed his eyes, leaning his back against the bedroom doorframe, pulling her with him. She stood between his legs.

Angels created his kind?

"You're sure?"

"I found the old experiments. Lux DNA was used to create the first vampire, so you and I are distant cousins. And you have a third DNA strand, just like I do, as a result. Now it makes sense why your fang serum contains the Lux morphing hormone. We gave it to you."

Could her story be true? He rubbed his eyelids with his palms. He had angel DNA? He wasn't an abomination, a demon—he could be redeemed?

A weight lifted from his heart. Hope blossomed.

"I'm sorry I judged you," she said. "I had no business doing so."

He opened his eyes and stared into her beautiful emerald ones. He had never loved someone as much as he loved her. Cupping her cheeks, he kissed her reverently. "Will you become mine again?"

A soft giggle escaped her lips. "You are possessive, you know that?"

"Why is that wrong? I don't understand."

She smiled. "Yeah, I don't think you ever will. But that's all right. It's part of who you are and I'm going to try to accept it—just don't be too overbearing about it, okay?"

"Overbearing?" He leered at her. "I promise to always possess you gently. Unless you want it rough—"

She slapped his chest lightly, a frustrated smirk on her face, and the tension between them broke. "You're terrible sometimes."

"Terribly good."

"Prove it."

"Oh, I intend to."

With vampire speed, he had her out of her dress, scooped her up, and laid her on the bed. Just as quickly, she grabbed a hypo from the nightstand and pressed the device against her thigh, making a light hiss.

"Bite first or—" she began.

"Lady's preference?"

"That you were naked already."

He stripped off his shirt and pants. "Better?"

"Better." She took his bracelet from his hand—he hadn't put it back on yet—and started to place both items on the nightstand.

He stopped her, touching the silver cylinder. One more thing stood between them—her initiation ceremony. He had to protect her without revealing too much. "Not to interrupt things, but I, ah, I need to ask you something. The stabilizing hormone—could you take it every day, twice a day, once you finish giving your presentations and return? Even if we don't make love that night?"

"Why?"

"I can't answer because of that...that thing I can't tell you about without violating the Covenant, remember? You agreed I shouldn't tell you. I just need you to promise you'll take a dose twice a day. It won't be for long."

She looked confused for a moment.

"Please trust me on this."

Her face relaxed. "All right."

He crawled into bed, looming over her on all fours. "Now, bite first or—"

"Well, since you're so interested in making me yours again—"

He struck before she finished, sliding his fangs into her neck, the penetration feeling like biting a grape, her skin resisting, until her warm blood burst forth and mixed with his fang serum. He took a deep gulp, and his erection pressed against her thigh.

The fire, the desire, the love flowed through him with each draw he took.

Her hands sought him out. He lifted his hips, and she touched him, spreading the moisture around his tip. In fluid strokes, she slid her hand along him.

His intense love and need to possess her overwhelmed him, and with the next draw on her blood, he almost came in her hand.

He pulled from her grasp, licked the wound closed, and kneeled between her legs. After licking the blood from his lips, he slid his tongue along her folds until he sucked her nub into his mouth. The two tastes—rich blood and salty juices—blended, delighting his taste buds.

With both hands, he reached to pinch her nipples. She gave a gasp of pleasure. He rolled her tips with his fingers as his tongue stroked the sensitive nerve bundle between her legs; he was careful not to pierce her with his fangs, increasing the pace, squeezing her nipples and tonguing her nub until she screamed his name.

Just the appetizer, mi amor.

He gave her no time to recover. Spreading her legs even more, he buried his *pene* deep into her.

Madre de Dios, *she is so wet.*

He wrapped his arms around her and rolled her on top of him. Fanning the fingers of one hand along her belly, he ran his hand across her smooth skin, and as she began to slide up and down on him, his thumb found her spot. He drew small, slow circles around it.

He watched her, her beautiful breasts bouncing above him with each cycle, her eyes closed, her head back, her hands gripping the sheet at his side, hanging on like she rode a bucking horse. His hips moved in rhythm underneath hers, his thumb never stopping its circles.

Her mouth dropped open, a mewl escaping her lips, and her eyelids fluttered, her breathing labored. She was close—he could tell when her movement shifted and became more languid.

He kept watching, not wanting to lose himself before she did. He sped up the circles his thumb made, and she cried out, riding him faster and faster, and suddenly gripped his wrist, connecting with the crystal.

Her orgasm rocketed through his mind, and he joined her, coming in a blinding explosion, his body bathed in pleasure—hers entwined with his.

She collapsed on top of him, and he held her close for a long, long time.

Chapter 50

Tuscany Bay Resort—That Same Night

"Out here," Marcus said, pushing Ari out the hotel room door and into the hallway. Before he closed the door, he glared at Lance Griffin, who was handcuffed to a chair, watching television, and pointed a finger at the prisoner. "You stay there. You make one move and I'll hear it, understand?"

Marcus flipped the latch so the door wouldn't completely close and lock behind him.

Ari crossed his arms and threw his head back like a prize stallion, tossing his curls off his forehead, his brown hair sexily tousled. "Why the bum's rush?"

"I'm on guard duty. I didn't want him to see us do this." Marcus pulled Ari into his arms for a deep kiss, sending a *zing* right through him. If only he didn't have to keep an eye on the prisoner.

When they broke, Ari asked, "How often do we need to renew the bite?"

"Every thirty days to be safe."

"Then I'll see you then."

"Not before?"

"Now, Marcus—"

"Surely you want to come for the trial. If all goes as Tig plans, I suspect we'll be underway in a few weeks. It promises to be interesting."

Ari gave a grudging look. "I might stop in to catch your performance."

"That would be a good thing. A very good thing indeed." Marcus ran his fingers through Ari's hair, letting the silky curls wrap around his fingers. Damn, he had it bad. "Prosecuting Jones will be a stressful time for me. I may need some relaxation."

His paramour laughed. "Sounds like a job right up my alley."

"I thought you'd see it my way."

"But what about Nicholas? You're sure this won't be an issue?"

"I told you. We're not exclusive."

Nicholas understood the terms—they weren't mates until they combined the bite with sex. Something Marcus was more than willing to delay for the moment. Being lovers with Ari put him in a position to learn everything there was to know about Tig's investigation and Cerissa's research lab—two projects in which he was deeply and personally interested.

Marcus wrapped his arms around Ari and kissed him thoroughly before saying au revoir. After all, there was no sin in taking pleasure in his work.

MARINERS LODGE, SAN DIEGO—A SHORT WHILE LATER

Tig scrolled through Cerissa's message. The scientist had included an executive summary along with her more detailed report on the motel blood but was hedging her bets—Cerissa wanted samples from Jones's maker and any offspring he made to confirm her theory. So the results weren't perfect, but they indicated a likelihood of a match. That would have to do for now.

The evidence pile was growing higher.

Tig was scheduled to resume her interrogation in a few minutes. Jones had spent the past forty-eight hours in custody at the Mariners Lodge. Plush accommodations, from what she saw. That would change when she extradited him to the Hill.

But so far, the lodge's council had been slow to grant her request. The problem wasn't the treaty—the treaty permitted extradition. The problem was that no one had much experience with what level of evidence was needed to invoke the provision.

Consequently, her interrogation of Jones had become a mini-trial, with the lodge's council listening in. Their concern over whether one of their own would receive a fair trial in Sierra Escondida was annoying, but understandable.

Well, Cerissa's report is one more nail in Jones's c—

She couldn't finish the bad cliché, even in her mind.

Tig switched off her tablet and gathered her paperwork into a briefcase. She'd been using a small office Quentin had offered her. For the past two nights she had dug deeper into Jones's background, building her case against him. So far, there were no eyewitnesses to his involvement in the murders, but she didn't always need them to score a conviction, especially when the circumstantial evidence was so damning.

She opened the door to leave. Ari was standing there, one hand raised as if to knock, and she stepped back. "How did you get in here?"

"Jayden cleared me through. He told me you'd be here tonight. I have something for you."

Beware of geeks bearing gifts.

She suppressed a grin and herded him into the small office. He took the guest chair, and she perched her bum against the desk. "Well?"

"Jayden gave me the results of the phone company subpoena. The answers came in today. I examined the data on the burner phones and compared it to what Ma Bell gave us." He paused. "Drum roll, please."

"Just get on with it."

"Hey, don't be so impatient. I could have hacked their system. It would have been faster."

She crossed her arms and frowned at him.

"All right. It turns out we only have one of the phones that was listed as 'private caller.' My guess is the other phone is still in the hands of the Cutter." He handed her a four-page printout. "This is what you're looking for."

The first two pages were a series of texts between Jones's burner phone and Lance Griffin. By each text, Ari had listed the originating phone number's last four digits. Nothing new there—she had enough to tie Jones to the bullet purchase—but the last entry held her interest. It was a communication between the burner phone and Angelo Pascala. The texts she'd seen before, but she now had the number that was listed as "private" on Pascala's phone:

    7366 (Jones's Burner) 9:22 p.m.: I'm here.
    0429 (Pascala) 9:23 p.m.: Come on up.
    7366 (Jones's Burner) 9:24 p.m.: On my way.

"The phone company confirmed those texts were sent and received through local towers in Mordida," Ari added.

Tig continued to stare at the texts. "Whoever used the burner phone was in Mordida and in contact with Pascala."

"Exactamundo."

The phone was found in Jones's possession, and if he'd been the one to use it, the texts clinched the link between Jones and the delivery of silver bullets to Pascala. She looked up at Ari. "Good work. Anything else?"

"Remember the Trojan on the winery's server?" He held out three personnel files. "I've narrowed the culprit to these three. I'm going to hack them to seize samples of their programming to figure out which one."

"No, you aren't." She had looked the other way when the town attorney enlisted Ari's hacking skills and cut other corners. But she was sworn to uphold the treaty, which meant going through proper channels. And with Jones in custody, the pressure of time was off. They would do it the right way. "I'll ask Marcus to issue search warrants to demand samples of their coding."

Ari gave an exaggerated frown. "You're no fun."

"This isn't about having fun. It's about having enough hard evidence to make the charges stick." She pointed a finger at him. "And you won't go behind my back, either, or you're out of a job."

He raised his hands in surrender. "You're the boss."

"I'll be in touch once I have the warrants." She slid the text printout into her briefcase and then phoned Jayden to see Ari out. She couldn't let her consultant wander around the lodge unattended. "Wait here for him."

Ari straightened his back, clicked his heels, and saluted her. "Yes sir, sir," he said with a hint of sarcasm and an infusion of mockery.

She rolled her eyes.

Civilians.

She closed the door and strode across the hallway to the observation room. Quentin waited there for her, Wilma with him. Through the one-way glass, they would watch her question Jones. He was already sitting in the interrogation chamber.

"Has your council approved extradition yet?" Tig asked.

"They are debating it now," Wilma replied. "When you start questioning him, they'll observe again by closed circuit."

Tig opened the door to the eight-by-eight-foot room. Jones sat at a plain table, silver handcuffs lined with leather around his wrists and the center chain fastened to an eyebolt drilled into the table. The silver would keep him weak and the leather would protect his skin from burning.

She took the chair opposite him. "Have you fed?"

"Yup, if you count the spoiled swill they gave me."

Yeah, bagged blood was pretty awful if you were accustomed to fresh from the vein. But she didn't care so long as it provided nutrition. "I wouldn't want you to claim you confessed because we mistreated you."

"Won't happen, 'cause I got nothin' to confess."

"Well, let's see whether you do. I've been thinking about why Dr. Patel was targeted in the last attack. And it didn't make any sense until I looked at this."

Tig took a file from her briefcase and slid twelve typewritten pages across the table to him. "Your screeds. You wanted a donor blood shortage to justify relaxing grazing laws—"

"Nope." He shook his head vehemently. "You're doing this 'cause you don't like my politics. You're so crooked, if you swallowed a nail, you'd spit up a corkscrew."

"Let me finish. You wanted a donor blood shortage, and Dr. Patel's promise of an increased supply threw a wrench into your plan. So you ordered her death."

"No way, Jose. I'm being sacrificed like an innocent lamb. And all y'all took the bait."

"Who do you think set you up?"

He shut his mouth, his expression angry.

"Really? Not talking? I would think you'd be anxious to tell us who framed you." Tig leaned in, locking eyes with Jones. "When the Carlyle Cutter tried to shoot Cerissa and shot Zeke instead, he was driving a rental. The credit card used was issued to Charlie Roberts at your address."

Jones's eyes got big. "That don't make no sense. All my plastic's in my wallet, which you took, and they all got my name on them."

Hmm. The driver's license logged by the car rental company turned out to be a fake—Charlie Roberts's name and Jones's address. She pulled a page from the file she held and put it in front of Jones—the sketch of the Cutter. "Who is this man?"

"I don't know."

"Really? Where's your mate?"

"Back east, visiting her parents. Haven't talked to her since you locked me up in this prison."

"Her? The name in V-Trak is Charlie R. Jones."

"Charlie's a girl."

"That's interesting. For some reason, the male or female box wasn't ticked."

"I'm not surprised you bureaucrats can't get anything right."

Tig leaned back in her chair, watching the prisoner closely. "I did a little digging. Your mate's birth surname is Roberts."

"So?"

She tapped a finger on the sketch of the Cutter. "This man is a serial killer. He sometimes goes by the name Charlie Roberts."

At first, he shrugged off the connection. Then a moment of understanding flickered in his eyes, followed by fear. He shut it down real fast, but not fast enough.

"So?" Jones repeated, trying for nonchalance and failing. "Don't mean nothing. My mate's definitely a woman."

"How can we get in touch with her?"

"By phone."

Tig wrote down the number as he said it. The same one in V-Trak. She had already tried phoning Roberts, and the call went to voicemail each time.

"Do you know her family's address?"

"Not in my head."

"It's strange," she said, sitting back in her chair. "Your mate's family information is also missing from V-Trak."

"Like I said, you bureaucrats couldn't find your fangs if they were sunk in a vein."

She laid Jones's regular phone on the table, the one he appeared to use all the time. "Is her family's address in here?"

"Nah. It's back at my apartment. Too much work to type it in. I got an old-fashioned address book I keep all that shit in."

She would check later to see if the address book was in the evidence box. Otherwise, she'd send Zeke and Liza back for it.

Quentin had asked around, and no one affiliated with the Mariners Lodge had ever met Jones's mate. No photo in V-Trak. Could the Carlyle Cutter be Jones's mate? Jones had parried her questions about Charlie well enough. She would raise the matter again once she had the address book in hand. It was time to turn to a new topic.

"Let's talk about the burner phones we found in your apartment," Tig said.

"I told ya, they aren't mine."

"Then how do you explain these fingerprints?"

She put another three photos in front of him: the fingerprint dust raised on each phone, the transfer card containing the print, and the overlay match to his.

"Simple," he said with a sneer. "They're as fake as a whore in church."

"Not by a long shot. Quentin provided two witnesses. They were present when Jayden did the work. Those fingerprints are yours."

"Proves nothin'."

"Then let's see what you have to say about this."

She showed him the email placing the ammunition order and a copy of the check. "You ordered two boxes of rifle bullets. You paid for them with this cashier's check." She laid down another document. "Here's the sworn declaration of the silversmith who made them."

"The guy's a liar."

She added a screen grab from the bank's video to the stack. "You purchased the check at Royal Beach Bank."

He narrowed his eyes. "It was to pay for new pews for the church. Someone broke in and stole the damn paperwork before I could mail it off."

Yeah, good luck selling that story to a jury. Jones hadn't filed a police report on the so-called "theft." Jayden had already contacted the San Diego police department to confirm it. "You purchased ammo—not pews—and kept one box at your apartment, the carton we found. You delivered the other to Anthony Pascala." She showed him the printout of text messages. "Your burner phone texted to him, confirming the delivery at his motel."

"I told ya, ain't my phone."

To the growing paper stack, she added the currency transaction report and credit card company statement. "So, who is the owner of 'On the Vine, Inc.'?"

"How should I know? They donated the cash. I thanked 'em and used it for the pews. At least, I would've, if someone hadn't stolen the damn check."

Tig gave a slight snort of disbelief. His answers were so good that she almost asked if he'd taken up tap dancing professionally.

"And then we have this report." She glanced in the direction of the camera. "The technology we're using is still being tested, but the preliminary results: the blood found in Pascala's room has a high probability of belonging to you."

"Yeah, right, 'high probability,'" he scoffed. "Well, that sounds like you can't prove the blood's mine, and if it was, anyone could've planted it in the motel, like they planted those phones and the ammo box in my apartment."

Tig leaned back in her chair. "Here's what I figured happened: you delivered the bullets and didn't want Pascala to remember you. So, you bit him, and then had him drink your blood, to give you an extra edge."

"Nope. You got the whole thing all wrong. Ya see, I'm always exchanging blood vials with other lodge members. Since we get grazin' permits here, we need them to heal our bites, something you, being from that stuck-up community, wouldn't know about. Anyone could've put some of mine on a tissue and left the tissue there."

"And how did you know your blood was on *a tissue*? I didn't say what we found it on."

He turned redder than his hair. "I—I am *done* here."

"Because you're guilty."

"The only thing I'm guilty of is stupidity. I'm a stupid son of a gun. I thought I had to do this to save our people. But I'm nothing more than a patsy." He crossed his arms as much as the handcuffs would let him. "And that's all I'm gonna say."

"Fine with me. Wilma?"

The intercom clicked. "The council voted to sign the extradition order."

Tig stood. "Isaiah Jim Jones—you are under arrest for murder and conspiracy to commit murder. You'll be taken to the Hill for trial. You have the right to legal counsel."

"I'm innocent, I tell you. Wilma, they set me up. Don't let them take me."

The intercom clicked off. "You better think of a better explanation," Tig said. "No one is going to buy what you're selling."

Except it bugged her. In the face of this evidence, why did he keep proclaiming his innocence? Ballsy? Or was he the patsy he claimed to be? If that was the case, why didn't he name the person who framed him?

And the Carlyle Cutter—he was still on the loose. Maybe they could horse-trade with Jones—name the co-conspirators, tell her where to find Chuck, and maybe the council would take the death penalty off the table.

Not bloody likely. Not with two Hill deaths.

Well, it didn't matter. Her job was to gather the evidence for the town attorney to present at trial. If a deal wasn't struck, a jury would be impaneled. They would be the ones to judge the thorny issue of credibility. For now, everything pointed at Jones, even if he claimed to be a victim.

She'd done her job. Now it was up to Marcus to do his.

Chapter 51

Rancho Bautista del Murciélago—five nights later

Five more communities, five more investor meetings, five more nights away from Henry—and Cerissa now had enough investors to move forward with the project. No more presentations were planned. She returned home exhausted, ready to take a break from work.

Home. Our home.

She searched the house for Henry—it was almost nine at night. No sign of him. Had he gone back to Father Matt's for another appointment?

When she told Henry the date she would return home, she had been vague about the time. They had talked by phone nightly, but she hadn't flashed back. She was swamped with wooing investors and doing research at the Enclave, popping back and forth between the two duties. He understood, even encouraged her to focus on work and finish the tour, so she could return home—home to stay for good.

Her arrival had to be public, so she drove the rental car back to the Hill rather than flashing in. That way, the guard at the gate would log her entry.

From the emails they exchanged, Karen was feeling better and gossiping up a storm about Jones's arrest, which had resulted in a collective sigh of relief in the community. The preacher had been arraigned before the council and held over for trial. At the arraignment he'd pled not guilty. In about four weeks, a jury would be impaneled.

The Protectors continued their wait-and-see policy. If the vampire communities put the VDM out of business, the Lux wouldn't interfere.

Still, certain inconsistencies bothered Cerissa. She and Ari had compared notes. New Path didn't look like a hotbed of conspirators. The vampires attending the church seemed like plain folk—disgruntled plain folk, sure, but not the type to conspire to start a war. Ari had hacked their email and found no indication of their involvement.

And Jones didn't act like the typical egotistical sociopath who would use assassination to get his way. Something about it all felt *wrong*. He continued to claim his innocence, the evidence against him was all circumstantial, and they had no leads on any co-conspirators.

If anything, his sermon, where he talked about his father returning legless from the war—well, he struck her as someone who had an overdeveloped sense of responsibility for the care of others, and she could relate.

Thanks to her *amma*'s abandonment and her *pita*'s early death, she had suffered from the same thing, feeling guilty when bad things happened, until she recognized the truth: guilt was like the snake adorning the neck of the Hindu god Shiva, and that snake would lie unless she controlled it.

Her power didn't extend to halting all evil in the world, and she had to stop listening to the snake. It had driven her to take Zeke along rather than cancel her trip to New Path Church. Her one poor decision started a chain reaction that almost ended her relationship with Henry.

Never again.

Jones had the same thing going on. In her view, he might throw himself on a bomb to protect his people, but not start a war.

She had included her opinion in her report to the Protectors. And she'd sent an edited copy to Tig—her impressions of what happened at New Path Church.

It was on their shoulders now.

There. That's a good first step for letting go.

She still had to figure out why adrenaline-enhanced blood had such a hold on Rolf—too little data. But there would be time to dig into Rolf's issues later. She didn't need to get everything done at once.

Maybe the Hill would be receptive to her ideas now. She wanted blood samples from more vampires to provide a larger base for test comparison. *Hmm.* Henry might be able to talk his friends into cooperating—it would be a valuable beginning.

Her stomach growled.

Time to take care of that.

She peered in the freezer and found frozen leftovers.

Woohoo!

While she waited for Henry's return, she could enjoy his home cooking again. She was so tired of restaurant food. Forty minutes later, she was full and feeling better.

When the doorbell rang, she scrunched her eyebrows together. She wasn't expecting anyone, and checked the security cameras before opening the front door. What she saw on the monitor made her stomach tighten uneasily.

She unlocked the heavy oak door. "Father Matt, what's wrong? Has something happened to Henry?"

"Get in the car and I'll tell you." He turned away, not waiting for her answer.

"Wait—"

He gestured to her and glanced at this watch. "Come on. We don't have much time."

She grabbed her purse from the foyer table, locked the front door, and then slid into the passenger seat of his metallic-blue Prius. The butterflies in her stomach performed backflips while he steered the car down the steep curving driveway.

"What's happened?"

She waited for Matt's explanation, but he remained silent.

"Matt, what's wrong?"

"Be patient. All is okay."

Patient? At Robles Road, he turned left, taking them deeper into the Hill community and toward the town hall complex.

Where is Henry?

She had tried phoning him when she first got home. He hadn't answered—that was why she'd figured he was with Father Matt. She had tried calling and texting Karen, but no answer. Then she called Jayden. He hadn't picked up either.

"Matt, is Henry all right?"

He didn't answer—his eyes were focused on the road.

"Matt?"

He glanced her way. "Henry's going to be fine."

"What do you mean by that?" She tried to sense Henry's presence. The crystal should have told her whether he was in danger. Either he'd gotten very good at blocking the connection between them or something very bad had happened. "Has he been hurt?"

"It's not what you're thinking."

"Then what is it? Do you know where he is?"

"I'm taking you to him. He's expecting you."

"Henry didn't say anything about this."

Where *were* they going? One attempt at kidnapping her had failed. Would they try again?

No, she refused to believe Matt was involved in the conspiracy, but his continued silence didn't reassure her. Then a different thought sprang to mind.

"Did he violate the Covenant again?" She covered her open mouth. The consequences would be horrible if he had. The threat of a hundred lashes still hung over his head.

The priest gave her a sideways glance. "Don't worry. Everything's fine."

"I don't think so. He would have told me if something was happening tonight."

"He couldn't." Matt signaled the left turn to enter the country club parking lot. "You'll see—nothing's wrong."

"This makes no sense. Henry knows I don't like surprises."

"Cerissa, do you understand the role ritual plays in a culture?"

She swung around to glare at him. "What are you talking about?"

"Ritual. Why cultures have rituals—"

"I'm not interested in discussing sociology. I want you to tell me what's happened to Henry!"

"Rituals can be used to bind people together as a community," he continued like he hadn't heard anything she said. "To let us know who we are in relationship to each other."

He drove toward the parking lot behind the country club. The front lot was full. He pulled into one of the few open spaces in the back.

Her eyes got wide. "Why is everyone here?"

"You'll find out," he said, opening his door. "Let's go."

"No." She wouldn't let them blindside her. "I'm not moving until you tell me what this is about."

"Ritual." He got out of the car and opened her door. "Cerissa, do you trust me?"

She sighed and looked up at him. "I have no reason not to."

"Then come along. You don't want to embarrass Henry, right?"

"I want to know what's going on."

Matt offered her his hand. "Come with me and you'll soon find out."

She narrowed her eyes. His was a friendly face, an honest face. She'd liked Matt from the first time she met him. She couldn't believe he'd bring her harm.

He seemed unperturbed by her reluctance. "You want to see Henry, right? Come with me."

Staying in the car wasn't going to get her questions answered. She accepted his hand and got out. He led her through the back door of the country club and into a dressing room. Lockers lined one wall. Mirrors, chairs, and makeup tables occupied the other wall. She assumed the room was used by band members who performed at the Hill dances.

Matt took a cocktail dress off a hook and handed it to her. "Put this on."

She examined the fancy outfit. The fabric was dyed in the community's vivid blue, and the dress had a low scoop neck, three-quarter sleeves, a short skirt, and, according to the label, should fit her.

"Henry gave us your size. Karen picked this one out."

"Karen's in on this?" The dress reflected her friend's tastes. A creeping suspicion came over Cerissa. Was Henry throwing some sort of surprise party for her to celebrate her return?

"Put your clothes and purse into a locker; you won't need them. Once you've changed into the dress, come out into the hall. But first."

He took a small container out of his pocket, which was about the size of a room service jelly jar, the kind served with breakfast toast at fancy hotels. He unscrewed the lid, dabbed his little finger into the thick goo, and the tip came out a bright blue. He reached toward her forehead.

She pulled back. "What are you doing?"

"I'm going to put a small dot on your forehead."

She continued to move away, putting her hands up. "That's pretty intimate, to touch someone's third eye."

Matt kept moving toward her. "I've never heard anyone compare it—" Then he stopped. "Are you Hindu?"

"My father was. But Hindus aren't the only ones who…" She stopped—she couldn't explain her real reason. Unless she was close to someone, she hated having them touch her where her Lux third eye was. She stepped back a few more paces. "Must you apply the dot?"

Looking into the mirror, he expertly dabbed a solid blue circle onto his own forehead. "You can do it; just be careful not to smear the pigment. It's stage makeup." He turned the jar over to show the label: *Ultramarine Greasepaint.* "It means you're one of us. For the ritual."

Okay, forget about a surprise party. This was too weird. She dipped her pinky into the thick base—the consistency was similar to zinc oxide ointment, a cream she'd given patients in the past for treating diaper rash—and copied what he'd done. "How do I look?"

"Fine. You'll want to tie your hair back once you've changed. There are various bands and clips in the dressing table's drawer. I'll wait for you in the hall." He closed the door, and she turned the lock.

What had Henry agreed to on her behalf?

Damn him. Why didn't he tell me about this?

She wasn't comfortable with human customs, let alone vampire ones, which were in a whole different class of weird. She threw her purse into a locker and pulled her t-shirt over her head to toss it in.

Nothing to do but go along.

She stripped off her pants and slammed the locker door shut.

She wiggled into the dress. The bright blue, stretchy fabric looked good against her dark skin, but the color clashed with her green eyes. Oh well.

A pair of black high-heeled designer shoes in her size sat on the dressing table. She slipped them on too. They pinched a little, so she morphed her feet a shade smaller, allowing the mass to transfer to her calves.

She gazed into the mirror and pirouetted. The skirt was short—whatever ritual was planned better not require her to bow. If she did, whoever was standing behind her would likely get a show of her French cut panties.

She took a hair band out of the drawer and pulled her hair into a ponytail. Twisting around, she peered into the mirror. Her hair fanned out across her back, static electricity from the dress frizzing the waves out. She morphed the strands into a long braid, which she circled and pinned—being Lux definitely had advantages.

But it also had its disadvantages. She'd been in human form for over twenty-four hours. The stress of whatever Matt had planned was making her antsy. She returned to the locker and found the hypo in her purse, recalling Henry's request that she use the stabilizing hormone twice a day. A little extra stabilizer wouldn't hurt—it would carry her through the night until she could morph and rest.

She applied the hypo to her neck and took one more look in the mirror—no mark.

There. As ready as I'll ever be.

She dropped the device into her purse and closed the locker again. When she opened the door to the hallway, Matt was standing by a small table. On it sat a large polished box, like a display case. The top was solid wood rather than glass.

"Over here." He gestured for her to join him, raised the lid, and hastily stepped back.

She was startled by what she saw: a collection of oversized symbols. Various types of crosses, Stars of David, moons and crescents, a double-headed axe, even non-religious geometric patterns, like triangles, circles, and hearts, lay before her. Some solid, some outlines of shapes.

All silver.

"Select one," he said.

"This makes no sense. Silver jewelry is banned from the Hill."

"Just take one, all right? It's for the ritual."

Matt was gloveless—he couldn't hand one to her; she had to pick it up herself.

"You're sure? Henry won't be mad?"

"I'm sure. I keep telling them we need to brief the bright ones, but the council thinks it's better if you don't know in advance. Trust me and go along, okay?"

Before this, she'd thought vampire customs were weird. Well, they just got weirder. She selected a non-religious symbol, wrapping her fingers around a large, solid star. Henry would understand the joke even if no one else did—she believed her people came from the stars, even if their presence had inadvertently started humanity's belief in angels...or even Jinn.

She held up the star and looked into the hallway mirror so the camera in her lenses caught a glimpse of the strange outfit and symbol.

"Follow me." Matt took her hand and led her outside into the night. While she'd been gone, "June gloom" had moved in and the weather had cooled off. The lightweight dress she wore made the brisk air more noticeable. Goose bumps crept up her arm, and not just from the cold night.

The outdoor amphitheater was ablaze with light and filled with both vampires and their mortal mates, all wearing outfits in the same vivid ultramarine shade.

She froze.

Under the bright lights, the spectators seemed to glow, each bearing a blue dot on their foreheads, exposing those third eyes. She unconsciously lifted her hand to cover hers.

"Relax," Matt said. "Nothing to worry about. You look fine." He grasped her elbow and guided her to the stairs at the side of the stage. "The rest of the journey is yours. I'll be out there rooting for you."

He gave her a peck on the cheek and put his hand to the small of her back, and the pressure he applied got his message across—she was to start climbing.

Nerves made her stomach churn—what the hell was going on?

"Up you go," Matt said, prodding her from behind. "They're waiting for you."

The five metal steps seemed insurmountable. Then she saw Karen.

"Come on," Karen said in a stage whisper. She wore a silk dress in the same vivid bright blue, hugging her curves.

Before Cerissa could take step one, she heard the mayor's voice. "Who are we?"

The crowd responded, "We are the town of Sierra Escondida."

"Who are we?"

"We are the community of the Hill."

"Come on!" Karen raised her stage whisper to almost a yell.

"There's no way out," Matt said.

That wasn't reassuring. She clutched the silver star and took her first step.

"Who are we?" Liza asked.

"We are vampire and mortal," the crowd responded.

Cerissa's eyes widened at hearing the honesty of the chant, and she stopped mid-step.

"Who are we?" Liza asked again.

"We are those who honor the Covenant."

Karen gestured impatiently at her. Matt pushed her from behind, and Cerissa stumbled forward, climbing another two steps before catching herself by clutching the cold metal rail.

Karen grabbed her arm and yanked her the rest of the way onto the stage. "Relax. It's going to be okay."

The mayor resumed the lead. "Why are we here?"

"To welcome a new mate."

"And whose mate do we welcome?"

"The mate of Enrique Bautista Vasquez."

Cerissa watched Rolf, Yacov, and a few other vampires escort Henry to center stage. He didn't look good. His skin had an ashen hue and his eyelids drooped, half-closed. His black hair, normally bound back with a leather string, hung loose around his shoulders in disarray, and he hunched in on himself.

Were they holding him upright or restraining him? Either way, his condition alarmed her.

At the sight of Henry, the crowd broke into a round of jeers, hoots, and catcalls, like a rowdy group at a bachelor party. He was the only one not wearing the ultramarine color. Black slacks and a white shirt, unbuttoned at the neck, set him apart, and his forehead was naked of the blue dot.

Why?

Marcus stepped forward, brushing his neatly trimmed mustache outward with his thumb and forefinger before speaking. "Is there anyone here who challenges Henry for this mate?"

No one had better say a word. If Zeke so much as clears his throat, I'll find the nearest piece of wood and stake him.

When no one answered, Marcus repeated, "Is there anyone here who challenges Henry for this mate?"

She couldn't figure out why he said it twice. Did they think she'd cheated on Henry because she'd been out of town for a week? The third time he intoned the question, she realized it was part of the ritual.

"Dr. Cerissa Patel," the mayor called out, looking at her. "Step forward."

Slipping a piece of paper into her hand, Karen whispered in her ear, "See the X on the stage? Walk to it and stop."

"You must be joking. This is choreographed?"

"Just do it."

Cerissa walked downstage and stopped as instructed, growing less afraid of the unknown and more irritated. Henry should have warned her. Instead, he had urged her to resume her work for Leopold. Now she smelled a proverbial rat.

A vampire rat, that is.

Wait... Maybe he did try to warn me. He'd said there was a secret he couldn't share. Is this it?

"Cerissa, who are we?" the mayor asked.

She read the paper Karen had slipped her. She didn't need it. She had already guessed the answer. Her lone voice rang out clear: "We are the town of Sierra Escondida."

"Who are we?"

"We are the community of the Hill."

"Who are we?"

"We are vampire and mortal."

And Lux. Wait until they figure that one out.

"Who are we?"

"We are those who honor the Covenant." Why hadn't she read the damn thing more closely? The mayor stepped forward carrying a thick, oversized binder, the kind one might find in a legal library, except the outside was covered in a golden embroidered tapestry. He handed the volume to her. It was heavier than she expected; she had to grip the loose-leaf binder against her chest to keep from dropping it and morphed her muscles to comfortably handle the weight.

"Cerissa, do you vow to be bound by the Covenant, to follow its rules and regulations, and keep faith with us, never telling any mortal from the outside world what we are?"

"I agree," she said, and swallowed hard. At least the vow didn't prohibit her from telling the Lux.

The mayor leaned in, saying in a voice meant only for her, "Learn these rules well. I don't ever want to see you in front of the town council for violating them, understand?"

"Yes, mayor," she said softly.

"Now hand the book to Karen."

Cerissa did as she was told.

The mayor stepped toward the crowd again. He swung his hands up like a conductor about to lead an orchestra, his large paunch riding upward with the movement of his arms. "What sets Hill vampires apart from others?"

The crowd replied, "We have learned restraint."

"What sets Hill vampires apart from others?"

"We control our lust for blood."

"What sets Hill vampires apart from others?"

"We never harm our mates."

The mayor turned. "Henry."

Hearing his name, Henry roused from his stupor.

"Come forward to claim your mate."

When he opened his lidded eyes, they glowed red. She had never seen them look so wild before. Solid black eyes could signal anger, hunger, or sexual arousal, but red meant blood-crazed, usually from starvation.

Karen whispered, "He's been fasting while you've been gone."

"That's terrible. Why would he?"

"To demonstrate his control. Now stand still and be quiet."

Henry slowly stalked to the center of the stage, his red eyes transforming to solid black when his gaze locked on hers, a wisp of his lust entering her mind, but it didn't last long, and his hunger won out, his eyes glowing red again. He stopped four feet away.

Tig stood to the side of Cerissa, wearing civilian clothes. Rolf and the others positioned themselves near Henry. Were they there to protect her in case Henry lost it? His control of the crystal wavered as he struggled to block his hunger from entering her mind.

"Henry," the mayor began. "How long have you fasted?"

"Five nights," Henry replied. His voice was weak and ragged.

"And you are hungry?"

"Yes."

"But you won't attack."

"No."

"No matter how provoked?"

"No matter how provoked, I will not harm her."

The mayor gave some signal. Rolf, Yacov, and the others tore Henry's shirt away. Cerissa's stomach dipped, leaving her with a bad feeling about this. Except for the gold crucifix he wore, he was naked from the waist up.

"Cerissa," the mayor said. "Under the Covenant, you are forbidden to harm your mate, with two exceptions. The first exception: if he attempts to hurt you, you may defend yourself."

"What is the second exception?" She regretted it as soon as she spoke the words.

"Tonight, you will do so to demonstrate his commitment to the Covenant."

She looked at the silver star in her hand and understood its significance.

"No." She shook her head slowly. "I cannot."

The crystal made her unable to harm Henry.

"Now, my dear," the mayor said softly, "you must. It's part of the ceremony." He took hold of her arm and guided her hand toward Henry's chest. "Open your hand and place the star against his skin."

She pulled back. "It'll hurt him. I can't."

Rolf strode over to join them. "Weakling! I told you she would wimp out."

He grabbed for Cerissa's hand, yanked her out of the mayor's grasp, and bent her hand to reach Henry's face. Henry didn't flinch as the star approached his cheek.

The speed with which she moved caught everyone by surprise. She elbowed Rolf's stomach before flipping her knuckles under his chin, lifting him up. She sent him sprawling.

"Don't ever touch me again!" she yelled at him.

"Someone's been drinking Henry's blood," one of the vampires in the front row said, loud enough to be heard throughout the amphitheater.

The crowd broke into laughter. Tig and Jayden grabbed Rolf and dragged him off stage.

Cerissa rubbed her fist, trying to soothe the stressed tendons. Vampire blood wasn't what had made her strong enough to send Rolf flying.

The mayor backed away, sending a message to the audience: he wasn't sure what she might do next.

She caught Henry's gaze. "Do you want me to do this?"

He knelt before her. "Please. You must."

She had his permission. A permission she hoped he never gave again. "Give me your hand."

She bent over and kissed the back of his hand the way he had so often kissed hers. She moved quickly, replacing her lips with the silver star. Karen whispered, "Hold it for five."

The crowd began to count.

"One…"

The pain on Henry's face tore at her heart. Why were they doing this? It made no sense.

"Two…"

The acrid smell of dying flesh accosted her nose. She could tell he was struggling for control of the crystal's connection, trying to block his pain from her, and she knew when he lost it—his agony drilled into her brain.

"Three…"

She gasped. It was like a hot iron had touched her own skin, and the searing burn turned her breathing ragged. Her mind screamed: *Make it stop. Make it stop. Make it stop.*

"It's almost over," Karen said.

"Four…"

Just say it, just say it, just say it, just say it, just say it.

"Five."

She released his hand. He fell back on his heels, holding his wrist, his eyes glowing a deeper scarlet. A black, angry star disfigured his beautiful hand. She clutched her stomach, panting. As he regained control of the crystal, the searing sensation faded from her mind.

"Okay, Henry," the mayor said. "Show them what you're made of."

She watched Henry close his eyes and take a deep breath. He opened them and looked up at her. Hunger and pain were all she saw in their red depths.

Henry rocked forward, placing his hands flat on the stage as if he were about to stand. Instead, he lowered himself and kissed the top of her foot. Slowly, he raised himself and kissed her knee, followed by her thigh just below her skirt's hem.

Then he stood. The look in his eyes was frightening, but he didn't do what his eyes threatened. He took her hand and kissed her palm, and then straightened, until he was looking directly at her, standing before her.

With great difficulty, he asked, "May I?"

She reached for him, pulling him to her. "Yes, Henry, yes."

His fangs pierced her neck. Her nipples pebbled in response, lust pooling between her legs. She blushed—feeling those things in front of an audience unnerved her.

But thank goodness she'd used the hypo. Suddenly popping into Lux form would have been a disaster.

He took four gulps before letting her go and stepping back.

"Henry—"

"*Mi amor.*" He locked eyes with her. The red receded and his chestnut brown irises returned. They shone from the inside like stained glass.

"You need more," she said.

He licked the open wound to stop the bleeding. Why wasn't he feeding? Five nights? He must be starving. She modified her blood, not letting it clot, and felt the flow trickle down her throat in two little trails.

"Stop that," he whispered into her ear.

"But—"

"Stop."

"Henry—"

"Now. Stop it."

She reversed the process. He licked the wound again and the blood clotted. The crowd cheered wildly. She didn't understand. None of these strange rituals made sense to her. The mayor pounded Henry on the back, congratulating him. Even Rolf was back on stage, praising Henry's restraint. Tig helped him put on an ultramarine blazer, and Rolf dabbed a blue dot on Henry's forehead.

Karen leaned close to Cerissa. "Henry's proven himself—he's committed to the community's rules." She walked away for a moment and came back rolling a small table. On it was the Covenant and a beautiful hand-crafted wooden chest. "Put the silver star in here," Karen said, motioning toward the box.

Cerissa threw it in, relieved to be rid of the damn thing.

"Step back, Henry," the mayor said. He turned to Cerissa. "Welcome to the community, my dear." He kissed her European style, once on each cheek, and then he kissed the clotted bite. She pulled back, shocked.

Karen kept her from moving too far away. "Just go with it. They won't feed. It's part of the ritual. They do it to symbolically demonstrate the same control Henry did."

The mayor dropped a handful of gold coins into the wooden box and stepped aside.

Cerissa had no time to respond. Another vampire appeared before her, welcoming her into the community and repeating what the mayor had done. They formed a line, climbing the stairs at the front of the stage, until she found herself facing Zeke.

Concerned, she glanced over to Henry. How would he react? He was surrounded by Rolf, Tig, and the mayor. Zeke's cerulean eyes looked cautious.

"Welcome to the community, ma'am," he said, dropping more gold into the box. He kissed her on one cheek, and when he kissed the other, he added, "Someday you're gonna wish it was me you chose." He kissed her neck, licking his lips as he sauntered away.

That was tacky.

"Oh, Cerissa, oh, dear!" Gaea repeated the ritual and hugged her. "I'm so happy you two worked things out."

"I still want to know how you found out."

"Oh, dear, I can't give away all my secrets." Gaea tossed a couple of gold bars into the chest and stepped away.

When Rolf approached her, he smiled grimly and performed the ritual kiss. "Just remember, payback's a bitch," he whispered in her ear before tapping his fist lightly against her chin.

So, he wasn't going to forgive and forget. Yet the four bars he'd dropped in the chest was the largest single donation so far. Did the gold mean he now accepted her as Henry's mate, or did it represent his need to always be the biggest and the best?

Yacov murmured his welcome when he kissed her checks and her neck, and his long beard tickled her exposed collarbone. He tossed a handful of gold coins into the box before pressing a drawstring bag into her hand.

"Cut diamonds, my dear. Henry will know what to do with these when you're ready."

From the weight, she placed the value at over twenty thousand dollars. "I can't accept these."

"Of course you can, dear lady." He folded his hand around Cerissa's so she couldn't give them back. "Shayna and I are so glad you've joined our little community. You've made Henry a happy man."

She hugged him. "Thank you, Yacov."

Tig was next in line. "I didn't know you had the heart of a warrior," she said with one of her rare smiles, and then kissed Cerissa as the others had done. "An impressive strike, for a mortal."

"I'm sorry. I shouldn't have hit Rolf."

"Not at all. Rolf had no right to touch you. I'm sure Henry is proud of you," the chief added, clasping Cerissa's shoulder before dropping gold coins in the box and moving on.

"Leopold!" Cerissa exclaimed, when she saw who was next in front of her. "What are you doing here?"

The scrawny vampire kissed both her cheeks and her neck. "Just as sweet as I remember." He handed her a bar of gold with a parchment note wrapped around it, his wax seal holding the whole package together. "Did you expect me to stay in New York when my own envoy was being officially welcomed into Sierra Escondida? I think not."

She looked at the bundle. "What is this?"

"You can read the note later, my dear girl. I have formally renounced my claim. Henry owes me nothing from the sale of Enrique's restaurant."

She wrapped her arms around Leopold and hugged him. "Don't worry," she said. "Our project will make you much richer than the restaurant ever would have."

"I know," he said, a crooked smile lifting his thin, angular mustache. "I'll see you later at the party."

After the fifty-five vampires welcomed her to the community, their human mates crowded on stage, teasing her about the size of her chest. "The gold's yours, not Henry's," Karen explained. "To fund your freedom, should you ever need it."

By now, she was so overwhelmed that she said nothing. Jayden motioned toward the country club—the crowd was moving that way. "Let's go in. They won't serve refreshments until you're in there. They have to toast you first."

All she wanted to do was to see if Henry's hand was all right. He still looked wan and weak. "When does Henry get to feed?"

"Anytime he wants," Karen replied. "He's being macho, showing off. He put on quite a performance."

"Huh?"

"Restraint. He could have bit your calf, your thigh, or your wrist, but he held out and made it to your neck, and after asking your permission. Believe me, he was showing off. Come on, if we go inside, he'll accept whatever they have ready for him."

"Whatever what?"

"They got a blood donation from a frat party—an inebriated college kid, you know? They're going to get him drunk."

Cerissa rubbed the back of her neck. "I'm on information overload. Let's go get something to drink so Henry can."

Chapter 52

Rancho Bautista del Murciélago—Later That Night

"Haaave I told you how beauuutiful you are to-to-night?" Henry said, slurring his words.

"Only for about the eleventh or twelfth time." Cerissa did her best to support him as he leaned against her. "Let's get you upstairs and into bed."

He swayed on the step and leered at her, the small paper bag in his hand swinging. "Yessss, bed."

He'd been like that during the entire drive back. Father Matt had driven them home in his Prius. They'd been in the tight back seat, and Henry had hung on her in a way he'd never do in public, kissing her neck and running his hands over her arms.

It was a good thing Henry's car was parked in the garage. In his condition, she would have fought with him over the keys if he'd tried to drive.

Matt carried in the chest and the Covenant before saying goodnight.

She thanked him, closed the door, and left the gifts—the gold and jewels—in the foyer. She needed to deal with Henry first. What did you do with a drunk vampire? The donor had at least a three-point-zero blood alcohol level. Or was Henry so wasted because he'd been fasting?

They reached the top of the stairs. Her high heels sank into the second floor's thick carpet, and she held her arm tight around his waist to keep him steady. "How is your hand feeling?"

He flexed his fingers. The motion tugged at the black necrotic skin. He stumbled and fell forward, taking her with him. He caught himself against the bedroom doorframe and pulled her into his arms, kissing her deeply.

Yes, his breath had a faint odor of alcohol, along with the metallic taste of blood.

When she broke for air, she asked, "Henry, was that a marriage ceremony?"

"Do you want to be married to me?"

"You didn't answer my question."

"No, w-we are not married," he said, his Castilian accent becoming thicker, the R's rolling heavily. "You—you are a member of our community now, bound by the rules of the Covenant. The initiation ceremony was about you."

"Why the fasting and the silver?"

He pounded his chest with his fist. The paper bag rattled. "To demonstrate my commitment to our way of life—you are safe as my mate."

"Sarah," she whispered.

"You understand." He nodded. "Never again."

"You're a good man, you know?"

"Thank you, *cariña*."

He started toward the bedroom and abruptly turned, almost tripping. She helped steady him.

"I almost forgot." He reached into his pocket and held out a key fob tied with a shiny red ribbon and a flowerlike bow.

She took the offering from him. "What's this?"

"My gift to you. A key to the Viper."

Her eyes widened. "You're giving me your car?"

He snatched it back, looking appalled. "No. I'm giving you a key to *our* car. *Our* house, *our* car. Shared."

She brushed her fingertips over his face, caressing the stubble. "You trust me with your baby?"

"*Our* baby. But I'd like to be there the f-first time you drive her. I don't want to have to replace the clutch."

"Beast," she said, accepting the key again and holding it to her chest. She valued this gift far more than the gold and diamonds.

"*Si*, your beast."

"And how is my beast feeling?" She took his hand in hers and examined the blackened star. The smell of dead flesh was pungent. "Will the burn heal?"

He held out the sack he was carrying. "It will soon."

Cerissa waited for an explanation, but none was forthcoming. He broke from her embrace and stumbled to the bathroom. She followed him. He braced himself against the sink and placed the bag on the counter.

"Do you need help?" she asked.

"Open it."

She pulled out a jar. Thick blood was visible inside—it reminded her of dark red molasses. "A peanut butter jar?"

"The only one Shayna had handy. She cleaned it first."

"That is not a sterile environment."

"It does not need to be. Vampire blood, not mortal. Yacov's. Take off the lid."

Yacov was very old. His blood would be potent. *Hmm.* Maybe she'd save a small sample for testing later.

She unscrewed the lid. Henry held his hand over the sink and tried pouring the liquid on the necrotic flesh. He winced when it hit. The blood beaded like his skin was made of wax and rolled off.

"Wait," she said, "I have a better way to do this. Hang on to the sink and don't do anything."

She waited to see if he would follow her instructions before leaving him alone. When he remained motionless, she ran into the bedroom and searched through her medical kit, finding what she needed.

He was still hanging on to the sink when she returned.

At least he's an obedient drunk.

"Don't move," she instructed. She sprayed a liquid on his hand. He jerked his hand back.

"Did the spray hurt?"

"No, it is cold."

"It's supposed to be. The cold will numb the burn. May I try again?"

He gave his hand to her, a look of dumb trust on his face. She sprayed a light mist. This time, he didn't jump. "How is it?"

"I do not feel the pain."

"Good. It's working." She continued to apply the numbing spray, waving the aerosol back and forth, the mist evenly covering the angry scar. She would never have used it on necrotic human flesh. Vampires healed in a way humans did not. When she was satisfied enough spray had been applied, she let his hand go and selected an old-fashioned syringe with a very fine needle from her medical kit.

He flexed his hand. "That feels better."

"It's temporary." She filled the syringe with liquid from the jar. "You shouldn't feel this."

"I am vampire. I can tolerate great pain without attacking."

"I know. I saw. You've proven yourself. Now let me work, all right?"

He shut up, and she injected blood directly into the necrotic flesh. She sensed him watching her, but she ignored him and finished hastily. "There. Do you think that's enough? The surface doesn't look like it's healing."

"Even with the blood, a silver burn takes time to heal." He raised the jar and swigged the remainder of the contents.

When he finished, she twisted the lid onto the jar and dropped the container into her medical kit. There was enough residue left to experiment with. A red trickle ran from the corner of his mouth.

"You're a messy drinker," she said, pointing to it.

Looking in the mirror, he used the back of his other hand to wipe the trail away. He licked the blood off and smacked his lips. "Good to the last drop."

"Just like the wines you make."

"Better." He flexed his injured hand again, making a fist and then stretching his fingers.

"Hmm," she said. "I might be able to develop an easier delivery mechanism than injection."

"What d-do you have in mind?"

"Let me see if it works first. Tomorrow night, I'll take another blood sample from you to experiment with."

He shrugged. She took that for a yes.

She reached for his hand. "How are you feeling now?"

The black mark appeared slightly faded, but it still looked like she'd branded him.

"You would pick the star," he said.

"Don't blame me." She pointed a finger at him. "It was supposed to be symbolic. My people were from the stars. Poetic."

"The star is one of the larger symbols. Women who pick the star are believed to be afraid of their mates. Or angry at them."

"I'm neither of those things," she said, and kissed him. "If you had told me about the ceremony, I would have picked something smaller."

He may have been drunk, but he didn't take the bait. "May I use your toothbrush?"

She smiled. She knew what that meant. "Go ahead."

She waited patiently while he sloppily brushed his teeth. Then something occurred to her. "You're just lucky I remembered to take the stabilizing hormone."

He grinned cockily. "I had every faith you would."

Yeah, right. At least nothing bad had occurred. She took the toothbrush from him, rinsed it and brushed her teeth. When she finished, she turned to walk out of the bathroom and toward the bed, figuring he'd follow her. Instead, he reached for her and stumbled.

"Come on, my stalwart vampire." She braced an arm around his back and led him to bed. "Let's get you undressed."

"Handsome and stalwart."

"And humble," she said.

"It is the truth."

She let go of him, and he flopped face first on the bed.

He lay there while she took off his shoes and socks. "You need to turn over if you want me to take off your pants."

He obliged. She unzipped and removed them while he unbuttoned the coat, revealing his bare chest. She smiled at him. He was wearing nothing but tight black briefs and a vivid blue sports coat. He looked like one of those silly advertisements for men's underwear, right down to his washboard abs.

She tugged at this arm. "Come on, sit up, so I can take the coat off you."

He stripped off his underwear and reached for her. "I do not want to wait that long."

She laughed and fell into his blue-coated arms.

Chapter 53

A Hotel Conference Center—the next night

The President stared out the high-rise window. He was due to preach in an hour. First, he had a few things to take care of.

His patsy had been transported to Sierra Escondida. Would Jones keep his mouth shut? Or would a favor need to be called in to eliminate the idiot?

Fortunately, Jones's mate was safely locked away.

Charlie Roberts, the President thought with a snicker. The Scarlet Brethren were watching over her—a powerful incentive for Jones to remain silent.

And using her name on Chuck's ID was a smart way to frame the preacher and remind Chuck who the boss was—two birds with one stone.

Very efficient.

The President twisted the ruby ring's band around his finger as anger welled up inside him. The Hill had put on a little morality play last night, and Beta had been at the heart of it.

An initiation ceremony.

Bah.

When he reshaped the world, no vampire would ever starve again, for ceremonial purposes or otherwise, let alone *kneel* to a mortal.

He picked up his phone and punched in the Director's number. "Ditch the SUV," he said, not even pretending to speak in code.

"Do you think it's really necessary? It's registered to one of our subsidiary companies. Our competitors don't know the name."

How dare he question me?

The President clenched his jaw. He hated explaining things to underlings, but this one required special care. "They know about On the

Vine and they have a partial license plate number from your SUV. Charlie Roberts needs to disappear. Use one of the other corporate debit cards I gave you to get more money. Take a taxi to the airport and rent a car there using one of your other IDs. I am going to discard this phone and buy a new one. You do the same, using the cash."

"Got it."

"Then go to our site on the dark web and enter your new phone there. IT will relay it to me."

"Yeah, I got it, I know the drill," the Director replied. "But you haven't explained how that police chief bitch found my apartment in Mordida."

"Watch your tone." No one spoke to the President that way. "How doesn't matter. The *bitch* knows too much about you for you to stay in San Diego right now. Once you rent a car, drive to the safe house. Wait there for instructions."

"All right. I should be there in a couple of hours once I change cars."

"Good. I have an idea. We need to lie low for a few weeks. Let them think they captured the real ringleader. And keep your hands to yourself. We want them to believe you've gone to ground."

There was silence on the other end of the line.

"Did you hear me, Mr. Director?"

"I heard you."

"I've been considering what you told me—about the work your contact does on the Hill. I have a way to deliver our *goods* to all five targets at once. Your contact's position will be integral to the plan."

"Anything would be better than this cat-and-mouse game we've been playing," the Director said.

This cat-and-mouse game would be over already if you weren't so incompetent.

But the Director was highly strung, and shaming him only resulted in more dead bodies—and the more dead bodies, the greater the likelihood mortal police would find the Director. The President wasn't willing to sacrifice his court torturer just yet.

"I will call you tomorrow night when IT gives me your new number," the President said. "Be careful. Don't take any chances with getting caught. Your old identity must disappear completely. No mistakes."

"Don't worry. There won't be."

"There better not be if you want your year-end bonus," he said, and disconnected the call.

A Note from Jenna

Thank you for reading *Dark Wine at Dusk*. I hope you enjoyed it.

Cerissa, Henry, Tig and Jayden will return in Book 4 of the Hill Vampire series, *Dark Wine at Death*.

They have a lot to do to solve the mystery of the VDM. Who is the President? Will they discover that in time? And how will they stop the Carlyle Cutter before he kills again?

To accomplish their mission, Cerissa and Henry must learn to work as a team. Will Henry be able to keep his promises? The next phase of their relationship will answer an important question!

Death is slated for publication in Spring 2020.

Want to be among the first to know *Death's* release date, and receive special announcements, exclusive excerpts, and other FREE fun stuff? Join Jenna Barwin's VIP Readers and receive Jenna Barwin's Newsletter by subscribing online at: https://jennabarwin.com/jenna-barwins-newsletter/

Did you enjoy *Dark Wine at Dusk*? <<<gets on knees and begs>>> Please let me know by leaving a short review. One sentence is all you need write. And please consider telling your friends or posting a short review on your favorite review site. Word of mouth and reviews are an author's best friend and much appreciated. <<<begging over>>>

Although this book has been through many rounds of editing, it's always possible for errors to slip through in the publishing business. If you find errors, or have any comments about the book you want to share with me personally, please contact me at: https://jennabarwin.com/contact.

Happy Reading!

Acknowledgements and Dedications

To my husband Eric—thank you for all you do to make my life as a writer easier, including all those errands you run and home projects you complete while I stayed glued to the computer, pounding away at the keyboard.

To two wonderful author colleagues—Caitlyn O'Leary and Ophelia Bell—thank you! You both have been extremely generous with your time and knowledge about the indie publishing world.

To Tari Lynn Jewett and our #CharmedWriters group—your support and companionship during writing sprints make the lonely job of writing a lot less lonely.

To Kay H.—thank you for putting up with my learning curve, and for your gentle suggestions and encouragement. You know just the right thing to say when I need to hear it.

To my editing team—it takes a team to polish a story and ready it for readers. Katrina, Trenda, and Arran—you are all fantastic! You push me to make the story better, and I sincerely appreciate it. Any errors in grammar, clarity, or plot are mine, not theirs. Their full names are:

- Katrina Diaz-Arnold, Refine Editing, LLC
- Trenda K. Lundin, It's Your Story Content Editing
- Arran McNicol

And thank you to my book cover designer, Christian Bentulan, who picked up the gauntlet and did outstanding work on the cover design. You did a marvelous job matching the first two covers!

There are many other wonderful people who have helped me improve my writing, and also helped me tackle the business of being a writer. The generosity of other writers, who have freely shared their expertise, is greatly appreciated. Thank you everyone, for your support and help!

Printed in Great Britain
by Amazon